CHILDHOOD
SWEETHEART

BOOKS BY WENDY CLARKE

CHILDHOOD SWEETHEART

WENDY CLARKE

bookouture

Published by Bookouture in 2022

An imprint of Storyfire Ltd.
Carmelite House
50 Victoria Embankment
London EC4Y 0DZ

www.bookouture.com

ISBN: 978-1-80314-534-1
eBook ISBN: 978-1-80314-533-4

For everyone who loves my books

PROLOGUE

The most painful goodbyes are the ones that are never said and never explained.

The brothers stand silent, little more than a gull feather's width between them, as their father points to the boat that's been dragged onto the stones at the loch's edge and unbuckles his belt.

From the edge of the forest, Seth sees the fear that crosses the face of one boy, the defiance etched in the hard stare of the other. He's too far away to hear the lecture they're getting but can guess the words. How the underwater currents could pull them away. How a sudden squall could whip the usually still water to a frenzy. How easy it would be on a freezing winter's day such as this, for Loch Briona to take a life. Lowering his binoculars, he calls to his dog and steps back into the shadows.

The father's hand tightens around the battered leather belt. From the window of the white house at the top of the hill above the lodges, Moira sees her husband, the man she loves despite everything, slowly draw it from the loops of his trousers. Sees her boy flinch and prays he won't incite his father's anger further.

As he folds his arms, squares up to the man as he's always done, the little girl, Ailsa, squats on the concrete steps that lead to the wooden lodges. She sees the other boy, her best friend, pull at his brother's shoulder. Knows he'll be pleading with him not to do anything stupid. But, before she can find out what happens, her mother takes her hand. Tells her it's not their business and leads her away.

Three sets of eyes.

A moment in time. Shaping all others.

Eleven years later, long after the cruel hand of death has visited, they will all have changed. The weak, the strong, the guilty, the innocent. Forever shackled to the past. Some alive. Some dead.

All regretting.

ONE

AILSA

Ailsa pulls the last of the sheets from the washing machine in the cold outhouse and presses her thumbs into the small of her back. Through the grimy, small-paned window she can just make out the Scandinavian-style lodges where birdwatchers and walkers stay from spring to autumn. The silver-freckled surface of Loch Briona bathed in late September sunshine at the bottom of the grassy slope.

Just out of sight is the lodge she shares with her son, Kyle. It's larger than the others, set a little apart, its wooden steps leading to a raised deck affording a view of both the loch and the dark swathe of pine forest that surrounds the holiday complex on two sides. With its kitchen-living area, functional bathroom and two bedrooms, it's all that she and Kyle need.

When Moira had asked why she hadn't taken the bigger of the two bedrooms for herself rather than give it to Kyle, Ailsa had lied, saying she'd thought the view of the loch would be calming for her son. The real truth she'd kept hidden. There was no way to explain that she hadn't wanted that room because of the boathouse. The wooden structure that jutted out onto the water on spindly legs just visible if you pressed your forehead to the glass.

Ailsa closes the washing machine door, trying to banish the image of the building's weathered doors and rotten floorboards. The phantom smell of fish. She doesn't mind having a smaller room if it stops her remembering what happened there when she was a child. Not much older than Kyle.

Too scared to tell anyone in case they didn't believe her.

Too young to truly understand its significance.

Straightening up, Ailsa goes to the laundry room door where a glance at the sky shows dark clouds gathering. Banks of them. Solid as countries and casting shadows on the hills behind the main road that looks down on Loch Briona Lodges. Ailsa smiles at the term 'main road'. Moira's name for it, not hers, but it's as main as they get on Bray, stretching from the harbour town of Trip, six miles to the east, all the way to Balmoor in the west. Another road joining it at the point where the forest turns into moorland. Connecting it to the main town of Elgin on the other side of Loch Briona and often impassable during a harsh winter.

Moira's not back yet, the parking space next to the house still empty. She's been Ailsa's employer for the last eleven years and even now, when she's in her uniform of battered wax jacket and wellingtons, it's easy to forget the woman came from a wealthy family. Very easy. Not that Ailsa likes the word 'employer'. Like the term 'main road', it strikes a false note, giving her relationship with the older woman a status that's too formal. Yes, Moira might pay her wages, but, over the years, she's been more of a mother to her than her own, and without her, she'd have no job, no home and certainly no stability for Kyle.

But, as she cleans the chalets and sweeps the wooden decks, the loch stretching out below her, serene or untamed as the weather sees fit, the thought is often there in her head. Intrusive but unspoken. How does Moira continue living here faced, every day, with the tragedy that blew her family apart? A devastation of such magnitude that it left in its wake a void that she and Kyle had struggled to fill.

Not that it had been easy for her either. Moira wasn't the only one left to mourn.

The clouds have bunched and darkened, shutting down the sun. Ailsa shivers and steps back into the cold, stone room and rubs at her arms, the fabric of her cardigan wrinkling beneath her fingers. Yes, Moira might have lost her son, Callum, but because of that terrible night Ailsa had lost someone too. She'd lost Jonah.

She closes her eyes a moment, just his name enough for her heart to give its familiar lurch. She doesn't often think of him, tries not to, and this is exactly why. It's just too painful. The hurt still as raw as it was the day he left.

Ailsa turns away from the window, bending to lift the end of a white sheet that's dragging on the tiles. But as she tucks it in with the rest, something feels wrong. Out of kilter. Just as it had earlier that morning.

Knowing she's being silly, Ailsa drags the plastic basket along the tiled floor, and stuffs the bedding into the dryer. She can't put her finger on what it is that's worrying her. What caused her to push away the breakfast of bacon and scrambled eggs Moira had made her earlier that morning. Replacing her usual strong coffee with a cup of weak tea in the hope that it would calm her churning stomach. All she knows is that whatever this feeling is, it's taken hold and grown. And it's unnerving.

She shivers and pulls her cardigan around her. The feeling comes again – like milk curdling in her stomach. Usually, when she feels like this, it's due to something Kyle's done or said, but there have been no problems for a while. Her son's hours of sleep are less erratic, and he usually only wakes once or twice now. Settling quickly when she goes into him. No, it's something more than that; she's just not sure what.

The metal door of the dryer is cold against Ailsa's hip as she presses it closed. Thinking she hears a cry, she straightens and listens. She's left the door to the outhouse open. The one to the kitchen of the old house too in case Kyle needs her.

Is it her son she heard? She hopes not.

She'd left him engrossed in his Lego on the rug in front of the range in Moira's kitchen, knowing from experience that it was better to let him stay than make him come with her if he didn't want too. She'd be able to hear him through the open doors if he wanted anything and there was no danger of him wandering out on his own. The world is a frightening place for Kyle. A complicated jigsaw with the pieces moved into the wrong places. On his own, he'd be forever trying to rearrange them to make them fit better. Sometimes, Ailsa knows how that feels.

The cry comes again. Louder than before. There's no mistaking it now. It *is* Kyle. Her son needs her.

Leaving the tumble drier rumbling, Ailsa kicks the washing basket aside and runs out into the small yard that houses the toilet and shower block and the wooden sauna. Moira's house is one of the largest buildings on Bray, situated further up the hill where it can look down on the loch and the holiday lodges, and by the time Ailsa reaches the porched side door, she's out of breath. She stops and listens, scared of what she's going to find when she goes in. Trying to work out what might have happened.

The side door leads into a small lobby full of shoes. On the wall is a wooden shelf underneath which are several hooks – Kyle's anorak the only coat hanging there. He's quiet now, and not wanting to startle him, Ailsa steps over the walking boots and wellingtons on the floor to the kitchen door, positioning herself so that she can see him. He's exactly where she left him half an hour ago, kneeling beside the Aga. But, instead of the intense concentration he'd had on his face earlier, he's rocking. Forward and back. Forward and back. Forward and back.

A glance at the floor in front of him shows her what's happened. Lego bricks are everywhere, the remains of the tower he'd been constructing. A tower, once completed, that would have been identical to the one he built yesterday and also the day before.

When the tower fell, the pieces had scattered into a kaleidoscope of colours and random patterns that Kyle must have found hard to cope with. Ailsa looks down at them, seeing them through her son's eyes. Understanding what they represent to him: confusion, chaos, discord. The scattered pieces lying on the rug are in stark contrast to the orderly rows of individual colours Kyle had carefully placed before starting this latest project. Thirty pieces in each row – something Ailsa knows because he told her. Just like he told her the exact measurements of the tower on its completion.

Relieved that his outburst is nothing more than a bout of frustration at having failed in his task, Ailsa goes into the room. Putting her churning stomach down to something she ate, and knowing her son hates it when she's ill, Ailsa composes her face.

'All right, Kyle?'

Kyle looks up, his eyes meeting hers as she's taught him, but he doesn't return the smile she gives him. Instead, he frowns. 'Did you know that a dog's sense of smell is forty times better than ours? Did you know that they can sniff at the same time as breathing?'

Ailsa closes her eyes for a fraction of a second, then opens them again. 'Yes, I know that, Kyle. You told me yesterday. And they don't sweat.'

Kyle nods. 'Yeah, Mum. Good remembering. Some are faster than a cheetah too.'

His obsession with dogs is a new thing. It used to be spiders and, before that, car number plates, though there aren't that many to be seen on the small island of Bray. Most visitors preferring to leave their car on the mainland in order to travel on the more frequent foot passenger ferry. Those who have come to birdwatch, or visit the rutting grounds in autumn, are happy to make do with the local bus service or Douglas's cab, when he isn't serving behind the bar at The Stag down by the harbour in Trip. At Loch Briona Lodges, they go one better with Moira collecting the guests from the ferry in her new Land Rover.

She can hear Moira now, her wellingtons crunching on the gravel drive. She told her she was driving out to Ewan's croft where she'd been promised a lamb for the freezer. Ailsa goes out to meet her, taking in the woman's smart black trousers that balloon from her wellingtons and the red Fair Isle jumper, its pattern of vivid blue and yellow circling her neck. Covering both is the usual open wax jacket that had once belonged to Moira's husband, Hugh, its green material worn at the elbows and in the creases. The quality of its waterproofing tested on a daily basis in winter.

The sight of it still makes Ailsa go cold. How can Moira want to wear it after the way he treated her? It's like she's clinging on to Hugh in some ghoulish way, unable to let go. Ailsa knows what the people in the village say when they see her in it, for gossip travels quickly on a small island. *She should burn everything the bastard left behind. That's what I'd do if my husband ran off and left me for one of his bits on the side.*

Ailsa knows Moira hears the gossip too, but it's not for the islanders to judge. She must have her reasons for wanting to keep him close, for despite him being a violent drunk, she'd clearly loved him. And they say love is blind.

The wind has picked up, playing with Ailsa's hair, flapping it around her face. 'You were gone a while. Get what you wanted?'

Moira glances over her shoulder at the Land Rover parked on the gravel drive. Something crosses her face but passes again before Ailsa can read it. 'I suppose so. Managed to get away before Ewan started off on one of his rants about the birders camped at the croft. If he doesn't like it, he shouldn't have them stay.' She gives Ailsa a tired smile. 'Anyway, how's your morning been?'

'Fine.' Ailsa points to the outhouse. 'With so few guests this week, I've managed to get the last lot of sheets into the dryer. I'll make up the new beds as soon as I've taken them out.'

Moira comes over to her and kisses her cheek. Her skin is cool, sweet-smelling, the press of her earring sharp against Ailsa's jaw before she releases her.

'Darling girl. What would I do without you?'

Another gust of wind blows between the buildings. Ailsa captures her hair in one hand, then, taking a band from around her wrist, secures it in its elastic embrace. As she does, she wonders, as she often does, how Moira always manages to look so well groomed. As though she's stepped out of an office in the city rather than a four-wheel drive on a windswept isle off the north-west coast of Scotland.

As if reading her thoughts, Moira's hand moves to her fair hair, which is pulled back tightly from her face into a neat bun. There are faint shadows under her eyes and the planes of her cheekbones seem sharper than usual. Her lips a little pinched.

'Are you all right, Moira?'

Moira drops her hand to her side. 'Yes, of course. I just didn't sleep too well last night.'

'It wasn't Kyle, was it? He had a bad dream, but he quietened quickly.' She thinks back to her son's pale face, his forehead filmed with sweat. He'd been shouting. Something about a dog. She thinks of the questions he asked her a moment ago. The sooner he moves on to a new obsession, the better.

Moira gives her a reassuring smile. 'No, of course not. You

mustn't ever think that.' She points to the house. 'Your lodge is nowhere near the house and, even if it was, the walls are so solid, a bomb could go off and I'd not hear it. Anyway, how *is* that wee man of yours? Built his tower yet?'

Ailsa looks over to the house. 'To be honest, it was a bit of a disaster, but you know Kyle, he'll carry on until he's finished. And then he'll probably make another one – I dread to think what will happen when he runs out of bricks.'

'If that happens, we'll buy him some more.' Moira puts a hand on Ailsa's arm. 'The lad can't build an empire without the required building materials. I'd better go and take a look.'

Without taking off her wellingtons, Moira walks through the small porched lobby that leads into the kitchen. Ailsa follows.

'How's my handsome wee boy then?'

Ailsa remains in the doorway, not wanting to interfere. It's good for Kyle to interact with other adults, and Moira knows how to manage him. He's stopped rocking now and seems more relaxed.

Moira crouches down beside Kyle and Ailsa's pleased to see how she makes sure to leave a big enough space between the two of them to make him feel comfortable. Moira points to the Lego tower. 'Building another Empire State Building for me to look at?'

Kyle squints at a piece of Lego shaped like a window. 'No, don't be stupid, the Empire State Building is in America.'

'Kyle. Don't be rude. Moira was only being nice.'

Moira looks up at her. 'It's fine, Ailsa. Don't worry. I need to pick my words more carefully. You'd think I'd know after all these years.'

'The Empire State Building is three hundred and eighty metres high unless you count the spire and then it's four hundred and forty-three metres.' Kyle fits the window into the side of the tower. 'It was finished in 1931.'

Moira laughs. 'It's older than me then.'

'Thirty years older. Your birthday is September 30th, 1961. That makes you a Libra.'

Moira looks at Ailsa and raises her eyebrows. 'I swear that boy's a walking encyclopaedia. I'll make us some tea and then there's something I need to talk to you about.' She glances over her shoulder at Kyle and lowers her voice. 'Alone.'

Stepping over the Lego bricks, she lifts the kettle from its stand and fills it from the tap. Her back is to Ailsa, but there's something in the way she's standing, the slight tremor of her hand as she holds the kettle still under the gush of water that alerts her to something. Despite Moira's easy words to Kyle, there's something different about her today. She'd seen it in the way the woman's eyes had flicked to the clock while they were having breakfast. In the sound of the vacuum cleaner in the living room – a job *she* would normally have done.

It comes to her now what it is. Moira's nervous. She'd not recognised it earlier, but now she can see it clearly in the woman's forced jollity. The way she hums as she pours water onto the teabags, something she never normally does.

Ailsa places the flat of her hand over her stomach. It's why she's been feeling this way, as though serpents are writhing inside her. She relies on Moira to be strong. Dependable. It's that knowledge that helps her cope with her own life.

With Kyle.

With her own nightmares.

'Don't worry about me. I've just had tea,' she lies. Whatever it is that's troubling Moira, she doesn't want to know. 'I need to get on with the laundry or I'll be late for Kyle's lessons and he'll never let me hear the last of it. Are you all right to keep an eye on him for half an hour?'

Not giving Moira a chance to answer, Ailsa lifts her coat from the back of the door and puts it on. 'Maths at eleven o'clock, Kyle. I'll be back before then.'

'Maths at eleven o'clock,' he repeats. 'Don't be late, Mum. Don't be late!'

Ailsa hears the anxiety in his voice and knows she has to calm him. 'I won't be late, Kyle. You know that. Moira will be here if you want anything.'

She lets herself out into the yard but hasn't gone far before she hears footsteps behind her. 'Wait, Ailsa. I'm too old to run.'

Ailsa stops and lets Moira catch up. She looks at her affectionately. 'You're sixty, Moira. That's hardly old.'

'Fifty-nine years, fifty-one weeks and five days if we're going to be precise.' Moira glances back at the house. 'I'm sure Kyle would approve of that. Anyway, it's my birthday I wanted to talk to you about. I've been thinking I'd like to make it a bit of an occasion. A celebration.'

'Oh.' Ailsa's finding it hard to hide her surprise. She's never known Moira to waste time on a birthday before, and 'celebration' and 'occasion' aren't words usually found in her vocabulary.

The writhing serpents in her stomach settle. She's been worrying over nothing. Is it any wonder Moira's not been herself today? Entertaining is not something she's used to, and it's easy to guess what she wants to talk to her about.

'Would you like me to help organise it, Moira? Who were you thinking of inviting? Douglas and Reyne? Ewan?' She's struggling to think who else. Moira has never had a wide circle of friends.

'No. None of those.' She looks up at the clouds that, for a moment, are holding on to their rain. 'I'm thinking of inviting family.' Her eyes return to Ailsa and she swallows. 'Well, actually, that's a wee lie. You see, I've already done it.' She stops, seeing Ailsa's face. 'Please don't look like that, love. I know it's a shock, but I managed to get hold of my son. He'll be on the morning ferry tomorrow.'

Ailsa says nothing. Without realising it, her hands are

clasped in front of her so tightly that the points of her knuckles have whitened. She knows she should breathe, but it's like she's forgotten how.

Moira's arm is around her shoulder. 'It will be fine, hen.'

But it won't be fine. Her whole life is about to be tipped upside down.

Jonah is coming.

She feels the gentle pressure of Moira's hand on her shoulder as she draws her closer. She's worried. Needs to know Ailsa's okay. She tries to muster up a smile, but it's more than she can manage.

For with Jonah's return, the memories will surface again. Not just the ones from the night Callum drowned but earlier ones. Without wanting to, her eyes leave Moira. They sweep the hillside of wooden lodges and come to rest on the boathouse, half-hidden by the rocks.

A place she only visits in her darkest dreams.

TWO

JONAH

It's colder than Jonah remembers. So much colder... windier too. He pulls up the collar of his jacket and does up the top button. Over the last decade he's grown soft. Grown used to the milder weather of the city where, in summer, the buildings press in on one another trapping the heat. The crowds giving an illusion of warmth in the winter. He's forgotten what it can be like out here with the prevailing winds blowing in from the sea. The rain ever-present in the dark pregnant clouds above his head and the damp that seeps into your bones, settling there to leave you cold for days after. Leaning his arms on the wet wooden rail of the ferry, he strains for the first sighting of Bray, the place he used to call home.

And, as if conjured up by thought, he sees it. Still just a dark smudge on the horizon but there, nonetheless. Soon he'll be able to pick out the houses, the cliffs, the beaches of his childhood.

He shudders and pulls his scarf over his chin, covering his beard.

The ferry's turning for the final leg of the one-and-a-half-hour journey from the mainland and, as they draw nearer, the island becomes more defined, his memories morphing into reality. There are the dramatic mountains, remains of ancient volcanoes dropping down to the sea, their rocks encrusted with the white icing guano of sea birds. There's the small harbour. There's his whole goddamn fucking life in front of him, laid bare. Moving ever closer.

But they're not there yet. There's still time for him to change his mind, buy a return ticket and not set foot on the island. For the thought appals him and he can't quite believe he's done the one thing he said he'd never do. Return.

He runs fingers numb with cold through sea-damp hair and tries to control his thumping heart. He knows he's mad to be here, but desperation had made him buy the ticket to Inverness, drive a hire car over a hundred miles to the port and get on this ferry. It had been something in his mother's voice on the other end of the phone that had snared him. Stopped him getting to sleep later that night in his cheap rented room. He couldn't put his finger on what it was, but it was something... and he hadn't been able to ignore it. Couldn't afford to.

Jonah turns and leans his back against the rail, pinching the soft skin between his eyes. They're sore from lack of sleep and the damp, salt wind that fusses his hair and stiffens his beard. There's no going back, though. Already, the engine has changed. Its resonations deeper. Louder. The vibrations of the deck beneath his feet more pronounced. Soon they'll be docking, and he'll have to follow the other passengers onto the jetty. Tamping down the memories.

Knowing he has to eventually, Jonah forces himself to turn back again. Face the island that's so close now he feels he could almost touch it. He draws in a deep breath of sea air into his lungs and makes himself look properly. In front of him are the pastel-coloured houses strung along the quayside like beads on a necklace. To the right, The Stag where he and his brother used to drink. He chews on the inside of his cheek, not wanting to remember. Not wanting to go there.

Above his head, guillemots and gannets circle. He remembers how the two of them used to watch them, lying on the short turf, a hip flask of whisky, siphoned from their dad's bottle, flat on the grass between them. They'd relied on the bastard being too pissed to notice any was missing and thankfully they'd been right. For if he'd found out what they'd done, there would have been no safe haven from his anger.

Jonah thumps his forehead with the heel of his hand. There he goes again... remembering when he'd vowed he wouldn't. The plan was to see his mother, suffer the family meal she'd begged him to attend, wish her a happy birthday and see if the instinct to come home had been correct.

Not drag up the past.

Clang. Clang. Clang. The anchor is dropping. They're here. Picking up his rucksack, he hoists it onto his shoulder. He's travelled light; it's how he always travels. For over the years, he's lived in more places than he cares to remember, leaving again as soon as he starts to feel settled. He wouldn't have stayed in London so long if it hadn't been for Gemma. He'd liked her well enough, and they'd tried to make a go of it, but when she'd told him she was leaving him, that she was tired of his mood swings, he hadn't argued. Maybe if he'd tried harder. Stopped the drinking sooner. Talked to her...

But he knew that nothing would ever be different. For to change the future, he'd have to change the past and that was impossible.

He wonders what she's doing now. Knows that, in all likelihood, she'll be with someone else. Someone worthy of her who will treat her well. Not leave her always looking over her shoulder. Choosing words carefully for fear of causing a fight.

The few passengers that didn't alight when the ferry stopped at the first two islands are heading towards the exit.

The ramp has already been lowered, and Jonah waits his turn to walk down it onto the concrete pier. He walks quickly, paying no attention to the smaller boats moored up on the other side, their halyards clinking in the wind, or the couple walking their dog on the pebbled beach. Knowing that a moment's hesitation might see him running back to the ferry. Carrying on to Rum or Canna or somewhere else that doesn't hold such shit memories.

He hears the rumble as the ramp is raised, grits his teeth and walks faster. He'd expected his mother to meet him, but she'd messaged to say she'd left her old car in the car park of The Stag earlier that morning and had caught a lift back with Douglas when he did his mail round. She had some things to do and, this way, he could arrive at the house at his leisure.

She doesn't want to be in the same car as me, he thinks, then checks himself. The thought is ridiculous since it was *she* who'd invited *him*, not the other way round.

He's reached the road and the first of the candy-coloured houses that face out to sea. Above the door is written Village Shop and Post Office, and he considers going in to get a packet of crisps, but as he digs his hand into the pocket of his jeans for his wallet, he's assaulted by memories. He and his brother standing at the back of the shop next to the newspaper stand. Their pocket money tight in their fists, eyeing up the sweet display. Snickers bars stuffed into pockets when Heather the shopkeeper's back was turned. Her voice carrying after them as they ran off down the street to cadge a lift back with the mail man. *Get back here, Callum, you wee tyke. I'll tell your father of yae.*

Always Callum. Never Jonah. Everyone knowing which brother's idea it would have been. Then would come the turn of the head. The flash of a smile capable of getting a young boy both into and out of trouble. Not bad days. Not when you consider what was to come.

Jonah sees Heather through the shop window, her head

bent to an open newspaper on the counter. A little stouter. A little greyer. If he goes in now, he'll have to endure her sympathy and he's not ready for that. *Still alive. Lucky bastard* – he might as well have the words tattooed on his forehead.

Except he's not lucky. His brother's death is something he has to live with every day of his fucked-up life. His absence affecting him in more ways than he could ever have imagined. Survivors guilt the therapist had called it, but he's having none of it. He'd never been the one in any danger.

No, it's more than that. So much more. For no one tells you what it's like to have his face with you every day. His voice. Taunting you with the fact you could have saved him, if only you'd been stronger.

Ignoring the open door of the shop, Jonah turns right, heading instead towards the white bulk of The Stag. His mother's old Land Rover is parked between a van and a large recycling bin, as she said it would be, but he doesn't cross to it. Instead, he crosses the rough patch of muddy grass that serves as a beer garden and pushes open the door of the pub. Surprised at how it smells the same as it always did. Beer and damp carpet. Though what made the landlord decide carpet was a clever idea when the only footwear the floor sees is muddy walking boots and wellingtons is anyone's guess.

It takes Jonah's eyes a moment to get used to the gloom. The place has had a bit of a spruce up since he was last here. New colour on the walls, or maybe it's the lighting that's different. It's difficult to tell. Shame they didn't think to rip up the carpet at the same time.

Behind the bar, a young lad is standing head bent to his phone. He isn't anyone Jonah recognises and for that he's grateful. The fewer people who know he's here, the better as far as he's concerned. He can't be doing with any of the questions his presence could generate. Can't face the softening of their voices. Their sympathy. He wants none of it.

Jonah taps his card impatiently on the bar top and the lad looks up.

'Aye?'

'I'd like a drink if it isn't too much trouble.' He's unable to stop the sarcasm that's crept into his voice and the lad has registered it. He eyes him suspiciously.

'New here?'

'You could say that.' Jonah massages his brow with his knuckles. He's going to have to keep a check on his emotions. Life is slow on Bray, always has been, and he should remember that. He doesn't want to stand out; being here is bad enough without having people gossip about him. 'Sorry, it's been a long journey.'

'So what will you be wanting?'

Jonah eyes the various bottles of whisky in their optics.

What he really wants is a single malt, but he resists the urge and orders a Coke instead. Muttering his thanks, he takes it to a table well away from the two men in waterproof jackets and hiking boots hunched over a map. Apart from the barman, the three of them are the only ones in here.

Jonah wipes the condensation from his glass, then takes a mouthful, pretending it's something stronger. He'd managed a year dry before his latest fall from the wagon and he's still angry with himself for having been weak. Succumbing to pressure from so-called friends in the pub one evening when he'd been feeling low. He'd always sworn he'd never end up like his drunkard father, but the numbing balm of alcohol is the only thing that can drown out the demons in his head. The ones that have taunted him since his brother's death.

However much he wants a drink, he won't give in to it. *Can't* give in to it.

Slipping his hand inside his jacket, Jonah rests his palm against his heart. Registering the thud of it. Immediately, he regrets the action and pulls his hand away. It's no longer his own chest he's feeling beneath his fingers, but his brother's. He tries to force the thought away, but it remains in his head. The bunched material of his brother's T-shirt sodden with seawater is as real as if it was happening again. The flesh cold beneath his palm. He's sitting astride his slim, muscular body mouthing the words he'd read somewhere would help him in his terrible task.

Nellie the elephant packed her trunk and said goodbye to the circus.

A bloody kid's song, the link between life and death.

Before his eyes, his brother's sternum dips and rises as the heels of his hands press to the rhythm. Over and over. The boat rocks. His body's exhausted.

'All right, mate?'

Jonah looks up. Turns his head to the voice. One of the walkers is staring at him curiously. Did he cry out?

'Aye. Fine.'

But he's not fine. For as he'd carried on mouthing the words, carried on pumping, the nineteen-year-old he'd once been had known in his heart it was useless.

He was trying to revive a brother who was already dead.

THREE

AILSA

Ailsa stands and watches Kyle. He's sitting at the table in front of the big picture window in the lodge they share, his head bent to the exercise book she bought in the shop in the harbour last time she was there. It's where he does his lessons after she's finished cleaning the lodges, and she's thankful that he doesn't seem to mind.

Although it's not yet midday, it's dark in the large living area as the blinds are half-closed. Any movement outside will be a distraction for him and she has to make this work. Has promised the education authority as much.

Ailsa watches Kyle a moment longer, then moves into his view, making sure he's seen her before speaking. Her voice calm and measured.

'How are you getting on?' she asks. She's not a natural teacher, and there are times, especially when he's studying maths, when she wonders whether it should be *him* teaching *her*, instead of the other way round.

'You set me eight problems and I'm on number seven. They're easy, Mum. I want you to make them harder. I like it when Moira teaches me. She makes them really difficult and it's better.'

Ailsa smiles. It hadn't been her intention for Moira to take over some of Kyle's maths lessons; it had happened organically. She'd popped in one morning to tell her about a new booking they had at the lodges and, while she was there, had helped Kyle with something he was stuck on. She had explained it simply and clearly, and Kyle had asked if she could work with him another time. Since then, Moira has helped out whenever she can.

'Moira's busy today but maybe tomorrow. Would that be okay?'

Kyle nods. 'Tell her to make it hard.'

'I will.'

When Kyle had attended the local primary school, he'd been top of his class in mathematics and often it makes her feel guilty. She doesn't want to be accused of holding him back by deciding to homeschool, but she hadn't been happy for him to stay on, despite Mr Dickson's assurances that it would be for the best.

I want you to consider your decision carefully, he'd told her as she'd sat awkwardly on one of the hard grey chairs in his office after telling him her plan. *Since Kyle was diagnosed with autism, he's getting additional needs support in class and we really are very lucky to have such a good primary school on the island.*

Ailsa hadn't considered herself lucky, though. She'd considered herself tired. Anxious. Out of her depth. Every moment away from her son, as she waited for him to come home and hear about his day, a torture in case it hadn't gone well. But it had been her anxiety over his eventual transition to secondary school, an anxiety so acute that it would keep her awake at night, that had decided her. The noise... the larger class... the new curriculum. How would he ever cope?

So, she'd thanked the head teacher and told him she had a copy of his Individualised Education Plan and would be home-schooling Kyle. That she knew what she was doing. Hoping he wouldn't see through the lie.

Looking at Kyle now, she wants to plant a kiss on his sandy head but resists, knowing he'd hate it. Every day, since she'd realised he was different to the other children in his nursery, playing alone, not wanting comfort if he fell, she's been guided by him, pushing aside her own needs. For, whatever else she might think or feel, she knows she's a good mother to Kyle. Loving him with a ferocity that sometimes scares her.

Ailsa goes to the window, prises apart the slats of the blind and looks out. The holiday centre is unusually quiet this week, only a couple of the lodges occupied. It happens sometimes and it gives her a welcome break. More time to spend with Kyle.

A middle-aged couple walk past with their dog. It's on an extendable lead and, every so often, it makes a dash for freedom before the woman pulls it back in. They're moving between the lodges, and before they disappear, Ailsa sees the dog cock its leg against the side of one of them. The woman hasn't noticed and she can't be bothered to open her window and call to them. Also, she doesn't want Kyle to see it as it will set him off and in a bid to quench his thirst for his latest obsession, he'll ask her what feels like a thousand questions, most of which she won't be able to answer. She drops the blind again, glad to see his head is still bent to his work.

Since she took Kyle out of school, she's been surprised at how much support she's had from online charities and the homeschool communities who have offered guidance and suggestions. It's made her realise she's not so alone in her quest to do the best for her son. His old additional support needs assistant, Jill, has also been in touch, even though there was no requirement for her to do so.

'Tell you what, I'll look online. Find something to stretch

you.' Ailsa stops, realising how confusing what she's just said could be to him. 'I mean something harder that you'll enjoy.'

'Thank you, Mum.' Kyle nods his head vigorously, and Ailsa makes a mental note to use the expression as an example later.

Recently, she's been working with him on situations just like this one, comments that can lead to misunderstandings. She's bought him a bright orange exercise book where he can draw the literal meaning of an expression, then write underneath what the person really means when they use it. Yesterday's was *head in the clouds* and she smiles as she remembers the drawing he'd done: a giant with a ring of clouds around his neck. Today's slip-up will be a good one to add to it.

Not now, though.

As Ailsa remembers the thing she has to tell him, her smile falls away. 'Kyle. Darling. Look at me, please.' She sits down next to him and waits for him to make eye contact with her. When he does, she carries on. 'You know how yesterday you met someone you haven't seen in a while. Ewan's daughter, Caitlin.'

Kyle frowns. 'Yes. I didn't like her hair. It looked like she'd put her finger in a socket.'

Ignoring his comment, Ailsa carries on. 'Well, there's someone else you're going to meet today.' She waits, judging his reaction. He seems calm enough even though new faces are stressful to him. It's why she tries not to let him make contact with the ever-changing visitors at the holiday centre, taking him with her when she cleans the chalets only after they've left. Leaving him in Moira's kitchen when she does the laundry.

'Don't you want to know who it is?' Her stomach is starting to churn. She doesn't want this any more than Kyle does.

'No,' he says. 'I don't.'

'I know, sweetie, but it will be better if I tell you... so you're prepared. The man who'll be coming here today is called

Jonah.' She stops, closing her eyes for a second before carrying on. 'He's Moira's son. He's smart and kind. You'll like him. Everybody does.'

But how can she know this? She hasn't seen Jonah in over a decade. Has heard nothing from him. The man she's remembering is the person he used to be, not the one he's become.

A stranger.

She traces her palm with her finger, remembering the feel of his hand in hers. Remembering too the shape of his head as he'd bent to his books the way Kyle does now, and how she'd linked her arms around his neck, pressing her cheek to his. He'd been her first and only friend and she'd loved him so much.

'I won't like him.' Kyle's voice breaks the spell. Then louder. 'I said I won't like him.'

It's only now that Ailsa sees the danger signs she'd missed earlier: how the pads of his fingers are white against the red pencil as he presses it into the page until the lead is in danger of breaking.

Before she can do anything, he gives out a loud wail, but Ailsa knows better than to panic. She looks at her watch, seeing that it's twelve thirty already. Past his lunchtime. She hasn't been keeping track of the time, and he's worse when he's hungry. Why had she chosen now of all times to bring this up?

She takes the pencil from his hand and closes his book. 'I know it's upsetting to see all these new faces, but sometimes we have to do things we don't like. I want you to take a deep breath in and then let it out again, just like I showed you the other day. It will make you feel better. Then we'll have something to eat. Good idea?'

Kyle folds his arms. 'I want Marmite sandwiches.'

'Then that's what you shall have.' He had the same yesterday and the four days before that, but Ailsa hasn't the strength to persuade him to try something else. She's just relieved to have diverted him from what could have been a long and tiring tantrum. One that would most likely have left her in tears and Kyle red-faced and exhausted. 'Why don't you come and help me make them?'

She twists the plastic rod to open the blind fully, letting in the September light. Today the loch is still. Mirror-flat. A man on a paddleboard, his wetsuit seal-black, moves past the rocks and out of sight. When it's calm like it is today, it's hard to imagine the surface whipped into waves, the swell big enough to rock a boat so badly it can take a life.

She shivers.

Living in the place where the tragedy happened hasn't been easy, but what else could she have done? Where could she have gone? For the first months after Callum had drowned, when the small community was still reeling from the shock, she'd been so numb she hadn't cared where she was.

And then Jonah had left too. Taking off straight after his brother's funeral without a word. Unable to cope with the guilt of living when his brother was dead. Unable to look at the loch without remembering. Or that's what she told herself. Abandoning her.

Her own way of coping had been to reinvent herself. Becoming a harder, more brittle version the girl she'd once been. Not caring what she did or who she did it with.

And when, after she could no longer ignore the tiredness, the sickness and the button on her jeans she could no longer do up, she'd reluctantly gone to the doctor and discovered she was pregnant, she hadn't cared about that any more than she'd cared about anything else.

FOUR

JONAH

'Jonah Wallace. As I live and breathe.'

Reyne, landlady at The Stag, stands in front of him, her hands on her hips, feet planted on the worn carpet, and Jonah knows he's sunk. There'll be no getting away from her, and by the time evening comes, everyone will know that Jonah Wallace is back.

He stares at the greying hair piled up on top of Reyne's head, at the heavily made-up eyes, the top that barely contains her full beasts, and composes himself. How he acts now will dictate how Reyne will portray him when she leans over the bar top to pass on the news to anyone who comes in.

He jerks his head to the seat next to him. 'You gonnae sit?'

She will anyway and it's easier to pre-empt it.

Reyne pulls out a chair and parks her backside. Beams at him. 'I thought, for a wee second, I was seeing a ghost.' Her smile fades as quickly as it arrived. 'Not that I thought... oh, dear Lord.'

'You're all right. I know it must be a shock after all this time.'

'Aye, that's exactly what I meant.' Her smile returns and

Jonah knows she's grateful to him. 'What's it been? Nine years? Ten?'

'Eleven.'

'Goodness. Ken you believe it. Has it really been that long?' She reaches out an arm and pats his hand, and Jonah knows the question is going to come. 'How are yae?'

He swallows. What is he supposed to say? That he hasn't a job? That he can't sleep at night? That he hates himself and who he's become? No, those things he has to keep to himself. Instead, he forces a smile.

'I'm good, Reyne. Yourself?'

'Oh, I can't complain.'

Jonah looks around. 'Apart from the colour of the walls, the old place looks much the same.'

Reyne shrugs, the shoulders of her top wrinkling, mirroring the lines of her cleavage. 'You know how it is on Bray. Nothing much changes. It's what your father used to say... why he always preferred this place to the pubs in Elgin.' She jerks a thumb at the optics. 'The whisky might have had something to do with it too, of course. Best on Bray.' There's a heartbeat's pause before she continues, her eyes not quite meeting his. 'Seen anything of him since you've been on the mainland?'

Jonah's fingers tighten around his glass. She's fishing for gossip like she always used to. As she says, nothing changes. 'No. Why the hell would I?'

'No need to snap my head off. I've just heard talk, you know. That he was seen in Mallaig, with his fancy piece.'

'Seen by who?'

'Oh, I don't know. Someone who knows someone. We hear it all in here.'

'Tittle-tattle. Why do you even listen to it?'

Reyne gives a small smile. 'Passes the time. It's not as if there's a lot else to do once the season's ended and the bulk of the visitors have left.'

He tips his glass and takes a large mouthful of his drink. 'I should be going. Ma will be waiting.'

Reyne looks disappointed; she's always had a soft spot for him. His brother too. 'How long will you be staying on Bray?'

'A few days.' He looks at his watch. 'I need to sort some stuff out, then get back to the mainland.' He's not going to tell her about the people who knock on the door of his flat in the middle of the night. The ones who appear when he least expects them with their threats and their demands.

'That will be your job I suppose.' She pulls her top back over her shoulder. 'The last I heard, you were studying business at Edinburgh, or something of the sort, which would have been years ago now. Moira keeps things close to her chest. Clams up whenever I mention you, in fact.'

Jonah looks away. 'I left. It didn't work out.'

He pictures the student union bar full of people he didn't want to be friends with. The few lectures he'd attended, making him want to scream. How could he study when his mind wouldn't settle for more than a few minutes at a time? Was it any wonder he'd been thrown out at the end of his first year? What had followed was a series of dead-end jobs: bar work, security, night shift at the local supermarket. Mind-numbing work that meant he could switch off. Not have to think... or remember.

'Such a shame. Everyone had such high hopes for you.'

Jonah bites back what he wants to say in reply. Instead, he gives a thin smile. 'Thanks for that.'

Reyne's face falls. 'Don't take it the wrong way. It's just that your mum had her heart set on you taking over the lodges from her someday. Wasn't that always the plan?'

A hard darkness settles somewhere in the vicinity of his breastbone, and Jonah moves his fingers to it, massaging the place. Trying not to think of it. Those same fingers. His brother's chest. Heart no longer beating.

'Yes, that was always her plan.' He fixes her with a hard stare. 'But you know what they say about the best laid plans.'

Suddenly, he can take no more of it. He stands, shoving his chair back so that it bangs against the wall. 'Fuck this. I dinnae need this shit.'

Leaving his Coke half-drunk, he picks up his bag and strides to the door, ignoring the walkers who have looked up from their map and are eyeing him warily.

'Oh, for goodness' sake sit down, Jonah.' Reyne is frowning, her arms folded. 'You haven't finished your drink. Your mother's not going to want to see you this way. Not after all this time.'

Ignoring her, he pulls open the door and steps out into the weak September sunlight. The wind is gentler than it had been earlier and it's a wee bit warmer, the clouds having pulled away from the sun. He'd forgotten this about the weather. How it can change so suddenly and unpredictably... just like his mind.

Having reached the car, he crouches and finds the key under the wheel arch where his mother said she'd leave it. If only he'd trusted his instincts this time. Told her it was impossible for him to come back... made up some excuse or other and stuck to it. But he'd heard from her tone that something wasn't right, and it had been enough to drag him here.

He climbs in and turns on the engine, remembering the feel of the worn leather seats. The jolt of the gearstick in his palm as it finds reverse. This was the car in which he and his brother had learnt to drive, and they'd loved the imagined freedom it gave them even though there were few roads on Bray and even fewer places to go.

Jonah backs out of the space, exits the car park, then heads inland. He drives on instinct, deft as a homing pigeon, and as the pastel houses of the harbour reduce to small dots in his rear-view mirror, the landscape in front opens up to him. Huge swathes of peat moorland, its pattern of hummocks and hollows as familiar to him as his own skin, backed by the ever-present sharp ridges of the Bray Mountains. To either side is moorland, the few rowans that crouch there bent and twisted by the wind.

The road is narrow, a single-lane, and Jonah drives with his window open, breathing in the peat-scented air. Occasionally, he'll pass a cluster of grey stone houses with flat fronts and sloping roofs, or a whitewashed croft cottage. The road rising towards the foothills before descending again into the shelter of a glen.

Jonah can no longer see the ocean. He's driving through a landscape that has started to don its autumn mantle, turning from deep green to golden brown as the heather and grasses die back. Despite himself, as the cold air blows in through his window, he feels his head start to clear, the tightness in his chest loosen. His mother had been right on the many occasions she'd said it to him... this place has a way of getting into your very soul.

He continues on autopilot, driving through a landscape sculpted by wind and rain. Not passing anyone on the narrow road. The only eyes to see him belonging to the wild goats standing in groups on the short-cropped grass. The road rises and Jonah drops a gear, hearing the engine work. He rounds a steep bend and then slows, his heart thumping against his ribs. He's at the crest of the hill, the land falling away to his left.

There it is. The sign to Loch Briona Lodges.

He slows. Below the road, at the bottom of a gravel drive, he can just see the roof of his mother's large white house, a smattering of wooden chalets dotting the green grass slope in front of it. A few clustered around the shore of Loch Briona. Parking the car at the edge of the road, Jonah gets out and looks down on the place he once called home and the dark loch beyond it.

It's the place that's haunted him every night of his adult life.

The place his brother died.

Jonah stands with his hands in his pockets, remembering. I was a kid then, he thinks, his eyes skimming the pale shore, the steel-grey loch, before alighting on the woods on the eastern edge. Remembering.

They were *both* kids then. Him and his brother. Unaware of the horrors life would bring them.

A weight settles on Jonah's chest making it hard to breathe. Nothing could have prepared him for how the years would change him. How they'd chip away at who he used to be, sculpting him into an adult he could only ever imagine in his nightmares.

But what of Ailsa, the girl he'd wanted more than any other? What nightmares had the years brought her?

.

FIVE

AILSA

Then

Ailsa trails behind the others, wishing she hadn't said she'd come. Wondering what had made her think it was a good idea.

Callum is ahead, skirting the edge of the treeline that separates the holiday lodges his parents own from the dense pine-fragrant woodland. When he reaches the shoreline, he stops and waits for the others before carrying on again. Pushing back branches where he needs to. Skilfully navigating the rocks and water-filled pools at the loch's edge.

There are five of them, including Ailsa. Walking alongside Callum are two teenage boys of around his age. She's seen them hanging out with him at school and she doesn't much like the look of them. Bringing up the rear is Jonah, looking as though he'd rather be anywhere but here. She knows how he feels. Ailsa looks round and smiles and he smiles back shyly. There's a fresh crop of acne on his cheeks, but Ailsa doesn't care. If anything, it makes him look more grown up than the hint of fair fuzz under Callum's chin and the silver stud in his ear.

It's chilly in the shade of the trees, and Ailsa steps out onto the open shore in the hope the afternoon sunlight might warm her.

'Get back, idiot.' Callum's voice is sharp. 'Jesus.'

He stops walking and his eyes bore into her before his attention moves to Jonah. 'Why the hell did you bring her?'

'He didn't bring me. I wanted to come.' Ailsa had intended her voice to come out confident, but, instead, it sounds defensive. Like a child remonstrating with its mother rather than the twelve-year-old girl she is.

Jonah's at her side now, she can feel the rub of his sleeve against hers.

He points an accusing finger at his brother. 'Why can't you leave her alone? She's not doing any harm.'

'And she's not doing any fucking good either.' Callum gives Ailsa a withering look. 'She's a bloody waste of space.'

He jumps down from the rock he's been standing on and comes over. At thirteen, he's head and shoulders taller than Ailsa – long-limbed and lean like his father, Hugh. Like Jonah. At the thought of the man, Ailsa looks back the way they came, as though he might appear. There's nothing to see, though, only the narrow strip of sand and pebble beach, the grass slope beyond dotted with the wooden holiday lodges her mum cleans. No Hugh striding down the steps from the white house at the top of the slope. No harsh voice calling them back. She's glad as Callum's made no secret of the fact that if his father knew where they were going, there'd be trouble for everyone. The brothers especially.

'What are you looking at?' Callum's voice cuts through her thoughts. 'Yes, you. I'm talking to *you*.'

Ailsa turns back. 'Nothing.'

'Stay at the back and keep quiet.' He narrows his eyes at Jonah. 'Can you vouch for her? How can you be sure she'll keep her mouth shut?'

'She will.' Jonah looks at her, rubbing the back of his neck. 'Won't you?'

With an effort, Ailsa controls her voice. 'Of course.'

'Make sure you do or I'll have a word with Ma about your mum's job. It shouldn't be too difficult to find another scrubber.'

Laughing at his own joke, Callum turns away and carries on up the beach, the two boys from his class shadowing him. The taller of the pair is called Bram, she remembers now, and as he catches up with Callum, he punches him on the arm and says something she can't hear. The boys laugh louder and something inside Ailsa shrinks.

Despite the way he talks to her, she's caught his furtive glances when he thinks she's not looking. Has noticed how his words are more vicious when she's with Jonah, as though he's trying to prove something. She doesn't understand it. Doesn't like it.

'Take no notice.' Jonah glares at Callum's back. 'He's an idiot.'

She likes it when he takes her side. It makes her feel like she's not so alone. There's a high-pitched *twee twee,* and Ailsa turns her head towards the sound. A sandpiper is standing at the edge of the loch, bobbing its back tail feathers. As she watches, it dips its long beak into the water.

There's a splash and the bird lifts away, flying low over the loch on stiff, shallow wingbeats. Callum laughs, picks up another stone and aims it at a bird perched on a rock to his left. When it misses, he swears and carries on walking.

Ailsa watches him. 'I'm glad you're not like him.'

'He can't help how he is.'

Jonah stops and glances back at the lodges, not needing to say more. Callum's inability to stay quiet, to not answer back, makes him take the brunt of his father's anger.

She looks at Jonah, at his pained expression. Unlike his brother, he'd learnt quickly. Kept out of his dad's way if he could. She'd seen him on days she came down to the lodges after school to meet her mum, ducking out of sight of him. She also remembers something Moira had told her mum – that, as a baby, Jonah had hardly ever cried. She wonders now if it's possible that even at that young age he'd known the sound would irritate Hugh. Could babies understand that much?

Ahead of them, Callum has put his finger to his lips. He points at the trees and mouths *come on*.

The only reason Ailsa's here is because of Jonah. From the first time her mum had brought her to the lodges, he'd been nice to her and now, several years on, he's the only real friend she has. So what if the other kids think he's odd? She knows he isn't. If keeping himself to himself is strange, then she must be too. But the best thing about him is how much he loves Bray, even as much as she does. The heather-covered moors, the burns that run down from the high hills, cold to their bare feet even in summer; the ever-changing sky and the pine-scented Scottish air. Everything.

'We don't have to go,' Jonah says, but she knows he wants to. He always wants to do what Callum does, even if he doesn't like it.

'I don't mind. We're only going to look, aren't we? It's not as if we're actually going to *do* anything.' She stops, unsure. All she knows is they're going to check out the place where Seth lives. Her mum calls him a loner, but she's heard what the islanders say about him. As someone who's had her own fair share of name-calling, she wonders if he knows. Or if he even cares. Her mum said he used to live in a run-down crofter's cottage on the other side of the island, but recently he's moved into an old caravan in the trees down by the loch. No one knows why, but Callum says it's so he can spy on the holidaymakers in the lodges and steal their things when they're out kayaking or bird-watching.

Ailsa joins the others at the edge of the forest. She came

with them because of Jonah but also because, despite the nerves that have gripped her stomach, she's curious. Wonders what it must be like to live on your own in a forest with only an Alsatian for company.

'Stay close and stop when I tell you to.' Callum's voice is commanding. He's used to being the leader, takes pleasure in it. 'I'll go first.'

From the beach, the treeline looks unbroken, but when they enter the wood, the pines in front of them seem to move apart like trees in a fairy tale. It's just an illusion though, simply a trick of the eye, the way the firs have been felled making them appear animated.

The ground beneath their feet is soft with shed needles, the air, pine-scented. They're at the edge of a clearing, and from behind the tree where she's hiding, Ailsa can see Seth's caravan. It's white, quite new-looking, and she wonders how he managed to get it there as there's no real path.

'What if he sees us?' she whispers.

'Then we'll run.' Jonah reaches a hand behind his back and shakes a fallen leaf from his hood. 'Bloody fast.'

Despite her heart beating unnaturally hard and fast, Ailsa relaxes a bit. They're doing no harm here... simply checking things out. Wasn't that what Callum had said? And Jonah wouldn't be with them if his brother was planning anything else. She glances sideways at him, wishing she felt more certain.

'Look, there he is.' Callum points a finger at the grimy window near the front of the van.

Ailsa looks where he's pointing. Yes, there's definitely a shadow of a man behind the glass. As she watches, the shape moves out of view, then back again.

Her skin prickles. If he looked up, would he be able to see them? Would he know they were there? A gust of wind shivers the leaves of the trees around her. In the shadow of their canopy, it's cold, the scent of pines replaced by old wood smoke and something sweeter... more pungent.

Ahead of her, Callum's now crouching down. He's waiting, but she's not sure for what. The other two boys crouch as well, but Jonah stays where he is beside her. She doesn't like his expression. It's wary. Uncertain.

Now it's Ailsa's turn to doubt. She'd thought it might be fun to spy, but now she's here, she's not so sure. The boys are whispering together and, in the hunch of their backs, the smirks on their faces, she knows, with a sudden certainty, that scouting the place had only ever been part of Callum's plan.

She tugs at Jonah's sleeve. 'Don't let him do anything stupid.'

'He wouldn't.'

But they both know that's not true. Callum is a law unto himself at times.

There's a sound and Ailsa freezes. The caravan door is opening, and Seth is coming out. In front of her, the boys crouch lower, their giggles barely contained.

Ailsa holds her breath and presses her back against the tree, terrified they'll be heard or, worse still, seen.

She watches Seth as he extends an arm patchworked with dark tattoos to empty the mug he's holding onto the forest floor. From inside the caravan, a dog barks. He turns. Tells it to hush. Now he's facing them again. Tenting a hand to his eyes. Scanning the trees.

Ailsa shrinks back against the tree's rough bark and waits for the moment he'll know they're there. But it seems they're in luck. Seth hawks and spits, then turns and steps back inside the caravan, closing the door behind him.

A quick glance at Jonah's face shows that he's as relieved as she is.

'Come on, Callum,' he hisses at his brother. 'Let's go.'

Callum wipes his hands down the sides of his jeans. 'You do what you like. We're going to have some fun.'

On the right-hand side of the clearing, a little way away from where they're standing, are the remains of some sort of building. Two sides of a stone wall, the rest of the building reduced to rubble. Crouching low, Callum breaks cover. Runs to the pile of masonry and picks up a large lump of stone. He looks over at the others, his cheeks ruddy with excitement.

'Come on. What are you waiting for?'

'Don't,' Jonah says to the other two boys. 'Don't be idiots.'

But Jonah doesn't have the charisma of his brother and his words aren't going to stop them. With a nod to each other, they straighten and skirt the edge of the treeline. When they reach Callum, they bend to the rubble, weighing the rocks in their hands like children on a beach choosing the best stone to skim.

Ailsa's blood runs cold. 'What are they going to do?'

'Isn't it obvious? Bloody idiot. I think we should get out of here.'

'Shouldn't we stop them? Can't you talk to him?'

Jonah shakes his head. 'What's the point? Once Cal's got an idea in his head, there's no stopping him.'

There's a metal clang and Ailsa's and Jonah's heads shoot up. Inside the caravan, the dog barks, louder than before. It's Bram's rock that's hit its target, the dent in the metal side of the van where it's made contact clearly visible.

Callum punches the air. 'Beauty!'

He picks up his own rock just as the caravan door flies open. Seth stands there, the dog straining at the end of the rope he's holding. 'Little fuckers!' he roars. 'Get away from my van.'

Callum flips him the finger. 'Who's going to stop me?'

Pulling back his arm, he lobs the rock at the caravan. It hits the window and the air in the clearing is filled with the sound of shattering glass.

'Little shite.' Seth's face is mottled red. 'I'll tell yae father of you.'

Callum pulls a face at him. 'I couldn't give a shit. Anyway, he knows what you are. Everyone knows... hanging around the school like a bloody perv. Don't think we haven't seen yae.'

Seth's eyes flash dark and Ailsa's scared. He's an adult and whatever Callum thinks of him, he shouldn't be talking to him like that.

'Let's go.' She pulls at Jonah's arm. 'Please, Jonah.'

'I can't leave him.'

'Why not? You said yourself he's an idiot.'

'I can't explain it.' He rubs his nose with the back of his hand. 'I just have to know what he'll do. So I can fix it.'

There's no need for either of them to wait, though, as Callum and his friends are already running back to them. Pushing past them, they disappear into the trees, heading in the direction of the loch.

Seth is striding across the clearing, the dog ahead of him, straining at the rope leash. Fear flashes through Ailsa. She shouldn't have listened to Jonah. Should have gone when they had the chance. It isn't as if Callum waited for *them*.

The dog's angry barks are filling the clearing and a bird flies up from one of the trees above her head. She wants to run, but fear roots her to the spot.

'You're lucky I didn't let him loose on you.' Seth is in front of them now, holding onto the dog's collar. Ailsa's never seen him close up before, and his heavy dark eyebrows and sallow skin does nothing to calm her racing heart. 'Do you want to know why I didn't?'

Ailsa nods dumbly. Moves closer to Jonah, wishing she'd never come. She doesn't want to look at the dog, whose growl is as terrifying as his bark had been. Doesn't want to think about what damage its teeth could do.

But it's not her Seth's looking at but Jonah. Fixing him with eyes that in the shadow of the forest's canopy look almost black. His voice has a strange nasal tone as though he's recently had a cold. 'Well, do you or don't you?'

Ailsa wants to run, but Jonah stands his ground. 'I don't care. Tell me if you want.'

Leading the dog by the lead, Seth walks around Jonah, slowly, deliberately, the previous year's pine needles crunching under his dirty boots. It makes Ailsa shudder, but Jonah doesn't look scared. Why not? Is it because, having lived in the shadow of his father's temper all his life, he's used to situations like this?

Seth stops in front of him, presses a finger to his chest. 'I didn't let him loose because you're not like him. You're different.'

Jonah steps back, places a hand where Seth's finger was, over his heart. 'Am I?'

'Go on.' Seth points in the direction of the loch. 'Get on with you.'

Without saying more, Jonah turns and walks away.

'Wait for me, Jonah.' Ailsa runs after him, trying not to trip over the knots and weaves of the forest floor. Trying harder still to block out the sound of the dog's plaintive whine. The sound of Seth's laughter.

When they break out of the trees and the loch is in front of them, she pulls him round, still breathless from the effort to keep up with him. 'He's right, Jonah. You are different. Why were you so surprised he said it?'

But Jonah doesn't answer. Instead, he pulls the hood of his top up and walks on. Following the prints his brother's trainers have left in the patches of sand between the stones.

Leaving her behind.

SIX

JONAH

At first sight, nothing's changed. There is the large white house with its small-paned windows looking down on the holiday complex. There too is the dense green forest and the handful of lodges placed at discreet intervals on the grass slope leading down to the loch. Further up the beach, he can see the old boathouse, a rowing boat pulled up on the beach beside it.

Surely it can't be the one he and his brother used to go out in? Not after all this time. Without thinking, Jonah's hand lifts, his fingers reaching around to his shoulder, half expecting to feel the tenderness where his father's belt had landed. The stab of pain when he moved that had made him screw up his eyes and pretend to be ill so that he could miss school.

Realising what he's doing, Jonah drops his hand to his side. Forcing himself not to think of it. Those days are over. Gone. Nothing is the same.

He closes his eyes a second. It's this place. The memories it drags up. Once, despite everything, he'd loved it here, especially when they both were kids: playing out on the loch, swimming, fishing from the wooden boat. That had been in the days before their dad's drinking got worse. Before he got into the habit of taking his frustrations out on them all.

But that was then and this is now. He no longer loves the place. Loch Briona and the lodges that look out onto it are cursed. Jinxed. Nothing but bad luck has happened here. And any dreams he'd once had for this place have long gone. Dying alongside his brother.

Not wanting to go inside just yet, Jonah walks past the house. Instead of taking the steps past the laundry room and the toilet and shower block he and his brother helped to build when they were teenagers, he weaves his way between the lodges until the grass slope ends and he reaches the small beach.

Jonah looks around him. It's quiet here, so much quieter than he remembers, and he wonders why. Loch Briona used to be a thriving holiday centre, every lodge booked until late in November when the deer rutting season, a time to see the majestic stags locking horns in a battle for supremacy, had finished. Today, it looks as though most of the lodges are empty. Just a couple showing evidence of occupation, the detritus that comes with visitors: walking boots by the door and an open umbrella propped up against the wooden rails of the decking. A light is on in the window of a lodge he's just passed, despite it being morning, but the rest are dark behind their panes, their doors padlocked.

Could the reason be that people know what happened here? Even though the scenery here is beautiful, you couldn't blame someone for not wanting to stay in a place where the spectre of death still hovers.

Jonah jumps down onto the stones, his feet crunching beneath him. He's dreamt about this moment in his darkest hours. Dreading it. But he has to face his fears and get it over with. For his own sanity, rather than dwell on the bad things, he needs to remember the good times he and his brother spent on the loch. The fun they had.

It's not working, though. Already, he's back there. On the water. Hands pressed against his brother's chest as he pumps. Loch water pooling in the bottom of the boat. His brother's glassy stare.

There's a sound behind him and Jonah jumps. Turns around. 'What the fuck?'

A boy stands on the pebbles, a multi-coloured Lego building in his hand. Behind him, the door of the lodge, the one where he'd seen the light, stands open.

'I don't know you.'

'What?'

Jonah eyes the boy with curiosity, taking in the pale freckled face. The flop of sandy hair across his forehead. He looks to be around eleven or twelve, and it's an odd thing for a boy of that age to say. Back when he was living here, they didn't get many kids at Loch Briona, mainly birders and walkers. It seems things have changed. He looks around, but there appears to be no adult with him.

He tries a smile. 'Should you be talking to strangers?'

The boy shrugs. 'You're not a stranger. I've seen you before.'

'I thought you said you didn't know me?'

'I don't.'

Jonah shakes his head. 'Jesus. Anyway, it's unlikely you've seen me before as I've not been here for eleven years.'

The kid's eyes alight on something a fraction to the right of his shoulder. Something that's clearly more interesting than he is.

'I've seen a photograph of you,' he says eventually. 'It's on Moira's sideboard in the dining room. It's in a silver frame. You're her son and the other person in the picture is the dead one.'

The boy's manner is direct. Disconcerting.

'Okay. So, you know who I am, but who are you?'

'I'm Kyle. I live there.' He points to the lodge behind him.

Jonah looks where he's pointing, then back again. There's something about the way he speaks, his expressionless face. Might he have autism? He takes in what Kyle's wearing: the yellow polo shirt that's buttoned up at the neck, the stiff new-looking jeans. The trainers he's wearing look new too. Not a smudge of dirt on them. In fact, he looks as though he'd be more at home in a town on the mainland than on this windswept island.

The boy hasn't stepped onto the pebbles but is standing where the path ends and the beach begins.

'How do you know my mother?' Jonah's curious to know. 'How do you know Moira?'

Kyle opens his mouth to speak, but Jonah doesn't get to hear the answer. Someone's hollering the boy's name. The sound coming from one of the chalets further up the grass slope. A woman's leaning over the wooden rails of the raised deck waving her hand. A vacuum cleaner next to her.

'Come here, Kyle.' He hears the panic in her voice. 'Come here *now*. You know I don't like you going near the water.'

Kyle stays where he is. 'I'm not by the water,' he shouts back. 'I'm standing on the step and I'm talking to this man.'

As the woman runs down the lodge steps, Jonah takes in the wild, un-styled hair, the faded jeans ripped at the knees, the baggy knitted jumper in a multitude of colours that hangs lower at the back than the front. And, in all these things, he knows her instantly. Ailsa. Just the sight of her making his palms sweat. His breath catch.

She shows no recognition, though, her panic too all-encompassing. Reaching the boy, she grabs him by the shoulders and pulls him to her chest.

Kyle's body stiffens. His head thrashes back, catching her on the jaw. 'Get off. Get off me. Get off.'

The boy's earlier composure has been replaced by a wild panic. His face is contorted. His distress clear to see.

Jonah steps forward. 'What's the matter with you? Can't you see the kid's terrified?'

It's as if his words have brought her to her senses. Ailsa's arms fall to her sides. 'Oh, Jesus.' She steps back. 'I'm sorry, Kyle. I was just so scared when I saw you down here.'

Released from her grip, Kyle's face returns to neutral. 'Can I play Minecraft now?'

Ailsa takes in a deep breath and releases it. She gives a smile that doesn't reach her eyes. 'Yes, but just for half an hour, then it's time for your lessons.'

'I know, Mum. You don't have to tell me.'

Turning, he walks back up the path, his white trainers bright against the dark asphalt. He climbs the steps to the chalet, Ailsa's eyes watching him all the while.

When the door has closed behind him, she turns and gives Jonah her full attention. Soon she'll realise who he is, and he'll have to speak to her, properly, in a way he hasn't spoken to anyone for a long while. For the last eleven years, his conversations have consisted of nothing more meaningful than drunken words in a pub, which he's forgotten the next day, or pillow talk with some girl or other he's picked up. None of it important.

And he knows why it is. It's because he doesn't want them to get close. See the man he's become, not the person he used to be. The one he keeps hidden behind a mask of indifference. The one he hates.

'Is he always like that?'

Ailsa doesn't answer. She's staring at him as though he's an apparition. Taking in his overlong hair and beard, the sunglasses he likes to wear even when it's not bright. The moment she knows it's him is reflected in the pinch of her eyebrows and the slight parting of her lips. In the sharp intake of breath.

And he waits for what's to come.

'Jonah.' Her voice is soft, strumming the strings of his memory. It's all she says.

A thousand thoughts crash into his head. Hard. Fast. Hitting their mark, then retreating. The taste of her lips. The softness of her skin. The way she'd once looked at him. Nothing's changed. She still has this hold over him... even after all these years.

'Yes.'

'I didn't think you'd come. I don't think Moira did either. Not really.'

Jonah looks out over the loch where dark clouds are leaving uneven patches of shade on its flat surface. On a day like this, it's hard to remember what it can be like when the wind picks up and the currents run strong.

He shivers. 'I wasn't going to. I don't know why I did. There's nothing for me here any more.'

But he does know. He knows only too well.

He can't meet her eye. It's been so long and so much has happened since the last time he saw her. However much he wants to believe she doesn't feel any animosity towards him, it's futile. What she's thinking is the man standing before her let her down. Left without a word, leaving her to pick up the pieces and comfort his grieving mother when it should have been him.

She stands a few feet away from him at the end of the path leading to the water, just as her son had. It's like she doesn't want to come closer. Is scared to. And who can blame her. He's not the person she was once in love with. Can never be that person... not after everything that happened.

Ailsa's voice breaks into his thoughts. 'Have you seen Moira yet? Does she know you're here?'

He shakes his head, his hair falling into his face and he's aware of how much it's grown since he last saw her. He tucks it behind his ears. 'No.'

'You have to do it sometime, Jonah.' She looks at his small rucksack. 'Did you bring her a gift?'

'What?'

'A gift... for her birthday. It's why you came here, isn't it?'

There's a note in her voice that alerts him. Something about her question. It gives him hope... but he mustn't let his guard down. Not after all this time. He doesn't need the complication.

'Yes, that's why I came.' He looks up at the big house. 'How has she been?'

Ailsa's voice hardens. 'You'd know if you ever spoke to her.'

'It's been difficult.'

'And you think it hasn't been for me?'

Jonah shoves his hands in his pockets. 'I know I let her down. Disappearing like that. Dropping out of Uni. Fucking up my life. I just couldn't face her. Couldn't deal with all the emotion. I was a coward and took the coward's way out, but that's who I am, Ailsa. The person you never really saw. The one I kept hidden from you.'

Ailsa's face softens. 'You weren't a coward, not really. Everyone copes in different ways when they lose someone. You were grieving, that's all. Moira will understand.'

'I didn't get her anything.'

'You brought yourself, Jonah. And that's all she asked for. See her now. It won't be as hard as you think.'

He looks at her light-brown eyes with their heavy lids, the long sandy lashes she hasn't bothered to coat with mascara. He hears the kindness in her words. Senses in them her desire for reconciliation – not just him and his mother, but all of them.

She's right that he has to see her, but her belief that it won't be as hard as he thinks is far off the mark. Seeing Moira again after all this time will be hell on earth.

A sharp rapping sound takes his attention. It's the boy, face pressed to the window of his lodge. His knuckles resting against the glass.

Realising he hasn't asked Ailsa about him, he does it now. 'The kid?'

'Don't call him that. His name is Kyle. He's my son.'

He scratches the side of his face. 'I didn't know you had one.'

Her jaw is set. 'There are a lot of things you don't know about me, Jonah. You weren't the only one to change after Callum died.' A flush comes to her cheeks. 'I went off the rails a bit. Toughened up and hung around with Sorcha. Slept around. I mucked up my Advanced Highers and was pretty difficult to live with. Mum had already become disillusioned by island life and decided we should leave Bray for the mainland. What she hadn't banked on was me refusing to go with her. Moira was wonderful. She said I could have Mum's old job and live in one of the lodges. Mum didn't argue.' Her hand rests on her stomach. 'A month later I found out I was pregnant.'

Jonah tries to picture it. The evenings spent at The Stag or at the club in Elgin – the only one on the island. Picking up men. Shagging them in the back of a car maybe. He can't imagine it. Doesn't *want* to imagine it. He thinks of all the one-night stands – the beds he's left and the doors he'd crept out of before their owners woke. Far be it for him to censure.

'Go on.'

'Kyle is the best thing that ever happened to me.'

'And the father?'

She shakes her head and Jonah knows in that gesture that either she doesn't know who it was or, if she does, she's never told him.

'So you brought the kid up by yourself?'

'Not by myself, no. I had Moira. She lets me live here rent-free, and, in return, I help her with the lodges. Just part-time, though.' She glances up the hill to her chalet, but her son's face is no longer pressed against the glass. Instead, he's sitting on the deck watching them. 'Kyle needs me.'

Jonah scratches his head. 'What's wrong with him? Why isn't he at school?'

He'd noticed straight away that he was different. The shifting gaze. The direct questions.

'Nothing's wrong with him.' Ailsa's tone is fierce. A lioness defending her cub. 'He's smart and funny. He just sees the world a little differently to you and me.' She pinches her lips together, signalling an end to that particular conversation. 'I need to go now. It's time for his lessons.'

She turns and walks back up the slope, raising her hand in greeting to a couple who are just leaving one of the lodges, raincoats covering walking trousers, boots already covered in mud.

'I'll see you around then,' Jonah calls.

When she doesn't answer, he turns away again, his face clouding. There's no place for the feelings Ailsa has stirred up in him. No place at all.

'Damn her!'

Picking up a flat stone, he skims it hard and fast across the water before turning and walking purposefully up the slope to his mother and the hell that's awaiting him.

SEVEN

AILSA

Ailsa's just letting herself into the lodge when she sees Moira's car pull up outside the house. She hadn't realised she'd gone out. Instead of going to her own front door, the older woman takes the path down the hill, and as she gets closer, Ailsa sees how her face is set.

When she reaches the lodge, Moira stands at the bottom of the steps, untying her headscarf. She looks tired, the lines around her mouth deeply etched, making her look older than her sixty years.

Ailsa holds open the door. 'Did you need me for something, Moira? Would you like to come in?'

Moira looks around her; she seems distracted. 'Have you seen Jonah? Is he here yet?'

'Aye. You've just missed him. I found him down by the loch and sent him to find you. I'm surprised you didn't pass him.'

Moira looks back up to the house. 'I didn't.' Her eyes meet Ailsa's again. 'How did he seem? In himself?'

Ailsa looks away, wanting to keep to herself the way he'd made her feel. Still trying to process why a part of her still wants him as much as it ever did. Even though she knows it's pointless. 'It's hard to say. It's been so long.'

Moira folds her scarf and puts it in the pocket of her coat. She looks up at Ailsa. 'I know it's been a long time, and that's why I want to give him a chance. He's my son, Ailsa, and that bond will always be there. I will come in if it's not inconvenient.'

'No, it's fine.' She glances in at Kyle. He's sitting at a table by the window, a textbook open in front of him. 'You're always welcome.'

Moira nods, then fingers gripping the wooden handrail, she climbs the steps and follows Ailsa into the lodge.

'You're late, Mum.' The legs of the chair tap on the wooden floor as Kyle rocks. 'I started without you.'

Ailsa places a steadying hand on the back of her son's chair to still it. She smiles. 'Good on you. You see, Kyle, you are perfectly able to get on by yourself for a few minutes.'

She turns to Moira. The older woman is leaning against the arm of the settee, studying Kyle, the fingers of one hand tapping out a rhythm on the back of the other. She looks deep in thought.

'What would you like, Moira? Tea or coffee?'

Moira drags her eyes away from the boy. 'Aye, tea, if it's not too much trouble.'

There's a half-finished mug of tea from earlier on the table. Picking it up, Ailsa walks through to the back of the lodge where the kitchen is and empties the dregs into the sink. As she gets another mug from the cupboard and makes the tea, she hears Moira talking to Kyle. Something about her birthday and how much fun it will be.

'Will there be dogs?' she hears him reply. 'I like dogs, but Mum won't let me have one.'

Ailsa stiffens, the kettle steaming in her hand. This conversation could go badly wrong as the last time she said no to his request, he kicked off. She should have warned her.

As if waiting for this moment, a sudden barking drifts in through the open chalet door. It's not close, but all the same, Kyle's head shoots up and he runs to the window. 'Can I go and see it?'

Ailsa thumps the kettle down on the worktop. She doesn't want to have another conversation about it now. It's Seth's dog they can hear. It must be out on the beach, its bark carrying on the still air. Ailsa tries to ignore it, pouring water into the mugs, fussing with the tea bags. She knows that dog... is scared of it. Not that she sees it much, only on the odd occasion when Seth takes the bus to the harbour to buy food. She thinks of its intelligent eyes, the pointed ears, the sharpness of its muzzle, and shivers. Whenever she sees it outside the shop, tied to the rail by the thick rope around its neck, she gives it a wide berth. Its owner too.

It reminds her too much of the other one. The one he'd had before. The one that bit her.

'Mum? Can I?'

'No, it's your lesson time.'

As if they have a will of their own, Ailsa's fingers snake under the sleeve of her jumper, seeking out the narrow ridge of the scar that runs down the inside of her arm. If her mother had known the truth, the animal would have been reported... but it wasn't the dog's fault. She squeezes her eyes shut, guilt consuming her. No, it wasn't his fault at all. And she shouldn't think uncharitable things about its owner either, as for all his adult life, the man has been the victim of hurtful gossip. Guilty of nothing more than reacting to it. Is it any wonder, considering what he's had to put up with over the years? Yet, despite everything she tells herself, there's something about Seth's appearance, his manner, that makes her glad he keeps himself to himself.

The dog has stopped barking and she sees, with relief, that Kyle has sat down again. The breath she lets out is long. The crisis has been averted... for now, anyway.

Putting the mugs, and a glass of Kyle's favourite lemon barley drink on a tray, Ailsa carries it into the living area. As she puts it on the coffee table, Moira shakes her head. *Outside*, she mouths.

Wondering what it is that can't be said in front of Kyle, she puts his drink next to him and smiles. 'I'm just going out on the deck with Moira. We won't be long.' She taps a finger to the book that's open in front of him. 'See if you can get on with these two questions on your own and I'll check them when I come back in.' She shows him her watch. 'I'll be ten minutes that's all.'

'Promise?'

'I promise.'

Kyle thinks for a minute, then nods. 'All right.'

She goes to the door and opens it, shivering as a gust of cold wind blows in. It's not really the weather for sitting outside. Stepping out onto the deck, Ailsa lifts the top of the bench seat and takes out a couple of tartan blankets. She holds one out to Moira. 'Here. No need for us to freeze to death.'

Moira takes it from her and pulls out a chair from under the rattan table. She sits, wrapping the blanket around her legs, and Ailsa does the same.

Out on the loch, a gull cries and both women turn towards it. It's Ailsa who turns back first, not wanting to know where the older woman's thoughts have taken her.

'What did you want to say to me?'

Moira pulls her gaze away from the grey water, throws a glance at the closed door. 'What I have to say is for your ears alone.'

Without warning, the curdling sensation in her stomach

that Ailsa had experienced the previous day returns. 'Now you're worrying me.'

Moira smooths a hand over the top of her head. 'I'm sorry, but this isn't easy.'

Ailsa's fingers bury into the soft wool of the blanket either side of her lap, finding the solid edge of the chair and gripping it as though to a life raft. 'Is it about Jonah?' Why she thinks this she doesn't know. It's just a feeling she has.

Moira taps her nails on the glass tabletop. 'What I have to say does have something to do with him.'

Ailsa shifts in her seat, her breath catching in her chest. A sixth sense telling her she isn't going to like this. 'So what is it?'

The tapping stops and Moira links her fingers. She fixes Ailsa with a steady gaze. 'It's something I need to ask you, and I think, deep in your heart, you know what it is.'

A gust of wind rattles the lodge door and Ailsa's eyes flick to it, hoping it won't unsettle Kyle. 'I really have no idea.'

Moira sighs. 'It's not something we've talked about properly, but now is the time for us to be open with each other.' Reaching out a hand, she takes Ailsa's, her fingers cold against her skin. 'All right, I'll spell it out if that's what you want me to do. Although you've never said as much, I believe that Kyle is Jonah's son. That I am his grandmother.' She leans forward, chest pressing against the edge of the table. Her face earnest. 'Am I right?'

Something inside Ailsa freezes. Why is Moira doing this? Why after all these years? Haven't they been happy living as they've done without questions... without the need for answers? But Moira is looking at her expectantly, and she knows she won't get away with silence.

She needs time to think. Time to stop the racing of her heart. 'What's made you ask this question now?'

'Isn't it obvious? My son hasn't been back on the island since...' She stops, swallows. 'Since the tragedy. He doesn't write. Only answers my calls when he needs money. It's clear he hates this place. Hates me.'

Ailsa's shocked by the hurt in her voice. She'd thought she didn't care. 'He doesn't hate you. How could he? You're his mother.'

'I know my son. I may be his mother, but he also thinks I'm his judge and jury. He's hurting. He thinks I blame him.' She looks away at the stretch of water that took both her sons, one to an early grave, the other to another life. 'And I'll be honest with you, Ailsa. I'm petrified he'll leave again. He deserves to know the truth, and when he does, things might be very different.'

Ailsa stares at her, unable to believe what she's hearing. 'You want to use my son... *my* son... as a pawn to keep Jonah here? If I hadn't heard it with my own ears, I wouldn't believe it.'

Moira's hand rises to her throat, her fingers touching the deep hollow there. 'That's not what I meant. I just think Jonah has a right to know.'

Ailsa looks at her coldly. 'Jonah has a right to nothing. He left us. You. Me. All of us. You know what I was like after Callum drowned and Jonah took off. I was a mess. I've never lied to you about what happened. I changed. Pushed my way into Sorcha's group and started hanging around the pubs in Elgin. There were guys I slept with whose names I didn't even know. I'm not proud of it... it was just what happened. My way of coping. Kyle's father could be anyone. Nothing's changed, Moira, just because your precious son's come home.' Pushing the blanket to one side, she stands. 'You know, I think you'd better go.'

Moira looks at her a moment, then, her fingers gripping the arms of the chair, pushes herself up. She closes her eyes, her body swaying a little, and Ailsa fights the urge to steady her. Why should she feel guilty when it's Moira who's brought this on herself? Why couldn't she have let things be?

Recovering her composure, Moira folds the blanket and lays it on the back of the chair. 'I'm sorry you feel this way, Ailsa. I'm just doing what I feel is right... for us all. If Kyle is my—'

Ailsa cuts her off. 'Kyle is nobody's but mine. Please leave before I say something I'll regret.'

Moira walks unsteadily across the decking, grasping the handrail as she takes the steps down. When she reaches the bottom, she looks back up.

'He has his eyes. His hair. Why did you think I wouldn't see it?'

'For God's sake, Moira.' Ailsa's tone is sharp. 'You're seeing what you want to see. Nothing more. And if you say anything to Jonah, I swear I'll—'

'I'll say nothing today, but I'll make no promises. I know my own flesh and blood when I see it. I only wish I'd said something sooner.'

Ailsa turns away, but as she grasps the door handle of the lodge, she turns back.

'If you *do* say something, we'll leave Loch Briona. I'll do it, Moira. You know I will.'

Ailsa's chest tightens. She doesn't want to leave, this is her home, but she will if she has to. Jonah's return has already started to upset the status quo of her life, and she doesn't like it. It's not good for Kyle.

It's only now she notices her son's face at the window, his forehead pressed to the glass. He won't have heard what they've been talking about, but he'll have seen their expressions, know that she and Moira have had an argument. Once, he wouldn't have been able to do this, but Ailsa's put a lot of work into helping him recognise the visual cues of emotion – exaggerating a facial expression and asking Kyle how he thinks she's feeling, playing snap with visual cue cards. Every day, every week for the last few years.

And this is the first time she's regretted it. He'll be struggling to process what he's just seen. Will want to know the cause and will ask her why she's angry with Moira. Ask what the woman's done to make her brows pull together and her lips press in a thin tight line like the picture on his card.

It's a conversation she doesn't want to have with him.

Not today.

Not ever if she has anything to do with it.

Moira is looking at Kyle too, and Ailsa sees the effort it takes for her to compose her face, to push through the hurt and the disappointment to make a smile for him. He smiles back at her as she taught him, and as Moira's face brightens, Ailsa's anger dissolves into guilt once more.

Is she doing the right thing? She's too wound up, her emotions too all-consuming to know for sure. Walking to the rail, she leans over and watches Moira make her way up the hill towards the house where her son will be waiting for her. She stops at the side door before going in, and Ailsa wonders if Moira's plucking up the courage to face him. Her heart thuds. Will she tell Jonah about the conversation they've just had, or will she respect her wishes?

Ailsa leans her forehead on the wooden rail and mouths a silent prayer. *Please don't let her. Please. Please.*

EIGHT

AILSA

Then

Ailsa stares out of the window. Between the buildings on the opposite side of the road, a slice of grey-blue sea is just visible, the Skye Cuillins a blot on the distant horizon.

'Ailsa. I asked you to give me your answer to question five.'

Mrs Kendrick's voice jars in her head, unwanted, and she looks up, her brows pinched together. She'd been miles away thinking about Jonah. It's something she's been doing a lot recently, and she's not sure what to make of the thoughts that come unbidden, whenever she's doing something she doesn't like, such as helping her mum strip the beds in the chalets at Loch Briona at a weekend. Or English, which she'd only chosen as it was the lesser of many evils... she taps her pen against her notebook.

Hating to be caught out, Ailsa runs her pen down the page until she reaches question five. She starts to read from her notes. 'George kills Lennie by shooting him in the back of the head to save him from a more painful death at the hands of Curley.'

'He did indeed.' Mrs Kendrick nods her approval, then fixes

Ailsa with her dark eyes. 'I'm sorry if I interrupted your daydream. But there will be plenty of time for that when term ends.'

'Aye. Sorry.'

There's a murmur of voices behind her. A laugh that's smothered. Ailsa feels herself redden.

She looks at the next question on the sheet in front of her, then back at the text, skimming down the page to find the answer to it, but just as before, the words blur and swim. In their place is Jonah's face, just as it had been before, his image as clear as if it were printed on the page. The fair hair that he only has cut when he's made to. The high cheekbones. The blue eyes that do something funny to her insides when he looks at her.

Placing the book back on the table, Ailsa turns to the window again, watching a gull hover above the building opposite before alighting on the roof tiles. When was it she'd started feeling this way about him? When had the friendship changed to something else entirely? In her eyes at least.

The gull lifts off again, rising above the rooftops and flying away towards the sea. For there's the crunch. The question she asks herself as she lies in bed each night. Does Jonah feel the same?

Usually, the two of them hang out after the school bus drops her off on the road halfway between her house and the Loch Briona Lodges. It's where he's been working the past year, having deferred his place at university until the following September at his mother's request. He hadn't been happy about it, had told her so more than once, as he'd been itching to leave the island. His mother had insisted, though, telling him that helping out at weekends was one thing, running the place full-time an entirely different proposition. This way, by the time he takes up his place at university, he'll be prepared. Will have a foundation upon which to grow the business skills he'll learn there.

That's what she says anyway.

Ailsa looks at her watch. Only half an hour until she can be out of here. Only a few more months until her exams and then she'll be finished for good. School makes her feel closed in. Claustrophobic. Like her mum, she needs air. Space. The salt-tang smell of the sea and the heather-and-peat scent of the moors.

Mrs Kendrick is droning on. Something about the goals shared between George and Lennie. She stops talking and Ailsa looks down quickly, not wanting to be singled out again. Isn't it enough that her clothes set her apart? A fact for which she has only herself to blame. She runs her hand down her thighs feeling the coarse linen of the baggy checked trousers she chose this morning, worn a few inches above the heavy brown brogues and the heather-coloured ankle socks. Today, she's wound a scarf of her mum's around her head, tied at the top in a floppy bow. The effect is a strange merging of bohemian and plain odd – or at least that's what the other girls think. She's heard them discuss her when they think she's out of earshot.

She doesn't care, though. Let them laugh. She knows she's odd. Different. It's the way it's always been. Her mum's the same. A free spirit, coming over to Bray on a whim when she was barely out of her teens. Meeting her dad and staying. She's still here – even though her dad never stayed the course. Never even waited until she was born.

Ailsa feels a point of a pen in her back and turns. 'What?'

It's Sorcha. She's leaning across her desk, the loose neck of her T-shirt gaping, the swell of her breasts, aided by the push-up bras she favours, visible to anyone who might chance to look. And from the way the boys in the seat across the aisle are nudging each other, Ailsa's not the only one who's noticed.

'Just wondering if you're going to the Winter Ceilidh?'

Ailsa tenses. 'Why? What's it to you?'

'I was interested. That's all.' Sorcha glances at the girl

sitting beside her. It's Bethany, Ailsa's best friend back in juniors. 'We just wondered what you'd be wearing if you *did* go.'

Sorcha's face is poker-straight, but she's unable to keep it up. Her mouth puckers and tears form in her eyes from the effort to stop it. A snort of laughter escapes her, causing Mrs Kendrick to look up, and she covers her face with her hands, her shoulders juddering. With effort, she gains control, sitting back in her chair, her breasts pushing into the soft fabric of her top. It's an action she's practised many times over the course of her higher school years. One that's honed to perfection.

'Settle down, please. Anyone would think I was teaching S1 rather than S6.' Mrs Kendrick gets up from her table and comes over. She stands in the aisle between Ailsa and Sorcha's desks. 'Is there a problem, Sorcha? Something I should know about?'

Sorcha wipes away a tear from the corner of her eye with the back of her hand, leaving a smudge of mascara. 'No, Mrs Kendrick. Sorry.'

Ailsa has dipped her head to her book, but she feels her teacher's eyes on her.

'Ailsa? Everything all right?'

'Aye. Fine.'

She taps a finger to the textbook in Ailsa's hand. 'Good. Then I suggest you both knuckle down if you want to have any chance of passing your exams.'

With a sigh, Mrs Kendrick leaves them and goes back to her table.

'Bitch,' Sorcha mutters under her breath.

For a moment, Ailsa thinks the insult is meant for her, but when she glances behind her, she sees Sorcha's eyes are fixed on their teacher not her.

Ailsa turns back again. Ashamed of the relief she feels.

·　·　·

By the time the bus drops her off at the nearest stop to her house, it's almost empty, most of the pupils attending Bray High School coming from the main town of Elgin on the other side of the loch, or one of the other smaller towns on the more populated eastern side of the island.

Ailsa likes this part of the journey – when the bus falls silent and she's left with just the memory of the inane chatter she's had to listen to on the forty-minute drive. Conversations filtering through the gaps in the seats from the back of the bus about clothes and programmes she's never watched because her mum doesn't believe in having a TV. The boys are no better than the girls. Show-offs. Pressing their feet against the back of the chair in front, their voices overloud.

Now it's just her and a younger girl from one of the crofts further down the valley and she's glad she's sitting near the front so she doesn't feel obliged to talk to her. Instead, she presses her forehead against the window and looks out at the changing scenery. The road has climbed, winding through the heather-clad, lower slopes of the Ben. And below to her right, Loch Briona lies flat and grey. Its pebble shores, with their rocky outcrops, lacing its edge like an uneven petticoat.

Also from here, she can see Elgin, though it's too distant to distinguish the houses or the waterside pub. Forty-five minutes along the windy narrow road by car or bus or twenty as the crow flies across the water. There used to be a ferry, but now the only way to get across is to sail or to take a boat with an outboard like the one Jonah and Callum keep moored up on the wooden jetty at the holiday centre. Once, a couple of summers back, the three of them had tried to kayak there, but the wind was brisk, the current strong, and they'd given up. By the time she got back, windswept and exhausted, her arms had felt as though they'd been involved in a wrestling match.

'Your stop.' The bus driver turns in his seat and smiles at her. 'Unless you want tae go back again.'

Ailsa pulls a face and stands. 'You must be joking.'

'I was. See you tomorrow then.'

'I suppose.'

She jumps down onto the short turf and raises a hand, watching the bus drive away. Normally, she'd go straight home, sit in her small kitchen while her mum shows her the wool she's dyed or the feathered dreamcatcher she's made from nature's detritus collected from the beach. Today, though, she can't face it. Wants to put off the moment when her mum will ask her how she got on in her revision lessons and she'll have to lie. For despite her claiming to be a free spirit, living off the land as much as their small holding will allow, she's keen for her daughter to leave the island and make something of herself. Not fall into the trap she did of thinking life is easy without a proper job and a proper income.

So, instead of going home, Ailsa walks the other way, following the road down towards the loch. She's only just reached the sign telling motorists that Loch Briona Holiday Lodges are 250 metres ahead when she hears the roar of a motorbike engine. Turns just in time to see the bike round the corner. It's going too fast, its front wheel skidding on the stones, and she has to jump backwards to stop it from hitting her.

The bike swerves to a stop and Ailsa stands where she is, her heart hammering. Her legs feeling as if they might give way at any moment.

Reaching up a hand, the rider lifts the visor of his helmet. 'What the fuck were you doing in the road? I could have killed you.'

Ailsa stares at his red face. The ice-blue eyes. She wants to shout that it was his fault, that he was going too fast and should be more careful, but she doesn't. Instead, she folds her arms around her body and says nothing. Jonah's brother, Callum, has always had this effect on her. Making her feel tongue-tied. Awkward in a way that Jonah never has.

He rests his hands on his leather-clad knees and jerks his head in the direction of the chalets that can just be seen between the trees. 'Going this way?'

She nods.

'Cat got your bloody tongue?'

Heat rises up Ailsa's neck. 'I thought I'd see if Jonah wanted a hand with anything.'

Callum doesn't try to hide his amusement. 'I bet you did.' His eyes give her the once-over. 'I wouldn't bother wasting your time there. Believe me, he wouldn't be interested in you. He's bloody fussy. The person who ends up snaring him will be some posh bird who's studying to be a lawyer or a doctor.' He powers up the bike, letting the engine roar. 'Not some local girl who looks like she's made her own clothes, even if the girl in question *is* hot.'

Ailsa's just thinking about what to say in reply when his face breaks into a smile, changing his features.

'Want a lift?'

She shakes her head. 'No, thanks.'

'Please yourself.'

He drops his visor and shrugs, powering the bike away. Leaving her standing at the side of the track, confused. That's always been the problem with Callum. The way he blows hot and cold – one minute insulting her, the next minute acting as though it never happened. Jonah once told her he'd been the same at school. It could have gone either way, but, somehow, despite often being in trouble, he'd manage to charm most of the teachers into ignoring his misdeeds.

His dad had been the same. Hot-headed. A womaniser. How Moira had put up with him so long was beyond anyone's comprehension, and when at last she'd seen the light and thrown him out, told him his latest woman was welcome to him, the whole community had breathed a sigh of relief. He'd kept her very quiet, the last one, and speculation was rife as to who it might have been, but whoever it was, the result had been the same. Hugh had taken his wife's advice and left Loch Briona and good riddance. Only Moira had mourned. Maybe she hadn't really meant it.

Their dad's leaving had affected the boys greatly. Differently. Callum had treated his dad's departure as might a vanquishing soldier. Becoming cockier than ever – his status elevated from bad apple to family protector. He'd told anyone who'd listen that he didn't care that they'd lost a father – the person who practically ran the holiday complex, repairing lodges and felling trees that had weakened in the winter storms and become a danger to the visitors. He didn't care because *he* could do those things to help his mother. They didn't need the bastard. Hugh's departure with his latest fancy woman was a blessing for everyone.

Jonah, on the other hand, had taken it badly. Had taken time off school, and on his return had become more withdrawn than before. So, Ailsa had taken a step back from their friendship, knowing him well enough to realise that it was better to give him space and time to adjust.

Ailsa carries on down the road towards the lodges, and as she reaches the large house, a glance through the reception window shows Jonah, his head bent to the computer.

Not sure if he can see her, she knocks on the glass and he raises his head, a slow smile altering the contours of his serious face. For months after his dad left, he didn't smile at all, but now, if she's lucky, she'll catch one and hold it to her heart in case the next one is slow in coming. She's thankful that they're coming back now. Those smiles she loves.

And with the return of those tentative smiles, has come a departure: the black and yellow bruises that used to bloom on the brothers' skin, unmentioned. Cheekbones. Arms. The soft flesh above the kidneys she'd once seen when Jonah had reached for something on a high shelf in the kitchen.

That's something none of them will ever miss.

Jonah comes out to meet her. He stands shyly with his hands in his pockets, shuffling his feet on the stony path.

'Have a good day?'

'If you can call memorising quotes from Steinbeck good, then, yes, it was.'

He smiles. 'Oh dear. Fancy a walk?'

'I was hoping you'd say that. My head feels fit to burst.'

'Yeah, mine too. I'm trying to get my head around the accounts. Let me just get my jacket.'

He reappears with a battered leather jacket and shrugs it on. 'Anywhere in particular?'

Ailsa shrugs. 'I don't care.'

'We'll go this way then.' Jonah leads the way down to the water's edge and turns right. 'Hear about Seth?'

'No, what about him?' She wishes the man didn't live so close. Having him there, just a mile or so from their homes, makes her uneasy.

'Police took him in for questioning.'

'Really? Why?' She wants Jonah to hold her hand so badly it hurts.

He doesn't, though. Instead, he takes her arm, and she has to be content with that. 'The rumour mill has it a boy's gone missing.'

'Where from?'

'I'm not sure.'

Ailsa's breath catches. 'You think Seth did it?'

He shrugs. 'Who knows? He's kind of crazy, so maybe he did.'

'Living alone and not wanting to be part of society doesn't make you crazy, Jonah. If it did, my mother would be tarred with the same brush. Lots of people choose to live off-grid. Anyway, who told you this?'

'Callum.' He steers her around a lump of driftwood. 'He seems to know everything.'

'Callum's a stirrer. It wouldn't surprise me if he was the one spreading the rumours about Seth and that boy himself.'

Jonah's face settles into a frown. 'He wouldn't do that, Ailsa.'

'No, I'm sorry.' Ailsa kicks herself. What made her say such an idiotic thing? She knows how fiercely protective the boys are of each other. Criticising one is like criticising the other. It's just that she's still mad at Callum for almost running her down at the top of the road.

'That's why I thought we'd go this way for a change,' he continues. 'Today, there'll be no danger of us bumping into him or him setting the dog on us.'

Seth is known for warning intruders away from his property with obscenities and the loosening of the thick rope that serves as a lead around his dog's throat. It makes Ailsa shiver.

'The dog,' she says suddenly. 'What will happen to it?'

'They'll have found somewhere for it if they keep Seth in. Don't worry, the police won't want a dead dog on their hands.'

'I suppose not.' She doesn't tell him she'd be happier not going anywhere near Seth's place. She's just glad to be with him. The thought of the odd man makes her shiver, though. His small, dark eyes. The fine straight hair. The binoculars always trained on something.

Harmless, her mum calls him, but she's not so sure.

Especially after what Jonah's just told her.

NINE

JONAH

Jonah hears his mother before he sees her: the back door opening, then closing, the rustle of material as she hangs up her waterproof on one of the hooks on the thick stone wall. He'd let himself in, knowing it's what she'd expect him to do, and has been waiting in the over-stuffed chair in the kitchen next to the Aga. Bent forward, elbows on knees, his eyes trained on the doorway.

Her boots are next. He hears the rubber thunk of them as she pulls them off and drops them onto the tiles before placing them next to her shoes. She'll be moving his aside too, most likely, for when they'd been a family she'd always be cleaning up after him and his brother. After his father too.

At the thought of his old man, Jonah shudders. Over there by the window was where he'd once pinned him to the wall, his large builder's hand twisted in the fabric around his throat. He stares at the faded wallpaper and frowns. What had he done that time? If he's honest, he can't remember. It would have been something and nothing, of that he's sure. A wrong word. A chore not done. It didn't really matter what. His mother had diffused that one, though. Managed to calm his father down. Get him out of the house before his fist could swing.

There had been home-made biscuits after. Whispered words of comfort. Promises made that it would be kept between the three of them, for he remembers now how his brother had walked in, his hair windswept from an afternoon mucking about on the loch. He'd looked from one to the other, seen their serious faces, and had known as he always did. As they *all* always did.

Just another fucking day in paradise, Jonah thinks.

He looks around the room. How could he have thought it was normal to live like that? Was it because they'd never known any different?

Ailsa knew, of course. Only a fool wouldn't. She'd seen the black eyes and the bruises. Seen, also, the way the two of them were around their dad. Always watchful. Always waiting. Eyes, ears, the small hairs on the backs of their necks... every part of them marking time until the next outburst.

And then it was over. As quickly as it had started. The drunken, womanising bastard was gone, out of their lives. Their mother taking charge for the first time in her life and good riddance to him. In many ways things were better, but they were still left with the gossip. The humiliation of it. The spectre of Hugh still hanging over the place. Over them all.

'Jonah.' His mother's in the doorway looking at him. 'I'm glad you came.'

He stares back at the woman he hasn't seen for eleven years. The moment he's been dreading for just as long.

He's not sure why, but the sight of her shocks him. It's not that she's changed that much considering the time that's passed – maybe her hair's a little greyer, her frame a little thinner – but these are things he'd expected. The natural passing of time. No, it's something else. Something in the way she's standing, shoulders stooped as if she's carrying the weight of the world.

Shadows under her eyes where once there hadn't been. His instinct to make the journey had been right. He's certain of it.

She's studying him too, as though trying to work out the answer to a particularly difficult problem, and it makes him unexpectedly sad. It hadn't always been that way.

He pulls himself together. 'Ma. How are you?'

That he's here at all, after all this time, sitting in his childhood kitchen with its wooden table etched with the lines and grooves of his younger self, is absurd. That they're speaking to each other as though they're strangers even more so. After all they've shared.

His mother lifts a hand to her head. Her hair looks thinner. Finer. Neat though, drawn back behind her head in a bun as it's always been.

'How am I? Really? Tomorrow I'll be sixty, Jonah, and for that I'm thankful. There was a time when I thought I might not make it that far.'

The words are like a punch to his gut. Is she referring to his father or her anguish after his brother's death? It's not something he wants to ask her. Not now. Not ever. The time for those questions has long passed. There's no place for them now.

He scratches his neck. 'I should have brought you a gift... for your birthday.'

'Did you want to?'

Jonah shakes his head. 'To be honest, I didn't think about it. I never really believed I'd come.'

'None of us did.' She takes a step towards him, and Jonah stiffens. He thinks she's going to embrace him, and when she doesn't, straightening the collar of his jacket instead, he's oddly disappointed. He was right all along. She blames him... just as he's always believed. And why wouldn't she?

'I saw Ailsa,' he says, his voice feigning an indifference he doesn't feel. Wanting to change the subject.

'Yes. She told me.' She lifts his coat from the back of the

chair and returns to the lobby, and Jonah imagines her hanging it on the hook next to her own. A hook that might as well have had *Jonah* written above it like at school. A hook that something tells him will have been empty of coats for as long as he's been gone. The one on the other side of it too.

'She looks well,' he says, when she comes back in.

A strange expression crosses his mother's face, gone again before he can recognise what it is.

'Aye. She's been a wee treasure. I don't know how I would have managed without her, if I'm honest.'

The words she hasn't said lie between them unspoken. *After you left.*

But he'd had to. What other choice had there been? Staying on at Loch Briona could never have worked. Not even with Ailsa there. Not if he wanted to survive. But in boarding the ferry to the mainland, he'd simply swapped one hell for a different one. For his guilt had travelled with him. Growing with each passing day. Tormenting him whether asleep or awake.

Jonah knows he should leave it, but he can't. 'You could have sold. No one would have blamed you.'

'No!' The word is sharp. 'Too much of me is here to ever leave. You of all people should know that.'

He bites back what he really wants to say. That the place is corrosive. Eating away at you until there's nothing left. 'Yes, I suppose.'

He gets up and walks to the window. It's started to rain, teardrops running down the pane. When it's like this, the loch steel grey, the clouds dark and heavy, it's hard to imagine why people come here.

'So what were you planning... for tomorrow. Did you want to go out? The Stag, maybe?'

He's not going to suggest taking the motorboat across to

Elgin. That's something neither of them would be able to cope with.

Moira leans her back against the wooden table, her face brightening into a smile. 'I'd like to stay here. Use the dining room and make an occasion of it. Ewan has given us one of his lambs, and I thought I could cook something nice for us all.'

'All?' He hadn't expected that. For some reason, he'd imagined it would be just the two of them... alone, so they could talk.

'Yes. Ailsa and Kyle too. It would be wrong not to include them.'

He thinks of the strange boy he'd spoken to. Peering out at him from under his fringe. 'Wrong? How so?'

'I'm not going to dignify that with an answer.' She looks at him. Assessing him. 'The two of you used to be so close. I thought you—'

'No, Mum, you didn't think. You never do. That's all in the past. We're not those people any more. Jesus. Why won't you ever let me just forget? Is it any wonder I never came home?'

Her face falls and her eyes are so wounded he has to look away.

'I'm sorry, Jonah. For me, that time when you were boys is as fresh as if it was only yesterday.' Pulling the chair from underneath the table, she sits heavily. 'It's how I keep him alive. I'm sorry if it makes you uncomfortable, but it's true.'

Jonah's shoulders sag. He runs a hand down his face. 'No, it's me who should be sorry.' Knowing he should make an effort, he crosses the room. Places a hand on his mother's shoulder. 'You tell me what you want me to buy for tomorrow and I'll get it.'

She smiles up at him. 'Bless you.' Lifting his hand, she presses it to her cheek. 'Things will be different now, Jonah. Now that you're back.'

He resists the urge to pull his hand away.

Things *will* be different. How could they not?

TEN

AILSA

Ailsa wakes from a dream, the details of which have been forced from her mind by the piercing scream that comes from Kyle's room. Without bothering with a dressing gown, she leaps from her bed and hurries to her son's bedroom on the other side of the lodge.

'It's all right, Kyle. It's just a bad dream.' It's an effort to keep the anxiety from her voice. 'I'm coming.'

Still shell-shocked from having been woken so abruptly, she pushes open Kyle's door expecting to find him sitting up in bed as he often is when waking from a nightmare. Usually, his eyes would be screwed up tight, his fist pressed to his lips, but not tonight. No, tonight, Kyle's bed is empty, the duvet a heap on the floor.

Her son is at the window, his arms folded above his head, the skin of his forearms pressed against the cold glass. The blackout curtains that help him get to sleep at night have been pushed aside and he looks so small, so lonely. Ailsa looks at her little boy, taking in the Spider-Man pyjamas that stop mid-calf, showing off his skinny ankles – the ones he won't let her replace, however much she cajoles. Her instinct is to scoop him up. Smother him with comforting kisses. But she can't. There's nothing he'd hate more.

'Kyle... sweetheart.' Not wanting to startle him, she moves to his side. It's a moonlit night and she sees how pale his face is, his skin reflecting the moon's white orb.

Kyle doesn't respond. He's staring at something in the darkness.

'What is it?'

Kyle's bedroom faces onto the path that leads down to the shore of the loch, lit with an occasional ornamental lamp. At the bottom, moonlight silvers the water. She presses her forehead to the window, trying to see what he's seeing, but there's no movement. Nothing to see except for the wooden hulks of the nearby lodges and the tall pines that enclose the holiday site.

Kyle opens his mouth, and although Ailsa is ready for it, the sudden scream he gives is a dagger to her heart. It's a terrible sound, and she's grateful that it's not the height of summer when there are more people here, as the wooden chalet walls are thin.

What has caused this?

Trying to control her own fear, Ailsa steadies her voice. 'There's nothing out there, Kyle. Come back to bed and we can talk about what has made you so upset.'

To her surprise, Kyle lets her take his hand and lead him back to bed. He sits on the edge but won't get in. His rocking making the bedsprings squeak.

His voice is flat. 'I don't want the man to climb in the window.'

Ailsa's eyes flick to the blackout curtain. 'There *is* no man, Kyle. It was just a bad dream, but I'll check if it will help you to sleep.'

Getting up, she leaves his bedroom and goes into the living room. Unlocking the door to the patio, she opens it and looks out. Everything's still. From somewhere in the forest, a dog barks. The sound plaintive. Lonely. Carried through the night on the breeze that plays with Ailsa's hair. Kyle has heard it too as when she goes back to him, his hands are over his ears. His eyes screwed up tight.

'We can get a dog to protect us. Yes, Mum. Say, yes.'

'No, love. There's nothing to protect us from.' She tries for a confidence she's not feeling. In the dead of night, what she thinks she knows for certain can loosen and fray.

Kyle's speaking again, quicker now, the words tripping from his tongue as they do when he's been over-stimulated. 'Dogs sweat through their paws, but the area isn't large enough to cool them so that's why they pant. Their noses have a special pattern, and no two dogs have the same. Like our fingerprints.'

Ailsa watches his pale face, wondering how best to deal with him. His broken sleep has caused him to become stuck in his thoughts. A loop he'll find hard to get out of by himself.

Coming round in front of him, she holds up her raised palm. Sometimes, words aren't enough and it's the signal they use to signify that he's stuck.

'It's late and you're tired,' she says. 'Mummy's tired too. It's time to end the conversation and sleep, darling. I'll stay with you if you like.'

'In case the man gets me?'

Ailsa's breath freezes in her lungs and she stares at him. 'What man?'

'The one who was outside. The one who was looking at me.'

Getting up, Ailsa walks to the window once more. The night is still, no wind to move the branches. She'd seen no one before and there's no one there now.

'It was a dream,' she says again. 'Come on. Into bed and in the morning, I'll make us pancakes. You'd like that, wouldn't you?'

Kyle doesn't answer, but he does as she asks, pulling the

covers right over his head until all she can see is the top of his sandy hair.

She blows him a kiss even though he can't see it. 'Good night, darling. I'll see you in the morning.'

But as she's closing the door, her eyes are pulled to the window once more. She must have been right; Kyle had been having a bad dream. But he'd been so scared. So sure.

She touches the silvery scar on her arm.

What if she's wrong?

What if someone really was watching him?

ELEVEN

JONAH

Then

Jonah glances at the girl walking next to him, her wild fair hair blowing in the wind, her cheeks flushed. He's known her since forever and she's the sister he's never had. The one he wishes he'd had instead of his idiot brother. Hot-headed. Arrogant. Thinking only of himself.

Ailsa's told him about her run-in with him as she'd walked down the drive. Idiot! He hates that he's been tarred with the same brush as Callum. It's something he's spent his life fighting against. Yet, the more he's fought against it, the tighter the invisible bond between them has got. And now he's scared the knots that bind them can never be severed. Not without consequences. For he's not blameless either. There are things he's done that make him no better than Callum.

Ailsa skirts a line of rocks. Looking back at him, she smiles. 'You okay?'

'What? Yeah, sorry. I was miles away.'

'Somewhere good?'

He feels a twist in his gut. 'No, not really.'

The ragged strip of beach they've been walking on has curved away from the holiday lodges and they're now alone. If he didn't know better, he'd think they were miles away from anywhere. Anyone. It's how he likes it. Not sitting at a desk in reception getting to grips with the accounts. Not watching his brother up a ladder fixing one of the chalet roofs like his father had once done. Not listening to Callum shouting at their mother.

This is what he likes, not the business but the stark beauty of where they live. The ever-changing water of the loch. Mirror-flat on a fine summer's day, its siren beauty calling the boys to swim and canoe. Daring them to disturb the mountains reflected in its glassy surface.

Best of all, though, is when the place is as it is today, those same peaks white with snow. The bitter air chilling your bones, reminding you you're alive, when the truth is you're dead inside.

He looks across at Ailsa. The blue woollen coat Ailsa wears to school over her blazer looks too thin for the time of year. She'll come down with something if she's not careful.

'Warm enough?'

She pulls the collar up, looking pleased that he's asked. 'I'm fine.'

He nods. At least it's not raining... or sleeting. That's worse, not one thing or the other, the freezing rain making it hard to see. Impossible to drive. The snow, though, when it comes, is beautiful. Transforming Loch Briona and the lodges into a fairy-land. One that only the family will see for the holidaymakers will be long gone.

'How was school?'

'Same as always. Boring. Pointless.'

Jonah frowns. For him, learning makes you powerful, opens the world to you, but he's given up trying to make Ailsa see it that way. He knows she's brighter than she thinks, but what good is an education if it doesn't set you on the path you desire. And what does she desire? He wishes he knew. The only thing she's told him is that she doesn't ever want to leave Bray.

He thinks of his mother and the plans she has for him when his university course is over. He'd thought things would be different with his father gone, thought she'd favour Callum and his practical skills over his ability to number crunch, but nothing's changed. She's made it clear. Jonah's future is running Loch Briona. It always was and it always will be.

'Do you think Sorcha's pretty?'

The question comes out of the blue. Jonah thinks about it. He doesn't really know her, just seen her a couple of times at the lodges, slipping into one of the empty ones with Callum when their parents' backs were turned.

'I suppose so. If you like that sort of thing.'

If he's honest, he thinks Ailsa is much prettier, more natural. Her style less conventional. Not designed to impress or flatter as Sorcha's is.

'Callum seems to like her.' Ailsa's not looking at him, but she's waiting for his answer as though it's important to her.

'My brother likes anyone who comes on to him, and half of those who don't.'

Ailsa casts a quick glance his way. Her voice sounds resigned. 'I think she is.'

'It's lucky then that we don't all have the same taste.' It seems the right thing to say and, when he catches her smile, he's pleased. He'd hate for Ailsa to be like Sorcha. Obvious. Calculating. But whatever he thinks of the girl, he's glad she's caught his brother's eye, taking Callum's attention away from Ailsa. An attention that disturbs him in a way he can't explain.

To their right are the woods that form a living barrier between the loch and the mountain road. First birches, their trunks shedding bark like old skin, then, further along, the tall Scots pines that he loves so much.

'Come on.'

He holds out his hand and Ailsa takes it, looking pleased. They step into the trees and walk between the tall trunks, patterns of leaves shifting on their faces.

'Jonah, look there.' Ailsa stops and points.

They've reached the clearing where Seth's rusting caravan is, and now he's not sure why he took her this way. He looks in the direction she's pointing, knowing it can't be Seth she's seen beneath the high green canopy as the guy's at the police station in Elgin. No threat to them.

Ailsa stands with her hands pressed to her mouth, then, before he can stop her, she runs into the clearing.

'Ailsa, wait.' He follows her. 'You don't need to go in there.'

But it's too late. He hears her cry out and is filled with cold dread at what might have caused the sound.

Pushing into the clearing, he sees her and stops, seeing what she sees. Seth's weathered caravan stands alone in its circle of trees, wheels sunk into the soft pine-strewn earth. It's never been much to look at but now its rusting hulk is daubed in shiny red paint. The words painted there clear to anyone who might happen to venture this far from the chalet site.

Guilty. We know you did...

Jonah stares at the paint that runs from each letter like blood. The sentence that hasn't been finished.

'Who would do such a thing?' Ailsa moves closer, her shoes crunching on the pine needles.

'I don't know.' But he does. He knows only too well. He's seen his brother's handiwork before. On the side of the school's science lab and on Douglas's cab the morning after he'd refused to give him a lift back from The Stag when he was pissed as a fart.

He'd thought he'd grown out of it. Clearly not.

'He doesn't deserve this. Whatever happened to innocent

until proven guilty?' Ailsa folds her arms and shakes her head. 'It makes me sick.'

'Me too.' And it does. When he gets back, he'll be having words with the idiot.

A low growl comes from nowhere, silencing them. He feels the clutch of Ailsa's fingers on his sleeve and knows he needs to be brave for the two of them.

His eyes scan the area, searching for the noise. It doesn't take him long to see Seth's dog lying under the caravan, its nose pressed to the ground. The rope around its neck attached to one of the van's metal legs. Next to the creature is a battered metal bowl containing only a small amount of water.

'Poor thing.' Ailsa moves closer. 'It must be thirsty.'

'Don't.' Jonah jumps forward and pulls her back. 'You didnae know the dog.'

'I know enough to see that it's scared.'

She moves a step closer, palm held out in front of her. 'It's all right, boy. We're not going to hurt you.' She shoots Jonah an accusing look. 'You said it would be okay. That someone would take care of it while Seth's at the police station.'

'I thought they would.'

'That water's not going to last long.' She's level with the dog now and it gives another low growl followed by a sharp bark. 'Don't be scared.'

'Ailsa don't—'

But it's too late. Ailsa has reached out her hand to the bowl and, in that instant, the dog comes alive. Springing from beneath the caravan. Jaws snapping.

Ailsa pulls her hand back but not before the dog's teeth make contact with the soft skin of her forearm. Jonah jumps forward, grabbing the empty paint can that's lying beside the caravan steps and swinging it at the dog's nose. It's enough to make it let go and Ailsa staggers back, her arm clutched against her chest.

Dropping the can of paint, Jonah runs to her. 'Are you all right?' He lifts her arm and inspects the gash that runs from elbow to wrist. 'We need to get you back. Get this looked at.'

Ailsa looks down. The mark left by the dog's teeth a red trail against her winter-white skin. 'It's just a surface wound.'

'Even so, it needs cleaning. Maybe even a tetanus injection. That dog's dangerous. It should be put down.'

'No!' It's said so sharply he blanches.

'I thought you didn't like dogs.'

'I don't.' She casts a nervous look its way. 'It's just that I think it was scared... and I know how that feels.'

He wants to ask her what she means, but she's hurrying on.

'Its instinct is to guard and it's not fair to blame it.' She points to the paint can hanging from Jonah's fingertips. 'It must have been there when whoever it was defaced the caravan. It's probably why they never finished.'

He looks down at it. Sees the red dribbles of paint that run down the outside. The same red as the door of the sauna he and his brother helped their father to build. He'll need to get rid of it.

But first there's Ailsa to worry about. Digging into the front pocket of his jeans, he brings out a handkerchief and unfolds it. 'Here, it's clean.'

He lifts her arm and carefully wraps the handkerchief around it, trying not to react when she winces as he ties the ends. 'That will stem the blood until we get back at least. Let's get out of here. The place gives me the creeps.'

'In a minute.' One careful step at a time, Ailsa moves back to the caravan. Making sure she's out of reach of the dog, she picks up the water bowl that now lies upturned between them and steps away again. Crouching, she unzips her school bag and takes out her water bottle, emptying it into the metal bowl before pushing it close enough that the dog can reach it.

Jonah watches all this. Seeing how kind she is. How her

concern for the dog has overridden any pain she feels from the creature's bite. If only he had that empathy. That need to put others before himself... but he doesn't. Not really. Otherwise, he'd be happy to stay at Loch Briona and take over the family business as his mother wants rather than wanting to run away. It puts him to shame.

But he hates it here. It holds too many bad memories.

'Come on.' He takes her good arm. 'We need to go. I'll ring the police when we get back and let them know about the dog. Say we heard it barking and were worried.'

'And the van?'

'They'll see it when they get there. It's just a stupid prank – we don't need to get involved.'

He wonders if Ailsa knows why he's saying it, concluding that it's most likely she does. She knows his brother as well as he does. Later, he'll come back and get rid of the paint can. Their mother doesn't need anything else to worry about.

Blood is already soaking through the handkerchief. When they get back, he'll take a proper look at the wound. They've a decent first aid kit in the office and it might be enough.

'All right?'

Ailsa nods, but her face is pale.

'That's good. Let's go then.'

They walk with their arms linked until they hit the beach, the pine-strewn forest floor giving way to pebbles, and Jonah acknowledges the relief he feels at being out in the open once more.

The dog is barking again, but he doesn't want to look back and neither does Ailsa.

Maybe it was an oversight for, if they had, they would have seen the greying net curtain at the window of Seth's caravan move aside. Seen the hard black circles of binoculars pressed against the filthy glass.

TWELVE

AILSA

Ailsa looks in the wardrobe, trying to decide what to wear to Moira's birthday meal. If anyone had asked, she'd have told them that it was the older woman she was making the effort for as she pushes the clothes along the rail. Deep inside, though, she knows it's not true. The hanger with the full blue skirt that she unhooks from the rail has been chosen because Jonah once said the colour suited her.

It's as simple as that.

Not that she has any thoughts of rekindling anything. That time has long passed. The knowledge they share a permanent wall that would take more than a sledgehammer to demolish. But, still, even after eleven years, it's hard to break the habit. She smothers a yawn. Her broken night has given her a headache. Made her grouchy.

'What do you think?' Ailsa carries the skirt to the living room and holds it up to her waist, turning to Kyle who's at the laptop playing Minecraft, his face rigid with concentration.

Not expecting an answer, as once he's started a game, it's difficult to distract him from it, Ailsa studies his face. Seeing that he looks none the worse for his broken sleep last night. In fact, he'd woken earlier than usual, coming into her room and demanding his usual Rice Krispies. Turning his nose up at the pancakes she'd promised.

Should she have talked to him about the previous night and what he thought he'd seen? Probably she should have, but she hadn't wanted to upset Kyle's good mood. Not today. Not when the success of Moira's evening could depend on it.

'I think it will do.' Ailsa puts the skirt on the dining table and pulls a chair over to Kyle. 'Look at me, please. I have something important to say and then you can carry on.'

Reluctantly, Kyle turns. 'What?'

Ailsa breathes in deeply. 'Do you remember what I said to you yesterday... about Moira's birthday meal?'

Kyle's eyes fix on a space behind her. 'You said I had to be quiet and let the adults speak and that not everyone is interested in what I'm interested in.'

Hearing her words uttered from her son's lips, they sound cold. Insensitive.

'I'm sorry. That wasn't what I meant.'

He folds his arms, but still he won't look at her. 'Then why did you say it, Mum?'

'I just meant that although we all love hearing about your interests, sometimes you have to listen to what other people say too.'

'And if they're boring, can I tell them?'

Ailsa has to laugh. 'No. That wouldn't be a good idea. If you told Moira that, it would make her sad.' She pulls an exaggerated face to illustrate what she's said, the corners of her mouth dragging down.

Kyle looks at her briefly, then away again. 'That's how she looked when you were talking to her outside yesterday. Was she sad then?'

Remembering Kyle's face at the window, Ailsa sighs. As he hadn't mentioned it, she'd presumed he hadn't noticed anything was amiss. She'd also tried to forget the conversation the two of them had been having. Remembering her threat to leave if Moira said anything to Jonah. Praying she wouldn't have to carry it out... for all their sakes.

'She was a bit sad, Kyle, but she's better now.'

'Why was she sad?'

Ailsa draws herself up. In no mood for Kyle's constant questioning. The way he has of bullying her until she gives an answer that satisfies him. Wearing her down.

'I told you, she was—'

His voice rises. 'Why was she sad? Why was she sad? Why was she sad?'

Suddenly, it's too much. The broken night. Her concern over how Kyle will be tonight. Jonah's unexpected return.

'For God's sake. Give it a rest, why can't you?'

As soon as she's said it, she feels guilty. It's not Kyle's fault, and she mustn't take it out on him.

'I'm sorry, Kyle. I shouldn't have shouted.' Reaching out a hand, Ailsa covers Kyle's, trying not to react when he pulls it away. She smiles, pointing to her lips. 'See, I'm happy again now. You don't need to worry.'

Ailsa's scared he'll keep on asking her about Moira, but her outburst seems to have broken the cycle of his questioning. He turns back to the laptop and within seconds his fingers are tapping at the keys.

Picking up the skirt, she takes it back to the bedroom and lays it on the bed. Tonight will be fine. She's no need to worry.

Somehow Ailsa has managed to avoid Jonah all day, but it's only been putting off the inevitable. Locking the lodge door, she follows Kyle down the wooden steps, then takes the path up to the large white house at the top of the hill. In her bag is a bracelet she found in a little craft shop in Elgin made from sky-blue sea glass, and she hopes Moira will like it. Kyle is holding a bunch of dahlias, the stems of which are wrapped in damp kitchen roll and held fast in a polythene bag. They'd picked them earlier from the little fenced-off garden area she's created next to the lodge. It sets theirs apart from the visitors' and makes it feel more of a home.

As she passes one of the lodges, a man comes out and hangs a groundsheet over the wooden rails on the decking. He smiles and says hello before going back inside. She notices how moss has colonised the roof tiles changing them from grey to a damp green, sees how one is loose and has slipped. Despite their best efforts, the holiday complex is slowly falling into disrepair and unless they do something about it soon, their rental numbers are in danger of dipping even lower.

Not wanting to worry about it now, Ailsa ushers Kyle to the back door of the house and knocks on it. Her heart is hammering inside her ribcage, and she presses the flat of her hand against her chest, telling herself to calm down. Not to be so silly. This won't be the first time she's sat at Moira's family table and shared a meal with her. But of course it's not Moira she's worried about. It's been a very long time since she's shared the table with Jonah... and the last time was when Callum had been there too.

The door opens and Moira stands there smiling. She's dressed in an expensive-looking knee-length crepe dress and at her throat is the locket she never takes off. Her hair is down today, styled into waves that fall to just above her shoulders, but despite the blusher on the contours of her cheeks and the carefully applied eye make-up, she looks pale and tired.

Forcing herself not to stare, Ailsa ushers Kyle in. 'Kyle wanted to give you these,' she says, hoping he won't contradict her. 'And this is from me.'

She pulls the tissue-wrapped present from her bag and hands it to Moira. 'I hope you like it.'

'I'm sure I will, whatever it is.' Moira leans in and kisses her cheek. 'Thank you, darling, I'll open it later. And how's my wee lad?'

'Kyle, Moira's talking to you.'

He looks at the floor. 'I'm all right.'

'That's better.'

Ailsa takes off her coat and tells Kyle to do the same, then hangs them both on the hook at the end of the row, noticing that the one that used to be Jonah's is empty. They're first to arrive. From the range in the kitchen comes the delicious aroma of roasting lamb and rosemary, and she feels her stomach rumble. 'Where would you like us?'

'I thought we'd use the dining room. It's not often I have the chance to entertain.' Moira lifts the flowers from the bag and unwraps the wet kitchen roll from the stems. She smells them. 'These are exquisite. Are they from your garden?'

'Yes, they're ones that managed to survive the last storm.'

Moira looks towards the window where dark clouds are gathering outside. 'I'm not so sure another isn't coming, despite what the forecasters say.'

'It wouldn't be the first time they'd got it wrong.'

Unprotected as they are on the edge of the North Atlantic, the storms on Bray can be severe. It's something they all know only too well.

Kyle has left the room and soon they hear the plink plink of the old piano that has been in Moira's family as long as the house. Kyle loves it, and Moira has been giving him informal lessons. The other day she heard them play a simple duet together, and it had brought tears to her eyes.

'He had a bad dream last night, but he seems fine today.'

'I'm glad. I don't like tae see him troubled.'

It's as though the conversation they'd had the previous day had never happened and Ailsa's relieved. Maybe now she's had a night to sleep on it, Moira will have realised how rash she'd been in her assumptions. Jumping to her own conclusions, with no evidence.

Ailsa follows Moira into the dining room where the mahogany table takes centre stage between the heavy sideboard and the fireplace. The room is large, but the red-painted plaster on the walls draws it in, making it strangely claustrophobic. The table is set for four, one at each side, and Ailsa hopes she won't be opposite Jonah. Scared he'll be able to read her.

Today, Kyle seems distracted. Instead of practising the tunes Moira's been teaching him, he's playing the same four notes over and over and it's starting to grate on her nerves.

'Stop that now, Kyle.'

He stops for a moment, his eyes on his fingers, then presses down again, louder this time.

'Kyle, I said that's enough.'

'It's all right, love. Let me deal with this.' Moira skirts the table and places her fingers on the keyboard next to Kyle's. As he plays his four notes, she improvises a tune of her own to go with them, and Ailsa's amazed to see his face break into a rare smile.

'You see what wonderful music we can make even when we don't expect it? I have something new to teach you next time you're here. Something my father taught me. When you've practised enough, you can play it to Mum. Would you like that?'

Without looking at her, Kyle nods. 'Yes.'

'Then that's what we'll do... but not now. Now there's lamb to eat and an apple crumble that still needs topping put on it. Why don't you help me?'

Moira lowers the lid of the piano, and Kyle removes his fingers from the keys. He gets off the stool and follows her into the kitchen as obedient as a dog. Ailsa massages her forehead with the heel of her hand. How does Moira make it look so easy? Is it because she's already brought up two boys of her own?

Her eyes slide to the silver-framed photograph of the family that's on the sideboard. Moira and her husband, Hugh, flanked by their two sons, a photograph taken in this very room. She remembers when it was taken. It was on their anniversary. Yet, despite the happy occasion, the woman's eyes are wary, the boys' faces impassive as though they're mannequins placed there by the photographer. She shivers. The image reminds her of the photographs the Victorians would take of their dead relatives, propping them up amongst the living. Except in their case, they are all alive. *Were* all alive.

Shaking off the maudlin thoughts, Ailsa calls out to Moira. 'Anything I can do to help?'

'No, Kyle and I are doing a grand job, aren't we, lad? Pour yourself a wee dram if you have a mind to. Or there's wine if you prefer. There's a good red open on the side.'

'Wine would be lovely, thank you, but maybe I should wait until Jonah gets here.'

'I'm sure he won't mind. Just help yourself. Tonight is a special night, after all.'

Feeling the need for alcohol, Ailsa lifts the stopper off the cut-glass decanter and pours herself a generous glass. It's chilly in the room and she wonders whether she should suggest lighting the fire, but it's not her house so she doesn't.

Instead, she goes to the dining room window and stands to the side, watching the path she came up earlier. She's guessed Jonah is staying in one of the empty chalets and wants to mentally prepare herself for seeing him again. Not let him take her by surprise as he had before.

From the silver frame, she feels Jonah's brother Callum's eyes watching her, Hugh's too. So alike. They never thought much of her, and the feeling was mutual. It's an uncharitable thought, she knows, but she's glad they're gone. Loch Briona is a better place without them. Sometimes, when she sees Moira content in some activity around the lodges, chatting to a bird-watcher or happily sharing gossip with Reyne, she'll wonder what would happen if Hugh returned, his tail between his legs. Would Moira take him back after making such a fool out of her? Would she forgive him for not having bothered to go to his own son's funeral?

When she sees her in that battered old wax jacket, or polishing the frame containing his photograph, she's scared she might.

But what about Callum? If she could click her fingers and make him come back, would she? As she looks down at the loch, imagining a motorboat drawing nearer, two boys on it instead of one, she knows she'll never feel any different. Not when she remembers what Callum could be like. But then she remembers how traumatised Jonah was after the accident. How it broke him, Moira too. Her mum used to say that however much you despised someone, you should never speak ill of the dead. Not even if the words are inside your head. But it's hard not to.

She sees Jonah now. He's walking slowly up the path, his hands dug deep into the pockets of his jacket, his face set. Looking for all the world as though he's approaching hell rather than his mother's house.

She watches as he stops and looks back down the slope to the loch, just visible in the gloaming, the lights of Elgin beginning to twinkle on the other shore. After a few seconds have passed, he tips his head back to the sky and she sees the pain that's etched onto his face – the deep furrows between his brows, the tight pinch of his lips. And she can't help wondering what he's thinking. Whether he's remembering the night it happened. Whether it's his dead brother's face that's in his head... or hers.

THIRTEEN

JONAH

Jonah pulls himself together and turns back towards the house, forcing his feet to take him towards an evening he's been dreading since he woke that morning. As he passes the shower block, the toilets, the recreation area with its dartboard and pool table he and his brother had helped to build before the curse fell on their family, he keeps his eyes firmly on the gravelled path. Barely aware of his heart beating a tattoo in his chest. Barely aware of the face at the window that pulls back as he draws near.

He has a headache, the result of broken sleep. The nightmare he'd woken from the previous night refusing to lessen its grip even when he knew he was awake. He'd lain in sweat-soaked sheets, fear creeping into his bones, his organs. The face looking up at him from the water turning his body rigid. He'd left the curtains open, but the view of the moonlit loch, rather than calming him, had only served to meld the fantasy into reality. And, even when the sun came up, his brother's dead face had been there. Keeping him company through the day. Making him fear he was going mad.

He'd thought he'd managed to conquer these night terrors, but he knows he's only managed to supress them.

Reaching the back door, Jonah knocks – too hard, a demand to be let in rather than a request. It's because his nerves are frayed. He knocks again, harder still and the door opens, but it isn't his mother who stands there, head on one side, it's the kid he saw yesterday. The one with the pale freckled face and the strange way he has of looking past him.

The boy's face registers nothing, but, as he watches, his features change. Close in. 'Go away.'

'Hey, that's not very—'

'Go away!' Kyle's face is ashen, the freckles standing out more than they had a few seconds ago. It's as if he's seen a ghost. 'Go away! Go away!'

His eyes are looking past him into the darkening yard, and Jonah turns his head to see what he's looking at, but there's nothing there. It's clearly him he's addressing. In the distance a dog barks. A lonely sound. The boy listens. Falls silent.

Why does no one come and take the kid away? He can't be here on his own, surely. But just as he's about to push past him into the lobby and find out what's going on, his mother is there, the expensive perfume she's always loved following her. Kneeling beside the boy, she urges him to look at her and, with reluctance, he does.

'I think that's enough, don't you, Kyle. That's no way to greet my son now, is it? That's no way to greet anybody.'

Kyle looks at her, his head on one side. 'Are you angry?'

'No, not angry. Just disappointed. It's my birthday and I want everything to be lovely. I hope you do too. Say hello to Jonah now.'

'Hello, Jonah.'

The words hold no emotion, and it's as though the outburst of a few minutes ago never happened.

Jonah nods an acknowledgement. 'Is your mother here?'

He hadn't meant to ask, and his own mother's eyebrows raise a fraction.

'Of course she's here, son. Why wouldn't she be? She's part of the family.'

He massages his temple with the first two fingers of his right hand. That's where she's wrong, he thinks. No one would choose to be part of this fucked-up family. Least of all a smart girl like Ailsa.

'Shall I come in then?'

'Do you need to ask? This is as much your home now as it always was.' His mother steps aside to allow him into the lobby and he takes off his jacket. There are two raincoats he doesn't recognise hanging from a hook at the end of the coat rack. Ailsa's and her son's presumably. After a second's hesitation, he hangs his own jacket on the hook beside his mother's. It's what she would want and today he needs her to be happy.

'Why dinnae you go into the dining room and fix yourself a drink?' His mother bends to the Aga, opens the door and peers in. 'I'll be in with the dinner very soon. You stay here, Kyle, and help me put the vegetables into the dishes. Think you can do that, lovely?'

The boy nods and Jonah stares at the woman who he knows is his mother, but whom he doesn't recognise. Seeing her as he's never seen her before: confident, not afraid to express her love in front of others. Would things have turned out differently if Hugh had allowed her to show this side of herself when he and his brother had been boys? It's something he'll never know. He grasps the back of the wooden chair, bristling with an emotion he doesn't want to acknowledge. Her husband had made sure he was the main recipient of her affection... something that hadn't changed even after he'd gone.

'Are you all right, Jonah?'

'Aye.' Without looking at her, he leaves the two of them and goes into the dining room, wanting to be alone. But he'd forgotten about Ailsa. She's standing by the window looking pensive, her hair piled on top of her head in a messy bun, her red lipstick incongruous against her pale face.

An image comes to him of those lips pressed against his. The taste of wine on her tongue. He pushes the memory away. There's no place for it here.

He forces a smile. 'Ailsa?'

She gives a faint smile back. 'We meet again.'

Her hands move to her sides, smoothing the odd flared skirt she's wearing against her thighs. She looks nervous.

'Moira's been praying for the day you'd come home. Let's make this evening good for her.'

'Just Moira?' He hadn't been able to help himself and is relieved when she doesn't answer. Wishing to diffuse the tension, he scratches at his beard. 'Anyway, I haven't come home. Not really. It's just two days out of three hundred and sixty-five.'

'You're leaving so soon? Please don't tell her that. Not tonight anyway.'

He glances out of the window, but there's nothing to see but darkness. 'I won't, but that doesn't change the fact that I made a stupid decision. There's nothing for me here.'

'No. You've made that quite obvious.' He sees the flush that creeps up her neck, guesses what it means, but he can't let the thought of her distract him. 'But we were such good friends, Jonah. What happened to that?'

'You know. What happened changed us all. We were teenagers... we're not any more.'

Ailsa looks as though she's about to say something in reply, but before she can, he hears his mother coming through from the kitchen. She stops in the doorway, a platter of lamb held in front of her. The boy follows behind with a bowl of roast potatoes, the steam rising in the cold room.

'Yae haven't got yourself a drink.' She puts the platter down on the mat in the centre of the table and reaches for the whisky bottle on the sideboard. 'Here, I'll pour you a dram.'

The sight of the bottle is enough to make Jonah's salivary glands work overtime. He can almost taste the amber liquid, would do anything to have her pour him a large glassful, but he mustn't. He can't. Jonah swallows. 'Nae. I don't drink. Not any more. I've seen what it can do to people. I don't want to end up like my dad. Like Callum.'

Silence follows. It's as if the room is holding its breath, and Jonah knows it's because each one of them is remembering the past. A string of consequences spawned by the twist of a bottle cap. Each one of them affected in some way by the terrors it freed. Jonah runs a hand down his face. No, they don't call it the demon drink for nothing.

'You don't look like you do in the photograph. You look old.'

Jonah looks down. He'd forgotten about Kyle. There's something about the frank way he has with the things he says , the lack of artifice, that he finds amusing. Admirable.

He's also grateful for the interruption to their collective thoughts.

'That's because I *am* older. And I've got this.' He rubs his palm against his beard. 'Maybe I'll shave it off.'

'I think it suits you.' Ailsa turns away, disappearing into the kitchen to help bring in the rest of the dishes.

Jonah frowns and pulls out a chair from beneath the table.

'Shall we?'

'Aye, of course.' Beneath Moira's carefully applied foundation, the skin has a strange waxen quality to it. 'Why don't you take the seat by the window?'

He stares at the chair. It's the only one with arms... his father's old seat. He doesn't want to sit there, but how can he not? Feeling sick to his stomach, he pulls the chair out and lowers himself into it, feeling the sag of a cushion that had submitted to years of his father's weight.

Ailsa sets the bowl of vegetables and the gravy on the table and sits opposite Moira. No one speaks and the red walls of the dining room press in. They're waiting for him to do something, but he's not sure what.

'I expect you'd like to carve. Lamb was always your father's favourite.' Moira points to the carving knife and the two-pronged fork laid out on the cloth beside the joint of meat.

Jonah looks at the leg of lamb, its skin pierced with sprigs of rosemary, a slick of pale red juice pooling on the white china, and feels his stomach cramp. He doesn't want to carve. He doesn't want to sit in his father's chair. He doesn't want to take his place. Evil bastard. Why does his mother still insist on speaking about him as though he's still here? As though he'll walk back through the door at any time.

Opposite him, Ailsa's boy leans forward, knife and fork in his hands, rocking the legs of his chair in a way that's doing Jonah's head in. Why does no one stop him?

As if reading his thoughts, Ailsa puts a hand on the back of Kyle's chair to still it. She gives her son a warning look, then reaches for the carving knife. 'I'll do it if you like.'

'Nae.' Jonah clears his throat. 'It's fine. I don't mind.'

Pulling the plate of meat towards him, he stands and jabs the fork into the layer of golden fat. He carves the first slice, his mother's eyes on him all the while, her face inscrutable. When he's done, she smiles up at him.

'It's good to have you home, Jonah.'

He serves them all, and when the vegetables have been passed round, he lifts his glass, wishing it contained more than just water. 'Happy birthday, Ma.'

Ailsa lifts her glass of red wine. 'Yes, happy birthday, Moira. I hope it will be one to remember.'

Moira looks at the three of them in turn, studying their faces as if memorising them. There's a rumble of thunder from somewhere beyond the loch and the cut-glass light that hangs above the table flickers.

When she speaks, her voice is laced with melancholy. 'Yes, Ailsa. I fear it will.'

FOURTEEN

AILSA

Ailsa and Jonah are still sitting at the table, surrounded by the remains of Moira's birthday meal. Bored with their conversation, Kyle has taken himself to the kitchen, eventually falling asleep in the chair by the Aga.

'I covered him with a blanket.' Moira comes back into the room and takes her seat. 'He should be warm enough. Poor wee lad looked done in. You say he had a bad night?'

'He thought he saw something. It frightened him.'

'Really? Was it something in his room?'

'No, it was outside the lodge. I heard him cry out, and when I went into his room, he was standing at the window looking down at the loch.'

Jonah frowns. 'It would have been dark. How would he have seen?'

Ailsa traces the silver band around the rim of her coffee cup with her finger. 'The path's lit, so it would have been easy enough to see. He said it was a man and had got it into his head they wanted to get into the lodge. He was terrified. It took an age to calm him down.'

Moira looks at Jonah. 'It wasn't you, was it? I remember

when you were a teenager, you'd wander around the site in the hope it might help you sleep better.'

He folds his arms defensively. 'Why would I be hanging around the loch at that time of night? That's Callum you're remembering anyway.'

Ailsa's finger stops its tracing. 'I didn't say what time of night it was.'

'It's just an expression, Ailsa.' A new coolness has slipped into Jonah's voice. 'Anyway, I was asleep. More than likely it was one of the visitors.'

Ailsa's fingers find the scar on her arm. 'He heard a dog barking and it set him off. Question after question. I thought I'd never get him to sleep.'

Moira takes the cup and saucer from her and stacks it with her own ready to be taken out. 'It would have been a bad dream, that's all. Unless it was Seth's dog. I hope he's keeping it secure at night. You can't have dogs wandering around willy-nilly.'

Ailsa knows what she's talking about. She'd made Jonah promise not to tell Moira what Seth's previous dog had done, but he hadn't kept his promise. Moira had wanted to call the police and it had taken a lot of persuading on her part to stop her. She remembers how she'd pleaded, telling Moira it hadn't been the dog's fault, it had been hers for scaring it. Yet, although she'd felt sorry for the creature, the incident had left her with a fear of dogs, which, thankfully, she's managed not to transfer to Kyle.

'It wasn't on the site. It was further away than that. The forest. But you're right about the man, Moira. Kyle's dreams can be really vivid...'

Jonah frowns. 'I heard a dog barking last night too. He doesn't still live there, does he? In that caravan? I've always wondered what happened to him.'

'Aye, he still lives there. He doesn't bother us, and we don't bother him. It's how it always should have been.'

Jonah rubs the back of his neck, and Ailsa wonders if he's remembering how Callum and his friends had tormented him.

'You have to admit he's strange, though,' he says, after a minute. 'Always hanging around the site. That kid, the one who went missing—'

'They found him, Jonah. You know that. He'd simply got lost.'

'Yeah, well. I bet there's more to it than that. There always is.' He runs his hand through his hair. 'Anyway, what happened to the dog?'

Ailsa shudders. 'It died a few years back. He has another.' She doesn't want to think about the man from the woods or the dog. She pushes back her chair. 'I really should go. I'm glad you liked the bracelet, Moira.'

'I did. It's beautiful. Thank you, darling.' As she reaches across for Jonah's cup, the green glass changes colour in the light that hangs above the table. 'But don't go yet. I have something important I need to say to the both of you.'

'Can it wait until morning, Ma?'

Jonah's eyebrows pull together, and Ailsa knows what he's thinking. He needs to be away from this room, from them all. This evening's been a strain for him, and she's seen how hard it's been for him to answer the inevitable questions that have arisen: about where he's been living, about his job – anything that would help them understand a little more about the man he's become since moving to the mainland. His answers had been frustratingly vague. Questions turned around to form questions of his own. As deft as a politician.

Throughout the evening Ailsa's searched for clues, tiny pieces of the boy he once was, and has found them in the tip of his head. The self-deprecating smile. Tiny nuggets that she'll remember after he's gone tomorrow.

Now, he's looking at his mother, waiting for her to answer.

'No, Jonah.' She clasps her fingers and gives a tight smile. 'This can't wait.'

Hidden by the heavy damask curtains, the storm has begun. A sudden squall that throws rain at the windows and sends wind whistling down the chimney. They should have left before it started, but Moira had stopped any half-hearted attempt with a gentle hand on her arm or a question about Kyle.

As the long evening had worn on, the anxiety she'd felt when she'd arrived had mushroomed. She'd found herself studying Moira's every expression, every word, for clues and each time the woman turned to Jonah, she'd expected the worst. Had been waiting for the moment when she'd tell him her suspicions about Kyle. But it hadn't happened. How could it when the boy had been sitting with them at the table?

But now he's asleep. Now there's nothing to stop her.

Jonah pushes his chair back and crosses his legs. 'Ma?'

Moira straightens her back. 'I don't want you to worry about what I'm going to tell you. I want you to know that I'm fine with it.'

Ailsa closes her eyes and inhales through her nose until her lungs are full. This is it then.

She starts to speak, to say that Moira has no grounds for what she's about to tell Jonah, then stops. Staring at the snail trail of a tear on the older woman's face that belies her words. Not understanding.

This isn't about Kyle. It's about something else. Something bigger.

She folds her arms, self-protection never far from her thought. 'What is it, Moira? Please tell us.'

When Moira speaks, her voice is solemn.

'What I have to tell you is that by Christmas I will be dead.'

Ailsa sees how Jonah's face slackens with disbelief. She can't believe it herself. 'Is this a joke, Moira?'

'If only it was.' Moira pauses. Looks from one to the other. 'I have a brain tumour. I've been told it's inoperable.'

It's like someone's pulled the rug out from under her feet. 'But you can't. You never—'

Moira holds up her hand. 'No, let me finish. I know you'll have questions, but it's easier this way. For months now I've been suffering headaches. Blurred vision. I thought it was just migraines, but Dr Ross wasn't convinced. He sent me to the mainland for tests. I didn't want to worry you, Ailsa, so I told you it was migraines I was having.'

Ailsa's still reeling from the shock. Why hadn't she said something? 'I would have come with you. I would have done more at Loch Briona.'

'You do enough. More than enough. If it wasn't for you, this place would have folded long ago.'

Ailsa glances at Jonah, wondering if this last comment of hers is directed at him, but it doesn't appear to have been. Moira is sitting with her hands clasped in front of her, her face neutral, her eyes on her coffee cup, as though she's just told them the weather forecast or a piece of local news.

Jonah leans forward. 'But they can do something, right? Chemo or radiation or...' He stops.

'No, Jonah. I've told them I don't want it.'

'But why not? You have to fight this.' Ailsa's voice is wracked with frustration. 'You *must* fight it.'

'For what? A few extra months? I want to enjoy what time I have left. Not spend it making constant trips to the mainland. Dealing with nausea and hair loss. I want to be here, at Loch Briona.'

Ailsa doesn't trust herself to speak. A huge, painful lump has formed in her throat, and she can't look at Moira. The woman who's been more of a mother to her, these past eleven years, than her own. She turns to Jonah for some guidance; he's Moira's son, after all. He's leaning forward, his forehead resting on the heels of his hands, and she can't see his face.

Eventually, he gives a mirthless laugh and sits back. 'So this was the real reason you asked me here. Not to help you celebrate your birthday. Not because you wanted to see me, but because you wanted to tell me you're going to fucking die.'

'Jonah!'

Ailsa reaches across the table and touches his arm, but he shakes her off.

'You couldn't make it up, could you?' he says bitterly.

'It wasn't just that.' Moira's voice is patient as though she's speaking to a child. 'I wanted to talk to you both about what happens after.' She stops and presses her lips together, giving them time to digest her words.

It's too much for Ailsa. The tears she's been fighting so hard to hold back are spilling down her cheeks. She wipes them with the back of her hand, wishing she could turn back the clock to before Moira had told them this terrible thing.

'As my only surviving son, Loch Briona will of course be yours, Jonah. I know the last few years have been difficult for you and that you never completed your studies, but this is where you belong. You will make a success of this place and bring it back to how it was before... before...'

She stops and, in her head, Ailsa finishes her sentence. *Before I told Hugh to leave.* A time when the lodges were all full. When paddleboards and kayaks dotted the loch and when *Wallace* was not a name that made locals lower their voices or shake their heads. Hugh was a violent bully, but he knew how to run the place. If only his business head and his practical skills had been shared equally between his two sons.

Her stomach clenches at the thought of him.

She looks at Jonah, trying to work out from his expression what he's thinking, but his face gives nothing away. They have to keep it together. For Moira's sake. For their own.

'I thought, one day, you'd come back and have a family of your own,' Moira continues, looking meaningfully at Ailsa.

Unbidden, Jonah's nineteen-year-old voice is in Ailsa's head, as it has been since she found out he was coming home. Their foreheads pressed together. His tears streaming, unhindered down his face. *I have to tell you.* The secret she'd never asked to hear. Had not wanted to hear. 'Moira, please, don't.'

'I'm sorry, but the truth needs to be spoken.'

It's Jonah who breaks the tension.

'So what do we do now?' He looks around the room as though seeing it for the first time. 'My life isn't here. Hasn't been for a very long time. I'm fucked up, Ma. You dinnae know how much. I can't be the person you want me to be. It was Callum who belonged here. Callum who did everything. Fixed the lodges... built the outbuildings. Not me. Callum! And he'll never pick up a hammer or drill again. He's fucking dead.'

Moira's face hardens. 'You're wrong, Jonah. I know he was your brother, but his death is colouring your memories of him. You may not want to hear it, but he was a disgrace to the family name. A liability. He stole money, did you know that? He took from people what wasn't his to take. Drank his money away like his father. Yes, he was practical, but in time, there would have been nothing left for Loch Briona except bankruptcy. His death saved the place.'

The air in the room alters. Ailsa doesn't move. Is afraid to. Despite everything, Jonah loved his brother. She knows he did.

Ailsa sees how he pales, his eyes so wounded she has to look away. Will he defend him as he's always done – even though he has no need to now? She doesn't have to wait long for the answer.

'He's dead and still you can't give him any slack.' Blotches of red have crept up his skin. 'It's me you should hate, not him. I've done things too—'

He stops and looks at Ailsa, and she lowers her eyes. Why can't he stop? Just bloody stop.

There's a shout from the other room. Kyle's woken and he's always grumpy when he's not in his bed. Relieved at the distraction, Ailsa gets up. She kisses Moira on the cheek. 'We'll talk about this some more tomorrow. You need to rest.' She's going to say, *get yourself better,* but the words stick in her throat.

Moira's not going to get better.

Moira's going to die.

Not able to bear it, she surveys the table, littered with the detritus of the birthday meal. 'Leave this. I'll come back and do it in the morning.' She rests a gentle hand on Moira's shoulder. 'I mean it, Moira. Lay a finger on this and you'll have me to answer to.'

'All right, love. You clearly won't let me get away with it if I do and, to be honest, I'm exhausted. Take the wee lad back to the lodge. I have things I need to talk to Jonah about.'

Ailsa presses her lips together and nods. Kyle's calling to her, his voice rising, and she needs to get him to his bed.

'I'll see you in the morning then.'

'Sleep well, love.'

Ailsa collects their coats from the lobby and helps Kyle into his. He's not properly woken up and his eyes are still half-closed, his hair on end.

She opens the door and looks out. Seeing the rain hasn't stopped, she pulls up her hood, then reaches over and does the same for Kyle. 'We're going to have to make a run for it or we'll be soaked. Come on, I'll race you.'

Side by side they run down the path towards the lodge, rain sliding off their hoods, shoes muddy from the puddles they can't see. Her son's coat flaps behind him, his feet turned out as they always are when he runs. But her mind's not on Kyle and how he'll settle when they get back. Instead, it's fixed on what

Moira's just told her and what she might be saying to Jonah now she's gone. How he'll react to it. What he'll do.

She wants to run back and tell Moira she's wrong... that she doesn't know what she's doing, but she can't. She has responsibilities. If Kyle doesn't get at least seven hours sleep, they will all regret it come the morning.

No, it will have to keep.

They've reached the steps to the lodge and Ailsa digs into her pocket for her key, water dripping from her coat. The bottom of her skirt already soaked.

Kyle is ahead of her, his hand gripping the wet rail. He's only gone up two of the wooden steps when he stops, his head bent to the step above. Slowly, he straightens again, and she can see it. The fear. She recognises it in the way the muscles of his body have tightened. The hands that he's jammed into his armpits. All this picked out by the lamp at the side of the path.

Ailsa climbs the steps behind him and pushes back her hood to see what he's looking at. Rain drips down inside her coat, flattens her hair to her forehead and still she can't see it.

Kyle pulls at her coat and points. She sees it now. At the side of the step where the wooden rail has partially sheltered it. The muddy print of a shoe or boot. Another on the step above.

Not wanting to think what this means, Ailsa runs up the rest of the steps until she's standing on the deck. At first, she sees nothing else, but then she sees another print. It's below the living room window under the overhanging eaves.

'Kyle, come up here.'

She feels uneasy. Turning her back on the lodge, she scans the site, seeing nothing out of the ordinary. It's late and there are no lights in any of the windows. But there's no denying someone's been up to their chalet. She just doesn't know why.

Then she sees it – a flicker of light between the branches of a tree as the wind moves it. A torch?

But she mustn't overreact. It must be Jonah picking his way

through the rows of lodges to reach his own cabin. Now she thinks about it, the footprints might be his. He'd arrived at Moira's after they did and could have called for them on his way up, not knowing they'd already left. It's possible... but wouldn't he have said?

Kyle hasn't moved; he's seen the light too.

'The man! The man!'

She needs to get him inside. Calming her voice, she calls to him again. 'Come on, love. Let's get you home to bed. It's just Jonah, that's all.'

But he won't listen. His finger is pointing, the palm of his other hand covering his eyes. 'Make him go!'

Knowing how things could escalate, Ailsa hurries down the steps and takes Kyle by the arm, ignoring him when he tries to wrench it away. She pulls him up the stairs and, with difficulty, unlocks the door before bundling him inside.

She sinks down onto the settee. There's too much in her head to process. Moira's bombshell, the footprints round her lodge, Jonah's return that has dug the fresh earth from around her heart and laid it open like a wound. Despite what he'd told her on that windswept cliff when they were kids. A secret she'd never told anyone, but which had changed her life for good. Caused a series of events that had ruined them all.

The rain's coming down harder now, bouncing off the lodge roofs. Filling the potholes on the path. Behind her, at the boundary of the site, the Scots pines moan in the wind, their tall canopies protecting the caravan where Seth still lives. It's metal carcass stained with rust and the remnants of paint from a long-ago teenage prank.

For almost eleven years, Loch Briona has been her home. Now, suddenly, she no longer feels safe.

FIFTEEN

JONAH

Then

Jonah finds Callum at the boathouse down by the loch. He looks around to make sure no one is near as this isn't a conversation he wants anyone to hear.

'What the hell do you think you were doing?'

Callum looks up at him from the shadow of the stacked canoes. 'What are yae on about?' He bats at Jonah's leg. 'Get out of my light. I cannae see what I'm doing.'

Jonah stands his ground. 'Seth's van. Those words. Don't deny it, big bro, it was you. What did you think you were doing? You're nineteen for Jesus' sake... not twelve.'

Callum pushes himself up and rubs his hands down the front of his jeans. He jabs a finger into Jonah's chest. 'Who gave you the job of being my fucking conscience?'

'Someone has to do it.'

'Anyway, what's it to you? The guy's a perv. With any luck he'll be off this island before the day's out. It was a bit of paint, okay? The way you're going on, you'd think I killed the guy.'

The laugh he gives is too loud. Too wrong.

Jonah turns away. 'You're sick, do you know that?'

Callum's jaw tightens. 'Want to say that again?'

He doesn't. And what does that make him? An idiot. A coward. Just like his brother always taunted him with. If it's true, he doesn't care. No longer wanting to be near his brother, he strides back to the house. Glad that Ailsa hadn't been there to hear their conversation.

Despite what people think, he's not coping. Hasn't been for a long while. He's heard the gossip, which is that their father leaving the island is the best thing that could have happened to the family, but they're wrong. He hated the guy, but, in the last few months, he's come to realise he was the only one who was able to keep Callum under control. Keep him on the right path, albeit with the back of his hand. Without him, it feels as though nothing's changed – that he and his mother are still walking on eggshells. His father's boots were large ones to fill, but Callum's managing it just fine.

Rather than walk up the path through the outbuildings, Jonah takes the longer way through the trees. As he walks, he presses his fingertips to his temples, tap tapping to try to steady his nerves. This is never going to get better. Never. Not while he has to live in this place.

When he lets himself into the house, his mother is there waiting for him. 'Where were you? The phone has been ringing off its hook.'

Jonah closes his eyes a second. 'I've been stuck in this office all day. I'm allowed to have a break, Ma.'

His mother gives an exaggerated sigh. 'If your father was here...'

Jonah's heart freezes. Taking her shoulders, he steers her to a chair and makes her sit. 'Listen, Ma. You've got to stop this. He's gone and you have to accept it. He never loved us. We don't need him.'

Moira sinks her head into her hands. 'He's never coming back.'

The desperate sadness with which she says it is heart-breaking yet a body blow. He hates it when she talks like this... It scares him too. Hugh was their persecutor. Their tormentor. His presence intimidating and not worthy of her love.

Usually, she's fine, then other days, days like this...

He needs to get her through it.

Gently, he lowers her hand. 'No, Ma. You know it. There's nothing you can do that will change things. You still have us... me and Callum.' He puts a comforting arm around her shoulder, although, inside his chest, his heart is hammering. 'You must forget the past and everything that's happened. He's gone, and this place...' He points to the window. 'We'll make it work, I promise.'

At least that was something his father hadn't been able to get his hands on. The lodges had been in his mother's family for years, and her parents had left them to her in trust. Loch Briona Lodges were hers and hers alone, and there'd been nothing his dad had been able to do about it. Always good with his hands, and younger than his mother, he'd been a maintenance worker on-site when the two of them had met. Although he didn't know for sure, Jonah had always suspected he'd married Moira for her money. What a shock it must have been for him when her parents died on one of the mountain roads one winter, their car found in a ditch. Not just because he'd have to contend with a grieving wife, but because it was only then he'd found out he'd never get his hands on the place. For some reason unknown to Jonah, she'd never told him about the trust.

But his dad had soon realised what side his bread was buttered on. He might not own Loch Briona Holiday Lodges, but by expanding the number of plots and keeping the place in good running order, he'd helped to create a lucrative business for them to live on. He might not have had direct control of the site, but he had control over his wife and children. The result had been the same.

Until the day it had all kicked off.

Ma threw him out, he remembers saying to Reyne, his face still numb with shock. *I can't believe she actually did it.* He remembers her reply as well, knowing it was true and what they all felt. *It's for the best. He never deserved her.*

'He's not coming back,' his mother says again, her eyes looking up at him wet with tears. 'Never.'

'No, Ma.' He helps her up. 'Why don't you lie down for a bit? It's quiet at the moment. I'll hold the fort here. Look, I've been thinking. I don't have to go to Uni next year. I can stay here. Help you run things.'

She shakes her head, the old Moira returning. 'No. It's what we've always said you'd do. One of you boys needs to have the business knowledge to carry this place on after I've gone. We've talked about this, Jonah. The holidays are long, and you'll be able to come back and help out between your studies. In the meantime, Callum and I will muddle along. He'll make sure the lodges are well looked after. You don't have to worry; I won't be on my own here.'

'No, you won't.'

He smiles at her, unable to show what he's really thinking.

That it's precisely what he's afraid of.

SIXTEEN

AILSA

Ailsa parts the curtains at her bedroom window and looks out. The rain, which had been so heavy the night before, has stopped, the storm clouds blown away by the wind. Although it's still quite dark, there's a pinkish glow to the east and, as she watches, the sun lifts clear of the horizon. She smiles. That's what she loves most about Bray: the way the weather constantly changes, the sky moving from gunmetal-grey to clear blue and back again in the blink of an eye.

Her mother hadn't been so enamoured with it. She's in Spain now, with a man Ailsa's never met... Mario she thinks his name is. Every so often, she'll send postcards of golden beaches and indigo skies, palm trees and whitewashed houses. *Come and visit*, she writes in her haphazard handwriting. *Every day is like summer!* But Ailsa doesn't want to visit. She doesn't want to be in a place smelling of sun cream and sangria. Bodies lying prone on the beach. Skin weathering to the colour of a walnut. And, on the rare occasion her mother had come back to the island, she'd been restless, bored. Her heart and her attention elsewhere.

In recent years, those visits have been fewer.

She looks down at her pale freckled arm. No, she likes it here, away from everything, where the only crowds are the seals that bask on the rocks in the bay. The loudest sound, the Manx shearwater as they fly to their nesting burrows on the peaks once night has fallen. She likes their high-pitched cry, but it's a sound that has her son pressing his hands to his ears in alarm. He's happier when autumn arrives and they disappear to the southern hemisphere, leaving winter behind.

Not so different from her mother, she thinks as she puts on her dressing gown.

Not that the Hebridean sunshine doesn't make her feel good. Quite the opposite in fact. She likes it when the loch changes from deep blue to green and when the rocks that dot the small beach are warm beneath her legs when she sits and has her lunch. When she and Jonah were teenagers, on unexpectedly warm summer days, they'd swim in the shallower water near the shore without a wetsuit.

That was before things changed.

Before his brother died.

She shivers and drops the curtain. She never swims at all now. Even with a wetsuit. It's because she no longer trusts the water – knows how quickly it can claim you and make you its own. Even the strongest swimmer. Even Callum.

Wrapping her dressing gown around her, Ailsa picks up her mug from the bedside table and goes out into the living room. She can hear Kyle in his room. He's reading aloud from one of the books he insisted she buy for him, his monotone voice filtering through the thin wooden door. *A dog has eighteen muscles controlling their ears. These help them to change direction...*

Not wanting to disturb him, she empties the dregs of her tea into the sink and reaches up to get out two bowls from the cupboard. There's no point in asking Kyle what he wants for breakfast; it will be the same as always. They're nearly out of bread so, as she puts a slice in the toaster, Ailsa makes a mental note to buy some more when she goes into town. She'll ask Moira if there's anything she needs before she goes.

She stops, her hand on the kettle as the events of the previous evening come back to her. Moira's got an inoperable tumour. Moira's dying.

How could she have forgotten? More than that... how could she not have known? Not have seen?

She knows why. It's because she's been so wrapped up in her own life she hasn't been paying attention to anyone else's. Filling her days with laundry, the cleaning of the lodges, lesson preparation for her son. Trying to pretend to herself that things are normal. She's glad that Kyle can be a challenge, that the focus of her attention has, so often, to be on him, as it gives her little time to think about anything else... the past. The terrible memories. Jonah's confession and how it started a chain of events she couldn't stop.

There's a sharp rap on the door making Ailsa jump. It's only just gone seven, and she can't imagine who would be wanting to see her this early in the morning. Thinking it must be Moira, she goes to the large picture window and pushes back the curtain. But it's not Moira who's leaning on the rail of the deck waiting for her to answer; it's Jonah.

Holding her dressing gown closed with one hand, she opens the door. 'Jonah?'

'Can I come in?'

Ailsa looks out across the site. The sky is lightening now, a layer of mist hanging over the valley, hiding the loch from view. The peaks of the Bens behind Elgin rise above it. It's ethereal. Beautiful. Like a scene out of *Lord of the Rings*.

'I suppose so.'

She lets him in and closes the door against the chill air. It's strange to have him here in her lodge. Once they were so comfortable with each other but not any more. Time has forced a wedge between them, and it makes her sad.

Jonah stands in the middle of the living room, his feet astride, and she takes him in, in a way she hadn't been able to at Moira's. As a teenager, he'd been so slim, too slim probably, not surprising when he lived on his nerves. But in the intervening years between then and now, he's filled out. The muscles of his arms beneath the khaki shirt he's wearing, smooth and defined. His cheeks beneath his beard no longer hollow. It suits him.

It's only now she's aware how she must look, her hair messed from sleep, her thin nylon dressing gown barely covering the jersey shorts and strappy top she wears in bed. It makes her feel vulnerable.

'What did you want, Jonah?'

He pushes his hands deep into the pockets of his jeans. 'I'm leaving today. I thought I should tell you.'

'I see.'

She looks away to stop herself from saying more for there are too many questions she wants to ask: How could you leave your mother after what she told you last night? What will you do? What about Loch Briona?

What about us?

But she doesn't ask any of this. Instead, she draws herself up. 'Would you like a coffee?'

Jonah pushes back his shirtsleeve and looks at his watch. 'I've just time.'

'You've booked your ticket for the ferry?'

'Aye.'

He stands with his hands behind his back staring out of the window as she makes the drinks. He doesn't turn when she pushes Kyle's schoolwork to one side with her elbow and sets the mugs on the table.

'I've something to tell you,' he says eventually. 'It's important you know as it will affect you and the kid.'

'His name is Kyle, Jonah. He has a name.'

He looks round then. 'Sorry, yes, Kyle.'

She knows, in the pit of her stomach, that what he's going to say won't be good. 'Are you going to tell me what it is then?'

Jonah picks up his mug and takes a sip. He puts it down again. 'I need you to know that I'll be selling Loch Briona. After Ma. After...' He stops and swallows, his Adam's apple bobbing.

Ailsa says nothing; she doesn't trust herself to speak. She's aware of nothing but the aching sorrow that's expanding in her chest.

Jonah frowns. 'Say something, won't you?'

Slowly, she moves lips numb with shock. 'You can't sell. It's my home. Mine and Kyle's. It's the only home he's known.'

'That's why I told you... so you can think about it. Make arrangements. I need the money, Ailsa. I have debts. I owe people. What happened here messed with my head. I fucked up and this is the only way I can get myself out of it.' He holds out his hands. A desperate gesture. 'You have to understand.'

A coldness creeps through her. 'Your mother's not yet dead, but you're talking about her as though she is. How could you be so uncaring?'

Jonah covers his face, his fingers pressing into his forehead. 'Because that's who I've become, Ailsa. You can look at me all you want with those big hurt eyes, but it makes no difference. No one can hate me as much as I hate myself. My brother's death is my fault. I should have been able to save him.'

Despite everything, Ailsa finds herself softening. No one can know what it must be like to be Jonah. Having to live every day with the guilt of what happened. Knowing if he'd been just a second quicker, or if the clouds hadn't covered the moon when they did, things would have been different.

'It's not your fault. You have to let it go sometime.'

Jonah sinks onto the settee, his face twisting. 'I loved him, you know?'

'Yes, I know. Everyone could see how close you were, despite...' She looks down at her hands. 'Despite what he was like.'

'Evil.'

'No, not evil.' She fights to find the right word. 'Just damaged. Disturbed. Is it any wonder after what the two of you had to endure?'

Jonah shakes his head. 'You always did try to see the best in people, but you're wrong. Callum was more than those things. He thought he had the devil himself inside him. That when he'd had a skinful and it called to him, he couldn't stop himself from doing the things he did.' He stops, his eyes searching for hers. 'Don't waste your kindness on him.'

The back of Jonah's hand is against hers, the skin warm. It would take just a second to take it in hers. Her heart races and for a moment she lets herself remember the time she had kissed him, by the loch one night when the wind whipped the surface of the water into white ruffles. But however perfect that moment, she can't let her memory stray further... that would be dangerous. It's a place she doesn't want to remember.

It hits her suddenly. Even after all this time, just seeing his face makes her heart quicken. Her skin flush. Can he sense it? What a fool she is... in denial. He's never wanted her.

'Couldn't you stay just a little longer? So we can talk about what's happening here with Moira... with Loch Briona? Just a few days. That's all.'

'Mum. Mum.' Kyle's voice makes her turn. He's standing in the doorway, his arms rigid by his side, his fists clenched. He doesn't look at Jonah, but at the kitchen worktop with its box of Rice Krispies.

'I'm hungry.'

Jonah turns to her. 'Can't he get his own breakfast? How old is he?'

'He's ten. Nearly eleven. And, no, he can't get his own

breakfast. Not unless I want to be here all day while he counts out each Rice Krispie into the bowl.' She knows she sounds defensive, but it's how he's making her feel. 'Look, you wouldn't understand. Our day-to-day life might seem odd to you, but I know how to manage my son and I know what's best for him.'

'But how do you know what is? Wouldn't the mainland offer more to meet his needs?' Seeing her face, he stops and holds up his palms. 'I'm sorry. What do I know about parenting? It must be hard for you on your own and the last thing you want is me interfering.'

Ailsa stands. She looks down at Jonah. How could it be that only a minute ago she was wanting to reach out to him? Wanting to find out if she'd been wrong all those years ago. Wanting to blank out the past and what he'd told her.

How can she still have feelings for the man whose heart turned to stone when his brother died? The man who wants them out of here.

'You can go now.' She walks over to the door of the lodge and holds it open. 'I'd hate you to miss your ferry.'

Jonah gets up, a frown creasing his brow. 'Don't make this harder than it needs to be, Ailsa. Think about what's best for Kyle.'

With an effort Ailsa controls her voice. Her son is listening, taking it all in. Trying to process it: their words, their expressions. 'Don't talk to me about Kyle as if you know him or what's best for him. As his mother that's *my* job.'

Jonah shrugs. 'I was only saying.'

He leaves the lodge, and through the window Ailsa watches him take the steps two at a time, clearly relieved to be out of there. She presses her back against the front door and forces her features into the semblance of a smile.

'Come on then, Kyle. Let's have that breakfast.'

Her heart's beating fast. Time is running out and soon

Jonah will be on that ferry. She has to speak to Moira – as soon as Kyle's finished eating. As soon as possible.

They need to have the conversation Ailsa has avoided for eleven years.

Moira's dying and it's time she knew the truth.

It took Ailsa a while to persuade Kyle to come with her to Moira's, but now they are inside her kitchen.

'You didn't need to come, lass. I could have cleared up myself.' Moira puts a hand to her head and winces.

Ailsa looks at her with concern. 'Are you all right? Do you want me to call Dr Ross?'

'No, just give me a moment.' She pulls out a chair from the kitchen table and sits. 'Sometimes, it takes a while for my eyesight to adjust.'

'I can't believe you never said.' Ailsa places a gentle hand on her shoulder. 'That you've been coping with this on your own for so long.'

Moira sighs. 'I've had to cope with many things in my life. This is just one more. No better or worse than the rest.'

'I want you to play the piano with me, Moira.' Kyle rocks from one foot to the other. 'Can you play the piano with me? Can you?'

'Aye, I most certainly can... but your mum and I would like to have a wee chat first, if you don't mind.'

'I do mind.'

She laughs. 'Well, sometimes, we have to do things even when we mind them. Like the washing and cleaning the lavatory. Why don't you make yourself comfy by the Aga and your mum and I will go into the other room? That way you can play on that game of yours and we won't disturb you with our talk. Later, we can practise the duet I taught you. The waltz. Does that sound fair?'

Kyle nods and Ailsa's filled with a deep sadness for everything Kyle will lose when Moira's gone. Everything they'll *both* lose.

Ailsa follows Moira out of the room and closes the kitchen door behind her. On their way to the living room, they pass the open door of the dining room. The table is still covered in last night's dishes. She'll need to sort it later.

Moira sits down, her fingers massaging her temples, but Ailsa remains standing. *She's only sixty*, she thinks. *She's too young to die.* Her overarching desire is to look after the woman who took her in all those years ago, but instead, she's going to turn her world upside down.

'Moira.'

She looks up. 'Yes, love?'

'I have to tell you something. I didn't want to, but I don't have any choice. Not after what Jonah's just told me... that he'll sell Loch Briona when the time comes.'

Moira's face hardens. 'He told you that?'

'Yes. He came to see me just now. He'll be leaving soon.'

'Leaving?' She stares at her as though trying to follow her thread. 'He never said. Never even came to say goodbye.'

'I'm sorry. I really am. But what I have to tell you is important.'

Moira leans forward, her fingers grasping the edge of the coffee table. She looks up at the window as if expecting to see Jonah outside, then back at Ailsa. 'I know what it is you're gonnae tell me.' She reaches up to Ailsa and takes her hand, squeezing it. 'I was right, wasn't I? Kyle is my grandson.'

For years she's kept it to herself, but now she no longer can. 'Yes, he is.'

It should be a joyous thing. A relief to have told her, but it isn't. By telling Moira, she knows she's opened a can of worms. One whose lid can never be put back on, however much she tries.

SEVENTEEN

AILSA

Then

The ceilidh is turning out to be a disappointment – not what Ailsa had been expecting at all. It was supposed to have been fun, an opportunity to forget the monotony of school. Forget revision. Forget who was friend and who was enemy. But it had been none of those things, and she wishes she hadn't come.

The main hall of the community centre in Elgin is too brightly lit, the strip lighting doing nothing to enhance the atmosphere. The space not quite large enough to stop the rows of students, who are stripping the willow or joining hands to form wheels and arches, from bumping into one another. It's hot too as no one's worked out how to turn off the radiators.

Wanting a quiet place to be by herself, Ailsa pushes open the door of the Campbell Room and slips inside. It's a room that's normally used for mother and toddler groups, bridge evenings and the like, and her idea is to read some magazines or play a game on her phone until it's time for the coach to take them all back to their respective homes. But as soon as the door swings shut behind her, she realises her mistake. The room's not empty. Instead, there are six or seven girls from Ailsa's class sitting on a rough circle of beanbags over by the vending machine.

It's Sorcha who looks up first. She's sharing her seat with Bethany, her arm draped loosely across her shoulders, telling her something that's made her laugh. As her eyes lock with Ailsa's, she stops talking. Her mouth puckering.

'Yes? Did you want something?' She looks Ailsa up and down. Makes a meal of it as though she hasn't already seen her... or already commented on the dress she's wearing.

Ailsa stares back, hating her.

Sorcha has an older sister. She'd been to the Winter Ceilidh two years earlier and had told Sorcha that the dress code was formal – despite the lively dancing and the only seating being the hay bales brought in to make the place feel more rustic – more in keeping with the jigs and reels the band on the stage are playing. When Sorcha had passed the information on to Ailsa, she'd thought it was her way of calling a truce.

What an idiot.

At the thought of how she'd believed her, Ailsa's eyes close in shame. Without knowing it, her fingers find the velvet material of the hippy-style maxi dress she'd borrowed from her mum, crushing the soft fabric. She'd paired the dress with high narrow-heeled ankle boots and had thought the combination, although unusual, had fitted the formal brief. Wearing a dress like the others would stop her being the odd one out as usual.

How could she have been so gullible? So stupid?

Living furthest away, she'd been one of the first to be picked up by the coach. As she'd leant her head against the glass and watched the scenery slip by, the peat bogs either side of the road changing to pine forests before opening onto windswept moorland, she'd felt a prickle of excitement about the forthcoming evening. She'd managed to persuade herself that things would be good tonight. Had done what she would never normally let herself do: dare to believe people can change. That she'd be welcomed into the group. Be accepted.

The blissful state had remained until the next person had been picked up. As she'd walked between the rows of seats, Ailsa had seen the girl's jean-clad legs. The tartan shirt she had on under her coat. The trainers.

So different to what Ailsa was wearing. So very different.

And as more and more people had got on the coach, raising eyebrows at her long dress, it had become clear what had happened. She'd fallen for it. The joke was on her.

'Well?'

Ailsa realises she hasn't answered the question. Sorcha's waiting, something she doesn't like doing.

She lets go of her dress and forces herself to breathe. 'I was looking for some coffee.'

'I was looking for some coffee.' Mimicry is what Sorcha does best. It elicits a laugh from the others as it always does.

All eyes are on Ailsa. The girls are waiting, watching to see how she'll react. Their interest heightened, their gaze travelling between the two of them, wondering how this is going to pan out. Whether something will happen that can be shared when they're next back at school, to break the monotony of the island. It's how it's always been on Bray, and Ailsa knows it better than most. Molehills built into mountains. Petty differences raised to the status of feuds by a few choice words in the classroom.

Ailsa bristles. 'Don't worry. I'm not staying.'

'Jesus! Stop being so sensitive. I just asked what you wanted. There's no need to take offence at everything.' Sorcha reaches across Bethany and fishes between the beanbag they're sharing and the one next to it. When she straightens up again, she has a bottle of vodka in her hand. 'This is the only coffee we're drinking here, but you can do what you like. The machine's over there if you want it.'

She points to the vending machine behind her, its menu

lights glowing. The school have provided soft drinks in the main hall where the dancing is, but it's caffeine Ailsa is craving at the moment. She looks at the vending machine. It would only take a couple of minutes to insert her coins, a few more to wait for the boiling liquid to be dispensed into the cup, but she knows the faces the girls will make behind her back if she does. Hasn't the energy for it.

Normally, she'd ignore them and do it anyway, but tonight her confidence has taken a nosedive. Maybe it was the way everyone had stared at her when she walked into the community centre earlier. The whispered comments behind hands as she'd sat on the hay bale furthest from the stage. Most of the other students had come in groups or couples, but she had come alone. She tries not to think of the aching disappointment she'd felt when Jonah had messaged to say he wouldn't be able to come with her, after all; that he would have if it hadn't been for the last-minute guests who'd turned up at Loch Briona without a booking. He was sorry to let her down and would try to make it later.

Ailsa looks at her watch. It's already nine thirty. If he was going to come, he'd be here by now. The ceilidh is in full swing. She can hear through the closed door the caller as she shouts out the moves, the laughter as those with two left feet turn the wrong way or grab the wrong partner. If Jonah had been here, it would have been fun. She'd be in the main hall, laughing and dancing with the others – not standing facing the girls in her year like a defendant facing a courtroom of jurors. Waiting for them to judge. Waiting for Sorcha to mete out her punishment.

Just a look. Just a word. Not much but enough to scar her for days.

'Well? Are you getting coffee...?' Sorcha holds up the bottle. 'Or are you going to join the big girls and have a wee drop of this?'

Surprised to be asked, Ailsa glances at the door. 'What if we're caught?'

'Jesus, listen to yourself. You really think the teachers are going to care? They're hardly going to throw us out of school when we'll be leaving in a few months. They know full well what most of us have in our bags, but they're just too lazy to do anything about it. In any case, the school wouldn't want the bad press. Come on. Let your hair down.' She smiles, catching Ailsa off guard. 'It looks nice like that, by the way.'

Ailsa's hand rises to her head, her fingertips touching the two thin plaits either side of her head that she's drawn back across her wild hair and secured with a clasp.

'Thanks.'

'And...?' Sorcha points to the bottle before handing it to Bethany. 'Want some?'

Ailsa stares at Sorcha's slim fingers wrapped around the bottle. What she really wants is to leave the stupid ceilidh, but she can't. The coach the teachers have laid on to take those not living in Elgin home isn't leaving until eleven thirty. That's two more hours. How is she going to cope?

She's torn between staying and going. 'I don't know.'

'Come on, yae misery guts. Sit down. You're making the room look untidy.'

'Yes, have some fun for a change.' Bethany jerks her thumb at the door and pulls a face. 'The music's rubbish anyway. No one can blame us for wanting to have our own party.'

Ailsa breathes in. 'Okay.' There's an empty beanbag next to Sorcha and, reluctantly, she sits, the beans giving beneath her. Despite what she'd told herself earlier that evening as she'd got changed, she doesn't want to join this group. Not really. But neither does she want to go back into the hall and watch the couples dosey doeing or playing tonsil hockey on the hay bales. If Jonah had been here, it would have been different... but he's not.

She tugs at the hem of her dress and tries to find a comfortable position, but it's hard when the beans keep shifting. The eyes of the other girls are on her, and she can't tell if they're friendly or not. Neither can she figure out why they want her to stay.

'Here.' Sorcha hands the bottle to Ailsa. She points to Bethany's bag. 'There's more in there so don't feel you have to ration yourself.'

Ailsa raises the bottle to her lips. As she does, the beanbag gives a little and some of the liquid dribbles down her chin. Self-consciously, she wipes at the underside with the back of her hand.

'Go on, have some more.' Sorcha is smiling at her, a remarkable thing at the best of times. Everyone knows her smiles must be earned.

This time when Ailsa tips the bottle, she manages not to spill any. The vodka tastes of nothing in particular and she wonders why people bother with it. Except that already just those few mouthfuls are helping her shoulders to relax. Her body to mould into the soft contours of the beanbag. Maybe, if she has enough, she'll forget the terrible start to her evening.

Time passes and Ailsa begins to relax. Listening to the girls chat between themselves. Feeling included for the first time in a long while.

Sorcha nudges her. Gestures for her to hand the bottle back. 'Jesus... slow down!'

It's a while since she's seen Sorcha at the lodges, and she wonders why. She remembers the day she joined the school at the beginning of S5. Her family had moved from the mainland, and it hadn't taken her long to form a group of her own – one that was invitation only. Not long at all. She looks at her dark hair and lash extensions. It hadn't been long before she'd slept with Callum either. Everyone knew because she hadn't bothered to keep it quiet. Wore it like a badge of honour to make herself popular. Ailsa had seen how she'd set her sights on him the minute she'd seen him in the school canteen. Had sat next to him and flirted as though there was no tomorrow. Not that he'd minded. Sorcha's stunning and Callum was never going to turn down an offer like that.

Sometimes, she can't help wondering... Would Jonah have turned her down?

Through the thin community centre wall, the music is gaining momentum, getting ever faster. There are shrieks of laughter. Raised voices.

'Well?' She feels a dig in her ribs. Everyone's looking at her. She'd been miles away... hadn't been listening.

'Sorry, what—?'

'Have you and Jonah done it yet?'

A giggle to her right. A meeting of eyes across the beanbags that's hard for her to miss. Bethany biting her lip in the hope it will stop her from laughing.

'Have you two fucked?'

The coarse expression makes her take a sharp intake of breath. 'We're just friends.'

'Aye, right.'

That smirk. The raising of her eyebrows. How Ailsa would like to slap her... wipe the look off her stupid face, but she doesn't. Finding the bottle of vodka in her hands again, she takes a long mouthful to hide her embarrassment. The room feels too warm and when she looks at Sorcha's face, it disconcertingly splits into two. A blink merges the two together again, but there's no denying how strange she feels. Not like herself and she can't decide if she likes it or not.

Everyone's waiting to hear what she's going to say. This is her chance to change things. How they look at her. How they talk about her. She looks at each girl in turn. Is she the only virgin in the group? It's never seemed that important before, but now it does. If she says yes, will things be different? Better?

Sorcha is leaning forward, her chin on her folded hands. 'Go on then. Tell us.'

She tries to focus. Thinks of Jonah. He might be the quiet, serious one, but in her eyes, he's just as hot as Callum. With his over-long fair hair and full, sensitive lips, there must be girls who fancy him. She can't be the only one.

Ailsa forces herself to look Sorcha in the eye. 'Maybe.'

It's not a yes, but it will be enough to set the tongues wagging.

The girls are asking questions, but she's said enough. Mustn't give them any more. For with that one word, Ailsa knows she's started something. And even in her inebriated state, she wonders if she'll be able to handle it.

When the door opens, they all look up. Fall silent. Ailsa pushes the bottle of vodka down between the beanbags and sits up straighter, fully expecting it to be one of the teachers, but it isn't. It's Jonah who stands in the doorway, framed by the hall's bright lights. He's saying something, but his words are swallowed up by the noise behind him.

'I can't hear you,' Ailsa says, her words thick in her mouth. With difficulty, she pushes herself up. Falling back again as she loses her balance.

Jonah crosses the room to her. If he's heard the giggling, he gives no sign of it. 'Someone said I'd find you in here.' When he reaches Ailsa, he takes her hand and pulls her up, putting an arm around her shoulders to stop her swaying. 'What's happened tae you?'

Sorcha laughs. 'She's pissed.'

He frowns. 'Really?'

Ailsa forces a smile. She knows what he's thinking... that it makes her no better than his brother. 'I'm all right. I only had a wee drop. I just need some space, that's all.'

Jonah looks at her a moment, then nods. 'Of course.' He starts to lead her away, but Sorcha's tugging at his shirt. Looking up at him through her extensions in that way she has. 'Callum with you?'

'Aye, somewhere. Ma let me take the car, but Callum came on the bike. Thought it looked cooler.'

'Tell him I'm here.'

Jonah shrugs. 'If I remember.'

'Or you could always bring your own cute arse back here.' She pats the beanbag beside her. 'I'll keep this warm for you.'

Jonah ignores her, but Ailsa sees the redness that's crept up his neck. 'Come on, let's get out of here.' He looks down at her and his eyes hold such concern that she feels a rush of warmth. He must care about her to look at her like that. He must.

'There's water on the table out there,' he says, nodding at the door. 'That should do the trick... and a wee breath of fresh air.'

He leads her into the hall and pours some water into a plastic tumbler. Ailsa takes a sip. 'Thanks.'

'I wasnae going to leave you with that coven.'

The room is starting to spin, and Ailsa clutches hold of Jonah's sleeve to stop it. 'They're all right.'

'If yae say so.' He looks back at the part-open door of the Campbell Room and gives an audible sigh. 'Their idea? The drink?'

His question makes her feel stupid. Young... as though she doesn't have a mind of her own. She's almost eighteen for Christ's sake. 'I wanted to, okay?'

He looks at her a moment, then smiles. 'Okay.'

He says no more. Despite the smile, he's disappointed in her, she heard it in that one small word, and it leaves her unsettled. Jonah is her ally. Always has been. If she loses his friendship, she has nothing. 'Let's go outside.'

'It's cold. Have yae got a coat?'

'It's in there.' She points through the double glass doors of the hall. 'In the cloakroom.'

'We'll collect it on the way out then.'

The freezing air hits her as soon as Jonah opens the front door. Shocking her. Sobering her. 'Jesus!'

Jonah laughs. 'I know we wanted air, but it's blowing a bleeding hooley out here. It wasn't as bad as this when I drove over. Let's find somewhere out of the wind.'

The community centre is set back from the road, the coach that will take her home parked outside. Taking Ailsa's hand, Jonah ducks behind it, leading her through the car park in front of the building and onto the street.

'Let's cross.'

On the other side of the road, Ailsa can just make out Loch Briona, its surface ruffled by the wind. She shivers and Jonah rubs her shoulders.

'The wind's coming from the east.' He points to the sheltered picnic benches set on the grass that leads down to the water's edge. 'Come on. If we sit there, we won't feel it as much.'

In summer, the benches with their wooden sides and roofs are a magnet for the tourists that come to Elgin to visit the craft shops or sample the local whisky in the two waterfront pubs, but, tonight, there's no one here but the two of them.

Ailsa runs over to the bench and sits. The wooden seat is hard and cold beneath her dress, but she doesn't care. Jonah is with her and after her disappointing evening, it feels like a miracle. She waits for him to join her, but he remains standing.

'What?' she asks. 'What is it?'

'You don't have to be like them, you know.' It's dark out here, no moonlight, and she can't read his expression. 'It's all right to be yourself. You look good, by the way. Your dress... that blue... it suits you.'

Ailsa looks down at it, pleasure spreading through her at his words. 'Thank you. I borrowed it from my mum.'

'That's nice.' He sits now and Ailsa feels the warmth of his body next to hers. Outside the shelter of the bench, the wind is whipping the branches of the trees, sending the grass into a frenzy, but here it's like they're in their own cocoon. Protected from the wind. From prying eyes.

'Look,' she says, pointing across the dark water. 'There's the holiday complex.'

Jonah shifts on the bench. 'Aye, I see it.'

The far shore is in darkness save for the zigzag of small white lights running down to the water. Over to the right, more white dots pick out the position of the lodges that in winter stand empty.

Ailsa leans back against the wood. 'It's pretty.'

'I suppose, but it's good to be away from it.' Jonah says no more, and Ailsa doesn't push him. With Hugh gone, things should be so much easier, but since the day Moira threw his father out, it's like he's withdrawn into himself. Callum has something to do with it, she's certain of that.

Inside the wooden shelter, it's like they're in their own little world. The disappointment of the evening has turned to joy that Jonah came for her. The vodka has made her warm and fuzzy inside. Has bolstered her flagging confidence in herself. He said he liked her dress. Said the colour suited her. Why say that if he didn't mean it? Why say that if he didn't care?

She thinks of Sorcha – how she'd looked at Jonah from under her dark lashes. With her perfectly made-up face and her thick dark hair, who could resist her? And the thing she'd said to him before her lips had curled into a smile... had she meant it? With a terrible sinking feeling, she realises something. Sorcha could have him if she wanted. She could have anyone.

Ailsa's hand rises to her cheek. Why would Jonah be interested in *her* – a gauche, unworldly virgin – when he could have someone like Sorcha?

She feels the panic sharpen. She has to do something before it's too late.

Jonah is saying something, asking her if she's warm enough, but Ailsa doesn't answer. Instead, she reaches up to him and draws his face towards her. Her lips find his and she kisses him. Her first kiss. Maybe his too.

At first, Jonah doesn't react. His lips, chilled from the wind, are unmoving beneath hers, and she's scared she's made a terrible mistake. But then gently, oh so gently, he starts to respond, his hand cupping the back of her head, his tongue slipping between her parted lips.

And, as he pulls her onto his lap and she feels how his own body has responded to the kiss, she knows what she has to do. Breaking away from him, she unbuttons her coat and the top buttons of her dress. She takes his hand and guides his fingers inside her bra, feeling her nipple stiffen at his touch.

Jonah's looking at her with an expression akin to anguish, but this time when they kiss, there's no doubting his feelings. The drink has made her bold. Her hand slips to the fly of his jeans and he gives a moan.

The girls were right.

This is the only way to keep him.

EIGHTEEN

JONAH

Jonah was going to leave without saying goodbye to his mother, catch the first ferry out and not return until he had no choice. But something had stopped him. And that thing had been Ailsa. In the last eleven years, he'd given her little thought, not allowed himself to, but now, being back here, seeing her again, it's made him curious. She's unfinished business.

There's something about the boy too. He's been thinking about it and can't get the idea out of his head. There's a familiarity in the way his hair falls. The way he stands with his arms straight down by his sides, his hands bunched into fists. Like *he* used to.

He hikes his bag onto his shoulder. No, it's his imagination. It has to be. She hasn't said anything. He doesn't want to be a father. Never has. What do they say? The apple never falls far from the tree or something. Well, it's true. Their father's blood had been in them both. Bad blood. He'd heard the talk, *Callum's just like his father. Have you seen the bruises on his mother's arm?* But they had it all wrong. Ailsa might not want to think it, but the devil was in the both of them. Sometimes, weakness plays as big a part in a person's downfall as strength.

He can feel the boat move beneath him again. His cheeks aching with the cold. Halfway between Elgin and the holiday lodges. No moon. No stars. His brother's face beneath the water, his fingertips breaking the surface to reach his.

It's cold. Bitterly cold.

He could have saved him, if only he'd had the courage.

His brother's gone. There's just him now and his decision to never have kids was to ensure that the cycle would end. The bad blood no longer having anywhere to flow.

That boy, Kyle. The direct way he spoke to him – as though he knew him. Even though they'd never met. Yes, there's something about him. Something unsettling. And Ailsa, his mother, so protective of him. The boy that might be his.

Jonah presses the heel of his hand to his forehead. Please, don't let it be so.

He stands in the middle of the path and looks out across the roofs of the lodges to the loch beyond, thinking about his brother. Thinking about everything.

Callum isn't evil... just damaged. That's what Ailsa had said. *Disturbed.* If only she knew how wrong she was. With a drink inside him, Callum had been more than that; it was knowledge they both shared.

A door slams and a couple come out of the lodge to his right. The man bumps one large suitcase down the steps, then goes back for the other while the woman watches. Once, he would have helped but not today. There was a time when he'd thought the day would come when this place would be his to run, but now it is, he doesn't want it. His forehead folds into a frown. He'd told Ailsa this, and now he wonders whether, in her turn, she's told his mother. Why wouldn't she? He hadn't told her not to.

He should never have said anything. Isn't sure why he had. But, in his heart, he knows why. It was because he'd still been trying to get his head around everything. Trying to keep his thoughts from unravelling. Over the years he'd trained himself to be unemotional. To put his own needs first. It was how he'd survived. But everything's changed. His mother's illness. The return of the recurring nightmare he used to have about that terrible night eleven years ago. The suspicion that Ailsa's son might be his kid.

No. No. No.

He turns and walks up the hill. At the bottom of the steps leading to Ailsa's lodge, he stops. He needs to see her again. Find out the truth. But when he hears it, will he be able to handle it?

There's only one way to find out. His feet banging out a rhythm on the wood, he runs up the steps and thumps on her door, just as he did earlier. She thinks he's gone, may not want to see him, but it's too bad.

Then another thought comes to him. What if she won't say? She's kept this particular secret for eleven years, why not keep it longer? Hasn't she already proved she's good at keeping secrets?

Unless he's wrong.

Unless she hadn't kept it to herself.

He waits, then when there's no answer, goes to the window and tents his hand to the glass. The room is empty. He turns his back on the lodge and scans the site, looking for the metal trolley Ailsa uses to transport the bedding to the laundry... not seeing it. Maybe she's out; more likely she's at his mother's. He's noticed how in the years since he's seen them, they've formed a bond.

Pushing down his jealousy, he leaves Ailsa's chalet and walks up to the house. Taking the short way through the amenity yard. There is the laundry room, the trolley parked in the doorway. There is the shower and toilet block and the sauna he and his brother helped their father to build.

His stomach clenches at the thought of those days – the two of them sweating in a summer heat rarely experienced on Bray.

Desperate to do it right so as not to feel the back of their dad's hand. The cut of his belt.

Forcing the black memories away, he carries on walking, his head down, past the woodshed and the generator and in through the back door. Not bothering to knock.

He hadn't expected the boy to be in the kitchen, but he is, his head bent to his tablet. He looks up when he hears the door close but doesn't say anything.

'Didn't your mum teach you that it's good manners to say hello when someone comes into the room?'

The boy looks up again. He has his attention now. 'No, Moira taught me.'

'Well then?'

'Hello. Hello. Hello. Hello...'

Kyle's voice is rising, and Jonah shushes him with a finger to his lips. Surprised when it works. 'That's a good lad. You dinnae want to worry your mum, now, do you?'

The boy's lost interest again. He's staring at the screen of his tablet, swiping up as he reads. Jonah studies him. Seeing the long thin fingers that are just like his own. The tilt of the boy's head as familiar as the reflection in the mirror when he trims his beard.

He thinks they must have heard Kyle's voice. Will come running to find out what the problem is, but they don't. They must be engrossed in something. Something so important it's made them deaf to the kid. He has to know what it is.

Leaving the boy, he goes into the hall. Voices are coming from the living room, and he follows them. The door is pushed half-closed. With his foot, Jonah widens the gap. They don't see him. There's too much happening for that. Ailsa is standing by the coffee table. Moira, though, is at the window, her hands pressed to the glass as though wishing to escape.

'No,' she says. And as she speaks, she taps her forehead against the window. Once. Twice. Over and over.

Ailsa stands. Her face is wet with tears, her cheeks red. Going over to Moira, she puts a hand on her shoulder.

'I'm sorry. I should have told you sooner.'

'It isn't true. Kyle is Jonah's son. I know he is.' Moira moves away, and Ailsa's hand drops to her side.

Jonah waits for Ailsa's reply. His body rigid with anticipation. The colour drained from his face. He sees the way Ailsa's face tightens, is left in no doubt as to her feelings.

And when she eventually speaks, the words dredged from deep within her, they don't register at first. All he can hear, all he can see, is her pain. Her disgust. She's reliving a moment from the past, that's clear. And from the bitterness in her voice, it's a moment she'd rather not have brought back.

'I know that's what you want to believe, but it doesn't make it real. You might not want to hear it, but it's a fact.' She raises her head and looks at his mother. 'Yes, you are Kyle's grandmother, but Callum was his father... not Jonah.'

'If Callum truly is his father, then the way he was conceived...' She stops and shakes her head, the pain pulling at the corners of her mouth.

'You don't know anything, Moira.' There's a lack of conviction in her voice that gives her away. Jonah knows his mother has heard it too for she goes over to her and takes Ailsa in her arms, holding her as she weeps.

Silently, he steps back from the doorway. He's heard enough. Seen enough. And the knowledge weighs heavy.

When he reaches the kitchen, he stops, his mind numb from Ailsa's revelation. Kyle hasn't moved from his chair by the range and now Jonah looks at him properly. He will have heard of the lad who drowned in the loch over eleven years ago, but that's all. How is he going to feel once he finds out he lost his father that day? Jonah's gut twists. *Callum.* He knows what people said about him at the time. Knows what they think now.

Nothing good will come of everyone knowing, but it's too

late. Ailsa's told his mother now, and things will inevitably come
out. Bad things... he can feel it. It's what happens here at Loch
Briona.

With a finger to his lips, he drags his eyes from Kyle and
steps outside the house, shutting the door behind him. Poor
kid... better for him not to know whose blood it is that runs
through his veins. Better if he never has to know.

But at least Callum's gone and can never come back. That's
something.

A wave of emotions washes over him: guilt, anger, sorrow,
resentment. Jesus he could do with a drink. One thing he knows
for sure. He can't leave Loch Briona now.

NINETEEN

AILSA

'You do realise this changes everything, don't you?' Moira smooths Ailsa's hair from her face. 'You must see that.'

Ailsa steps back and rubs at her arms. She's still in shock from having told the truth after all this time. 'It shouldn't. Nothing's different. Kyle is still the same boy.'

Moira shakes her head. 'No... he isn't.'

Suddenly, Ailsa's worried. Kyle responds to Moira in a way that's different to how he is with *her*. He's more amenable, more engaged, and she doesn't want him to lose that bond. What if Moira rejects him now she knows Callum is his father? What if she hates him?

She waits, her anxiety growing. Instead of speaking up, she should have let things lie and taken her chances. But how could she have done that after what Jonah had told her? That when the time comes, he'll sell Loch Briona to pay off his debts. There was no way she could stand back and let that happen. This is Kyle's home... the only one he's known, and he hates change. He'd never settle anywhere else. She knows he wouldn't.

'Moira—'

'Just give me a moment, Ailsa. I'm sure you'll appreciate this has come as a shock.'

'I know. I'm sorry. I just thought you should know.' She looks down at her hands. 'Now that things are different.'

'Now I'm dying, you mean?' It's said with such sadness that Ailsa feels it deep inside her chest.

'Yes,' she says softly. Not wanting to lie.

Moira takes her hand. 'I'm sorry, Ailsa. I know you'll think I'm overreacting, but I was happy when I thought Kyle was Jonah's child. I thought it would bring us all together. That it would help him heal and that one day, after he'd got to know Kyle better, he'd come to see himself as a father. I always thought he had it in him to be a good one.'

Ailsa's throat is aching from the tears she's holding back. 'Why did you never ask me? You've had eleven years?'

'Because you weren't ready to tell me the truth... and because my boy wasn't ready to know. He was so lost, so disturbed by what happened the night he lost his brother, and it changed him... and I don't just mean physically. Lying there day after day in his bed, not speaking. Not eating. There were days when I was scared he would never get over it. Then to take off like he did, making it clear he didn't want me in his life unless it was for money. It broke my heart.' Leaving the window, Moira goes to the sideboard and picks up a photograph of Jonah. 'The two of you were so good together. Anyone could see it. In fact, the only ones who didn't were the pair of you. I'd hoped that by the time he was ready to come back to the island, he'd also be ready to accept his responsibilities. It's why I thought... it's why I got it so wrong.'

Ailsa crosses her arms, her thumb finding the raised scar on her arm. 'I'm sorry. I never meant to upset you. It's just that when Jonah said he had no interest in running the holiday site, I panicked. Jonah's your son, but Callum was your son too, whatever you thought of him. He always made it clear he wanted to make this place work. If he'd known about Kyle, he would have wanted him to grow up here. I'm sure of that. He would have wanted this to be his home.'

Moira drops her head to her hands, her fingertips pushing through the fine hair at her temples.

'Why are you being so long?' Kyle's voice breaks through the silence. He's at the door, stepping from foot to foot. 'I should be doing my lesson. It's time, Mum. Come *on*.' Crossing the carpet, he goes to her and tugs at her sleeve.

Ailsa pulls herself together. 'I'm coming now, darling. I hadn't forgotten.'

Kyle clenches and unclenches his fists. 'Will that man be there?'

'What man?'

'The man who was here. Will he? Will he? Will he?'

Ailsa glances at Moira. 'What do you mean?' Anxiety tightening her chest, she walks to the window and looks out, seeing only the laundry room, the wash block, the sauna. She shivers. 'Was it the man you thought you saw the other night? Was it the same one?' She looks back at Kyle, irritation rising. 'Oh, for goodness' sake, stand still and think, Kyle. Was it him?'

She doesn't usually raise her voice to him, but she's on edge, the events of the last couple of days fraying her nerves. She runs a hand down her face... please, God, don't let this send him off into one of his tantrums.

To her relief, Kyle stops his rocking. He shakes his head as though she's said something stupid. 'No, of course it wasn't him. He's only there at night. He looks in at the window.'

Ailsa's hand rises to her chest. 'He looks in at the window? You never told me that, Kyle. Why not?'

His face is serious. 'You didn't ask me.'

It's Moira who gets up. She goes over to Kyle and stands beside him, keeping the distance he likes, and smiles at him.

'We're asking you now, lovely. This man at the window. Do you think it might be a dream?'

But what if it isn't?

She thinks of the visitors in the lodges. It's possible it might have been one of them. If it was, it won't happen again as the last two checked out earlier and the next two bookings aren't for another few days. She frowns. If Jonah looks at the bookings online, he'll feel justified in wanting to sell. The business is barely viable. Hasn't been for years.

'No, he wants to get in.' Kyle points to the window.

It's said matter-of-factly, but, even so, it chills Ailsa's blood. There were those footprints on the steps to the deck last night, now washed away by the rain. Under the window too.

Who is it creeping around at night, frightening her son? Do they mean to harm her? Or, more disturbing than that, is it Kyle who's the magnet?

This has only started happening since Jonah returned and she has a bad feeling about it. Jonah, Callum, Hugh, Seth. They're all linked by one thing. The past. And the people they were then.

TWENTY

AILSA

Then

It's been three days since the ceilidh. Three days and three sleepless nights. Since then, Ailsa's hardly spoken to anyone. Has moved seats on the school bus so that she's not had to sit near anyone and has spent all her free periods at school at a desk in the furthest corner of the library, her head bent to her books. At home, she's hardly moved from her bedroom and when her mum has questioned her as to why she's been so quiet, she's shrugged and told her she's fine.

Yet, she'd agreed to go for this walk. Why had she done that when he's the last person she wants to be with? She looks at Jonah out of the corner of her eye as she climbs the steep path wondering why she's been so stupid. He'll know something's wrong and although she'll tell him there isn't, he has this ability to see through her lies. He'll question her until she's forced to tell him what's going on in her head and she can't tell him the truth. Can't tell anyone. Ever.

Yet he's strangely quiet. His hands pushed deep inside his pockets. His long stride making it hard for her to keep up.

'What's the hurry, Jonah? Wait for me.'

His message to her phone as she'd come out of her art lesson had been unexpected. So too had been his request to feign illness and meet him in the car park after lunch. He needed to talk to her. Needed to explain. It had made sense then, but now, as she follows him up the hill, she wonders why she'd bothered. What's up with him?

When she'd run over to his car, she hadn't asked him why he wanted to see her. Had simply slid into the passenger seat and clicked her seat belt in silence. And as he'd driven them out of Elgin, taking the narrow road out, heading for the coast, she'd closed her eyes and imagined she was somewhere else. Wishing she could wind back the days and start over.

When the sea had come into sight, they'd followed the road around the coast a short way, then parked up on a rough patch of land. Leaving the car, they'd let themselves through a gate where a sign directed them to a viewpoint and begun their climb. Hands not touching. Not speaking. Their breath becoming more laboured as the path steepened.

Ailsa looks up at the sky. The weather had been fine when they first set out, but now, as is so often the case on Bray, it's changed, a band of rain sweeping in from the south-west. Light at the moment but sure to get heavier.

All the while they've been walking, Jonah has kept his head down, eyes screwed tight against the wind, but it's only putting off the inevitable. Eventually, they are going to have to talk.

Up ahead is the stone pillar signalling they've reached the highest point and they walk to it in silence. Jonah's face is pale. Drawn. Something is eating away at him, and it's better they get it over with. She feels her throat tighten. They haven't spoken since the night of the ceilidh. Could he have guessed why she's been avoiding him? Avoiding everyone?

When they reach the trig point, Jonah leans his back against the stone. His eyes fixed on the ocean. The air smells deeply of the sea, a scent of salt on the breeze. Above their heads, guille-mots circle.

What is Jonah thinking?

It's raw up here, Ailsa's breath clouding in front of her. Above their heads, a seagull screams and she watches it. Just for somewhere to look. Somewhere that isn't Jonah. Who is going to speak first?

It's Jonah. His voice strained. Cracked. 'I'm sorry.'

It wasn't what Ailsa had been expecting. 'Sorry?'

'Yes.' The wind blows his fringe across his eyes. 'I need to tell you why it happened. I can't live with myself, Ailsa. I can't do this any more.'

Ailsa stands. Feet planted and eyes screwed tight against the buffeting wind. From somewhere to her right, she can hear sheep calling to each other. Rain is misting her hair, and she doesn't have a hood. It will only be minutes before the heavens open.

'What can't you do?' The wind forces her to raise her voice. 'Why bring me all the way up here to talk in riddles? Was it that night?' Up here on the clifftop it feels as if they're under siege, the wind attacking them from all sides. She moves closer to the trig point, crouches down in its shelter. Reaching out a hand, she pulls Jonah down too. 'There's nothing for you to be sorry about. It was my fault.'

Jonah's face is lost in the shadows of his hood. He hugs his knees and stares out at the grey sea. 'I love this island but the dark winters... the smallness of it.' He turns and looks at her, rain dripping from his hood. 'It makes you do things. Bad things.' He stops. Hugs his knees tighter.

What does he mean? What is he on about? She'd thought he'd taken her up here to talk about the night of the ceilidh, but now she's not so sure. She doesn't like the way he's talking. It's scaring her.

The wind is wailing around the stone marker. Jonah has his

walking jacket on, the neck zipped up so high she can't see his mouth, but the coat Ailsa chose that morning is already soaked through. If she'd known she'd end up here on this windswept cliff, with little protection from the rain that's sweeping across the island, she'd have worn something different.

She shivers and pulls her scarf up, using it to cover her head. 'I don't know what this is about, Jonah, but I'm freezing. Let's go back to the car. Find somewhere for a coffee or something.' She shakes his arm. 'Jonah. Did you hear me? If we go now, we—'

But it's like he's not listening. Has gone somewhere deep inside himself. He turns to her, reaches out both hands and takes her by the shoulders. His forehead is close to hers, strands of soaked fringe beaded with raindrops that drip down his cheeks like tears. 'I'm going to tell you something, Ailsa, and when I've done, you are going to feel differently about me.'

Ailsa feels something shrink inside her. 'Maybe it's better if you don't.'

'I have to.'

'Tell someone else then.' Instinct's telling her this is important.

But he shakes his head. 'It has to be you. There's no one else.'

'What about Callum?'

His grip on her sleeves tightens. His eyes lock with hers, desperate for her to understand. 'No! And you must swear that you'll never tell him what I'm going to tell you now. He can't know. Ever.'

'But why not? He's your brother. I thought you told him everything. Surely, if something's wrong, he would be the best person to tell.'

'I said no!' His grip on her coat loosens again. His hands fall to his knees. 'You'll understand when you know what it is. I just can't live with this any more. I don't sleep. I hide it well, but I can barely function.'

Ailsa's full of confusion. 'Why me, though? Why now?'

'Because on this small island, where everyone knows everything, I can trust you not to let this go further.' He takes her hand and smooths her palm with the pad of his thumb. 'It might help you understand things too. Why I'm like I am.'

Below them, whipped by the wind, the waves run onto the shore. Ailsa can hear them rather than see them. Building to a crescendo. A meeting of water and rocks before the waves recede again. Out at sea, the seagulls wheel and scream. Under normal circumstances, Ailsa would enjoy watching them being buffeted by the wind. Not today, though. Today, she only has eyes for Jonah. Ears for what he has to tell her.

Years from now, she'll look back on this moment and wish he hadn't spoken at all. But now all she can think is that he's chosen her to tell. *Her.*

They sit, Ailsa's hand gripped tightly in his, their backs against the hard stone of the trig point. She lets him talk, not interrupting. Keeping to herself the rush of conflicting emotions his words are stirring up in case he stops. And when his story comes to an end, reaching its conclusion – when she knows what he's had to live with for so long – she doesn't dare move or breathe.

For she's no longer the person she was before he told her.

He's finished now. The words have dried. He doesn't look at her, and she knows it's because he's terrified of what he'll see in her face.

Above them, the rainclouds hang heavy and judgemental. Ailsa can no longer feel the rain, or the wind. She can no longer feel Jonah's hand or even her own heartbeat. Her body's trembling. It's the shock, she knows it is, and she can't stop it. How could he have kept this to himself for so long?

Those words in her head – those words that can never be

unheard – they're weighted with such importance. Their unexpectedness striking her dumb.

Pulling her hand away from Jonah's, she reaches up to touch the wet stone of the pillar behind her. Its solidity connects her to the here and now, to reality, but it's the only thing that does.

Yet, behind Jonah's voice in her head, another is fighting to be heard. Her own.

He chose you. He chose you.

And, as she tips her head back against the stone, feeling the slap of the wind against her cheeks, rain needling her skin, she knows it's enough. She doesn't want to, but she'll keep his secret. Will never tell anyone. Because, despite the shock of it, she loves him and always has. Always will.

Ailsa pushes herself up. Out of the shelter of the triangulation point, the wind dominates and she holds on to the stonework for support. She's shivering uncontrollably and has a desperate need to go back. To swap this bleak place for the chaos of her home. For, whatever she might tell people, the house with its hand-made rugs and throws, the vases of dried flowers gathering dust and the smell of joss sticks that lingers in every room, is a place where she feels safe. She needs to be there to digest what's happened and think about how they can move on after this.

She holds out her hand to him. 'Come on. We need to go.'

Jonah looks up at her, his face a picture of misery. 'You don't want to talk about it?'

'No.'

She pulls him up and they walk down the hill in silence, the wind pressing at their backs. It's only when they're at the bottom and heading for the car that she risks looking at him. She doesn't know what she expects to see: guilt maybe? But it's not this. The only emotion his face shows is relief at having shared his burden.

They drive home in silence, the sea receding in the rear-view mirror and the weight of what he's told her between them. When he gets to her house, he stops the car and lets her out. Ailsa turns as she reaches the front gate, wondering if he'll be watching her, but Jonah is already indicating, edging the car out and pulling away. The tail lights of his car disappearing as he rounds the bend in the road.

Above her head, the sky is dark. No stars. No moon. At this time of year, it's like night-time is always waiting. Creeping in once the minute hand has passed three thirty. Cutting the afternoon short. It's what she likes least about the island – that and the Atlantic depressions that bring the gale-force south-westerly winds that can stop the ferries from docking and leave them without electricity for days.

Her mum looks up as she lets herself in. The kitchen is scented with the lavender the two of them had cut from the garden in summer and hung in bunches from whatever coat or picture hook had been available. The dried buds they'd harvested are now in a box on the kitchen table and her mum is stuffing them into muslin bags to give as Christmas presents.

'Good day at school?'

'The usual.'

'Well, it won't be long now. Just a few more months and then it will all be over.' She looks at the clock. 'Was the bus late? You're usually back before now.'

Ailsa keeps her voice neutral. 'Jonah gave me a lift.'

Her mum's fingers pinch and stuff. When the little muslin bag is full, she pulls the satin ties together and secures them with a neat bow. Eventually, she looks up.

'I think you might be seeing a bit too much of that boy.'

Ailsa bristles. 'I thought you liked him.'

'I do. It's just that you haven't been yourself since you went to the ceilidh. Quiet. Self-absorbed. Did something happen? I know you didn't want to talk about it before but—'

'Then why ask me now, Mum?'

'I suppose it's because I thought whatever it was that was bothering you would blow over. As far as I'm aware you haven't seen Jonah since that evening but now... look, Ailsa, I just don't want you getting too serious. It's not Jonah. It's the rest of them.'

'What? His family? What are you trying to say?'

Her mum puts the bag she's just tied in the box with the others. 'Just that things are strange at Loch Briona. The atmosphere is odd. To be honest, it gives me the creeps, and once I've done my shift, I get out of there as soon as I can. Moira's been good to me but...' She shrugs. 'I don't know. You'd think she'd be happy with that bastard of a husband gone, but it's the opposite. And don't be fooled, she's scared of the other one you know... that Callum. I see it in her eyes when he walks past. Like a deer that's being stalked. I don't know what's going on there, but I don't like it. If I were you, Ailsa, I'd stay away from the lot of them.'

It's not the first time her mum's said something along these lines and Ailsa's weary with defending them. She'd been stubborn before, her feelings for Jonah clouding her judgement, but now she knows her mum had been right all along.

She'll never be able to think of Jonah the same way again.

Nor Callum. Never.

How could she after that night?

She helps her mum clear the table, sweeping the dried buds of lavender into her hand and throwing them into the kitchen bin, letting the lid fall with a clang. When the table is cleared, she heats up some vegetable lasagne left over from the night before and they eat it in silence.

As soon as she can, Ailsa excuses herself and goes upstairs to her room. She'd wanted time on her own to think about what Jonah had told her and decide what she should do, but her exhausted mind has other ideas. Within minutes of her head touching the pillow, she's asleep.

. . .

'Ailsa, wake up.'

Ailsa lifts her head and looks at the clock; it's gone two in the morning. She sits up, rubbing her eyes, unsure what is a dream and what is real.

Her mum's in the doorway, her hair wild, her dressing gown open over the tie-dye T-shirt she sleeps in. Her mouth is moving, words coming out, but Ailsa is struggling to take them in – something about Moira having had a call from the pub in Elgin. Callum drunk. Causing trouble. He couldn't drive back in that state so could Jonah go and get him? Bring him back to Loch Briona?

Forced from her sleep, Ailsa tries to focus. There's something else. Something about a boat. Yes, a boat. Jonah hadn't wanted to do the long drive back to Elgin in the dark so had taken the outboard.

Her mother's voice fades in and out. Some words more prominent than others. *Accident. Shock. Freezing water. Dead.*

All this she hears as her mum stands in the doorway, a dark silhouette against the bright hall light. Her mobile still in her hand from when Moira called her. She's waiting for Ailsa to say something, but she can't find the words to reply to the terrible thing she's just heard.

Is Jonah dead? Is he? Oh, please God, say it's a mistake.

She raises pleading eyes to her mum, and she comes to her, understanding. She sits on Ailsa's bed with a heavy sigh.

'It isn't Jonah, it's Callum. He was drunk and fell into the loch. Jonah tried to save him, but he'd been in the water too long. You know how cold Loch Briona gets in winter. By the time he managed to pull him out, it was too late. Callum didn't stand a chance.'

Ailsa covers her face with her hands, surprised that her eyes are dry. Is she wicked to feel the way she does? Relieved? Now

Callum can never know what his brother said. Can never punish her for knowing it too.

For Callum is dead.

She hugs the knowledge to herself. Jonah could have died too, trying to drag his brother out of the water, but he didn't.

Jonah is alive and nothing else matters.

TWENTY-ONE

JONAH

'Make it a double this time.' Jonah pushes his glass across the bar, his forehead falling back down onto his folded arms.

'You've had enough.' Reyne folds her arms and shakes her head. 'Take my advice and stop now, Jonah, or you'll regret it later.'

'Don't fucking tell me what to do.' Lifting his head again, he looks at Reyne through half-closed eyes. She's just a blur with eyes that won't stay still in her face and a mouth that won't shut up. 'You're doing my head in.'

Reyne purses her lips. 'There's no need for that. For years I put up with that waste of space brother of yours, your father too, but you're different to them, Jonah. You know better. I'll make allowances for your foul mouth after what you went through, but my tolerance is only so great. Let me make it clear, if you were anyone else, I'd throw you out.' She straightens and points to the coffee machine. 'Let me get you a black coffee. It might help you to sober up before Moira sees you in this state.'

'I dinnae care. Just fill the fucking glass, will you?' A couple over the other side of the room have stopped their conversation and are looking his way. Pushing off from the high stool, he steadies himself and points a finger in their general direction. 'What are yae looking at? Bleeding twitchers.'

'That's enough, now, son.'

There's a hand on his collar. Another gripping the sleeve of his combat jacket. Douglas has come from nowhere, and he feels himself being bundled towards the door.

'Get your hands off me.' Jonah struggles, tries to shake him off, but the drink has made him uncoordinated, and, despite his age, Douglas's grip is still as strong as it ever was.

'Don't come back until you've sobered up... and until you're ready to apologise to my wife.'

Douglas pushes him through the door, and Jonah stumbles into one of the two bench seats that are outside the front, the wood making painful contact with his knee.

'Fuck!' He sinks down onto the bench, rubbing at his leg, the pain momentarily sobering him. Through the window he can see Reyne, a mobile pressed to her ear. Probably telling tales to his mother. Like he's a kid.

At the thought of his mother, anger floods him again as he remembers what happened less than an hour earlier. The way she'd talked about Callum as though she was glad he was dead. As though glad he hadn't been saved.

Jonah spreads his fingers on the wooden slats of the table and looks at them. They're long and thin, the nails blunt like his brother's. How could she say those things?

The rain has started, darkening his jacket and running down his neck, but he hardly notices. The pain is too deep. The betrayal too raw. He should get up, but the heavy darkness of his mother's words is weighing him down.

Through half-closed eyes, he sees his mother's old Land Rover in the car park opposite where he's sitting. He'd driven it here with no thought as to how he'd be able to drive it back. That had been the last thing in his head as he'd lifted the keys from the hook by the door and pocketed them. It's hard to focus and he knows he's incapable of driving back to the lodges but who cares? If he kills himself, no one will miss him. If he kills someone else... well, he's done it before. His brother's white face swims in front of him, and he waves a hand in a futile bid to vanish it.

Pushing himself up from the bench, he staggers over to the muddy Land Rover, but before he reaches it, Reyne is in front of him. Appearing from nowhere like the devil.

'Get out of mae fucking way.'

Reyne stands her ground. Holds the flat of her hand out to him. 'The keys, Jonah.'

'What?'

Her voice is stern. 'The keys. You might want to kill yourself, but I'm not going to let you kill anyone else. Or any goats that might be wandering on the road for that matter. Hand them over.'

'For fuck's sake.'

'Just do it, or I'll get the police to do it for you.'

Reluctantly, Jonah pushes his hand into his jacket pocket. The keys fall onto the ground as he draws them out and he fumbles to pick them up.

Reyne's there before him, pocketing them before he has a chance to change his mind. 'Sober up, there's a good lad. We hate seeing you like this. Really we do. Doug will give you a lift home.'

'Don't waste your time. I'm not worth it.'

Reyne folds her arms. Breathes in through her nose. 'You were never one to feel sorry for yourself, Jonah. Not even when things were going badly for the family. You did your best in difficult circumstances. Things will get better.'

'You don't know anything. My mother's dying. Did you know that?' He jabs a finger at his head. 'Brain tumour. How do you think that makes things better, eh? This place is cursed. Fucking cursed.'

Jonah stops. Even with a belly-full of whisky he knows he's overstepped the mark. This wasn't his news to tell, and he can see from the way Reyne's mouth has formed a perfect O that his words have come as a shock.

'Moira? It can't be true?' Reyne presses a hand to her chest. 'She would have said something, surely.'

Jonah dips his head. 'No one can know everything.'

'I should go and see her. See if there's something I can do.'

He shakes his head, and the scenery moves, causing him to grip the edge of the bench to still it. 'No, leave it. I shouldnae have said anything.'

'Do you know how long?'

He hears the break in her voice and shakes his head. 'No.'

'Dear Lord. What terrible news.' She purses her lips. 'Well, at least that good-for-nothing husband of hers won't be able to get his hands on the place. Your mother's parents must have known what a wrong'un he was when they left it in trust for her.' She looks past the car park to the gorse-covered moorland road that in spring will smell of coconut. A road that leads to Loch Briona and the holiday lodges. 'Though I wouldn't put it past him not to find his way back to the island when he hears. He may not live here any more, but you know better than most how loud the island jungle drums can beat once there's news to spread. Yes, Hugh will be back to try to claim what he thinks is his rightful share. You can bank on that.'

Her words are coming to him like a radio station that's gone off frequency. He presses his hands to his ears to shut them out.

'Don't say his name to me.' His voice is deep. Guttural. 'Ever... do you hear?'

He feels Reyne's hand on his shoulder. Hears how her voice has softened.

'I'm sorry, Jonah. I didnae mean to upset you or drag up bad memories. It's just that I heard a rumour that someone had spotted him on the mainland. But they could easily have got it wrong. Still...' She stops and looks back at the road. 'No harm in being prepared is there.'

Jonah's jaw tightens. His limbs feel heavy. His brain foggy. He can feel the rain soaking deeper into his clothes, but he doesn't care.

'He won't come.' Between the pub and the neighbouring houses, he can just make out the grey sea and the pier where the ferry dropped him off only two days ago. He clenches his fist, his hands clammy. 'He can't.'

'Well, let's hope you're right. Come back in and sit in the lobby until you've sobered up. I don't wannae be the cause of you catching your death. That's if you think you can behave yourself.'

'No, I'm all reet out here.'

He drags his eyes back to Reyne, taking in her worried face. She's shivering, wanting to get back into the warm. He lowers his head back onto his arms. Reyne's right about one thing. Things are changing quickly here on Bray, and he needs to be prepared for anything.

Like he had to be as a child. As a teenager. Always looking out. Always looking over his shoulder. Only, this time, he's doing it alone.

TWENTY-TWO

JONAH

Then

It's hot, the sun beating down on Jonah's bare shoulders. Picking up his T-shirt from the ground where he'd dropped it, he uses it to wipe the sweat from his face and the back of his neck.

He looks at what they've done and what there's still to do. The area by the house is a sea of rubble, piles of bricks stacked alongside bags of cement. They'd completed the laundry room the previous week, but there's still the ground to prepare for the new shower and toilet block.

Using a string line, he's already marked out a straight line for the footings from the existing wall of the laundry and has started digging the trench. He leans forward, his hands gripping the handle of the shovel he's been using and rests his head on them. It's exhausting work digging by hand. Back-breaking. If they'd hired a digger, it would have been done by now, but his dad was having none of it. He and Callum would build this block by hand. It would make men of them he'd said.

He lifts his head and turns one of his palms up to inspect, wincing as he straightens his fingers. The flesh is red and sore from hours of digging. Blistered in places, the pad of his hand below his thumb, bruised. Feeling in the pocket of his jeans, he brings out a handkerchief and ties it around his hand, using his teeth to secure the knot. It's not brilliant, but it will have to do.

At the side of the trench he's dug, a cement mixer is rotating. Callum is bent to it, feeding it with cement from the bags he's sliced open with his Stanley knife. Jonah turns away, hating to see the livid red lines across his back, yet to heal. His own skin is not as patterned as his brother's. He's learnt to keep out of his father's way when he's had a skinful and his mother has a knack of deflecting Hugh's rage from him. Choosing her words so that his brother will be the one in the full beam of his dad's fury.

Sometimes, it makes him feel guilty, weak for allowing her to do it, but at other times he doesn't care. Callum has no moral compass. Can hurt with tongue and hand as deftly as his father. He's seen it in the way he threatens the younger boys at school and in his victimisation of Seth. Even his mother keeps a wary eye on him, having been on the receiving end of his vicious tongue before his dad had caught up with him and shown him the error of his ways with his fist.

The only person he's never turned on is Jonah. Maybe that's why his love for his brother runs side by side with his hate. It makes him feel special.

Callum turns and nods to him, wiping the sweat from his brow with his forearm.

'Jesus, it's hot today.' He slaps at his cheek. 'Fucking midges.'

'Don't complain. The longer this dry spell continues, the quicker we'll get this finished.'

Jonah looks up at him from the trench. 'Seen him today?'

There's no need for Jonah to say who he's looking for; their father is never far from their thoughts. Callum follows Jonah's eyes to the white house. 'Nah. He went out somewhere. Took the Land Rover.'

Jonah nods. 'It's better with him not here.'

'Too fucking right.'

Today, the site is quiet. The holidaymakers tend to leave early, getting in their cars and driving to the best walking spots or taking the ferry for a day trip to the next island. He likes it when it's like this, the sun glinting off the mirror-flat surface of the loch. The wind in the pines, releasing their fragrance. It's days like today when he understands why people come here, but, despite his parents' wishes, his plan is to leave this place as soon as he can.

There's a movement up by the house. He looks up, hoping it's Ailsa. Will she have remembered it's his birthday? Seventeen. It should be something to celebrate, but he hasn't felt much like celebrating for years.

It isn't Ailsa, though. It's her mother, crossing the drive to her car, her work finished for the day. He knows she doesn't like him, doesn't trust him with her daughter's friendship, and who can blame her.

He rubs at his shoulder, kneading the bunched muscles that years of manual labour have turned hard and smooth. Next year, he'll be an adult. His father won't be able to touch him, and he won't have to do anything the bastard asks. He'll be untouchable. Invincible.

Yet, deep inside, he knows it won't happen. How can he leave his mother to fend for herself when his dad has one of his drunken rages? How can he leave Callum? If only his dad would leave. Take off with one of his women. Jonah frowns. He can't be the only one who knows what the randy dog is up to when he goes to the mainland on some pretext or another. The running of Loch Briona used as a cover for his illicit liaisons.

No, of course he's not the only one. Nothing gets past

Reyne's ears. Gossip spread over a drink at The Stag. Gossip that's made its way back to him.

'Doug threw me out of the fucking pub again.' Callum shovels more ballast into the mixer. 'Isn't my money good enough for him?'

'What do you expect? You're underage. How did you get there anyway?'

Callum taps his nose. 'Wouldn't you like to know?'

Jonah shrugs. He doesn't really care as long as he doesn't put himself, or anyone else, in danger. Turning his back on Callum, he leans his back against the rough edge of the trench and looks across the site to where the thick band of trees starts. It's been a while since Callum did anything stupid. As far as he knows, his victimisation of Seth has run its course. He thinks of the man in his caravan, the dog whose plaintive howling enters his dreams at night. Poor guy – he's never been able to shake off the rumours the kids spread. Callum's made sure of that.

At times, he wonders what it was that made Callum persecute the man, but the answer is obvious: the bullied often become, in turn, the bullies. Callum hadn't needed a reason... just a victim.

'Fuck this. Let's go fishing.'

Jonah turns. 'What?'

'We'll take the rowing boat. Catch a few brown ones before he gets back.'

'We can't.' He glances up at the empty car park.

'Why not?'

'Come on, big bro. You know why not. What if he comes back and finds us gone?'

Callum gives a snort of derision. 'What if I called you a bleeding Jessie? Come on, we don't get many days like this. It's perfect. We'll keep this wee baby turning and fill the foundations with the concrete when we get back.'

Jonah looks at his sore hands, then at the glistening loch. Would it hurt?

'All reet.' He leans his shovel against the side of the trench. 'Just an hour then.'

It's a relief to get out of the hot trench. Not bothering to put his T-shirt back on, he heaves himself out and sets off down the slope towards the loch. The boat is where it always is, pulled up onto the shore. Jonah jumps down onto the sand and goes over to it, gesturing for Callum to join him. 'Come on. Let's get this beauty in the water. Can you get the rods, Cal?'

His brother nods and walks across the sand and pebbles to the boathouse. He opens the door and disappears inside before appearing again with two fishing rods. Coming back, he lays them in the base of the rowing boat, then, together, they haul the boat into the shallows.

Jonah jumps in and takes up the oars, seeing the flex of Callum's shoulder muscles as he pushes the boat out further, his sandy hair falling into his face, water soaking the bottoms of his shorts.

Once Callum's in the boat, Jonah takes them out onto the open water with strong pulls of the oars, and as the land starts to recede, he feels himself relax. The anxiety he keeps bottled away inside him releasing the further they are from the shore. The boat glides through the silky water until Callum calls for him to stop. They're about halfway across the loch, and from here he can clearly see the grassed slope with the wooden lodges, the white house and the dense forest where Seth has his caravan. Putting down his oars, he picks up one of the rods. With a deft flick of the wrist, he casts the line out as far as he can. Callum does the same and in silence they fish, the flies dancing and bobbing on the surface of the water. The breeze ruffling their long hair. Caught up in thoughts that neither of them want to share.

But, despite the beauty of their fishing spot, Jonah can't

relax completely. Callum has his back to him and as he casts his line again, Jonah tents his eyes with his hand and looks back at the shore. Checking the parking area to make sure his dad's Land Rover hasn't returned. His heart rate returning to normal when he sees it's not there. Time passes. He's left his phone with his T-shirt by the building works, but they haven't been out long. Maybe half an hour? Surely no more. There's a tug on the line. Jonah sits up straight. Grips the handle of the reel ready to play the fish in.

He tries to tell himself the shout from the shore is his imagination, or the call of a water bird, but Callum has heard it too.

He turns. 'Fuck!'

Their dad is standing at the water's edge, his arms folded. They're too far away to see his face, but Jonah knows what colour it will be. Can picture the muscles working beneath the skin of his jaw, the vein that will be throbbing in his temple. Driving or not, he'll have had a skinful, stopping on the verge to reach for the silver flask of whisky he keeps in his glove compartment. Knowing it's unlikely he'll get caught.

'We'd better go back.' With insufficient tension on the line, the fish has released itself, but Jonah doesn't care. It had been a stupid idea, and he should never have gone along with it.

Callum doesn't reply, but he's already drawing his rod into the boat.

Jonah picks up the oars and rows the two of them back in. He's glad his back is to his father, that the only thing he can see is the wide blue water with its small island, framed by the backdrop of hills.

He empties his mind of what he knows is to come and thinks, instead of Ailsa – wondering what she's doing. He pictures her wild hair, the eyes that seem to look into his soul and, for a moment at least, he's happy. His father can do what he likes, but knowing she's his friend makes everything a little brighter. A little more bearable.

TWENTY-THREE

AILSA

Ailsa sees him straight away. He's slumped across the wooden bench outside The Stag, his jacket soaked, his eyes closed. Like this, his wet hair sticking to his face, he looks so vulnerable. Younger. More like the teenager she remembers than the man he's become since the accident.

'Jonah?' Holding her open umbrella over him, she shakes his shoulder, the material of his jacket wet under her fingers. 'Jonah, you can't stay out in this. Come on, let's get you home.'

Jonah raises his head and peers at her through bloodshot eyes.

'Home? Where's home.' The words are slurred. He's drunker than Reyne had let on when she phoned her.

'You know what I mean. Let's get you back to Loch Briona. You can have a hot shower, and I'll make you some coffee. Maybe later you can tell me what this is all about.'

'Where's the boy?' Jonah waves his hand vaguely. 'Where's Kyle?'

'He's at home with Moira. Why?'

But Jonah doesn't answer. He's staring at her with glassy, unfocussed eyes.

'Jonah, I'm talking to you.'

Pressing his hands on the bench, Jonah levers himself up. He sways a little, then points in the opposite direction to the harbour.

'I want to see him.'

'Kyle's back at the lodges. I just told you.'

'Not the boy. I want to see my brother.'

His arm waves a little before dropping to his side. Ailsa's knows what he's talking about – the small cemetery set back from the road. It's where they buried Callum. A place she's never been... not even for the funeral. She'd told them she had a sickness bug and they'd believed her. And even though she felt guilty for not being there for Moira, she knew Jonah would look after her.

There was no way she could go and pretend she was sad. No way at all.

'Why not come back another time, Jonah? When you're feeling better.'

'No.' He shakes his head and sits back down heavily. 'I want to see him now. There are things I need to tell him. I can't sleep, Ailsa. The dreams... every night.'

Ailsa sits on the bench beside him, ignoring the wet that's soaking into her jeans. 'What sort of dreams?'

'That night.' He gives a shudder. 'That night.'

'What about it? Tell me, Jonah. Maybe I can help.'

He gives a mirthless laugh. 'How could you help? *You?*' He thumps at his forehead with the heel of his hand. 'I need to tell my brother the truth. I don't need you to come.'

Pushing himself up again, Jonah lurches away from the bench. Not seeming to notice the puddles that are soaking the bottom of his jeans as he crosses the car park. Ailsa runs after him and follows him out onto the road, struggling to keep the umbrella from turning inside out. He's walking along the dotted white lines in the middle and, although it's quiet at this time of day, he's in danger of being hit by anything that comes round the blind bend.

'Jonah, wait. Don't be an idiot.'

Either side of the road are rowan bushes, their berries blood red. Behind them is the stone cemetery wall and the rows of gravestones. She doesn't want to see them, yet she can't let him go on his own. Not in this state.

Giving up with the umbrella, she closes it and pulls her hood up, instead. She hurries after Jonah, trying to avoid the puddles that have collected at the side of the road. He doesn't wait for her but strides on ahead, weaving slightly, his head bowed against the rain. When he gets to the cemetery gate, he kicks it open with his foot.

Ailsa catches up with him inside the stone wall. She closes the gate behind her and stands with her back to it, looking at the rows of weathered headstones. The ones closest to them dating back two centuries or more. A quick scan shows that several names appear time and again: Macleod, Macdonald, Stewart most frequently. Family names, going back generations like Jonah's. There are many Wallaces buried in this graveyard too; Moira has told her.

Ailsa has no idea where Callum is buried, but Jonah does. He's already halfway along one of the rows, not looking either side of him as he walks. Not interested in the stones that are covered in lichen, their inscriptions hard to read, but heading for the shiny dark grey ones near the back of the cemetery. When he reaches the row's end, he turns right, then stops at the third gravestone.

Ailsa slows, not just because she doesn't want to see where Callum lies, but because she wants to give Jonah space. He hasn't been back to the island in eleven years, and she knows it's because, like her, he's been unable to face it... face *this*. And it's taken a skinful of single malt to bring him here today.

There's a bench set back against the stone wall, under the

shelter of a sycamore tree, and Ailsa sits, waiting for Jonah to do whatever it is he's come here to do. The rain is coming down in needles, bouncing off the graves, giving the marble headstones an additional shine.

Not wanting to disturb Jonah, Ailsa searches for something to do, her eyes alighting on a nearby headstone. She's just reading the inscription when an unearthly sound makes her head jerk up. It's anguished. Tormented.

She steps out from the shelter of the tree to see Jonah. He's kneeling on the soaking grass. Forehead pressed against the black headstone. White fingers gripping the edges of the marble as though without his help it might tip and fall like his brother had. To her dismay, she realises he's crying. His broad shoulders shuddering after every intake of breath.

She moves closer, not wanting to intrude on his grief. *I'm sorry*, she hears him say, when at last the sobs die down. *I'm sorry*.

'Jonah?' The brothers were close, but she hadn't been expecting this outpouring of emotion. Not after all these years. It's unsettling. 'Are you all right?'

He gives no indication that he's heard or maybe he doesn't care. Just sits back on his heels and tips his head to the sky. 'I could have saved you, but I didn't. I chose not to.' Dropping his head into his hands, he's consumed by another paroxysm of sorrow.

His grief is terrible to witness, but, even worse, is what he's just said. *I chose not to.* What does he mean by that?

A thread of disquiet wraps itself around her. She doesn't want to know, but she has to. She goes over to him. Looks down on the broken shell of him. How desperately she wants to take him in her arms, but she doesn't. Mustn't. Not until she understands the meaning of what he's just said.

'Jonah,' she says again. 'What did you mean when you said

you could have saved him but you didn't?' She squats down next to him. 'Please, you have to tell me.'

Slowly, he turns his head. Looks at her through swollen eyes – a strange expression on his face as though only just remembering she's there.

Ailsa rests her hands on his shoulders. Presses her forehead against his. 'Please, Jonah. I have to know.'

She hears his breath catch. He wants to tell her, she knows he does. But if it's another secret, will she be able to cope with hearing it? Moving her head away from his, she studies his face. Whatever it is, she'll deal with it. She's never stopped loving him, and whatever he's done, she'll help him through it. But, even as she thinks this, there's a part of her that already knows it's going to be hard. That what he's going to tell her, she might not want to hear.

'Tell me about that night,' she says. 'Tell me the truth.'

The wind takes her words, tosses them over the headstones, and she's afraid Jonah hasn't heard them, but he has. He stands, his hands pushed deep into his jacket pockets.

'All right.' He sounds sober now. Different. His voice full of pain. 'But when you've heard the truth, you'll look at me differently.'

'I won't.' She needs to make him understand. 'I didn't before.'

'What do you mean?'

She looks away. 'You know.'

His eyes roam her face as though expecting her to say more and when she doesn't, he shrugs. 'I've lived with this on my conscience for eleven years and in all that time I haven't slept a full night. Not one. Do you know what it's like not to sleep, Ailsa? When the guilt creeps up on you, squatting on your chest when you let your guard down.' He's pacing now between the row of gravestones. When he reaches her again, he closes his eyes a second. 'You want me to tell you? All right, I will.' He opens his eyes again, looking directly into hers. 'And do you know why? Because if I keep it to myself any longer, I'll go fucking mad. The question is, can I trust you?'

'Of course.' Ailsa stands and presses a hand to his chest, feeling his heart beat inside his wet jacket. 'You always could.'

But even as she says it, she wonders if it's true. She's older now... not the teenage girl she once was. What happened when they were teenagers has changed her, changed both of them, and that's not all. Now she has Kyle to think about too.

The words are easy to say, but as they fall from her lips, there's a voice inside her head. An insistent voice that's urging her to caution. If she'd stopped to listen, she'd have heard what it was trying to make her hear.

That one secret from Jonah is enough.

That one day, she'll regret having asked him.

TWENTY-FOUR

JONAH

Jonah turns away from her. The only way to tell her his story is if he can't see her face or the look of disbelief, of disgust, that he knows will darken her eyes when she hears what he has to say. He tells himself he's a fool to be doing this, but he no longer cares. Even without her knowing, he's a condemned man. His brain taking on the role of prosecutor in his waking hours, of judge and jury after night has fallen and sleep has taken him.

'You know most of it.' He speaks to the short turf beneath his feet. To the hard line of headstones. Not to her. 'How Callum was drunk. How Ma sent me to get him in the boat.'

'Yes.'

'What you don't know is that we argued.'

He waits, listening for a clue as to what she's thinking. Hearing only silence.

At last, her voice comes to him as if from far away. 'What about?'

'It dinnae matter.' He rakes his eyes across the green and brown hills beyond the town, looking yet not seeing. She doesn't need to know, he thinks. 'The wind was blowing a hooley. It came from nowhere.' He remembers the pitch and toss of the boat. 'Before I knew it, he was in.'

He knows Ailsa's heard it before, but she doesn't know it all. The truth lies there waiting. The only thing needed to release it, a skinful of drink and being back here on Bray.

And the guilt. It needs that too.

'There's more, isn't there?'

'Aye. There is.' His eyes are dry now. His tears long spent. 'I tried to reach him with one of the oars, but my hands were numb with cold.' He pictures the smooth, hard wood of the oar, loch water dripping from it. Remembers how it had slipped from his grasp, sliding under the surface. 'I knew there wasn't much time. That his body would be going into shock and that he'd die if I didn't get him out of there.'

'But you did it, Jonah. You did everything you could. There's nothing to feel guilty about.'

His voice is bitter. 'You think so?'

'There was only you. You're being too hard on yourself.'

How trusting she is. How loyal to the boy who'd loved her. It makes him angry.

'What do *you* know about it?'

She's behind him. He can hear the rustle of her coat. He wants her there, but at the same time he wants her gone, for he's no longer sure of what he's doing. A part of his brain questioning why he's telling her.

He turns now and looks at her, taking in her worried face, her soft fair hair beneath her hood. A face he's always loved. 'I wanted him dead.'

His voice is deadpan. He waits for the ripples of shock to cross her face, but they don't. Instead, she's waiting, knowing there's more to be drawn up from his well of despair.

'Did yae no hear me?' His voice is harsh now, like the wind on a raw, winter's day. 'I said I wanted him dead.'

She nods sadly. 'I heard.'

'Then why dae you not speak? Why dae you not judge?'

'Because I know there is a reason.'

He blows a sharp breath of exasperation. 'Callum. Everyone said he was no good. Everyone said he was no better than our father. Well, it's true.' He points a finger at her chest as though wanting her to see the worst of him. 'For those minutes, as he struggled in the water, I wanted my brother gone. I wanted a new life without him. No longer tainted with his name. It was only a few minutes, but it was enough for the cold to get him. When I came to my senses and managed to get him back into the boat, it was too late.'

The tears have come again, taking him by surprise.

He drops down to his knees by his brother's grave and lets them fall, unchecked.

'I killed my brother, Ailsa. And you're the only one who knows the truth.'

TWENTY-FIVE

AILSA

Ailsa stands in the living area of the lodge, her arms wrapped around her. On the table Kyle uses for his schoolwork, is the mug of coffee she'd made earlier for Jonah. While he's been out of the room, she's been trying to get her head around everything, but it's hard when through the thin wall, the patter and splash of water falling onto the plastic shower tray is distracting her from what she ought to be thinking about.

For everything comes back to him.

Back to Jonah.

On the other side of that partition, he'll be standing, head bowed, under the showerhead. Water streaming down the taut muscles of his back. The fair hair on his chest darkening as he turns into the spray. She's trying not to think of what it would be like to take off her own clothes and join him. Imagining the smooth curve of his biceps beneath her fingers. The meeting of skin on skin.

It would be different this time.

Now that they're older. Wiser.

She opens her eyes. What's wrong with her? After what he told her in the churchyard, his eyes red from crying, his voice cracked, sex with Jonah should be the last thing on her mind... but it isn't. What her mum had called an infatuation has lasted more than a decade. She loves him as much as she ever did, and there's no point in trying to convince herself otherwise. Yet, how can she ignore what he told her? More importantly, how much can she forgive?

Yes, she loves him, but, in time, he wants to sell Loch Briona, leaving her and Kyle homeless. Her future is in the hands of a man who caused the death of his brother.

From the bathroom next door, the sound of running water stops and Ailsa busies herself with tidying Kyle's books, pushing away the image of Jonah stepping out of the shower and forcing it back to what's important. The two boys on the boat. The truth of what happened that night.

Those few deadly minutes when Callum had been in the freezing water had cost him his life, but can she hate Jonah for it?

Only a thin partition separates her from the man with blood on his hands. How desperately she wants to believe there was another version of the story. Another explanation. His words could simply have come from the depths of his loss and despair. It's been eleven years, time enough for his memory to play tricks on him. Amplifying the drama. Enhancing the light and shade of that night. Yes, that must be what's happened.

And yet...

Ailsa sinks onto one of the chairs, covering her face with her hands, her fingers pressing into her forehead. There's no hiding from it. She'd seen the truth in his eyes. Heard it in his voice. For those long terrible minutes as he'd stood and looked down on his brother, he'd wanted him dead. That's the simple truth of it. What she must come to terms with.

Ailsa lowers her hands, pressing the flats of them to the cold wet denim of her jeans. By the time she'd persuaded Jonah to leave the churchyard and come with her to the car, the rain had started to come down harder. Driving into the already full puddles and running down the road edges. She's cold too. The skin of her forearms raised into goose pimples.

But she doesn't rub them. Doesn't do anything. Just waits.

At last, she hears the bathroom door open. Jonah comes out, a towel wrapped around his waist, his wet hair pushed behind his ears. Ailsa forces her eyes away.

'I've made you some coffee. You'd better drink it before it gets cold.'

'I will.' Going to his bag, he rummages inside it and pulls out another T-shirt. Another pair of jeans. 'Thank you for letting me use your room.'

'It's okay. Now that most of the visitors have left, Moira wanted you to have a better lodge down by the loch. I was called away before I'd had the chance to get it ready for you.' She looks at her hands, then back up at him. 'That's if you've changed your mind. If you're staying.'

Jonah runs a hand through his wet hair. 'Aye I shall. For a bit, just while I figure a few things out.' He doesn't explain more but crouches to his bag again and brings out a faded blue sweatshirt. He looks up at her. 'Sorry you had to come out for me. It's been a while since I've had a drink and it got out of hand.'

'You never used to drink.'

'Didn't I? You know that, do you? What I was like back then? *Really* like?' He looks away. Zips up his bag.

Ailsa presses the back of her hand to her cheek, feels the flush of it. 'No. It's just—'

'You know nothing, Ailsa. Nothing.'

'I know you wanted Callum dead.' The words are a shock. She hadn't meant to say them.

'Yes,' he says simply. 'I did. Still do. But him being gone hasn't changed anything. Hasn't made me happy. The opposite, if anything. My life's a fuck-up. Go ask anybody.'

'Now you're just feeling sorry for yourself. You can't change the past, Jonah. You have to get on with it. Live with it.'

He turns his head to her. Gives her a sharp look. 'And what if I don't want to?'

'Then I feel sorry for you.'

He looks away again and she's unable to see his expression, but from the slump of his shoulders, the bow of his head, he looks crushed. Defeated.

She puts a tentative hand on his bare shoulder. Feels the warm dampness of skin still flushed from the shower. 'Jonah?'

He knocks her hand away. 'Don't.'

Ailsa stands back, her hand to her wrist. 'I just wanted to...'

Jonah stands, his face stony. 'I don't need your sympathy. Dinnae want it. Do you hear me?'

Something changes in her then. The unfairness of his words a pin to her bubble. 'Then deal with it alone. I was your only friend when we were kids, and you were mine, but we're no longer those children. I'm done with it all. Done with *you*.' She moves away. 'Your coffee is there,' she says, pointing to it. 'I hope you enjoy it cold. I'm going to get Kyle.'

Unhooking her bag from the back of the chair, she turns to go, but Jonah's hand is on her arm, his fingers dropping to her wrist, circling it. 'Don't go.'

'Why would I want to stay with a man who couldn't give a toss that his mother's dying? Who'd rather throw me and Kyle out of our home than address his problems? A pathetic drunk.'

His face is set hard. 'You really want to know what this is about?'

'Of course I do.'

He looks at her, then away, his face changing. 'All right then. It's not about Ma or the accident. It's about your boy. Kyle.'

'Kyle? What about him?'

'I know he's Callum's kid and there's no point in denying it.'

Ailsa stiffens. Shocked. He knows.

'How did you find out? Did Moira tell you?'

He shakes his head, water from the shower dripping off the ends of his hair and onto his shoulders. 'I was there. I heard everything.'

'There?'

'At the house. I'd planned to leave, was going to say goodbye to Ma, but I heard you talking.' His eyes darken. 'I heard what you said. What *she* said. Such hatred for Callum... she didnae even try to hide it.'

He stops, his voice breaking. Ailsa wants to say something to console him, but she has no words of comfort. She can't lie.

'Yes, Callum's Kyle's father, but there's no point in any of us pretending he was a saint. He did terrible things... you know that better than anyone, Jonah.' She stops. Revisiting the past isn't going to help any of them. 'The difference between you and your mother is that your love for Callum has always been greater than your hatred. I know how guilty you feel about your brother's death, but it's more than that, isn't it? There's something else you have to live with – that you deprived him of ever knowing his son and he died never knowing he had one.' She puts a hand to his face. 'I can't take away your guilt, but I can give you some advice. Despite what you think, you're a good man, Jonah. You always were. Don't crucify yourself over him. He's not worth it.'

He turns wounded eyes to her. 'No?'

'No. So stop playing the martyr.' Even to her ears, her words are hateful, but she can't stop herself. 'You need to sort yourself out, not pull up a bar stool every time you hear something you don't like. I know what this really is about. You can't stand the thought of Kyle being Callum's child, can you?'

Jonah pinches the soft skin between his eyes. 'Too fucking right.'

'And why's that? Is it because you're jealous? That you wish it had been you instead of him? Well, I'll tell you something for nothing. Better a dead father than an uncaring one.'

She sees his hand before she feels it. For one terrible, ridiculous minute, she thinks he's going to strike her, but he doesn't. Instead, he catches a lock of her hair, spiralling it around his index finger. Without thinking about what she's doing, she raises her hand and covers his, letting it fall back to her side when she sees the look on his face.

'I'm sorry.'

A muscle works in the side of Jonah's jaw. He lets her hair slide from his finger. 'No, I am.' He tucks the strand behind her ear. 'I wasn't thinking.'

From the table by the window, Ailsa's phone rings out. Jonah steps back. Fastens the towel more securely around his waist. 'You'd better answer it.'

'Yes.'

Going over to it, Ailsa picks it up and looks at the screen. 'It's Moira. She'll be checking when I'm going to pick Kyle up.'

Jonah nods. 'Ailsa. I don't want you to think—'

'It's all right, Jonah. You've said it all before.' She knows the hurt is written in her eyes. Can do nothing to hide it. 'I know nothing's changed.'

Jonah looks down. 'It's just this situation. Being back on Bray. Everything.'

As if trying to make things better, he takes her hand, but she pulls it away.

'You don't have to explain.'

'I like you, Ailsa. I always have.' He stops. Says no more and she hears the unsaid *but*. For one stupid moment, she'd let herself believe things were different now. That the years had changed his feelings. She can't believe how naïve she's been.

'I said you don't have to explain, Jonah.' Ailsa folds her arms. 'You were never very good at this, were you?'

'At what?'

'It doesn't matter.' Going over to the table, she picks up Jonah's mug. He's forgotten to drink his coffee and now it's gone cold. She takes it to the sink in the kitchen area and empties it, knowing his eyes are on her. Knowing he'll hear the angry thump of china on the metal draining board.

'No, go on,' he says, his voice curious now. 'Please, don't stop now.'

'All right then. You were never any good at communicating with me.' She leans her back against the worktop.

In the living room, Jonah finishes buttoning his jeans and pulls his T-shirt over his head. 'What do you mean by that?'

Ailsa's thoughts spiral to the past. 'Despite everything you said, you and me... it's always felt like unfinished business.'

He's pulling the T-shirt over his stomach but stops. 'I can't go back there, Ailsa. It would do neither of us any good. You and me...' He shakes his head. 'I'm sorry.'

'Why are you sorry?' Ailsa leaves the kitchen area and comes back to him, standing between him and the door, as though by doing so, it will stop him from leaving.

Jonah picks up his bag and walks to the door. 'Let's just say that one day you'll be glad I left. Glad that we never moved on from what we were.'

'Which was?'

Jonah looks at the ceiling as if it might give him the answer, then back at her.

'I'll let you decide that. But it was a bad idea. And getting too close to me now is no different.' He walks to the door, brushing past her. 'It's too dangerous.'

Ailsa stays where she is, trying to understand what he's saying to her. He's talking in riddles. 'Dangerous? How? Look at me, Jonah. Talk to me.'

'It doesn't matter,' he says, his attention returning to her. His eyes stony. 'But one day, believe me, you'll thank me for it.'

TWENTY-SIX

JONAH

Jonah's seat is an upturned boat that's been dragged up onto the pebbles by the shoreline. He's been sitting here since Ailsa went to collect Kyle, thinking about the things he's learnt in the short time he's been at Loch Briona. That Callum is really Kyle's biological father. Ailsa's true feelings. His mother's mortality.

Now he looks at the rows of lodges that will, some day in the not-too-distant future, be his to do with as he pleases. And what pleases him is to sell the place, even though it will hurt Ailsa to do so.

He narrows his eyes as he scans the weathered decking of the chalets. The windows that haven't been cleaned for a good while. The loch where fewer and fewer people come to boat and fish, if Reyne's information is correct. Toxic. That's what it is... toxic. Not just the holiday complex, but the island of Bray itself. For even though it's wild and beautiful, its moorland and peat bogs open and windswept, there's a claustrophobia to the place that he can't bear. A cloying melancholy. It's a feeling that had descended on him the minute the ferry, that had dropped him off at the harbour, had turned and left again for the next island on its schedule.

Leaving him alone.

Leaving him vulnerable.

'I thought I might find you here. I take it you've sobered up?'

Jonah raises his head at the sound of his mother's voice, watching as she steps off the path onto the little beach and walks towards him.

'I'm fine.'

When she reaches the hull of the upturned boat he's sitting on, she touches it with her hand to check it's dry, then leans her back against it.

'Are you really? Remember, I spent the best part of my life with a man who said the same thing. Only he wasn't, was he?' She looks at him meaningfully. 'All right, I mean. Far from it. You know sometimes it's like he's still with me. Watching me. Steering me on the right course. I've never said anything to Ailsa as she wouldn't understand, but you're different. You're his son.' She grips his arm. 'I see him sometimes.'

Jonah closes his eyes for a beat. 'Jesus, Ma. Not again. Don't do this to yourself.'

'Oh, don't look at me that way. It's comforting to think he's still here.'

Jonah looks at her, aghast. 'How can you say these things? The bastard hit you. Hit *us*. It's not real what you see.' He taps his temple with his first finger. 'It's the cancer talking, Ma, making you imagine things. He's never coming back here.' He bites the side of his cheek. 'You're right about one thing, though. You must never say anything like that to Ailsa... to anyone.'

He stares at his mother, taking in the gabardine raincoat that was his father's. The face whose lines and shadows now have an explanation. He must remember she can't help it – doesn't know what she's saying. Yet, still, he's unsettled by what she's just told him, and a shiver goes down his spine at the thought of the man: the memory of his fist, the spittle at the corners of his mouth as he called out him or his brother for something they may or may not have done.

'Ailsa says she's told you. About Kyle.'

The sudden change of subject is disconcerting. 'Aye. She told me.'

So Ailsa hadn't told her he'd overheard, that he'd been eavesdropping – that's something. He's glad she doesn't know that he was there. Sneaking away again after, like a thief in the night, desperate to find an antidote to the pain in the bottom of a whisky glass.

His mother gives a careful smile. 'I won't lie. It was a shock to me too. A huge shock.'

She waits and Jonah realises it's his cue to say something. 'Aye. I would imagine it was.'

'Is that all you have to say?'

'What more *is* there to say?' He gives a bitter laugh. 'The boy's Callum's kid and there's nothing you nor I can do about it.'

His mother sighs. 'All this time. I never thought... never guessed. I had no idea the two of them...' She closes her eyes and gives a small shake of her head. 'She didn't even like him.'

'I know.'

What he wants to say is it was worse than that, she despised him and was as scared of him as everyone else was, but he doesn't. Instead, he presses the toe of his boot into the pebbles.

'Did she tell you what happened? *How* it happened?'

'She didn't need to. I could read most of it in her face, and I know my son well enough to make a guess at the rest. Callum could be charming when he wanted to be. Maybe he tried to persuade her... who knows.' She looks at Jonah and away. 'What I do know is she wanted *you*, Jonah, not him, and that would have been enough to take what wasn't his. Any way he could.'

Jonah's throat constricts. 'You reckon that's what he did, do you?'

She looks at him. 'I'm afraid I do. Unless you know something different?'

'Why would I? I just don't think you should condemn him when he's no longer here to give his version of the story.'

His mother pulls a handkerchief from her sleeve and blows her nose. 'All those years, I thought you and she...' She stops and tucks the handkerchief back in her sleeve. 'That poor child. That poor, wee bairn.'

She stops abruptly as if aware she's gone too far, and Jonah knows he should leave it, that no good will come of upsetting her further. But he can't let it go. Can't let her get away with it.

'Callum was your son,' he says, his voice coming out louder than he intended. 'He's dead, yet you can't help yourself, can you? Talking about him that way. Vilifying him.'

He thinks she'll be shocked, but she simply looks sad. 'You always did have this ability to stick up for him. Gloss over the things he did and paper over the cracks in his deviant personality.' She looks away from him, towards the frigid Loch. 'When even *he* knew he'd gone too far.'

Jonah throws his head back and laughs, the sound drifting away on the wind. She's too much. Talking this way when she still wears her bastard husband's old coat as though it were a second skin. Has constructed a new version of the past. Not wanting to see what *he* sees. Remember what *he* remembers.

'Yes, Callum's dead,' she carries on, as though she hasn't heard. 'But I'd speak of him the same way if he was alive.' Her eyes flick up to his. 'I know he was your brother, but there's no hiding from it. Even *you* know you can't hurt someone who doesn't have a heart.'

Jonah stares at her. He's heard enough.

Shaking his head, as if to evict her words, he stands, but his mother's fingers are gripping the sleeve of his coat. Pulling him down again.

'Don't go. There's something more I need to say, Jonah.'

'If it's about Callum, I don't want to hear.'

She looks at him and then at her hands. 'Not directly. It's about Kyle.'

'What about him?'

'Loch Briona is his home. Ailsa's too.' Her smile is uneasy. 'What I have to say might not be what you want to hear, but I'll say it anyway. He needs to be provided for. When I'm gone.'

Jonah's eyes are fixed on her. 'What's that to do with me?'

'It's not the boy's fault who fathered him and I need to make sure he has a home when I'm no longer here. I'm going to speak to my solicitor and let him know what I've just found out... that Kyle is my grandson on Callum's side.'

'You cannae.' He hadn't been expecting this. Not at all.

His mother looks out across the loch. 'I know your brother was a nasty piece of work, but this is Kyle we're talking about, and I have to do what's right. The trust my parents set up stated that on my death, my estate should be split equally between any children I might have and in the event of one of those children's death, to any children of their own if they have any. Before I knew Kyle was Callum's son, I thought that Loch Briona would go solely to you, but this changes everything. It will be put in trust for him and Ailsa will be the trustee, managing it on his behalf. That way, Callum's share will still go down his family line. You won't be able to sell the lodges unless Ailsa agrees.'

A coldness settles in Jonah's heart. 'Ailsa told you... about my plans to sell.'

She searches his face. 'I never had you down as heartless – that was your brother's speciality. What were you thinking of?'

His face freezes into a frown. 'Look at the place. It's rundown. No one wants to come here after what happened. I need that money... I owe people, Ma. If I don't pay them—' He stops, letting the words do their work.

He can't believe what he's hearing. Ailsa? His fingers grip

the edge of the boat. He mustn't respond. Mustn't retaliate in anger. He knows his mother and it will do no good.

But there *is* something.

'Are you sure Ailsa's the best person to manage the trust?'

The tone of her voice alters. 'Why do you say that?'

'She keeps him here. Keeps him with her at Loch Briona like a prisoner. Don't you think that's strange?'

Moira looks at him with a frown. 'Why strange? She's his mother and Kyle has needs.' She looks up at the sky as though searching for the right words. 'Ones that are a little different to most other children on the island.'

'She makes him worse. That much is bloody obvious. She wants him to be worse so she can have him with her. There's a name for people who do that, Ma.'

His mother's face hardens. 'You've been here five minutes and you know this, do you?'

It's not going the way he'd hoped.

'Sometimes, you can't see what's under your own nose. You're too close to it to see what's happening. You all are. But I saw it straight away. How she smothers him. Clings to him. Haven't you noticed? His worries are her worries. She passes them to him and makes him scared of the world. Scared of his shadow. Ailsa knows what she's doing and it isn't right. Callum would never have allowed it.' He dries to a halt.

She turns on him, eyes flashing. 'Callum's not here. You know that better than anyone.'

There's a sudden sickening in his stomach as he feels the boat rock beneath his feet. Feels his brother's ribcage beneath the heels of his hands. 'Of course I know.'

'Then dinnae be ridiculous, Jonah. See that you're talking nonsense. Ailsa's a good mother. Everyone says so.'

He shakes his head. 'Jesus, Ma. You're so blind... to everything. Just like you always were.'

He stares at the lines of her coat where the wax layer has

worn away at the elbows. The cord collar that's almost thread-bare. Beneath it, he can see the satin trim of her blouse and at her ears are the simple diamond studs her husband bought her for an anniversary. Earrings bought with *her* money not his, for he never had any of his own. What must people think of the woman with never a hair out of place, who wears the castoffs of the husband who beat her? Beat her children?

He knows what he thinks.

'Your condition...' He touches his fingers to his temple. 'It's not making you think straight. This place is falling apart around your ears. Ailsa's too scared to live a life outside Loch Briona so uses her kid as a shield. You're wrong to do this. For all our sakes, when the time comes, you need to let me sell.'

'When I'm dead, you mean.'

'Your words, not mine.'

Out on the loch, a red-throated diver, its bright summer plumage nearly gone, gives its eery, wailing call. It's a sound that's been with him since childhood, bringing with it memories of him and his brother. The oars of their kayak dipping. The tips of their ears and the backs of their necks reddening in an unexpected late summer heatwave long ago. He sees them now as they once were, heads tipped back, eyes fixed on the sky, watching the white-tailed eagle above their heads.

'You've made up your mind then,' Jonah says abruptly. Shutting the memory out.

His mother pushes herself off the boat. 'Aye. I have.'

Jonah stands too. Refocussing, he rests his hands on her shoulders. 'Then there's no more to be said.'

'No, there isn't, and if you see Ailsa before I do, will you tell her I want to see her. That I have something for her.'

'What?'

She gives a wry smile. 'Nothing you'd be interested in. Just a little something from the past I thought she might like to have. You'll tell her?'

Jonah shrugs. 'If I see her.'

Turning his back on her, he numbs his mind. Lets his feet take him along the shore to the steps. As he climbs, he's aware only of the tensing of his calf muscles. Nothing else.

As he passes Ailsa's lodge, he sees the face of the boy at the window. A face that stands between him and a fate that's not worth contemplating if he doesn't pay what he owes. A debt that rises with each year. One that they'll make him pay whether he has the money or not.

He runs up the wooden steps and bangs on the glass, making the boy jump.

'Tell your mum Moira wants to see her,' he shouts. If the kid doesn't pass the message on to Ailsa, then it's no skin off his nose. He's in no mood to see her.

There's no more to be said. Those were his mother's words.

If only she knew. There's a *lot* more to be said. A whole lot more.

TWENTY-SEVEN

AILSA

Kyle's scream wakes Ailsa from her sleep. Not again, she thinks. She'd told Moira these nocturnal episodes were getting less frequent, but now she's not so sure. Grabbing her phone, she pushes the duvet to one side, gets out of bed and hurries to his room.

'I'm here, darling. Right here.'

Not wanting to turn on the overhead light, knowing how sensitive he'll be to the sudden brightness, she uses the moonlight that filters through the gap in the curtains to guide her to his bed. She looks for the telltale hump of duvet but, just like before, the covers are flat. Kyle isn't there.

'Kyle?' She strains her eyes to see. 'Kyle. Where are you?'

She turns to the window, expecting to find him where he'd been the other night, but he's not. Then a sound makes her turn. It's coming from the other side of the room. Reaching across to the bedside light, she switches it on. At first, she doesn't see him, thinks it's a pile of clothes on the floor, and then she realises it's her son. Curled up in a ball, his knees pulled to his chest. His arms cradling his head.

She crouches beside him, her heart racing. Desperate to

take him in her arms. Knowing she mustn't. Outside, the wind that often blows up from the loch at night is trying to find a way in. Buffeting the wooden walls of the lodge. Rattling the door that separates the living area from the decking outside.

'You're safe, Kyle. I'm here. Nothing can hurt you.'

'Don't come in. Don't come in. Don't come in.'

At first, she thinks he's talking to her, but then she sees his wide-open eyes aren't looking her way but at the window. From his position on the floor, he'll only be able to see a part of it, as the bed will be blocking the rest, but it's clearly enough to terrify him. The edges of Kyle's memories don't soften with time as other children's do. He'll believe the man is there again, even if he's not.

'It was a bad dream. Like you had the other night. Nothing more. Come back to bed, Kyle. You must be cold down there on the floor.'

She reaches out her arms, thinking she'll lift him, but at her touch he kicks out with his feet. Lashes with his arms. Screwing up his eyes, he screams. The sound piercing in the silent lodge. Ailsa looks around her, desperately searching for a distraction.

Beside Kyle's bed is his tablet. She'd bought it for him on his last birthday so that he could look up information on whatever subject was his latest obsession. She opens the cover, relieved when the last page he'd been looking at comes up on the screen. *Alsatians as Guard Dogs: The Good, The Bad and The Ugly*. Something inside her twists and her fingers reach for the raised skin on the inside of her arm.

But she has to resist the temptation to slip into the past as Kyle's getting more agitated. His screams louder.

She looks at her phone. Sometimes, when he's like this, only Moira can get him out of it. But it's late. After three in the morning. Her finger hovers over the older woman's name, but she doesn't press it. Moira's ill and she has no right to disturb her. As it does every time she thinks of her, Ailsa's stomach clenches. One day, in the not-too-distant future, she'll have to do without her.

The thought is unimaginable.

To her relief, Kyle seems to be calming down. The most important thing is for her to stay in control. Kyle hates it when she's indecisive. Uncertain. He likes to know where he is in the world, and it's she who provides that solid framework.

'Come on, sweetheart. You're going to go back to bed now.' She lowers her voice slightly, making it a command rather than a question. Kyle needs to know what's required of him and when he does, he'll usually oblige. The springs give slightly as she sits and pats the cover beside her. 'I'll stay with you, and we can look at what you found out about the German Shepherds. You can tell me what you've learnt. That will be more fun than sitting on a cold, hard floor.'

Kyle is quiet now. He sits with his arms around his knees, his eyes on the blackout curtain.

'What does he want, Mum? What does the man want?'

Ailsa follows his gaze. The thick curtains are closed. Even if someone had been there, Kyle wouldn't have been able to see them, unless, of course, he'd parted the fabric and looked out as he had the other night.

Pushing herself up, she goes to the window and closes the curtains tightly. 'He didn't want anything. There was no one there. It was just a dream.'

'It wasn't a dream. I went out to ask him, but when I got there, he was gone.'

'You went onto the deck?' The hairs on Ailsa's arms rise. 'By yourself?'

'I just said I did.' He rubs at his eyes. 'I wanted to know why he had come and if he wanted to take me away.'

'Oh, darling.' Ailsa thinks of her wee boy alone out there. His bare feet treading the cold, hard boards. Trying to make sense of everything. Only knowing peace once he has all the parts of the jigsaw. All the answers to his questions. In circumstances like this, most children would be afraid to find out those answers, but, as in all other parts of his life, Kyle is afraid *not* to have them. Uncertainty his nemesis.

She steadies her breathing, trying to overcome her panic. 'Promise me you won't go out there again. Not on your own. Not at night.'

His eyes don't meet hers. 'Why not? You just said he wasn't real. That it was only a dream.'

'I know I did, but you're only ten, Kyle. It's not safe.' She stops, realising what she's said. She never used to think this way, but something's changed since Jonah came back. His appearance after all this time has unsettled her. Unsettled them all. She can't explain why she's always felt so at home here, so secure – it defies logic after all that's happened – but it's true. For the last eleven years, Loch Briona has felt like a haven.

But not any more.

Kyle has climbed into bed. To her surprise, he lets her sit beside him under the duvet, and as she leans her head back against the headboard and closes her eyes, he tells her about the dogs he's read about. The ones that guard the prisons. The ones that patrol the factory estates.

Ailsa shivers and pulls the duvet closer, not wanting to think about their sharp teeth. Their hot breath clouding the air. Tuning out his words, she lets her mind wander, instead, to the day of the accident.

Only, it wasn't an accident... Jonah's told her as much. He could have saved his brother, but he didn't, and she still doesn't know what she thinks about that. Needs to talk to him more about the night Callum died. And about something else too – the time they'd sat with their backs against the trig point, the rain sweeping in from the sea, and he'd made her listen to what was eating him up. The thing he could no longer keep to himself. She'd never questioned him about what he'd said, but now it seems mad that she hadn't.

She'd been seventeen then – barely more than a child – but that's no longer the case. Now she's a grown woman with a son and having Jonah back has made everything more real. In the eleven years he's been away, what happened at Loch Briona has changed him, but it's taken his return to make her realise how much it's changed her too.

Before Jonah leaves again, she needs to speak to him about Loch Briona.

Because, if she doesn't, this will never end.

TWENTY-EIGHT

AILSA

It's late when Ailsa wakes, daylight leaking between the gap in her curtains. She looks at the clock on her bedside table and sees that it's nearly nine. She must have forgotten to set her alarm. Wondering why Kyle hasn't woken her, she gets out of bed and slips on her dressing gown. The lodge is quiet. Deathly quiet. After his disturbed night, Kyle must have overslept too.

Crossing the passageway, she presses her ear against the plywood door and listens. Hearing no sound, she goes into the kitchen area and lifts down the box of Rice Krispies from the cupboard above the worktop along with Kyle's bowl. It's the same one he had when he was little, a picture of Spider-Man on its plastic base, and although it's too young for him, he's always resisted her attempt to change it.

She pours Krispies into the bowl and lays a spoon beside it, then fills the kettle. While she's waiting for it to boil, she opens the curtains in the living room, pushes open the door and steps out onto the deck, breathing in the fresh morning air. Leaning her arms on the rail, she looks out. Today, the loch is flat, white clouds reflected on its surface, and beyond the lodges, a breeze moves the tops of the pines. She loves days like this. Feels blessed to live in such a beautiful place.

When the kettle clicks off, she goes back in, but as she goes to pull the door shut behind her, she stops, her fingers on the plastic handle. Ailsa's eyes move to the lock and as she sees the key, her heart gives a small extra beat. She can't remember turning it when she went outside. She chews her bottom lip. No, she hadn't, she's certain. All she'd done was push down on the handle and the door had opened. Her mind runs through her journey from her bedroom to the deck, but now she's not so sure. Unlocking the door would have been automatic. Muscle memory – like cleaning her teeth or switching off the bedside light. Just because she doesn't remember doing it, doesn't mean she hadn't.

The lodge is as quiet as it was when first she got up. Shouldn't she have heard Kyle by now? Usually, he's up at seven on the dot. She tries to remember a time when he's slept in and fails. Even when he's had a disturbed night, his body clock wakes him – as dependent on regularity and order as the rest of him.

The sick feeling in Ailsa's stomach intensifies. She rushes to his room.

'Kyle?'

His curtains are still closed, but it's light enough to see that his bed is empty. How desperately she wants him to be hiding as he was last night, curled up somewhere on the floor, but he isn't. There's no sign of him. Clutching her dressing gown to her, Ailsa runs back through the living room and out of the chalet.

'Kyle? Where are you? This isn't funny.'

She leans over the balcony and scans the site, hoping to see him. Hoping to see anyone. But there's no one. Only the empty chalets and the dark forest that surrounds them.

'Kyle!' Her voice carries on the wind, but no answer comes.

Running back inside, Ailsa grabs her phone from the bedside table, then hurries out again, struggling with her coat as she jabs at Moira's name on the screen. At the door, she pulls on her boots, then, with the phone pressed to her ear, she runs down the wooden steps.

Come on Moira, answer.

The phone rings and rings. Eventually, it goes onto voice-mail and Ailsa glares at it in frustration. Why isn't Moira answering? If she takes the Land Rover and drives to the harbour or Elgin, she always lets her know. She looks up at the white house. If Kyle had gone up there, Moira would have rung her. Surely she would.

'It's me, Ailsa. Have you seen Kyle? Have you got him at the house? Ring me back as soon as you get this message, Moira.'

Ailsa has reached the concrete steps that lead down to the loch. She stops, uncertain. Should she hurry to the big house at the top of the hill or stay here and walk up and down the rows of lodges in the hope that Kyle might be hiding there. Playing some game or other. Ailsa's throat tightens. Kyle doesn't hide or play... not like other children anyway. It's not his way. The outside scares him. Confuses him.

'Kyle!' she calls again, more desperate now. Not caring that, if he hears her, the worry in her voice will upset him.

At each lodge, Ailsa ducks to look beneath the space at the base of the steps before running up them to the deck. But even as she tents her hand and peers through the glass of the picture windows, she knows it's futile. Once the visitors have left, the doors and windows are locked. There's no way Kyle would be able to get into them even if he wanted to.

Ailsa stops at the end of a row. What she needs is Jonah's help, two pairs of eyes being better than one. If she had his number, she could call him, but he's never given it to her. She stands with her hands on her hips. His lodge is at the bottom of the hill near the shore, and it would be just as easy to ask him in person.

Please, please let him be in.

By the time Ailsa reaches Jonah's lodge and pounds on his door, she's out of breath. 'Jonah! Jonah, are you in there?'

She peers through the glass, seeing nothing but the empty living room, the empty kitchen behind it. It doesn't look like he's there. Even so, she raps again, harder this time.

'Jonah!'

Not knowing what to do, Ailsa turns and forces herself to think. Panicking isn't going to help her find Kyle. Something made him leave the lodge, but he can't have gone far. To her right is the woodland of Scots pines, separated from the holiday lodges by a green wire fence. Sunlight flickers through the dark green canopy and from somewhere in the distance a dog barks. Ailsa frowns. It's Seth's dog. Might Kyle have tried to look for it? Would he have been brave enough?

The forest is only accessible from the beach, and if her son had wanted to reach it, he would have had to have taken the steps down to the shore. Surely he wouldn't have – Ailsa has forbidden him to go near the loch alone as he can't swim. It's not just Ailsa who has warned him but Moira too. She's never hidden from him what happened to Callum... how it was the water that took his life.

The dog barks again. It's a plaintive sound. With growing dread, Ailsa thinks of what she and Kyle read together the previous night. The webpages filled with information about dogs just like Seth's. She knows Kyle's obsession has grown recently, but surely that passion wouldn't have been enough for him to leave the safety of the lodge, take the path down to the beach and enter the wood.

And if he's done all these things, has found the caravan in the clearing, what would Seth have done when he saw her boy?

Ailsa's body grows cold, realising she hasn't a clue. Since

Callum died and Jonah left Bray, her contact with the man in his caravan has been minimal. Over the course of the eleven years, he's become even more reclusive than he'd been when she and the boys were teenagers. Despite the problems of the past, they've lived side by side without incident and she's hardly given him a thought.

It's only when his dog barks, a different Alsatian of course to the one which bit her all those years ago, that her mind turns to those days. Remembering how she'd followed Callum and his friends. Been there when he'd taunted Seth. A silent accomplice. Too scared to stop him. Just pleased that he and Jonah had included her. She's only glad she hadn't been there the night the man's caravan had burnt, a rag soaked in petrol forced through a broken window. Just the touch of a match needed to light it.

No charges had been brought, but everyone knew Callum had been behind it. For days after, he'd made jokes about it. Strutting around the site with the widest smile on his face until his dad's belt had wiped it off him. At least that's what Jonah had told her later. Seth had been out in his boat when the fire started... but what if he hadn't? What if he'd been unable to get out? Had died?

It had been Jonah's idea to raise money to buy Seth a second-hand van: a quiz night in The Stag, a sponsored silence at the school. People had been prepared to rally round and help in those days. But that was before the boy had gone missing. It was before the finger had pointed at Seth and the police had interviewed him.

Yet, even after the boy had been found on the moors a few days later, tearful and dehydrated, by a search party of police and islanders. Even after Seth had been released without charges, the taunts had continued. But you know what people are like.

Mud sticks.

Especially Bray mud.

It had been Jonah who had cleaned off the graffiti from Seth's van. Jonah who had been ashamed of his brother's bigotry. Yes, Seth was a loner, but there was no law against that. It didn't make the man a child snatcher.

And yet?

Ailsa is almost at the shore. Turning right, she starts to run. In front of her, on the boundary of Moira's land, just before the start of the forest, she can see the brick boathouse. As she always does, Ailsa averts her eyes, but in her heightened state of anxiety, it's not enough to stop the past pushing in.

She's there again, just twelve years old, inside the old building that smells of brine and rotten wood. The damp air fishy. Nauseating. Through the crack in the door is a thin yellow line. The only reprieve from the darkness as she crouches beside the boat oars and the fishing nets, waiting to be found.

She fights against the memory that follows, but it comes regardless. The yellow stripe disappearing. A hand pressed against her mouth to keep her quiet. Breath on her cheek. Fingers reaching up under her skirt to find the elastic of her school tights.

Ailsa blinks back the tears and edges around the dilapidated stone building. She'd been so scared; the game they'd been playing turned sour. Even now, she doesn't know who it was who had been in there with her, hiding in the shadows. Something had disturbed him, made him run out when her eyes were screwed tight shut, but what if he hadn't? What then?

But she knows all too well. Five years later she'd find out.

She screws her eyes up tight. She can't go there. Must resist the nightmarish pull of the past. Finding Kyle is what's important now. Nothing else. Even though it's painful, Ailsa looks at the boathouse again. At the closed door. If Kyle's in there, she needs to know.

She draws closer, her fingernails digging into the palms of her hands. 'Kyle?'

In a minute, she'll have to pull open the door and look in, but the thought appals her. What will she find there in the dark, damp space? She hadn't been much older than Kyle when it had happened, and she's never told anyone about it... not even Jonah. She'd been too ashamed – as though, somehow, what had happened had been her fault. Worried she should never have gone in there, that she'd been trespassing, even though it had only been to hide as part of their game.

Even though she fights it, her mind is running away from her, forming pictures she has no desire to see. An older Ailsa now, kneeling on the damp boards, her blue velvet skirt ruined, tears of misery and shame running down her cheeks.

Shivering with cold.

Shivering with the shock of what just happened.

Ailsa moves closer. 'Are you in there, Kyle?'

She should try the door, but something is stopping her. Some invisible force field. She's terrified of what she'll find. Desperate for Kyle to be in there. Desperate for him not to be.

She makes herself breathe. *Come on, Ailsa. Come on.*

'Mum.'

Ailsa turns. Hand to her heart. 'Kyle?'

Her son is there behind her. Standing in his pyjamas and dressing gown, his feet bare. His face pale in the gloom. She wants to pull him to her, hold him tight and never let him go. Only super-human effort stops her. That and the sight of what's beside him.

Ailsa steps back. 'Jesus, Kyle. Where have you been and what on earth are you doing with that thing?'

Kyle's brows pull together. 'It's not a thing, Mum. It's a dog.' He reaches down and pats it on the head, the rope lead loose in his hand. 'Good boy. You're a good boy.'

The Alsatian stands beside him, its amber eyes meeting

Ailsa's. The soft growl it gives comes from the back of its throat. A rumble of thunder that precedes a storm.

Ailsa's fingers slip inside the sleeve of her coat, feeling the raised skin of her scar. 'Leave the dog and come here, Kyle.'

'No, I don't want to leave it. It's scared.'

'Please, Kyle. Do as you're told.'

Kyle shakes his head. 'No. No. No. No. No.' His voice is rising and sensing his agitation, the dog growls again, louder this time.

'Okay.' She needs to stop this escalating. 'You can stay there, but you mustn't shout or you'll frighten him more.'

Kyle stops. Bending to the Alsatian, he ruffles its head. 'Sorry, dog.'

Despite the panic that had seen her running across the shore, Kyle's demonstration of affection for the animal is heart-warming to witness. She steadies her voice.

'Can you tell me what you were doing, Kyle? You know you shouldn't be out here on your own. I was worried.'

Kyle puts his head on one side. 'Were you?'

'Yes, of course I was. Anything could have happened to you.'

'Like what?'

The dog could have bitten you. You could have drowned in the loch. Someone could have been in the boathouse. You could have been taken.

Of course she can say none of this. The things that have happened in the past are *her* nightmares, and it wouldn't be fair of her to make them his.

'All sorts,' is all she can think of to say. 'But what I want to know is where you found the dog? Why he's here with you?'

'I saw him from my window, of course. He was on the beach. On his own. He shouldn't be on his own, should he?'

She eyes the dog warily. 'No, he shouldn't. We probably ought to take him back.'

'Is it Seth's dog?'

'Yes, I think it must be. Seth will be worried. We need to let him know he's okay.'

Although she doesn't like the idea of taking the dog back to the clearing in the forest where the caravan is, she hasn't much choice. She can't leave Kyle on his own, so he'll have to come with her. At least the dog seems to like him; he's sitting by his side and the growling has stopped. For the moment anyway.

'Come on.' Harnessing her courage, Ailsa takes the lead from her son's hand. 'We'd better go, and please, Kyle, don't leave the lodge again without telling me. You must promise.'

'Why can't I?'

'Because if I don't know where you are, I worry about you. You might not understand that, but I do.'

'All right.'

They make their way along the sand and rocks for a little way, the dog straining at the rope leash. Suddenly, it barks, the sound loud in the still air. Ailsa stops, pulling it back. Wondering what has caused its sudden excitement. Then she sees.

No more than a few hundred yards up ahead, a man steps out of the trees. He's wearing a worn black overcoat and army boats laced up over baggy trousers.

Seth.

A pair of binoculars hang from a cord around his neck, and as Ailsa watches, he lifts them to his eyes. She shivers, imagining her face framed in those two circles of glass, her image caught in them. Or is it Kyle he's looking at?

He lowers the binoculars again. Starts to walk across the sand towards them, his feet shuffling. His back bent. He can't be more than sixty, yet from the stoop of his shoulders, he seems much older. Even from this distance, Ailsa can see the hard set of his face. Is he angry that they have his dog?

The animal is pulling harder now, desperate to get to its

master. Ailsa looks behind her to where the empty lodges are. Out here on the shore of the loch, she feels vulnerable. Exposed.

Her mind turns to the footprints outside her lodge. Did they belong to the man who's coming towards them? Was it *his* face Kyle saw at the window? Moira's always said he's harmless, but how could she really know?

He's closer now. Close enough for her to see how hollowed his cheeks are, the stubble on his chin, and the thin hair, which was once so black, now grey. He lifts his hand. Points a finger at the two of them.

'*You*,' he says. 'You listen.'

Ailsa doesn't want to speak to him. Doesn't want to hear what he has to say. If he wants his dog, he can have it.

She drops the rope and, sensing freedom, the dog tears away from them across the sand.

'Come on, Kyle. Let's go.'

Even though she knows he won't like it, Ailsa takes his hand. She starts to walk away, but Kyle twists, forcing her to stop.

'I wanted to say goodbye, Mum. Let me say goodbye.'

'No. We need to go now.'

'But I want to say goodbye. I want to. I want to.'

He pulls at his hand to free it, but she holds on to it tightly. 'I said no, Kyle.'

The dog is running across the beach, sand from its paws flicking up behind it. When it reaches Seth, it stops and lies down at his feet, waiting patiently as the man bends and grabs the rope that's around its neck.

It's Ailsa's chance. Keeping a tight hold of Kyle's hand, she walks as quickly as she can towards the holiday park, ignoring the increasing volume of her son's complaints.

When she reaches the first lodge, she looks back. Seth hasn't come any closer but, even from this distance, she can tell by the way he's standing that the binoculars are pressed to his eyes again. After a few moments, he lowers them and pulls the dog into the darkness of the trees.

Ailsa carries on until she reaches the steps leading up to the white house, then stops and looks up at it, wondering if Moira is back from wherever it was she's been. Leaving Kyle studying a rock pool, the dog forgotten for a moment, Ailsa takes out her phone. Wondering if she might have left her a message.

There's nothing.

A kernel of unease lodges inside her.

Seeing Seth has unsettled her, but it's not just that. Something's wrong. She knows it. The site is too quiet, too empty, as if the heart of the place has stopped beating.

Kyle is standing on a flat rock, throwing stones into the water, watching the circles it makes spread across its surface. She goes to him.

'Let's get you back and I'll make us some cocoa. We've both had enough excitement for one morning.'

Her eyes flick to the boathouse, remembering her fear – not just earlier but that time when she was a child. The damp darkness that smothered her. The stench of fish and the fingers worming their way under the elastic of her tights. Fingers she knew, as she grew older, would have done more had they not been disturbed.

'Mum, Mum, look.'

Ailsa turns. Looks in the direction Kyle's pointing. She tries to make sense of what she's seeing. Tries to understand it. And, as she does, the kernel of anxiety grows, sending out tendrils that worm their way through the soft centre of her being and take hold.

TWENTY-NINE

JONAH

Jonah looks down at his mother. Even though he knows it's wrong to think it, fortune has smiled on him today, bringing his mother's life to an end sooner than any of them had expected. She's lying at the edge of the loch one hand outstretched above her head, the other at her throat. She looks peaceful – her eyes closed, the ends of her fair hair moving in the water like Medusa.

He feels nothing. Not the dark ache of a son losing his mother. Nor the despair at all that's been left unsaid. For there is no more to say. She hadn't loved him as a child, not properly, his father had seen to that. Children learn fast and it hadn't taken him long to learn not to love her too.

He looks down at her still face, his eyes dry, wondering if his brother's would have been too. It's something he'll never know. His mother's death will be a shock to Ailsa, but at least she's at peace. Ailsa will see that, and it might go some small way to softening the blow.

'Jonah.'

Ailsa's calling his name. She's further up the beach with the kid. Jonah looks back at his mother's body, knowing he should do something. Pull her away from the water. Check her breathing. Her pulse. But he doesn't. He's seen death before and he sees it now in her wide-open eyes, the waxy-white skin of her cheek that he'd longed to stroke when he was a boy.

'Jonah, what are you doing?' Ailsa's running towards him, the boy in tow. She stops a little way from him, breathless, her cheeks pink. 'Why are you kneeling in the water?'

As she speaks, she runs the flat of her hand across the top of her head, capturing her wayward hair with her fingers. For a moment he's transfixed, remembering how that small action used to affect him. What it did to him.

A movement brings him back to the present. Kyle has come up behind Ailsa. Standing with his arms poker-straight by his sides in that strange way he has. Fists clenched.

'What's happened?' Ailsa stares at the water lapping around his ankles. 'Your trousers are soaked through.'

He looks up at her, numb. Can't she see? Doesn't she know?

Ailsa's arms are folded around her body. Her expression fixed into a frown. It's then he realises that his body and the rock behind him are shielding his mother. Slowly, his senses come back to life and alongside it, the reality of what has happened. He points at Kyle.

'Get the kid away. Take him back to the chalet.'

The stones shift under Ailsa's feet. 'What are you hiding? Let me see.'

She comes closer, but like a rugby player blocking his opponent, he stands to protect his ground. 'I said get the kid away.'

'What's the matter with you?' She tries to push past him. 'Get out of my way.'

Jonah grabs her arm to stop her going any closer, but it's too late. She's seen.

Ailsa's face pales and she drops to her knees. 'Oh my God... Moira!'

He watches, helpless, as she presses her head to his mother's chest. 'We have to do something.' She looks up at him desperately. 'We need to call the doctor... or the coastguard. We have to get her to the mainland... to hospital.'

Jonah looks at her pale face, her panicked eyes, wondering why it is she doesn't see. How she doesn't understand. Surely he's not the only one to recognise death when it's staring him in the face?

Ailsa struggles to her feet. Takes her phone out of her pocket. 'It could be a stroke. It could be her heart. If we're quick enough—'

'Is Moira dead?' The boy stares down at her, his face a mask. For a minute, Jonah had forgotten about him. But there's something in the directness of the question that's strangely comforting. Of course he could lie, but the boy deserves a straight answer.

'Yes, she is.'

Ailsa's eyes move from Moira to her son. She wipes away her tears with the heel of her hand. 'We don't know that. I'm going to try CPR.'

Kyle looks at Jonah. 'Like he did on his brother? On Callum?'

'Yes, just like that.' She pulls at Moira's wax jacket, fumbling to find the zip. 'We have to try.'

Finding the tag, she yanks the zip down and feels inside the soaking coat for the woman's breastbone. She's just linking her fingers when Jonah pulls her back. He's had enough of this charade.

'Stop it, Ailsa. Cannae you see she's gone. Don't make this worse for yourself.' He looks at Kyle. 'Or for him. Her time came sooner than we expected, sooner than even Ma must have imagined, but she knew she didn't have long. She told us that herself.'

Ailsa rocks back onto her heels and covers her face with her hands. She's distressed, he can see that, but there's nothing he can do about it. Death is a fact of life. Something to be borne. Something to be lived with. It's always been that way at Loch Briona. He's learnt that the hard way.

Today the sky is blue, the sun glinting off the surface of the loch. The wind that had kept him awake last night, rattling at the windows and feeding his nightmares, has worn itself out and the sun is warm on his back. Crouching there by the water's edge in her denim jacket, Ailsa could be a holidaymaker about to skim a stone or a younger version of herself waiting for him and his brother to return from an afternoon's kayaking. That was a day he remembers well. As the sun had beaten down on them, they'd raced each other around the small island in the middle of the loch. He hadn't won, but despite the cloud of midges that had risen from the water and practically eaten them alive, he'd been as close to happiness as it was possible.

He remembers the day too for the smile on Ailsa's face as they'd paddled in... and for the welt his father's belt buckle had left on his skin as punishment for being late back.

Ailsa wipes away her tears with the sleeve of her coat. Gently, she lifts Moira's head and eases it onto her lap. With tender fingers, she strokes the wet hair from her face, not caring that her jeans are soaked through. 'What happened? Did you find her like this?'

'Aye.'

'Did she fall? Could she have slipped on the rocks?'

Jonah looks down at her and shrugs. 'I'm no doctor, but I'd say it was a stroke. Her time had come. It's as simple as that.'

She closes her eyes for a second, then opens them again, searching for his. 'And was it quick, do you think? I couldn't bear the thought of her having suffered.'

'Who knows?'

Ailsa's face tightens. 'Why do you say that? Don't you care? Jesus Christ, she was your mother, Jonah.'

'Aye, and I cannae be responsible for that.'

The look she gives him is withering. Taking out her phone, she dials the number of the responders, her voice choking with emotion as she tells them what's happened. As she nods and frowns Jonah studies her, wondering how it's possible for such small actions, such small expressions, to be so precious to him.

Ailsa ends the call, and he waits for the emotion to hit him. The grief to kick in. His mother is dead for Christ's sake. The woman who carried him in her womb for nine months is *dead*.

But there's nothing. Why would there be when he hasn't felt anything for years – not since the night of the accident. Not when he's sober, anyway. It takes a skinful for his emotions to rise to the surface and after what happened at The Stag the other night, he's not going to let that happen again.

He looks at his mother's lifeless body, the greyish cast to her skin.

We are the same, Ma, he thinks. *You and me, we are the same.*

Dead.

Kyle is standing watching him, his head on one side. 'Why aren't you crying?'

'Why aren't *you*?' Jonah doesn't want to be here any more, the spectre of death hanging over him. The curse of the place bearing down as never before. Pushing past the boy, he strides away across the beach until he reaches the steps to the lodges.

'Why are you being like this, Jonah?' Ailsa calls after him. 'Have you no heart?'

Jonah ignores her. He no longer wants to look at his mother's dead body.

More importantly, he doesn't want to have to answer that question.

THIRTY

AILSA

How long Ailsa's been sitting by the loch she's not sure. Kyle is a little way away from her, standing on a flat rock, his arms across his eyes. He's trying to process everything. Piece it together so it makes sense.

Eventually, he lowers his arms, the fingers curling into fists that whiten his knuckles. 'Where has Moira gone? Is she with Jonah's brother? Is she in heaven?'

Ailsa harnesses in her own distress. It's important she deals with this properly. 'She was ill, Kyle. Wherever she is, wherever she's gone, she can't hurt any more, and that's something we must be grateful for.'

Kyle presses his fists to his eyes. 'Did her heart stop?'

'Yes. It did.'

'What made it?'

'I'm not sure. It was her illness, that's all.' She shifts her legs to get more comfortable. It's cold here on the damp sand, and she wishes the responders would come.

'That man in the photograph. The one who has his arm around her...'

'Her husband, Hugh?' Ailsa gives a shudder and looks down

at Moira's white face. Why is her son asking about him? In the years since Hugh left his family, she's tried not to think of him and the harm he did to them. Moira's continuing love for the man is something she's never been able to understand. The holiday site was isolated. The island of Bray cut off from the mainland except for a ferry that in severe weather would sometimes not even run. He'd ruled the lives of his wife and sons. Made it hard for any of them to break away. And when, finally, she'd had enough and thrown him out, instead of valuing her freedom, embracing it, Moira had mourned for him.

Ailsa thinks of the old coat of Hugh's she'd started wearing once he'd gone. The photograph of him in its silver frame in pride of place on the mantelpiece. Stockholm syndrome is an emotional bonding between hostages and their captors... might it relate also to husband and wife? A way for Moira to survive the impact of Hugh's emotional and physical abuse?

'Yes,' Kyle continues. 'She says he's here on the island. That she forgives him and that they'll be together again.'

'When, Kyle? When did she say this?'

'It was when I was at the big house, Mum. She used to tell me stories about him.'

Ailsa looks up at the large, white building. Anger flooding her. Of course she had. Kyle was the only person who hadn't known him. She could talk about her husband to him without fear of judgement.

'She shouldn't have been talking to you about him. Hugh left Loch Briona years ago. He wasn't a good man, and he won't be coming back.'

'But he's here, Mum. I'm not lying. I'm not lying. I'm not lying.'

Kyle's getting agitated, and Ailsa knows she must stay calm.

'I know you're not lying, Kyle. I just think you misunderstood. Moira hasn't been well. It made her say things that might not make sense to us.' She stops, not wanting to confuse him.

'What I mean is, sometimes when you're ill, your brain can play tricks on you. It can make you imagine things or see things that aren't really there. Hugh wasn't a good man, but she still loved him, and, despite everything, she'd convinced herself she wanted him back. Probably imagined him here. Love is a strong emotion and there are different types of love.'

'You love me. You said so.'

'Of course I do, Kyle, but Moira's love for her husband was...' – she struggles to find the right word – 'complicated. Let's just say there are few people on Bray who would want Hugh back on Bray. He knows to stay away.'

Ailsa's fingers stray to the cord collar of the wax jacket Moira's wearing, wondering if it's true. Scared that it might not be. The person Kyle saw outside his window... surely it couldn't be?

'Am *I* poorly?'

Ailsa shakes her head, not understanding his sudden change of direction. 'Of course you're not poorly. Why would you think such a thing?'

'Because you said I imagined seeing the man at my window.'

Ailsa's breath catches. It's as if he's read her thoughts. She sees Hugh's face as she remembers it from the last time she saw him. The small dark eyes. The thin lips that never smiled.

'No, I didn't say that. I said you were probably dreaming.'

'Dreaming is made up too. You said.'

Suddenly, Ailsa feels immeasurably weary. Still cradling Moira's head in her lap, her hand on her damp hair, she turns her eyes to the loch. The clouds are breaking and light follows shadow across its vast surface. Usually, it would calm her. Not today.

'I know I said that, but the two things are different. I can't explain why, you just have to believe me.'

Her legs are cramping, her jeans soaked through. In the

distance, she can hear a dog barking. Seth's dog. The sound carrying on the still air. Above her, sit the lodges, their dark windows looking out onto the loch. There are no walking boots on any of the decks. No movement behind any of the windows.

The last visitor left a day ago and now Moira has left them too.

A chill breeze sweeps across the water, ruffling its surface and Ailsa shivers. Moira told Kyle her husband was here. Could it be possible? Strands of Moira's hair move in water that's no longer clear but tinged with red. Lifting her hand from Moira's head, she sees that it too is red. The shore is strewn with rocks and Moira must have hit her head on one of them when she collapsed.

If only Jonah would come back. He's left her here – a sentinel for his mother – and she's never felt more alone. Except she isn't alone. Her son is here too, and he's just told her something that could change everything.

She looks down at the woman in her arms. Poor Moira. Freed from her torment yet longing to be with her husband again. Her fingers gently smooth the woman's hair back from her forehead. 'Did you write to him? Did you tell him you were dying?'

Please, Moira. Don't let that be what happened.

Ailsa's holding her breath deep inside her body. She wants to be wrong. She wants Kyle to have misunderstood what Moira had told him.

Could Hugh be back? Could he be on the island?

The thought terrifies her.

In a metal tin under her bed is the envelope Moira gave her the previous day. She'd been in the kitchen when she'd heard Jonah's voice outside the lodge, but he'd gone by the time she'd got there. She'd got Kyle to tell her what he'd said, and, after their lunch, she'd gone up to the house to see Moira, surprised when she'd handed her the envelope. Although she'd asked what was inside, Moira hadn't told her. Just said that she should keep it somewhere safe and not open it until after her funeral at the earliest. Maybe never.

Ailsa had argued that she didn't want to think of that time, that it would be a long way in the future, but Moira had shaken her head sadly. It was as if she'd known her time would come sooner than anyone expected.

She can still feel the grip of Moira's fingers on her arm as she'd pressed the envelope into her hand. *There are things in here that will change everything – the way you look at the world. The way you look at people. Only open it if you are desperate and can't see any way out. If things work out the way you want, then burn it without reading it. Let things lie. Will you promise me that, Ailsa?*

Every instinct had been to read it later, but Moira had been good to her over the years and had stated her wishes. She owed it to her not to break her promise. So, instead of tearing it open once Kyle was in bed, she'd taken it out of her back pocket and placed it in the metal tin under her bed, pushing it under the pile of letters and postcards her mother had sent her. Vowing not to think about it unless she had to.

But Moira is dead now and would never know.

Uncertain, Ailsa leans forward and places her lips against Moira's cold forehead in a silent goodbye. No, this isn't the time.

But instincts are there for a reason, and she wasn't to know that one day in the very near future she'd wish she'd listened to them.

THIRTY-ONE

JONAH

'I'm sorry for your loss.' Jonah feels a hand on his arm. Looking up, he sees it's Sorcha. A little older. Now blonde. He'd heard she was still on the island but hadn't expected to see her. Had hoped he wouldn't see anyone from his past if he could help it.

'Aye, thanks.'

'She didn't deserve it.'

He frowns. 'What?'

Sorcha shrugs. 'You, know. What she had to put up with all those years with your dad. With Callum. I wouldn't be surprised if it was the cause of her illness.'

Behind them, people are milling about outside the church, waiting to leave. He can hear snatches of their conversation. He can't see Ailsa, or Kyle for that matter. The last time he'd seen them was inside the small church, Ailsa's head bent, her fingers steepled against her forehead. The boy rocking in the pew. Bored out of his mind.

Sorcha's hand is still on his arm. Jonah covers it with his own, his fingers tightening around hers. He gives them a squeeze. 'Thank you for your concern.' He squeezes harder, feeling the bones give and leans in close to her, his lips grazing her ear. 'Now get your nose out of my fucking business.'

She gasps. Pulls her hand away and takes a step back, rubbing at her fingers. 'Are you crazy?'

Before Jonah can reply, he sees Ailsa hurrying up the path towards them. She stops when she reaches them, clearly puzzled by Sorcha's face. The rigid set of her features.

'Is everything all right?'

Jonah lets out a breath he's been holding, relieved that Ailsa's arrived when she has. How could he have been so stupid? How could he have lost control in that way? It must have been the two glasses of whisky he'd drunk before making his way to the church and a funeral service he'd been dreading for days. The only way he knew he'd get through it. Knowing it would bring back memories more painful.

Sorcha pinches her lips together. 'Yes, fine.'

Even after all these years, there's a coolness between the two women that time hasn't tempered, and it fascinates Jonah. Sorcha's eyes are on him again, the fingers of one hand massaging the one he'd hurt. He waits for her to say something more.

Wonders if she'll let on.

Surprised when she doesn't.

'I know you're grieving, Jonah. That you've had a hard time. We'll leave it at that.'

She turns and walks away, and Jonah's eyes follow her. 'She's still here then? I'd have thought the woman would have escaped the island years ago. Found herself some rich bugger from the mainland who can't recognise a fake when it's staring him in the face.'

'That's not necessary, Jonah. She's all right.' Ailsa is watching Sorcha's departing back. Taking in, as he is, the tight, too short black skirt. The high-heeled patent court shoes. 'Anyway, what was that all about?'

'Nothing. The woman just winds me up. Always has done.'

Ailsa frowns. 'I never knew that.'

'There's a lot you don't know.'

Ailsa's face is drawn, dark shadows under her eyes. It's clear she's taken the death of his mother hard, but it's ridiculous. Despite what she might think, she hadn't known her... not really. Even after living together at Loch Briona for so many years. No, she hadn't known her the way he had when he was a boy. The way she had of putting her husband's well-being before her children's. Turning a blind eye to what he did because she loved him. Only his brother knew what she'd been like and he's no longer here.

The wave of emotion hits him hard. Takes him by surprise. He looks across the churchyard to where the marble headstone bearing Callum's name stands between the others. He can't see it from here, but he feels the pull of it. A magnet to his guilt.

Without warning, his terrified face is with him again, picked out by the hard, white circle of the flashlight. His hand breaking the water. Reaching out to him to be saved. Eyes full of fear.

'Jonah?'

Ailsa is looking at him, a question in the tilt of her eyebrows.

'Aye. Sorry. What did you say?' He forces himself back to the present, taking in the black knitted beret that's pulled over her wild fair hair. The black dress under her coat that's made of some odd velvet material.

She looks lost. Vulnerable.

Without warning, all the old feelings come rushing back and, even though he recognises the inappropriateness of his thoughts, he's never wanted her so much.

'I asked you what we're going to do.'

The question is unexpected, and Jonah rubs the side of his face with his palm. 'Do?'

'Now Moira's gone.'

'We'll go back to The Stag, and we'll toast Ma's health.

We'll let the fakes and the sycophants pay their respects and tell us how much they admired my mother and then we'll go back to Loch Briona and we'll talk about the future.'

He speaks quickly. Doesn't look at Ailsa while he says it. He has to make her see that selling is the only thing to do. That it would be madness not to. Okay, she hadn't agreed to it before, but now his mother is dead, she must understand that running the lodges herself would be utter madness. The losses his mother had admitted to would get larger with every year, and without money, a hefty loan, or a fucking miracle, the place would fall into disrepair. In a year or two, they'd be bankrupt.

The dozen or so people who had been standing in groups between the rows of gravestones are starting to disperse. Some are coming their way, others are letting themselves out of the iron gate in the stone wall and are heading down the road to The Stag where Reyne has prepared sandwiches and cake.

'I haven't changed my mind, Jonah.' Ailsa folds her arms across her body. 'Loch Briona is my home. Kyle's home. I won't sell.'

She turns to go, but Jonah grabs her arm. 'Yae have to.'

'I don't have to do anything.' She pulls her arm away. 'Moira has left the lodges equally between you and Kyle, and you can't do a thing unless you go through me.'

'Then buy me out.'

Ailsa looks at him as though he's just asked her to go to the moon. 'You are joking, Jonah.'

'Why would I be? It's the obvious solution.'

She shakes her head in exasperation. 'Where would I get money like that? Even if I got a loan, I'd never be able to afford to pay it back. No, Jonah. I can't buy you out, but neither will I sell.'

Ailsa looks across to where Kyle is standing with Reyne and Douglas at Moira's graveside, and Jonah follows her gaze. The boy's head is bent, his arms stiff at his sides in that strange, awkward pose of his. He's wearing a black jacket that's too big for him, most likely borrowed from someone. Just as he'd had to borrow a shirt and trousers from Doug. He pulls at the too tight collar. If he's honest, he's surprised Ailsa's left the boy so long as she and the kid are usually glued at the hip – more so now that Moira's no longer there to mind him.

The boy will one day own half the holiday complex and he doesn't even know it. Most likely wouldn't understand even if he was told.

Jonah's anger flares. Why has his mother done this to him?

Both boys had had it hard as kids, but everyone knew Jonah was the favourite. It didn't need to be spoken; it was just accepted. So why do this to him? Why change the habit of a lifetime?

His eyes leave Ailsa to trace the familiar line of purple and brown hills in the distance – the same ones they can see from the lodges. Was it to punish him for not saving his brother? Was that it? Or was it to punish him for something worse?

Goddamn his mother. Goddamn Ailsa.

There's a band of dark pressure behind his eyes. The same one he gets every time he recalls that fateful night. It presses and tightens. Stops him from thinking straight.

'Jonah, are you all right?'

He closes his eyes. Presses the pads of his thumbs to his eyeballs until stars appear. It's what he used to do when he was a kid. When his dad had taken the belt to him. It made the pain go away... for a bit anyway.

'Aye.' He opens his eyes again. Forces himself to take control. He doesn't want Ailsa to see this side of him. The weakness. He'd shown it once at his brother's graveside, and it's something he's vowed he'll never repeat. 'Aye, I'm grand. Just tired, you know?'

'Of course.' She looks at him with sympathy. 'The whole

thing has happened so quickly, it's been a shock for you. For me too.'

He's expecting her to leave, but she doesn't. There's something nervous about the way she's standing, the fingers of one hand clasped around the wrist of the other. Looking at him with those heavy-lidded eyes of hers, clearly deciding whether to voice what's on her mind. Something's bothering her, and he has no idea what. All he does know is he doesn't like it.

Ailsa looks over her shoulder at Kyle, checking again that he's okay, then turns back to Jonah. 'I can't stop thinking about that afternoon up on the clifftop when we were teenagers, Jonah. What you told me...'

He frowns. 'What I told you?'

Behind the hills, the sky is purple and swollen. No sun to speak of. More damn rain on its way, adding to the already swollen rivers. Ailsa is looking at him, waiting for him to speak. He knows he must be careful.

'Yes. We never really talked about it, and we should have. You took me by surprise, and I didn't know how to react. What to do with what you'd told me. I was young, not in the right place to process it... but I am now.'

'I see,' he says, playing for time. 'So what are you trying to tell me?'

'I just wanted you to know that if you were scared it made me look at you differently, then you were right. Can you blame me? In that short time on the cliff, it was as though you had become someone else. The boy I'd known had gone, replaced with someone I didn't recognise. I was shocked and we should have talked more, but we didn't. I was the only person who knew, and I guess you were scared too.'

Jonah's eyes slip away from hers, his heart thumping. 'Yeah.' He knows it's not enough, but it's all he can think of to say.

'Was that why you left after Callum died? Because you thought I'd turned away from you and couldn't give you the support you needed? If you did, then you were wrong. There's nothing you could have told me that would have changed our friendship... not once I'd had time to get my head around it. Despite everything, I'd have been there for you.'

'Would you, Ailsa? Are you sure of that?'

'I kept your secret, Jonah. I never told Callum what you'd shared with me, never told anyone. Isn't that proof?'

Her fingers pick at the fabric of her coat cuff, and he watches them, his mind racing. Wondering how this conversation is going to unfold. What revelations she'll offer up.

'Aye, I suppose so.'

'And that's why it felt like a stab in the back when you left. Going like that was cowardly. It made you no better than your father.'

Jonah stiffens. 'What did you say?'

Ailsa looks at the ground, then up again, forcing her eyes to meet his. 'I'm sorry, Jonah, but that's how you made me feel. When you left like you did, so suddenly after Callum's funeral, it was callous. Cruel. Your mother was still grieving, still in shock after what had happened. It wouldn't have been too much to ask for you to have waited until your university course had started. A few months would have been enough to make sure your mother was all right, but you couldn't wait to get away, could you? Only phoning Moira when you needed money.' She folds her arms. 'Where did you go, Jonah? How did you live?'

Jonah shrugs. Thinks of the back-to-back part-time jobs that had left him permanently tired, the cheap rooms in shared houses with their thin walls and sticky floors. Barely making ends meet. 'I managed.'

He doesn't want to talk about it any more, but Ailsa hasn't finished.

'I hoped things would change when you finally started the course. That it would give you something to focus on. I told myself that in three years you'd be back home – better equipped to take over the running of the lodges. Helping to make the place profitable again. But that wasn't what happened, was it? You dropped out... gave up. Not just on me but on your mother. On Loch Briona. No emails, no messages, no phone calls. You might as well have been dead like Callum.'

'You don't know what it was like.' Jonah shifts his feet, remembering the posh kids with their inane conversations about which girls they'd like to fuck at the fresher's ball. The lectures he couldn't get his head around. The cheap drink in the union bar that beckoned to him. Fuelling his guilt. His anger. 'After what happened on the loch, I was messed up.'

'That's not an excuse, Jonah. Have you any idea how hard it was, not just for me but for Moira, to have you leave like that and not come back?' She shakes her head sadly. 'Was it because you felt guilty? Because you knew you could have saved your brother?'

Jonah runs a hand down his cheek. Why had he told her? What had he thought would be gained by it? But, of course, he *hadn't* thought. It had been the drink that had made him do it.

'But it's not the thing that hurts me the most, Jonah. I thought that sharing your secret with me on the clifftop meant you trusted me and that, after the accident, you'd be able to share your grief with me too... but I was wrong. The way you cut me off after was hurtful.'

Jonah sees how her tears have left trails down her cheeks. He should feel remorse for what he did back when they were both teenagers, but he doesn't. He feels nothing. It is all too long ago. Too bleak.

'Maybe you misunderstood what I said to you that afternoon on the cliff. What I meant by it. Maybe we should talk about it now.'

Ailsa stares at him as though he's mad. Taking a handkerchief from the pocket of her coat, she dabs at her eyes. 'I'm sick of these games, Jonah.'

'I'm not playing games.'

'No? Then why ask such a thing?'

Jonah knows he must keep calm. Has to keep her on side. So much is riding on it. One careless word from him now and everything will crumble around him. He massages his forehead with the heel of his hand.

'I'm sorry. I'm an eejit,' he says carefully. 'I just want to hear your version of it... so I can be sure.' Despite the chill wind, sweat has formed on his brow and between his shoulder blades. 'Please tell me, Ailsa.'

Suddenly, he's scared of what she'll say. What she remembers of the words shared on that hillside when she was seventeen. Words that could be misunderstood. Words that could take him down. Words that should never have been spoken.

A mouth that should have stayed shut.

But she's distracted now, her attention taken by Kyle who's left Reyne and is running between the rows of gravestones towards them. In a few moments, he'll be with them, and he's both frustrated and relieved.

Kyle has reached them, is tugging at Ailsa's sleeve. 'I'm hungry.'

Ailsa looks down at him. 'I know, sweetie. It's past your lunchtime. We'll go to the pub and get something to eat.'

'I want Marmite sandwiches.'

Jonah sees her indulgent smile. Hates it. 'Of course, love. I asked Reyne to make them especially.'

Ailsa turns her son gently by the shoulders and ushers him in front of her until he shrugs from her grasp. They've only gone a few steps when she turns back.

'Tonight,' she says. 'We'll talk about it then.'

She walks away, Kyle trailing behind her, and Jonah stands frozen. Without warning, a violent nausea grips him, and he sinks to his knees, the flats of his hands pressing against the top of his head, his fingers interlinked. He can't fool himself any longer. Bury his head in the sand and act as though it never happened. However many glasses of whisky he's downed. However many lies he's told himself and others... It *did* happen.

And Ailsa knows the truth.

Another spasm of nausea makes him bend forward, his hand pressed to his stomach, his other hand reaching blindly to the hard stone of a nearby gravestone for support. He breathes slowly, in through the nose and out through the mouth and eventually, mercifully, the world stops spinning.

When he straightens again, Doug is at his side.

'You all right, lad?'

Jonah looks up at him. 'Aye. I will be.'

'Don't be ashamed. She was your mother, after all.' He looks around him. 'The bastard didn't come then?'

For a moment, he can't think what Doug's talking about. 'What?'

'Hugh. Thought he might have turned up like a bleeding bad penny, pretending to be sorry. Pretending he cared.' Doug scratches his chin. 'Wouldn't have fooled me, though, Reyne neither. We'd have known why he was here, the bastard. He'd have been seeing how the land lay. Planning how to take what was never his, more like. What he certainly never deserved after what he put you all through.'

Jonah looks away, not wanting to talk about him, but Douglas hasn't finished.

'Rumour has it he's been hanging around on the mainland. Biding his time. Once he knew your mother had passed on, the missus and I thought he'd be on the first ferry over here. Maybe I got it wrong. The years could have changed him, or the woman he left to be with might have shown him the error of his ways. Either way, he isn't here, thank the Lord.'

Jonah looks at Doug's concerned face, at the thread veins

that craze his nose and cheeks, a by-product of working behind the bar and the temptation of a late-night tipple. He's never liked him much.

There's a hollowed out feeling inside him. A strange numbness. Doug's guessed right. Hugh won't be catching the ferry to Bray.

But it's not because he's turned over a new leaf. Nor because he's been persuaded by some woman that it wouldn't be a good idea for him to be there.

No, the reason is more clear-cut than that. More permanent.

The reason Hugh isn't at the funeral is because he's dead.

THIRTY-TWO
JONAH

Then

Their father has Callum's neck in an arm lock. Dragging him to the cement mixer, he shoves his head towards the dark opening.

'Yae eejit. What if the mix had gone dry while you were out fishing? Think of the cost of the wasted cement. Not to mention the lost time.'

He pushes Callum away from him, watching as he stumbles, catching his shoulder against the metal edge of the mixer. He plants his feet and folds his arms. 'What did I do to deserve such a bloody waste of space for a son.'

Jonah stands to one side, glad that his dad's anger is directed at Callum. Guilt flooding him that he feels this way. *Don't react, Callum*, he says to himself. *For God's sake, don't react.*

But he knows his brother. Knows that he will because he always does. His father knows it too... is hoping for it.

Callum rubs at his shoulder, and for the first time, Jonah sees that his brother is almost as tall as the man who stands in front of him. They both are. How strange he hadn't noticed it before.

Dropping his hand to his side, Callum levels his gaze at his father. There's a strange intensity to his eyes that Jonah hasn't seen before, and it worries him.

Stepping forward, he pulls at Callum's arm. 'Come on, Cal, leave it.'

But Callum stands his ground. He ignores Jonah, his next words directed at his father. 'It didn't go dry so what are you belly aching about?'

Jonah's stomach clenches. The idiot. He's for it now.

His father takes a step forward. 'What did you say?'

'You heard. And while we're on the subject, if you'd hired a digger like we suggested, this would all have been finished by now. It's a fucking joke. You know that, don't you.'

Callum's always challenged his father but never like this.

A fear settles on Jonah's chest. He doesn't know how this will end, but he knows it won't end well. Every instinct cries out to help Callum, but he knows from experience that it would be futile. His interference has only ever made things worse.

His father's eyes haven't left Callum. He doesn't speak, but a nerve jumps in his eyelid, a sure sign of his anger. Pressing his lips tightly together, he drops his hands to the waistband of his trousers, his fingers feeling for the buckle of his belt. Threading the end through in a well-practised motion.

Slowly, he pulls the belt from the loops that hold it. Taking his time. Knowing there's no hurry. When the leather is free, he grabs Callum by the hair and draws back his arm. His face is triumphant, sure in the knowledge that by the time he's finished, Callum will have been taught the lesson he deserves, but he's misjudged his son. Lightning fast, Callum grabs his father's wrist. Twisting his arm behind his back so hard he cries out. The belt drops to the ground, and Callum kicks it to one side.

He lets go of his father and presses a finger to his chest.

'That's the last time you ever touch me, old man. If you try that again, I'll fucking kill you.'

Hugh's face darkens. 'You'll regret this. Your brother too.'

Grabbing Callum by the shoulders, he shoves him away, but Callum hasn't finished. Ducking his head like a bull in an arena, Jonah watches in horror as he charges at his father. Hears the *oomph* as his breath is knocked out of him. Sees the way the older man staggers backwards towards the trench.

With a yell that is almost inhuman, Callum lunges into him again. Hugh's legs buckle and he pitches into the trench Jonah had dug earlier, the soft earth muffling the thud.

Jonah stands rigid with alarm. His father will never let Callum forget this. Never let *him* forget it either.

'Christ, Callum. What have you done?'

But Callum's gone, legging it up the steps towards the house.

Jonah had been expecting a bellow of anger or at the very least an explosion of expletives, but no sound comes from the trench. His heart thumping madly in his chest, he hurries to the edge and kneels. He makes himself look down, giving a sharp intake of breath at what he sees. His father's lying at the bottom of the trench, one arm twisted awkwardly behind his head. Blood from where his head has hit a rock, soaking into the freshly dug soil.

Jonah jumps down and crouches beside him. His father's face is white. His body still. He looks away, his stomach churning. He's never seen a dead person before, but now he has. Callum has killed him. His father is dead.

THIRTY-THREE

AILSA

Most of the mourners have left The Stag and only a couple of stragglers remain, sitting on bar stools, picking at the few crisps that are left in the bowls on the shiny bar top. As they finish their drinks, Ailsa moves between the tables, picking up paper plates and plastic cutlery and dropping them into a large bin bag by her feet. Her head is throbbing from too much wine and the effort of being polite. Talking to people she barely recognises and giving answers to questions she knows have been asked out of politeness. Nothing more.

Reyne lifts the counter and comes out from behind the bar. She takes the bag from her.

'Are you all right, lass? You look done in.'

Ailsa pulls out a chair and sits. She looks up at Reyne. 'To be honest, I've a splitting headache. The last week has been difficult. Not only is it strange being at the site, knowing Moira isn't in the big house, but the two late bookings we had for next week have both cancelled.'

'Any idea why?'

'No. Jonah dealt with it. He's moved in there for the time

being. Just so that he can get to grips with what's going on with the lodges. It *is* his mother's house, after all.'

She doesn't say how odd it is to know he's there. How, despite their years of friendship, they've not been able to slip back into that easy way they'd had when they were together. She misses that. She misses the boy he once was.

'Of course it will be difficult. Trying to keep a business going while you're both still in mourning is no mean feat.' Reyne's hand on her shoulder is comforting. So is her smile. 'What about the lad? How's he been faring?'

'I'm not sure really. You know Kyle, he's difficult to read. I've tried to keep things as normal as possible, sticking to the routines he knows, but Moira was like a grandmother to him. Everything's changed so suddenly. None of us are acting as we should. It's hard for all of us but especially difficult for Kyle.'

'By *none of us* I take it you mean Jonah.'

Ailsa looks down at her hands. 'Yes, we're skirting around each other like strangers. I suppose that's because it's what we are.'

Reyne pushes the bag of rubbish to one side with her foot and sits opposite her. 'And the two of you used to be so close. I know Moira hoped that one day, when Jonah came back from university, you'd pick up from where you left off. Make a proper go of it.' She sighs heavily. 'None of us were to know things would turn out so badly for Jonah. It's what death does. Knocks the wind out of your sails.'

Ailsa presses her elbows into the tabletop and leans her head in her hands, her fingertips massaging her temples. 'It does.'

'Look, why don't you go back home for a bit. Leave the boy here. He's settled on the computer out back and is showing Doug how to play that game of his.'

'Minecraft?'

'If you say so. Games like that are a mystery to me. Anyway,

I'll get Doug to drop him back to you later.' She looks at Ailsa with concern. 'You look done in. What do you say?'

Ailsa thinks. When Kyle gets engrossed in his game, it can occupy him for the best part of an afternoon. Maybe it wouldn't hurt. 'You know he doesn't like skimmed milk only—'

'Ailsa. We know that.' Reyne smiles. 'He'll be fine with us. You go and have a lie-down. It will do you good. You look like a ghost.'

'Are you sure?'

'I wouldn't offer if I wasn't. I know how much you relied on Moira. We're happy to do our bit to help you out.'

Ailsa lets her eyes close for a second. She's dog-tired and a break from Kyle and his endless questions is probably what she needs. Just an hour or two.

'Have you seen Jonah?' She scans the now empty bar. 'I expected him to stay behind and help clear up.'

'Not for a while. I can ask Doug if you like.'

'No, you're all right. I'm sure he'll turn up.' Her neck is stiff, and she turns her head from side to side trying to release some of the tension that's been building throughout the day. 'If you're sure you're happy for Kyle to stay with you, I might do what you suggest. I haven't slept well recently.'

Night after night, she's lain in her bed, head turned to the window, wondering what the future holds. For her. For Kyle. Worrying about whether she'll be able to keep the place running with Moira gone. Just as anxious about Jonah's wish to sell.

Twice this week, Kyle has called out, and she's found him at his bedroom window, his hands pressed to the cold glass. He'd said he'd seen the man again, that he'd passed by the lodge, but now she's certain it's Kyle's imagination working overtime.

Even so, she'd gone to the patio door in the living room and tested the handle just to be sure she'd locked it. And when she was reassured that she had, she'd taken out the key and slipped it into the pocket of her dressing gown. Losing Kyle in the daylight had been worrying enough... but at night? It doesn't bear thinking about.

Ailsa stands. She smiles down at Reyne. 'Thank you. You're a lifesaver. I'll tell Kyle what's going to happen, then I'll go. Please, if you need me at all, just ring. I know what Kyle can be like. He might seem okay about it now, but in half an hour, things could be very different.'

'I will, love.' Reaching out a hand, Reyne pulls the black bin liner to her and ties a knot in it. She smiles reassuringly. 'And don't you worry about a thing, Ailsa. Your wee boy will be fine here with us.'

Ailsa had been hoping that when she got back to the lodges, the dark sorrow that had clung to her during the service, and at the wake in The Stag, would lessen, but it hasn't. If anything, she feels worse. The place reminds her of Moira. And of her absence.

Parking the car next to the white house, she takes the concrete steps down to her lodge, pausing a moment before climbing the wooden ones and putting her key in the lock of the patio door.

Before going in, she turns and looks back at the place that will soon be hers, well, Kyle's if she's going to be technical about it. With no visitors in the lodges, no Moira strolling around the place in her wellingtons and her dead husband's coat, the place feels desolate. Unloved. The empty eyes of the chalets staring out from under eaves that need repairing onto grey flat water and an even greyer sky.

Sometimes, when she looks down at the shore after the summer months have ended, she might see tufted ducks or shovelers, their bright breeding plumage turned mottled brown. Today, though, there are no birds to be seen, and it's hard not to feel as though their absence is out of respect for the woman who will never again walk beside the loch. That they too are mourning her.

The lodge is quiet without Kyle. Cold too. Moving over to the storage heater, Ailsa presses her hand to it to make sure it's on. It is, but still the skin of her arm is raised in goosebumps. Rubbing at it, she pulls the tartan throw from the back of the settee and lies down, wrapping it around her. She squashes a cushion and puts it under her head, her eyes fixed on the wide patio doors.

At first, Ailsa thinks she won't sleep but, eventually, her eyes close and the misery, the numbness, of the day dissolves into a dream. She's sitting in the small wooden rowing boat they keep for the visitors out on the open loch. The mountains behind Elgin on the opposite shore wearing their autumn colours of brown and purple. Sunlight gilds the fair hairs on Jonah's arms as he pulls on the oars.

She doesn't know where he's taking her, but she doesn't care.

She's happy... like she used to be when they were together. And even though she knows she's dreaming, it doesn't matter – just so long as it doesn't end. The sky is purple and amethyst, streaked with nectarine-coloured clouds. Above her head, an eagle moves in lazy circles. Jonah is smiling, saying something to her. She hears the words *beautiful, forever, secret*. Strains to hear more, but his voice fades in and out.

Ailsa looks around her. The sky is changing. Daylight guttering like a candle, to be replaced with a strange darkness. The eagle is no longer there, but in its place is a moon, as worn and thin as an old coin. She's cold. Too cold.

Jonah pulls at the oars. His words are ones she can't understand. His smile no longer reaching his eyes.

Ailsa tries to speak, but no words come out. She is mute. Dumb.

A dark, irrational fear engulfs her as she sits rigid in the boat, her eyes adjusting to the darkness. For behind Jonah, drawing nearer with every pull of the oars and lit by the pale, flat moon, is the boathouse. He is taking her there, and she has no idea why.

They have almost reached it. Jonah rows quicker, his back to the wide, black open space that will soon engulf them. Ailsa doesn't want to go there, but there's nothing she can do to stop him. He looks the same, yet there's something different about his face, something harder.

She knows she must wake up, but she can't. From the forest behind, a dog barks. It's not Jonah who rows her now, but Seth, his dark eyebrows pulled together, the tattoo on his forearm flexing and distorting with each pull of the oar.

A strong wind blows – coming from nowhere. The open door of the boathouse swings on its hinges. Back and forward. When it blows shut with an almighty bang, Ailsa sits bolt upright. Not sure if she's awake or still dreaming.

THIRTY-FOUR

AILSA

Ailsa rubs her eyes, disorientated. Is she still out on the loch or somewhere else? Slowly, her vision clears. She sees the table covered in Kyle's workbooks, the storage heater on the wall, the watercolour of Loch Briona. The same one that hangs on the walls of all the lodges.

The boathouse door bangs again.

But she's not on the loch. That dream is over.

Another bang. Ailsa freezes. It's coming from the patio doors. Clutching the tartan throw to her chest, she slowly turns her head to look. Crying out in alarm at the white, contorted face pressed against the glass. At first, she thinks it must be Jonah come to find her, but it's not a young face that peers in, it's someone older.

In that instance, she knows who it is. It has to be Hugh, come to stake his claim on Loch Briona Lodges now his wife, a wife who never divorced him, is dead. Does he know about Kyle? Does he know her son will soon have a half share of the site he thinks is rightly his?

A sudden bark makes her jump. The man isn't alone. There is a dog with him and now she sees her mistake. The fist that's pounding on her door doesn't belong to Hugh at all, but Seth and her error doesn't make her any more comfortable. As he straightens up, she sees him better: greying hair falling to his shoulders, skin weathered and lined, worn trousers pulled in with a belt that's seen better days.

The dog barks again and, without awareness, Ailsa's fingers move to her scar. She doesn't want to open the door, but she can't just leave him standing out there. It hadn't worried her before that she was alone on the site, but now the unease creeps in.

The rap comes again. He's seen her, so there's no point in pretending she's not home. Pushing the tartan throw aside, she gets up from the settee and walks to the patio doors. Unsure if she's doing the right thing, she turns the key in the lock and opens the door a crack.

The Alsatian looks at her with its amber eyes. She thinks it's going to bark at her, but it doesn't. She turns to Seth.

'Can I help you?'

Close up, and eleven years on, the man isn't as intimidating as she remembers from her childhood. When she thinks of those days, the image she has retained is of a face darkened with anger. But who wouldn't be angry with kids continually trespassing on their property, breaking the windows of their home, and scaring their dog?

It would be only natural for Seth to hate the person who had called him a paedophile. The person who had razed his home to the ground and destroyed everything he owned, but it's Callum who had done all those things. Seth has no reason to hold a grudge against *her*.

Seth doesn't speak but looks over his shoulder as though expecting someone. Out in the open, away from his forest home, he's clearly uncomfortable.

'Did you want something, Seth?' she asks again.

Seth turns back, his eyes meeting hers. He looks down at the dog and lays a hand on its head. 'I wanted to thank you for bringing him back.'

'It wasn't me who found him, it was my son. I'm just glad he didn't come to any harm.'

Seth shifts onto the other foot. 'I remember you. You weren't like the other kids. The boy neither. Not like his brother.' He narrows his eyes. 'I remember things.'

He's talking about Jonah, and she's glad he saw it too. Knows, as she does, that despite his life being far from perfect, as a boy he'd always done his best for others.

'Yes, he liked to do the right thing by people.'

Now he's thanked her, Ailsa expects him to leave, but he doesn't. It's as if there's something more he wants to say, and the silence grows until at last she can't stand it.

'Jonah will be back soon, if you want to speak to him,' she says, hurriedly to break the silence. 'And I'll be collecting Kyle in half an hour or so. Maybe you could come back later and thank him yourself. He'd like that.' It isn't true as Kyle hates meeting strangers, but she wants to be rid of him.

Seth stares at her with his small black eyes. 'I see things.'

His words conjure up visions and apparitions, and Ailsa wonders what he means. But then he points to the binoculars around his neck, and she understands.

'I watch the birds on the loch. The foxes that live near my van. I like to see the seasons change.'

The kids used to say he spied on them, and on the holiday-makers in the lodges, but that was long ago, probably not even true.

He folds his arms defensively as though reading her thoughts. 'There's no harm in that, is there?'

Ailsa feels the colour creep into her cheeks. 'No, of course not.'

'I see other things too.'

It's the second time he's said it. He seems harmless enough, but she wishes he'd go.

'Look, I really ought to be—'

'I seen your boy come back with the man.'

Ailsa frowns. 'What do you mean? Kyle is at The Stag with Reyne and Doug.'

'I know what I seen.'

'So you're saying he came back with Jonah?' She looks past Seth at the grassed slope filled with empty lodges. Why would he do that?

'Nae. Not that one, not the good one, the other.' He taps his greying head. 'He's not right. I wanted to tell you. Warn you. I couldn't come in the daytime. Not with him here. Not after what he did.'

Ailsa regards him coolly. 'So, it was you who's been snooping around the lodges at night. Peering in the window and frightening my boy?'

Maybe the rumours about him had been right all along.

The dog starts to whine, and he clicks his tongue to stop it. 'I wanted to warn you, but some people won't be told.'

Ailsa's had enough. 'Well, you've told me now. Thank you for letting me know that Jonah brought Kyle home. I'll go and pick him up from the house.'

She goes to shut the door, but Seth stops her, his fingers grasping her wrist.

'You won't find them there.'

Ailsa looks at him, eyes hard. She shakes off his hand. 'What do you mean?'

'Just what I said.'

He lets go of the door and pulls at the dog's rope lead. He walks across the deck, but Ailsa can't let him go. Not until she understands what he's telling her.

'Where are they, Seth? Where did Jonah take him?'

Seth has reached the steps. He starts to climb down and the dog follows, its nails scraping on the wood.

Ailsa runs across the decking. She stops with her hand on the rail and looks down at the man.

'Please, Seth. I need to know.'

Seth turns and regards her thoughtfully. 'I saw them on the shore by the loch. But it wasn't Jonah that took the lad. It was the other one. His brother. I like to keep myself to myself, dinnae like to poke my nose into other people's business, but when I knew he'd come back, I thought you should know.'

'I don't understand. Why not just tell me?'

'He's evil that one, and I knew what he'd do if he saw me.' Again, the glance over his shoulder. 'It's why I waited until dark.' He points to Kyle's bedroom window. 'I never meant to scare him.'

'Then why did you?'

'You had to know the truth, d'ya ken? That man's not who you think he is.'

A cold nub of fear settles within her. 'But it can't be Callum. Callum died over eleven years ago.'

Seth taps his binoculars, then points at the loch. 'Like I say. I see things. I've done my bit, and it's up to you whether you believe me or not. But I know what I saw.' He points across the site to the water. 'It's the other one that's dead. The good one.'

He goes down the steps, the dog clattering behind him, and Ailsa watches him walk away. He doesn't go as far as the shore but stops at the wire fence that separates the forest from the holiday site, pulling the wire from one of the posts and squeezing through before replacing it.

Ailsa's eyes follow him as he disappears into the trees, the dog at his heels. It's as if some sickness has befallen her, one that has injected ice into her veins making her unable to move. To think straight.

He's lying. He has to be. Seth is old. Crazy. Spouting

nonsense just to scare her. But why would he do that? What would it gain him?

Leaning her arms on the deck rail, Ailsa scans the shore. There's no one down there that she can see, but the beach is long and they might be out of sight. Why would Jonah take Kyle down to the loch? More importantly, why would he have collected him from Reyne's and taken him back here without telling her?

Ailsa's breathing has become shallow. With effort she tries to catch hold of it. Control it. She mustn't overreact. There will be a good reason for him having done this. Of course there will be. She looks down at her fingers grasping the rail. Sees how the skin is stretched thin and white across the knuckles.

Seth's words come back to her. *It's the other one that's dead. The good one.*

The water of the loch is flat today. Unruffled by any wind. It's hard to imagine how a life could be lost there. But now Seth's words start to break apart and fade, pushed away by others. The ones Jonah had spoken as he'd knelt by his brother's grave. He'd told her how he'd waited too long to pull his brother out of the freezing water. Had as good as said that, in those crucial minutes, he'd wished his brother dead.

Despite the dreadfulness of what he'd said, she'd made excuses for him: being back on the island had affected him, brought back all the old feelings of grief and guilt, and magnified them. The years playing with his memory. Changing it.

It was what she had believed.

What she had wanted to believe... because it was Jonah and she still loved him.

But what if she'd been wrong.

What if the man whose tears had mingled with the rain that day was not the person she thought he was?

With a sickening rush of adrenaline, she runs to the door of the lodge and slams it shut, then takes the wooden steps two at a time. Ignoring the concrete steps, she runs straight down the muddy grass, towards the narrow beach.

She has no idea what to believe any more... *who* to believe. But she does know one thing.

She needs to find her boy.

She needs to find Kyle.

THIRTY-FIVE

CALLUM

The boathouse is ahead of them, its weathered hulk pushing out onto the water of the loch.

The kid, *his* kid, stands looking at him, arms folded.

'Where are we going?'

Callum points. 'There. I bet you've never been inside.'

'My mum says I'm not allowed to go out onto the loch.' He looks at Callum accusingly. 'She says I'm not allowed to leave the lodge without her.'

'Yeh? Well, that's lucky then because you didnae. You were at Reyne's, not at the lodge. Did your ma say anything about not leaving The Stag without her?'

Kyle shakes his head.

'That's all right then.' He smiles. 'There's nae problem then, is there?'

Kyle thinks about it. 'No.'

'Good lad.'

Callum looks back at the lodges, then lets his eyes trail further to the car park next to his mother's house. There are three vehicles there. Ailsa's, his mother's new Land Rover and the older one he's been driving since he arrived on the island –

the one in which he'd collected Kyle. Reyne hadn't commented when he'd told her Ailsa had asked him to pick the boy up and he'd kept his face turned away from her so they wouldn't smell the alcohol on his breath.

'Did you know that a dogfish is a type of shark?'

He looks down at the boy. 'What?'

'I said did you know a dogfish is a type of shark. Mum says it's rude to say *what*.'

All the way back from The Stag, Kyle's been doing this, and it's hard to keep track of his random thought patterns. The kid must have a brain like an encyclopaedia. Callum forces himself to be patient. 'You don't get dogfish in the loch.'

Kyle ignores him.

'Did you know that fishermen don't like them. That they can bite through nets so they can feed on the fish.'

'No, I didn't know that.' He shakes his head. 'Jesus.'

Kyle looks at him with his head on one side. 'Are you angry? Mum says she's angry when she has that face.'

'I'm not fucking angry.' Callum rubs the back of his head. 'Look, I'm sorry, but it's been a difficult day. Ma's funeral... you know. So do you want to see inside the boathouse or not?'

'No. Mum says the water's dangerous.'

'You won't be on the water... not really. Anyway, you're with me, so you'll be safe.' He breathes in deeply. 'You're with your uncle Jonah.'

Reaching out, he takes Kyle by the arm. 'Come on. It's only there.'

As soon as his fingers curl around the boy's arm, he realises his mistake. Kyle doesn't like to be touched. It's been obvious from the way Ailsa holds back from him when he's upset. He's seen how much she wants to take her boy in her arms and how much strength it takes for her not too.

'Get off me. Get off me. Get off!' Kyle twists and pulls, his face reddening.

Callum lets go of him and turns away. 'Fuck.' He needs to be more careful, has to think of a way to let the boy know he can trust him. Kyle is all that's between him and the money tied up in the holiday site. The only thing between him and a brighter future.

His brain is whirring. He'd taken Kyle without a proper plan, the only thing in his head the knowledge that the boy is all that stands between him and his debtors. He needs to gain his trust. With luck, the rest will follow... like it did that night on the lake with Jonah.

'Stay here if you want.'

Trusting his instinct that the boy will follow, Callum sets off along the beach, smiling to himself when he hears Kyle's foot-steps behind him. They're nearing the boathouse, and for some reason, it's important to him that the boy be there when he goes inside.

The key is in his pocket. He needs to see for himself if the boat is still there. See whether his mother sold it or maybe bashed a hole in its fiberglass hull, letting it sink to the bottom of the loch. The way Jonah would have had he not dragged him out of the freezing water.

Stepping up to the door, Callum fits the key in the rusty padlock, teasing it until it releases. He pushes open the door, the cold dank air hitting him.

'Well? Coming in?'

He steps inside, his eyes adjusting to the gloom. There's a window at one end, but it's long since been boarded up, its glass having been used for target practice by the stones of unruly kids.

Callum stands on the wooden boards and lets out a slow whistle. The motorboat is there as he suspected, moving in the water. Kept here after all these years like some morbid memento to the tragedy. He crouches, resting his hand on the gunwale, surprised to see it looks much the same, despite the passing of time. Protected from the harsh Scottish winters by the walls and roof of the boathouse that has acted like some odd fucked-up shrine to his brother.

He straightens up again, the smell of fish and damp reaching him as it had the afternoon he'd hidden in the boathouse when he was thirteen. He hadn't expected anyone else to come in, so when he'd heard the door open, he'd stayed silent. Watching in the shadows as Ailsa stepped inside, closing the door behind her. Crouching, only feet away from him by the nets, in her school uniform. Her wild hair pale in the gloom.

Callum looks around the wooden building feeling bad about what he did, glad that the distant voices he'd heard had brought him to his senses. She'd been just a kid and if he hadn't got hold of his dad's whisky, hadn't been plastered, he'd never have done it.

His mind drifts away to another night – the night of the ceilidh. That had been different. Ailsa had been older then. It was *she* who had come on to *him*. It wasn't as if she'd complained when he'd left the motorbike at the top of the slope and led her here. And when she'd told him to stop, said she'd changed her mind, she hadn't meant it. Girls never did.

He points to the boat. 'So, what do you think?'

Kyle stands in the doorway but won't come in. 'Is it yours?'

Callum thinks. His mother is dead now. 'Yes, it is.' He knocks on the hull with his knuckles. 'Sturdy too. If you ever fancied coming out in it...'

'Mum says I'm not allowed in the rowing boat.'

'She said you weren't to go in the rowing boat, but she didn't say you couldn't go out in the motorboat, did she?'

As he had when Callum had mentioned leaving Reyne's without his mother, Kyle shakes his head. 'No, she didn't.'

'Which means it's okay, yeah?'

'I suppose so.' He takes one step into the building, then another. 'It smells in here.'

'It would. It was once used to store our fishing gear. It's been closed up for a long time.'

Kyle thinks about this. 'Is that the boat your brother died in?'

'Yes, it is.'

'If you fall into the water, you should float on your back.'

'Sensible advice... or swim to the boat if you can.'

Jonah's face is in his head again. His head tipped back, mouth gaping, eyes wide with panic. *Callum!*

Kyle sniffs. 'I can't swim.'

'No? Want to see what she feels like?' Callum steps down into the boat.

'Okay.'

'Good lad. I'll help you in.' He offers his hand.

'No. I can do it by myself.'

'Suit yourself.' He sits and waits as Kyle awkwardly steps over the rail and onto the bench seat. He wobbles a moment, then sits.

Callum looks at him. Ailsa will be thinking the boy is still at The Stag, and will be leaving to collect him soon. When she gets there, Reyne will tell her his lie. She'll wonder why he took Kyle home without checking with her first, but there's no reason for her to suspect anything untoward? Why would she when, as far as she's concerned, he's Jonah? The boy she loved, the man she loves still – something her eyes have been unable to hide. No, his secret's safe. Even their mother had found it difficult to tell him and his brother apart and even if she could, the mess he'd made of his face when he'd fallen in the boat, the black eye and the swollen, broken nose, had ensured that her suspicions had not been raised. Any differences in their personalities explained away by the tragedy he'd been a part of.

Losing a brother, in the way he had, would turn anyone to drink... to the gambling table. Would mess with anyone's head.

And if he'd dropped out of university, who could blame him after everything that had happened?

Callum thinks of the few lectures he'd attended. His absences and lack of interaction put down to his mental health when, in truth, he'd not understood a word the lecturers had spoken. Frustrated and bored, the student union bar had become his friend... gambling a way to pay for it. What had followed had been black years: waiting for that one big win that would change his fortunes, begging and borrowing in order to keep on top of the mounting debts he couldn't pay, women picked up and dropped, his guilt eating him up.

When he'd eventually turned to the loan shark, he hadn't realised how much worse things would get. He'd struggled with the extortionate interest rates, but the speed with which they'd sent round the heavies to put the frighteners on him had been a shock. They'd messed his face up good and proper. Re-broken the nose he'd had set after the accident.

He touches his face, remembering how he'd blamed his misfortune on the mother who hadn't loved him enough and on his useless, violent father. He pictures the body that lies beneath the shower block. Was that the secret Jonah had told Ailsa that afternoon on the clifftop? Does she think the person buried in the churchyard is a murderer?

It must be that. What other secret had Jonah to tell?

'I can't see any fish down here.'

Callum looks at the boy. He's leaning over the side of the boat, staring down at the water. Sandy hair so like his own.

His genes... his and Ailsa's. Something no one can ever know unless he wants Jonah's death to have been for nothing.

What was it Ailsa had said to him at his brother's graveside? *Your love for Callum was greater than your hatred.* If only she'd known how wrong she was. He'd never loved himself. He despised the boy he once was and the man he became later: a waster, a bully, a person able to inflict harm on a girl whose only fault had been to love his brother. A person who could watch his brother freeze to death in the frigid waters of the loch.

Because he wanted to be him.

Wanted to be Jonah.

Jonah. Jonah. Jonah. The one with the brains. The one with the girl Callum lusted after. The one his parents wanted to run Loch Briona.

The one his mother had loved the best.

Without realising it, tears of self-pity have snaked a trail down his cheeks. Eleven years ago, he'd decided the only way to have what Jonah had was to become him, but it hadn't worked out the way he'd intended. Now he can never go back... because, as Callum, he killed his father. And if the truth were ever to come out, the safest place for him is in the graveyard, the headstone with his name engraved on it watching over him.

But things are different now he's back on Bray. He can put the past eleven years behind him and be the person he's always wanted to be. As Jonah, he's blameless. As Jonah, he can live a better life. As Jonah, he can have Ailsa. And now, as Jonah, he can have Loch Briona.

If not for the boy.

If not for *his* boy.

Kyle is getting agitated now, rocking back and forward on the bench. His back to him, hunched over in his over-large funeral jacket. Just one push. That's all it would take.

There's a sound above his head. It's starting to rain, heavy drops clattering on the wooden roof. If they were to go back outside, they'd soon be drenched. Callum runs his hands down the knees of his jeans remembering the feel of cold wet denim. His imagination turning to the night he'd killed his brother. He's back there on the loch, yanking Jonah's sodden trainers from his feet. Dragging his waterlogged jeans down his legs and yelling his frustration to the wind when they became stuck around his ankles. All the while trying not to focus on his brother's skin.

The blue lips. Knowing that dressing Jonah's lifeless body in his own clothes would be harder still.

It was only as he'd pulled the boat up in the shallows that he'd realised his mistake. His own clothes had been dry. No drowning man wore dry clothes. With no other choice, he'd pulled Jonah's body to the edge of the boat, grunting as he'd heaved him onto the gunwale. Rolling him over the edge, he'd jumped in after him, gasping at the shock of the freezing water. Then he'd dragged his brother's body through the shallow water to the shore. Ready to face his mother. Ready to start a new life.

The rain is easing, and he thinks he hears someone outside calling. He waits, but now there's just the creaking of the boathouse doors in the wind.

Kyle's muttering to himself about dogfish.

Callum's head starts to ache.

There must be some way to get what he wants.

He stands, and with the boat rocking beneath him, takes a step closer to Kyle.

THIRTY-SIX

AILSA

Ailsa stands at the edge of the loch, her heart pounding. Are they out there somewhere on the water? Her son and the man she'd thought was Jonah. Might *still* be Jonah.

The afternoon had threatened nothing more than drizzle, but now the clouds have thickened. Moving in like a cavalry and depositing their burden of rain in that way they have on Bray. A sudden downpour that catches out the visitors to the island but leaves the locals shrugging and reaching for the whisky. The rain is stippling the loch. Already she's soaked, but the only shelter is the boathouse and she's not going there.

She turns. Hearing something – a noise like a twig cracking under the weight of a shoe. Scanning the edge of the forest, she sees nothing but the rough bark of the pines. The darkness beyond. Is Seth spying on her? Interfering? Is that his plan... to unsettle her with more of his wild stories? His lies?

But there's nothing to see in the trees. Nothing on the loch either. No boat of any sort to break the monotony of the pewter-grey water.

Where are they?

Pulling up her hood, she runs along the shore as she did the

day Kyle found Seth's dog. Calls her son's name to the wind and
rain.

'Kyle.'

A movement stops her in her tracks. Up ahead, the door to
the boathouse is opening and, moments later, Jonah steps out,
her boy behind him. They hurry towards her through the veils
of rain, Jonah's coat draped across Kyle's shoulders, and the
knowledge that he's safe makes her heady with relief.

But, that relief is quickly pushed aside by guilt as Jonah
smiles and all the old feelings rush back. Smothering everything
Seth told her. Squashing her fears. Her suspicions. How stupid
to have believed the man, even if just for one short moment.
Jonah's done nothing wrong. His only crime was forgetting to
tell her he'd brought Kyle home. His only wrongdoing that he
took him to the boathouse without checking with her first.

Her earlier worry and fear is overtaken by a sudden anger
towards Seth. How dare he put these doubts about Jonah in her
head, especially on the day of Moira's funeral? It's revenge,
that's all. Revenge, not for doing wrong themselves, but for
being witnesses to Callum's misdeeds when they were younger.
And to think she'd allowed herself to start believing his
nonsense.

She stops in front of Kyle. Sees how his hair is plastered to
his face, his cheeks white beneath his freckles. He's not looking
at her but at something in the forest, but when she turns her
head to see, there's nothing there.

'What on earth were you doing?' The question is addressed
to Jonah. 'What were you thinking taking him down to the
loch?'

Jonah pushes his wet hair from his face. 'Reyne said you'd
gone back for a rest and the kid was bored. I offered to take him
home. I didn't think you'd mind.'

'You could have let me know.'

'I'm sorry. I would have told you, but I thought you'd be

asleep and didn't want to disturb you.' He looks down at Kyle. 'You had fun with your uncle Jonah, didn't you?'

Kyle's shivering. 'We saw the boat.'

Ailsa looks where he's pointing and understands. 'You shouldn't have taken him there.'

'I didn't know Ma had kept it. I wonder why she did.'

'Uncle Jonah said he'd take me fishing one day. Can I go, Mum? Can I go?'

Something inside her shifts. She doesn't like the thought of Kyle in the boat where Callum lay dead. 'We'll talk about it later.'

It means nothing. Of course it doesn't. Jonah is his uncle. It's a perfectly reasonable suggestion.

They stand side by side. So alike. Seeing them together like this makes her happy yet sad too. Not for the first time, she wishes Jonah had been Kyle's father rather than Callum. But even if he had been, there could never be anything between her and Jonah. Not after that afternoon when he'd taken her up onto the clifftop and made her listen to his secret. A secret that would ensure she'd never look at him the same way again.

The rain is a grey sheet driving in from the loch. Elgin no longer visible on the opposite shore. Ailsa hadn't changed when she got back from Reyne's and, below her coat, the material of her black velvet skirt is sticking to her legs. Kyle's dark grey trousers are shiny, the fabric turned black with the rain.

The chill wind is getting stronger and Ailsa shivers. 'Let's go back. I need to get Kyle into some dry clothes.'

'Aye. When you're done, why don't you come up to the house? I'll make up the fire and we can talk... about Loch Briona.' He pauses. 'Like you wanted to.'

They've started to walk back along the beach, Kyle trailing behind them. 'You know I can't do that, Jonah. It's not a conversation I want to have with Kyle around and I can't leave him, not while Seth—'

Jonah slows, his eyes narrowing. 'What about Seth?'

'Nothing.' She hesitates. 'I just wondered if it might have been him Kyle saw the other night outside the lodge.'

Why didn't she say she'd seen him earlier? That he'd come to her chalet and told her a pack of lies? What's made her keep this to herself?

Jonah looks at where the trees meet the sand. 'Maybe I'll pay him a visit later.'

'No, don't,' she says quickly. 'He's harmless enough.'

It's like he's not listening. 'Or, better still, I'll do it now.'

He veers away towards the trees, but Ailsa grabs his arm to stop him. 'Stop it, Jonah. I could be wrong. Kyle could have been imagining it... or dreaming. You can't just go barging in there.'

'Why not? He's a meddling—'

'He's an old man who wants to keep himself to himself. What's got into you?'

Jonah looks at the hand on his arm. As if remembering himself, he shrugs. 'Maybe now's not the right time, but he needs telling.'

He breaks away from her, walking ahead with long strides. Ailsa stands watching him, the rain plastering her hair to her head. Feeling like the girl she once was. Always following. Waiting to be noticed.

Behind her, Kyle is dragging his feet in the patches of sand, seemingly oblivious to the rain. She glances at the trees as she waits for him to catch up. Maybe she should be glad that Jonah wanted to have it out with Seth. Maybe she should be happy he cared enough to do something. Yet, some instinct tells her that going to Seth's caravan wouldn't have been a good thing.

Ailsa shivers. The rain has penetrated her clothing, reaching her skin and chilling the very core of her. She looks at Kyle in Jonah's coat. He must be freezing. She wants him to hurry, but any insistence on her part will only make him slower.

When at last they reach their lodge, she's surprised to see Jonah waiting for them, sheltering under the wooden eaves.

'I'm sorry. I overreacted back there.'

'Yes.'

He sucks in his lips. 'It's been a difficult day.'

Ailsa takes in his soaked shirt, the cheeks above his beard that are white with the cold, and her heart softens. 'It has. I know.'

Jonah looks up the slope to the white house. 'Like I said. Why don't you and Kyle get yourselves changed and then when you're ready, come up to the house? If the kid gets tired, you can put him to bed in the spare room and take him home later. Ma told me you'd done that before, and he'd been okay with it. You look done in, Ailsa.'

Ailsa closes her eyes a second, her hand on the wooden rail. Yes, she is tired. Tired and cold and confused.

'Maybe just for a short while.' She takes Jonah's coat off Kyle and hands it to him.

Jonah nods. 'Good lass. You've spent years looking after Loch Briona, it's time someone looked after you... for one evening at least.'

Without saying more, he turns and climbs the hill to his mother's house. Ailsa watches his disappearing back, then, not caring whether he likes it or not, takes Kyle's hand and hurries with him up the steps to their chalet. They'll join him later. Why not?

Back in the lodge, Ailsa gets clean clothes out for Kyle and leaves him to get changed. In her own room, she goes to the window and closes the curtains. It's only five thirty, yet the rain clouds have darkened the sky to the colour of evening.

Unlike Kyle's room, with its view of the loch, her view is of the upper lodges and Moira's large white house at the top of the hill. She's just pulling the second curtain closed, wondering what Jonah's doing, when a light goes on in the living room window. Someone's standing there, hands locked behind their head. Jonah. He's looking down at the site and, for a split second, Ailsa's reminded of a picture in a long ago storybook. Of a king surveying their kingdom.

She pulls the curtains tightly shut and sits on the bed, wondering why the image is so unsettling. Wondering why the thought of spending the evening with Jonah no longer has any appeal.

Is it that she doesn't want to have what she knows will be a difficult conversation about Loch Briona... about the past?

Or is it that she can't get Seth's words out of her head?

It's the other one that drowned. The good one.

THIRTY-SEVEN

AILSA

When Moira had still been alive, Ailsa wouldn't have thought twice about walking straight into the kitchen through the back door, but somehow, with Jonah living there, it doesn't seem right and so she knocks.

Straightaway the door opens and Jonah's standing there, a smile on his face, a glass of malt in his hand.

'Come in,' he says, standing back. 'Give me your coats.'

Ailsa does as she's asked, taking off her own, then holding out her hand for Kyle's. Jonah takes them from her and as he hangs them on one of the hooks by the door, Ailsa feels a pang of sadness. Moira's coat is no longer there, just Jonah's, still wet from the downpour, water drops blackening the stone floor below.

'What can I get you? Tea? Coffee?' He points to his glass. 'Or something stronger.'

Ailsa hesitates, her eyes lingering a little longer on the coat rack. Something's wrong, but she can't think what it is. She pulls her eyes away.

'I'll have a coffee and Kyle will have a hot chocolate. Moira keeps...' She corrects herself, embarrassed. '*Kept* a jar of it in the cupboard above the kettle. I can make it myself. It's no problem.'

Jonah frowns. 'Don't be silly. You're my guests tonight.'

His cheeks are flushed pink from his whisky or from the shower he's just had judging by the damp hair that he's pushed behind his ears. He's swapped his dark suit and tie for jeans and a faded black sweatshirt. Ailsa's pulse quickens. Despite everything, the way he makes her feel has never changed. She wants to reach out a hand and place it on his cheek, feel the soft graze of his beard beneath her fingertips, but she can't do that... any more than she could do it to Kyle.

She looks away, not wanting him to see what she's feeling. 'Thank you. Are we in the other room?'

'Yes, I've lit the fire. You go on in and I'll bring the drinks through when I've made them.'

'Okay.'

When Moira was alive, they didn't use the living room much, spending most of their time in the kitchen with the range to warm them. Although Jonah's lit a fire, the room feels unlived in, the overstuffed furniture like something from a country house hotel. There's nothing of Moira in here, the only indication that this is her house a photograph of her boys. A school photograph, taken when they were eight or nine. Their faces pale against the blue background. Their sandy hair brushed back from their faces by some helper who hadn't known what they usually looked like.

When she was younger, even Ailsa hadn't been able to tell them apart and as the years had gone by, the similarity hadn't lessened. Ailsa looks closer. And yet, there's something about the eyes of the boy on the right that are different. More knowing. Was that Callum? The elder of the two by thirty minutes. *Big bro*, Jonah had jokingly called him, even though he was the more mature of the two by far.

'I don't like him.'

'What?' Ailsa looks away. Kyle is perched on the edge of the settee, his hands under his thighs.

'I don't like him.' He points at the photo.

'You don't know him, Kyle. You'll like him when you get to know him better. When you get used to him.'

'I won't. I won't. I won't.' Kyle's voice is rising, and Ailsa hurries to his side. Leaving a comfortable space between them, she sits next to him.

'It was kind of him to take you home today... to suggest a fishing trip sometime.' Although she hadn't meant to bring it up, she'd seen how his eyes had lit up and it's the only way she can think of to get him out of this.

Kyle's face remains stony.

'I still don't like him. He stares at me when he thinks I'm not looking. Like this.'

He pulls a face to show her, but before Ailsa can reply, the door pushes open and Jonah comes in, two mugs in one hand, a glass of whisky in the other. He smiles.

'Coffee for you.' He hands Ailsa a mug. 'And a hot chocolate for the lad.'

He places the mug on the table next to Kyle, then lifts the glass to his lips, its contents dark amber in the firelight.

Tonight, in his dead mother's house, there's something different about Jonah. A strange, forced joviality that doesn't feel right. He takes the chair next to the fire and they sit in silence, watching the flames in the grate rise up the chimney. The only sound the crack and spit of the logs. Despite its appearance, the settee is comfortable, the fire-lit room warm. It makes Ailsa sleepy.

In the hall, the grandfather clock strikes eight. She's never really noticed it before, but now its rhythmic chime sounds solemn. Like it knows Moira's hand will never again insert the key into its face and wind it.

Kyle yawns, not bothering to cover his mouth. It's been a

long day, and Ailsa knows from experience that if he gets over-tired, both his sleep and hers will be disturbed by nightmares. Maybe, in a minute, she'll try and persuade him to go upstairs to Moira's spare bedroom. Jonah's right, sometimes, when Moira had invited them both over for supper, Kyle would go up to the room and sleep. Later, Ailsa would wake him and take him home. On the odd occasion, she'd even managed to leave him, coming back in the morning before he woke and realised where he was. If he goes up now, it will mean she and Jonah can talk about the future of Loch Briona.

But that's not all she has to talk to him about.

It's time he knew about his brother. How it is that Kyle is Callum's son.

'Finish your hot chocolate, Kyle.' She puts her bag on her lap and unzips it. 'I brought your tablet. You can take it up to the spare bedroom and play something on it. If you get into your pyjamas, it won't matter if you fall asleep. I'll wake you up when it's time to leave.'

Kyle shakes his head wildly, so the hair flaps across his face. 'I don't want to go to sleep. I don't want to stay here.'

Ailsa glances at Jonah. 'It's only for a while, not the whole night. I can see you're tired.'

'How long, Mum?'

'What do you mean?'

'How long? How long?'

'Until I come and wake you?' She looks at her watch. 'An hour. Two, maybe.'

Kyle bangs his forehead with the heel of his hand. 'Which?'

'Two, Kyle. I'll come up in two hours and take you home.'

'Promise?'

'Promise.' Ailsa reaches into her bag and takes out the tablet. She hands it to him. 'Here.'

Jonah clears his throat, then lifts the glass to his lips. There's only a small amount of whisky left in it. She hadn't seen him drink at the wake, but he's certainly making up for it now.

Seeing her looking, Jonah puts the glass on the small table beside the settee. 'Problem?'

'No, of course not.' She stands and beckons to Kyle. 'Come on, sleepyhead. Let's go up.'

She's relieved when Kyle gets up without a fuss and follows her out of the living room. The spare bedroom is at the top of the stairs across the landing. When Kyle had started sleeping there on the odd occasion, Moira had told him they could call it his room. She'd painted the walls blue, like the loch on a summer morning, and swapped the plain white duvet for a Spider-Man one like his one at the lodge. Despite his hatred of change, Kyle had never objected to sleeping there.

Ailsa pulls his pyjamas out of her bag. 'Change into these. You'll be more comfortable and if you want to sleep, you can.'

'I haven't cleaned my teeth.'

In her hurry to go out, she'd forgotten to pack his toothbrush. Ailsa paints on a bright smile. 'Never mind. You can do them when we get back. I'll remind you.' She plumps up the pillow and lifts the duvet, hoping the compromise will satisfy him. 'In you get.'

Reluctantly, Kyle does as he's told. 'Ten o'clock then. One hundred and twenty minutes.' He checks his watch. 'One hundred and fifteen now. That's when you'll come and get me.'

'Yes, that's what I said. Try and get some sleep if you can, Kyle.'

She brushes his hair from his forehead, the most he will allow her to do, and blows him a kiss. When she reaches the door, she hesitates. 'Was Uncle Jonah good to you earlier, you know, when you were down on the beach? What I mean is, was he...' She searches for a word he'll understand. 'Was he kind? Like Moira was to you?'

Kyle shrugs and shuffles himself up the bed, the duvet

tented over his knees, the tablet balanced on them. He doesn't answer the question but asks one of his own.

'Will the man come tonight?'

'The man?'

'At my window.'

Ailsa thinks of Seth. His nervousness. His wild suppositions. Shuffling his feet on the deck of her lodge and looking over his shoulder as though expecting trouble. *He's evil that one. And I knew what he'd do if he saw me.*

What was Seth afraid of? What did he think might happen if he was seen? That his property would be defaced... his windows broken... the place burnt down.

Or worse?

Ailsa stands with her hand on the door, listening. Hearing no sound from downstairs. Why is she suddenly nervous? It was Callum who had done those things in the past, not Jonah. And it's Jonah who is downstairs waiting for her. *Jonah.* She has to believe it, or she'll go mad.

Yet, from the moment he'd arrived at Loch Briona, the difference in him had been stark. There had been a brittleness, a carefulness in his choice of words, that she'd not seen before. They were no longer easy in one another's company... their friendship consigned to the past. She'd told herself it was because he was older now. Because he had worries. Because his life hadn't turned out as he'd expected. She'd told herself it was how he had to be to cope with being back on Bray – the place where his brother had drowned.

But would the years have changed him so much? Taken the very essence of him, the kindness and sensitivity, and soured it?

Ailsa thinks of the debts he'd talked about. The drinking. The trouble he'd caused in The Stag when he'd first arrived. His thoughtlessness in taking Kyle from Reyne and Doug's without checking with her first. All of these things more Callum's style than Jonah's.

And that's not all. While she'd been settling Kyle, she'd worked out what it was that had snagged her when she'd seen Jonah's coat hanging in the lobby. For years, the boys had had their own coat hooks, but tonight the drips on the floor had come from the coat hanging from Callum's. The one Jonah had hung there.

Something and nothing.

Or something and everything?

Her eyes travel to the stairs, her imagination taking her to the place where Jonah sits waiting for her. What if it hadn't been Hugh who had wanted to come back for his share of Loch Briona Lodges? What if, instead, it had been his son, Callum – a man who's been living Jonah's life, just as Seth said? A man who, as a teenager, had left his brother in the freezing water of the loch for too long? Hating him for being the good one. Wanting to have what he had. Wanting to *be* him.

No, she can't think like that.

And yet...

And yet...

And yet...

It's crazy to even think this way, but she has to be sure. She has to know for certain.

THIRTY-EIGHT

CALLUM

'You're back.' Callum looks up and smiles at Ailsa as she comes in. 'Wouldn't he settle?'

She's been gone a long time. What has she been doing?

'No, he's fine. Playing Minecraft. What a surprise.'

She looks on edge, but it's not surprising. Taking the kid to the boathouse had been a stupid idea. He hadn't thought it through. When he'd seen Kyle leaning over the side of the boat, what had he imagined he was going to do? How could he ever have got away with it?

The whisky he's drunk is taking effect. Warming him. Dulling him. He hadn't meant to drink tonight, had wanted to keep a clear head, but since taking Kyle to the boathouse, the confusion he's feeling, and the frustration at his situation, has built up. A geyser waiting to burst through the thin crust of his sanity.

He's so close to getting what he needs – money to pay off his gambling debts. So close. But the one person stopping him is the boy... or rather the woman now sitting on the settee next to him. Not close enough that he can feel the warmth of her, but not so far that he can't smell her perfume. Light. Floral. Bringing back memories.

Jonah points to the second glass of whisky on the table. 'I fixed you a proper drink.'

'I haven't finished my coffee.'

'Don't worry about that. It will be cold by now.' He holds out the glass to her. Needing her to take it. Needing her to relax. Whatever it is that's stopping her from showing her true feelings for him, eliminated by the alcohol. 'Here. It would be a shame to waste it.'

'Okay.'

Ailsa takes the glass from his hand and takes a small sip. She looks different, her lips a darker red as though she's applied fresh lipstick. Is it for him? When he'd come to the island, his plan had been to play his part well, the part of his mother's favourite son. He'd ensure his inheritance was secure then, after she'd passed on, sell the place and be free of debt at last. Free to be whoever he wanted. No longer chained to his brother's name.

For, despite what he'd thought, being Jonah hadn't brought him happiness. It had brought him nothing at all... until his mother's phone call.

Christ, it had been difficult sitting in his ma's dining room on the night of her birthday, pretending to care. Pretending he hadn't guessed the reason she'd asked him to come. It would never have been because she wanted to see him. Loved him.

All those years calling himself Jonah. Thinking of himself as Jonah. Knowing it was the only way he could keep up the pretence. Trying to trick his brain the same way he was tricking everyone else.

There's a sound upstairs. Kyle moving around the bedroom. He'd come to Bray with a plan, but it was a plan made before he knew he had a kid. A boy whose father his ma had thought was dead rather than sitting on the settee next to Ailsa. A boy he can never claim as his own because he can never go back. Not after what he did to his brother. Or his father for that matter.

Or Ailsa.

But neither can he go forward, unless...

He looks at Ailsa, her face so pretty in the firelight. As she lifts the glass to her lips, her hand trembles slightly. What is she worried about?

The paedophile in the forest?

The responsibility of the lodges?

The boy upstairs?

As he thinks of Kyle, the half-formed plan that had come to him in the boathouse, morphs and gains clarity. He needs to make his move on Ailsa tonight.

He'd always wanted her, but it was only ever Jonah she'd had eyes for – the childhood friend who'd stolen her heart and never let it go. Seeing her again had only inflamed his desire, but, despite the hunger he'd felt to possess her again, he'd been strong. Making any type of move on her then would have been too dangerous.

He'd almost ruined things the afternoon he'd got rat-arsed in The Stag. Ailsa had let him shower in her lodge and he'd a hunch she wouldn't have said no if he'd given her a sign. He'd thought about her as the water had streamed down his body. Remembered the feel and taste of her. Nearly given in. But the stakes had been too high. What if that one simple act was enough to uncover his deception? The things he did with her, *to* her, screaming out *imposter*! So, instead, he'd stepped out of the shower, raised his arms above his head and pressed his naked body against the cold bathroom tiles to calm himself.

And when, later, he'd felt her cool hand on his damp shoulder, he'd knocked it away. Anything to stop himself succumbing. Pretending it was because he didn't want her sympathy. Jesus! He should be on the stage.

Ailsa shifts in her seat and the loose jumper she's wearing

slips a little down her shoulder to reveal a thin black bra strap covering pale, freckled flesh. How easy it would be to stand behind her and slip a hand inside the soft material. Seek out the sensitive bud with his fingertips. He closes his eyes, remembering. His body responding.

But he can't give in to it. Not yet. Not in the way he wants to.

He has to lure her... like a brown trout on the end of his line. He has to bide his time. Reel her in. This is not the moment to be making mistakes. Not if he wants his plan to work. Not if he wants them to be a family – him, Ailsa and the kid. The path he needs to take to stake his full claim on the lodges.

The way his father did.

'I'm just going to...' He holds up his empty glass.

Ailsa frowns, but he needs it. Has earned it.

Leaving the room, he goes across the hall to the dining room and lifts the stopper from the whisky decanter. As he pours himself a generous measure, topped up with water from the tap in the kitchen, he forces himself to concentrate. He must make no mistakes.

Ailsa is standing at the window when he gets back, staring out at the row of lights that illuminate the concrete steps down to the shore. What is she thinking? What is she remembering? There will have been things she and Jonah talked about. Things he'll never know. The time she spent with his brother when they were young is a minefield he has no option but to cross and his plan is to listen when she talks. Offer little of his own and glean as much information as he can. And if he gets things wrong, well then, he can always use the past eleven years as an excuse.

But what worries him most is the afternoon on the clifftop. The thing Ailsa mentioned at the wake. Something important happened there, he knows that. A secret Jonah hadn't wanted Callum to know he'd shared. It could, of course, be nothing important, but instinct tells him it is. Ever since Ailsa told him about it, it's been bothering him.

What was it Ailsa had said? *Despite everything, I'd have been there for you.*

What had she meant by that? What had his brother done that had been so bad he needed to keep it a secret? Why did he think it might change the way Ailsa felt about him?

He joins her at the window. 'What are you looking at?'

Ailsa turns, the whisky glass pressed to her cheek. 'Nothing much. Just the lodges.' She drops the curtain. 'I was thinking about the visitors who cancelled their bookings. Wondering why they did it. Did they speak to you on the phone, Jonah? Did they give a reason?'

'No.'

There had in fact been no phone call, just an email in which he'd told them the holiday lodges would no longer be available that week. That they'd be closing the site earlier in the season than expected. He'd returned their deposits and suggested alternative cabin sites in Elgin. They must have been okay with it as he hadn't heard back.

When he'd made the decision to cancel their bookings, he'd not yet formulated a plan, but he knew that when he did, it would work better without holidaymakers poking their nose into his business.

'It's strange, though, don't you think?'

Callum takes his whisky over to the settee and sits down. 'Not really. People change their minds and it's been pretty dreich on the island this last week. Can't say I blame them.' He pats the seat beside him. 'Come and sit with me. I know I haven't been easy since I came back here, but you deserve better. I want to get to know you again. Show you that, despite everything, there's still something of the boy you used to know in me.'

Ailsa sits on the edge of the settee. There's something in her expression, a guardedness, he can't read. He never could. That's what the sight of her does to him... scrambles his head. His thoughts.

'I want to know you better too,' she says at last. 'Especially now Kyle knows he has an uncle. After Callum died, it was as though *you* had too. You wouldn't talk to me. Shutting yourself in your room, closed off from everyone. When you left the island so suddenly after the funeral, there was so much left unsaid.' She looks sideways at him. 'That thing you told me on the clifftop... it was as though you regretted it and you never spoke of it again.'

Callum takes a mouthful of his whisky, surprised she's brought it up. He searches her face for clues. Finds none. Now she's raised the subject, it's no longer possible for him to ignore the terrible question that's been hounding him. Whether he's right in thinking Jonah talked to her about their father on that windswept hill. If he had, indeed, told her their secret – that Hugh was dead. Killed by his brother, Callum.

Would he really have been so disloyal? And if he *had* told her, how had Ailsa managed to live all these years knowing the bastard's dead body was just metres away from the lodges, interned beneath the footings of the shower block?

Maybe she'd managed it the same way his mother had. By telling herself he'd deserved it. Shutting the thought out. Pretending it hadn't happened even when the awfulness of it entered her dreams. Her nightmares.

It's amazing what someone will do for love.

The jumper has slipped from Ailsa's shoulder again and he's in an agony of wanting. He shouldn't have had that drink. Rather than pour himself another, he should have stayed off it, but he'd had to calm his nerves somehow. Just like his father, drink had always been his enemy. His undoing. Loosening his tongue, spiking his anger or lust, turning him into a loose cannon. His sobriety in the past few years had been the only thing standing between him and a prison cell.

He takes another mouthful. The other thing he's inherited from his father is the inability to stop once he's started.

'Let's talk about it now.' He returns his focus to her, keeping his eyes on her face. 'Tell me what you remember of what I said, and I'll try to explain it.'

Callum waits, thinking Ailsa will speak, but she doesn't. Instead, her hand slides across the settee cushions towards him, her fingers not quite finding his. Callum looks down at them. Every instinct screaming out to grip those delicate fingers in his own and press them to his throbbing groin, but he can't. He has to do what Jonah would do. Take it slow.

There are things he must know first.

'What I said—'

Ailsa's fingertips touch his own. 'Later. First, I want to talk to you about the night of the ceilidh.'

'The ceilidh?'

Callum stares at the photograph on the wall. The two brothers side by side in their school uniforms. He knows the part he played in that evening but what of Jonah? To go back there is too dangerous.

'Why talk about that night? It was so long ago.'

'I want you to remember it because it was the first time you told me you loved me. It was our first time...' She stops, her cheeks reddening. Callum feels the press of her fingers, sees how she's looking at him. Doesn't want to hear... yet does.

'When you made love to me,' she continues, 'it felt right – even though there was no bed, just that hard wooden bench. But we didn't care. It was the first time for both of us and that was what made it perfect.'

Callum frowns. Tries to get the picture in his head. Her and Jonah. He'd guessed something had happened, had thrown it in Jonah's face when they were on the boat the night he'd died.

Taunted him with it, but his brother had never opened up to him. It was what had made them have the fight. What had ended his life.

Ailsa releases her hand from his. Lifts it instead to his chest and he covers her fingers with his own, feeling the solid beat of his heart through them. Faster than it should be. His mind is racing, his brain already scheming. Thinking how this new knowledge will affect things.

She hasn't finished, though. Is still talking. 'I know it was me who came on to you, Jonah, but it was what we both wanted – you would have stopped me if it hadn't been.' Ailsa stops. Swallows. 'The lights of our lodges on the opposite shore looked like fireflies and the wind had whipped the loch into white ridges. Do you remember? It was like we were in our own cocoon. The wooden roof of the seat sheltering us, hiding us from the prying eyes of Sorcha and Bethany. I know that things changed between us after Callum drowned, and I understand why you pushed me away, but please, Jonah. Don't say that night meant nothing to you. Please don't say that you regret it.'

She's waiting for his answer, and Callum knows he needs to give her one. But he's worried. Whatever answer he gives, only she knows what happened that night.

Only she knows the truth of what Jonah did and what *he* did too.

THIRTY-NINE

AILSA

Then

'No, stop it.' Jonah pushes Ailsa from his lap. 'This isn't right.'

Ailsa stands in the entrance to the bench shelter, the wind gusting at her back, making her coat flap. She feels humiliated. Stupid.

With trembling fingers, she does up the buttons of her dress.

'What's the matter? What did I do wrong?'

'You didn't do anything wrong. It's just that you don't know what you're doing. I don't know how much of that vodka you had, but it's clearly enough. I should never have let it get this far.'

He reaches out a hand to her arm, but she brushes it off.

'Get off me.' How could she have got it so wrong? Been so stupid? He doesn't like her in that way... probably never has. And yet she'd been so convinced. It's not just the humiliation of his rejection – it's the condescending way he's speaking to her that grates. Just because he rarely drinks, doesn't mean she can't. 'Don't pretend you know my mind.'

'What were you thinking? That we'd do it here in the shelter? Anyone could have walked by – Sorcha, the coach driver, one of the teachers even. You might not care what people think of you, but I do. You're lovely and I know people who wouldnae say no if it was offered to them, whatever the circumstance, but I don't want to be that person, Ailsa. I care about you too much and I don't think this is what you want either. Not really. Not right now when you've had too much to drink.'

Inside, Ailsa is consumed with hurt and an embarrassment that's morphed into anger. He's right, but that doesn't make the situation any easier. 'Don't tell me what I want, Jonah. Don't tell me what I fucking do or don't want.'

She hates how she sounds. She doesn't usually swear, it's the alcohol, but that knowledge only makes her feel worse. Yes, she's had a drink, but that doesn't mean she's incapable of making a decision. If he'd asked her if it was what she wanted, she'd have said yes. And yet...

Yet there's another emotion fighting to push through the anger, and when she realises what it is, she's shocked. For the feeling is relief that she didn't go through with it. Not here in this wooden shelter.

Did Jonah really know her so well?

She feels a sharp tug on her sleeve. Jonah is looking up at her, his face creased with concern. 'I don't want this to spoil our friendship. You're the only one who makes this island tolerable. Stay. Let's talk.'

He's never said this to her before, but she's not sure she can believe anything he says now. 'Don't say things you don't mean.'

'I do mean it. I wouldnae say it if I didn't. You know I've been struggling recently.' He breathes in sharply. 'After Dad and everything. You've helped to pull me out of the black hole I was sinking into. Helped me start to believe there might be a future that's not so bleak.'

Ailsa leans her back against the wooden pillar of the shelter, her hair whipping around her face, and shakes her head. 'Don't play games with me, Jonah. Yes, I've been there for you, of course I have, because I...' She swallows. 'Because I like you. But you don't think of me that way. You responded to me because that's what happens when you're a man, but then you remembered that it was me. Ailsa. The girl who you think of as your bloody sister.'

'That's not true. Please, Ailsa—'

She's not listening. Instead, she pulls up the hood of her coat and runs back to the community centre. But, when she gets there, she sees Bethany in the covered entrance porch, her back pressed to the hard brick wall. Just as though she's been waiting for her.

'Jesus.' Bethany looks her up and down. 'The state of yae. Is it any wonder, Jonah didn't want a piece?' She gives a laugh. 'Don't worry, Ailsa. Maybe when you've grown up a bit... got some dress sense.' She points to the blue velvet fabric of Ailsa's dress and her lips curl again. Shaking her head in mock sadness, she sighs, then takes a drag of the cigarette between her fingers. 'Mind you, if an oddball like that turned you down, there's not much hope for you, is there?'

'You were spying on us.' The shock hits her full force in the solar plexus, sobering her momentarily. 'You all wanted this to happen. I can believe it of Sorcha, but you used to be my friend, Beth.'

Bethany cocks her head on one side and considers her. 'Did I? I don't remember that.'

The white light from the porch highlights the girl's face and Ailsa realises she no longer knows her. Not really. Since they sat together in primary school, she's changed. They both have.

With a smile, Bethany pushes herself from the wall and points in the direction of the shelter where Ailsa and Jonah had been sitting. 'Well, well. Won't you take a look at that.'

With a sinking heart, Ailsa makes herself look. She'd wondered where Sorcha was and now she knows. At this very minute, the girl is crossing the grass on the other side of the road. Has almost reached the shelter of the wooden bench. Jonah won't have seen her yet, but soon he will. When she's almost there, Sorcha stops and catches the waving strands of her beautiful dark hair, tucking them into the back of her jacket before pulling up the collar. There's no uncertainty in her actions. No neediness. She knows what she wants, and she knows what she'll need to do to get it... has tried it out on Callum, after all.

Ailsa's mind is racing, and she feels sick with dread. Jonah will stand no chance. More importantly, she and Jonah hardly know each other, so there'll be no friendship to lose if he gives in to her.

A few seconds later, Sorcha's ducked under the roof of the shelter and Ailsa looks away. Hating Jonah. Hating herself.

Bethany looks at her with a mixture of pity and contempt. 'Poor, Ailsa,' she says. 'Let's face it. He might not have wanted you, but he's never going to turn Sorcha down, now is he?'

Grinding out her cigarette on the wall, she flicks it into the darkness and shoulders open the door. There's a blast of folk music that stops as the door closes again behind her.

Ailsa's left alone. Betrayal, and the alcohol she's drunk, leaving a sour taste in her mouth. She presses the heels of her hands against her eyes. She won't cry. She won't.

The door opens again, and Ailsa drops her hands quickly, knowing it's probably Bethany unable to resist another opportunity to kick her while she's down. But it isn't. She forces her eyes to focus, thinking at first that it's Jonah who stands under the porch light, contemplating her with amusement, before realising her stupidity. How could it be when Jonah is in the shelter by the loch with Sorcha?

No, this is Callum.

'What's up?' he asks. 'Not something my brother's done, I hope.'

She gives a bitter laugh. 'Why would it be?'

He shrugs. 'Because he's an idiot, that's why.'

A girl's laughter pierces the night, the sound brought to them from across the grass by the wind that's whipping white-tipped waves onto the surface of the loch.

'I don't want to talk about it.' Her voice is brittle. Her words fuelled by resentment.

The laughter comes again and Callum frowns. Has he recognised its owner? If he has, he doesn't say. Instead, his voice is dry, matter of fact.

'Here, have some of this. It will make things look a wee bit better.' He fishes a metal hip flask from the inside pocket of his jacket, unscrews it and wipes it on his sleeve before handing it to her. 'Go on. I haven't got germs.'

'What is it?'

'Whisky. Jonah and I used to nick it from my dad, but now the bugger's gone we don't need to. There must have been half a dozen bottles hidden around the house. The outbuildings too.' He watches Ailsa put it to her lips and shakes his head, his sandy hair falling around his face. 'I wouldn't have offered it if I knew you'd be taking that pathetic sip... drink it properly.'

Ailsa takes a long mouthful, feeling the burn of it. No longer caring what she should or shouldn't do.

'You're not bad-looking, you know.' Callum's tone has altered. 'Not bad at all. I like the natural look. Not all tits and arse.'

Reaching out, he takes a lock of Ailsa's hair and contemplates it before pushing it behind her ear. His warm fingertips lingering at the side of her face before he draws his hand away again.

Before Ailsa has time to think about the meaning of this, he's holding out his hand to her.

'Come on.' Taking the flask from her with his free hand,

Callum tucks it back inside his pocket. 'I'll take you home. We can continue the party there.'

Without speaking, Ailsa takes his hand and follows him across the car park to where his motorbike's parked. He puts on his helmet and holds out the one that's hanging from the handlebars. Ailsa takes it, not wondering why he'd thought to bring a second one.

She puts it on and climbs on the bike behind him. A decision that would change her life forever.

FORTY

AILSA

Ailsa waits as Jonah looks down at his glass. Swirls the amber liquid.

'Please don't say you regret it, Jonah.'

She thinks he's not going to answer, that this has all been in vain, but then he looks up at her and speaks.

'Aye, of course I remember. What did you expect me to say? Christ, I've wanted to do this since the moment I got back.'

Reaching over to her, he slides his fingers into her hair, pulling her roughly to him. Then his lips are on hers. Urgent. His tongue searching.

Ailsa breaks away, her heart racing, nausea rising. She looks up at the ceiling. 'Not yet. I want to know what you thought that evening. I need to know you felt the same way I did.'

Jonah stares at her a long time as though searching for the right words. 'All right. I'll tell you how it was. It was my first time. My brother was shagging everything that moved on the island and I couldnae believe my fucking luck. Are you happy?' Seeing her face, he swallows, rubs his hand up and down the back of his neck as if worried he's said the wrong thing. Instantly, he corrects himself. 'But I loved you. Of course I did.'

The air in the room feels a little thinner and Ailsa's finding it hard to breathe. Can he see it? Because she's back on that clifftop the afternoon before the boating accident. The wind scouring the grass. Rain in the air. Jonah's words carried by the wind but still reaching her. His voice strained. *I need to tell you why it happened. I can't live with myself, Ailsa. I can't do this any more.* Needing to explain why he'd pushed her away at the ceilidh. Why he'd broken her heart.

I love you, Ailsa, but not in that way. I never meant to lead you on, but it's not just you... I'll never feel like that for any girl. It's something I've always known but was too scared to admit. Don't tell Callum. Promise me you won't tell Callum.

Ailsa forces herself back to the present. The man who sits beside her on the settee knows nothing of what Jonah told her the afternoon he'd died... because he hadn't been there.

There's a sound from upstairs. Kyle is calling her, and she knows she should go to him and see if he's okay, but it's like she has no control over her legs. The cold lick of fear inside has paralysed her.

She sees it now with monstrous clarity. Seth had been right all along. This is indeed Callum who sits so close to her on the settee, his beard unkempt, his overlong hair tucked behind his ears. Not Jonah, Callum – the blood of his heartless father pulsing in his veins. Callum, the one she'd felt no sorrow for the night she'd heard he'd died. Callum, the teenage boy who'd refused to stop when she'd said no. Glad to have something of his brother's at last.

She feels again the weight of his body pushing down on her. Her face pressed against the hard damp boards. The criss-cross of a fishing net leaving its impression on a cheek wet with tears.

She can barely look at him.

But how could it be?

She thinks back to what she knows. There had been the phone call her mother had received from Moira the night of the accident. Her mum had woken her, and she'd pulled on her clothes, her eyes still bleary from sleep. They'd run to the car and, in silence, had driven along the dark road to Loch Briona, the windscreen wipers ineffectual against the rain, the headlights of the car picking out the white huddle of sheep at the roadside. At the sign to the holiday lodges, they'd turned off onto the gravelled drive. The only thing in Ailsa's head, the only thing that mattered, the knowledge that Jonah was safe. Jonah was alive.

As they'd let themselves in, they'd seen him straight away, sitting at the kitchen table, his head in his hands. A blanket was draped over his hunched shoulders, and he held an ice pack against his swollen and bloodied face. Beside him sat Moira, her face white, her hands twisting. No tears. No words of comfort or condemnation for her son. The police were on their way, she said. They'd examine the boat and take photographs to add to a file that would be submitted to the Procurator Fiscal.

And as she spoke, Jonah had sat mute as the responders had checked him for hypothermia. Shock. Their priority now the living. He was still wearing the jumper and jacket he'd had on when they'd climbed to the triangulation point at the top of the hill that afternoon. The same afternoon he'd told her his secret. His hair was bedraggled, his trainers and clothes soaked through from where he'd anchored in the shallows and dragged his brother's lifeless body onto the shore.

And while her mum had held Moira's hands, filling the space in that room left by Callum's death with questions that had met with no answers, Ailsa had waited for the responders to tell them what was to be done. How long it would be before the helicopter arrived to transport Callum's body to the mainland. Not wanting to hear the crunch of the wheels of the gurney on the drive.

She'd taken everything at face value. They all had. Their main concern now for the boy who'd survived. The boy who'd tried in vain to save his brother. No one had thought to question Jonah's version of events, but why would they?

A few days later, they'd heard that the post-mortem had established the cause of death as hypothermia – no injuries to the body, or anything else, found that would cause concern. And when the Procurator Fiscal had decided a Fatal Accident Enquiry wouldn't be necessary, Moira had been able to plan the funeral.

A funeral that would see Jonah prostrate at his brother's grave. Black eye fading to mustard yellow. His nose still swollen and cut. A funeral neither she nor Moira could have known would be the last time they'd see him for eleven years.

Now the question comes to her... too late. Much too late.

What had *really* happened out there on that bitterly cold and fateful night?

FORTY-ONE

JONAH

Then

The air is frigid, the loch more so.

Jonah shouts, the wind forcing him to raise his voice. 'I'm not listening to any more of your crap. You're drunk, Callum. Give me the tiller. You dinnae know what you're doing.'

His brother's face is rigid, cold and disgust contorting his features. 'You have to be fucking joking.'

Behind them, the lights of Elgin twinkle in the dark sky. It should be pretty, but it's not. His mother's voice is with him. *Go and fetch Callum in the boat. He can't be trusted to get himself home.* Like Callum's a child instead of a grown man. But he'd gone anyway. What other choice did he have?

What a waste of everyone's time.

What a joke.

He'd had the wind behind him on the way there. Had crossed the loch in under twenty minutes, the moonlight and the lights of Elgin on the opposite bank, a guide. When at last he'd reached the jetty, he'd slipped the engine into neutral and lowered the anchor before letting the momentum of the boat bring him in. As the fender bumped the stonework, he'd jumped out and looped a line around the mooring bollard making the boat fast before running across the road to the pub. Hoping against hope his brother wouldn't be in too much of a state.

He'd found Callum on a high stool at the bar, his head on the wet wooden counter, his arms circling a glass of malt. And as he'd moved his brother's glass and shaken his arm to rouse him, the bartender had raised his eyebrows at him.

'Good luck, mate. You're gonnae need it with this one.'

How he'd got Callum out of the pub he doesn't know, for he certainly hadn't wanted to leave, but, eventually, he'd persuaded him to down the last of his drink. Then, with one arm around his brother's waist, had managed to steer a course through the pub's tables and chairs and out into the night.

The wind had picked up, whipping the normally flat surface of the loch into small waves. At the jetty, the boat rolled, straining at its ropes, and Jonah remembered how he'd stared at it, thinking that if he managed to get Callum on board, without him falling into the water, it would be a miracle. Amazingly, he'd done it.

The engine had sputtered into life, and he'd cast off, the boat rocking as he jumped in and steered them away. For the first ten minutes or so, their journey had been uneventful – the only sound the wind that was against them now, the boat's engine straining as they pushed into it. Ahead of them were the twinkling lights of the holiday complex – just fifteen minutes away if they were lucky and Callum behaved himself.

But Jonah should have known it wouldn't be that easy. With too much drink inside him, Callum could be unstable. Unpredictable. In one swift move, he'd forced the tiller from Jonah's hand and pulled back the throttle, the white wake just visible in the darkness behind them.

Now, Jonah glares at him in frustration, his temper rising.

'Stop being such a fucking idiot. You'll have us both in the water. Give it here.'

Shoving Callum aside, he takes back control of the boat and reduces the speed. Not caring that his brother has slipped on the wet deck, pitching into the wooden bench.

'Fuck! *Fuck!*' Callum's hands cover his nose. Blood drips between his fingers.

He looks up at Jonah with dark eyes, and Jonah knows that there's going to be trouble. Not only is he clearly in pain, but he's been humiliated and that's never sat well with him.

'Look, I'm sorry, Cal. Let me—'

'You think you're so bloody perfect, don't you? Just because you're going off to poncy university.' Callum's right eye is closing up. His voice is thick. Each syllable slurred. 'Everybody's golden boy. Well, let me give you some news.' He heaves himself up onto the bench and points a finger, sticky with blood, at Jonah. 'You'll never survive off the island. You're nothing but a coward. Too scared to stick up for yourself. Hiding away in corners. Hoping you won't be noticed.'

Jonah leans to the left, trying to see past his brother. Shocked at the injustice of what he's saying. 'That's not true. You know it's not.'

The lights of the Loch Briona Lodges are moving ever closer. Callum twists round to look at them. 'They never wanted me to have it, you know,' he says, waving an arm in the direction of the lights. 'I heard them talking about it, dear Ma and Pa. In their eyes I was never more than a handyman. Good with a saw. Good when the lights went out in a storm. The dogsbody. No better than the old man.'

Inside, Jonah's guts are twisting. He doesn't want to talk about this now. Not when Callum's drunk. Not when he's in this mood.

'I saw Ailsa today.' He'd said it to change the subject, but immediately he regrets it. What is he hoping to achieve?

Callum will only think he's trying to rub his nose in it... the fact that Ailsa likes him best. For although he's never said anything, only an idiot could miss the way Callum looks at her.

The wind is fierce, spray blowing into their faces. Despite his obvious pain, Callum gives a slow smile.

'She's good, you know.'

Jonah drags his eyes away from the lights on the shore. His throat tightening.

'What?'

'Ailsa. I said she's good.' Callum's eyes are half-closed, the skin puffing up around them, but they don't leave his. He's waiting. Seeing how he'll react. Whether he'll take the bait.

'Fuck off.'

Callum lifts the ends of his long hair and twirls it around his bloodstained finger. 'Ooh, Callum. Aren't you going to kiss me?'

'You're lying.'

Inside, Jonah's gone cold. If it was anyone else, he'd know what they were doing, but Callum doesn't lie... not to him, anyway. Sometimes, he wishes he would, for then he wouldn't have to know the dark workings of his brother's mind.

Please. Anyone but his brother.

Callum's laughing now, the blood dripping down his jaw giving him a clown-like appearance in the moonlight. 'Do you want to know what we did? What she likes.' He points to the deck of the boat. 'On her back like a whore.'

'You bastard.' Jonah's up from his seat, the boat rocking as he takes the few short steps needed to reach Callum. 'Don't you fucking speak about her like that.' Rudderless, the boat turns in circles, waves slapping at the sides. He grabs Callum's collar, twisting it at his throat, and presses his forehead to his. 'Take it back.'

But he knows Callum can't. He's told him now. Inside his chest, his heart has turned to stone. Nothing will ever be the same again.

Callum's face is red, his head forced back by Jonah's knuckles at his chin. His broken nose making him look like someone else. 'What do you reckon, little bro? Think she lies in bed comparing us. Giving us scores out of ten.' He laughs at his own joke. 'Callum ten. Jonah zero.'

Jonah gives a shudder. He knows why Callum's doing this. It's because of the huge chip on his shoulder that gets bigger by the day. His brother thinks he has everything and is scared that, one day, after he's come back from university, he'll be handed the running of Loch Briona too.

But Ailsa? The knot that's gripping his stomach tightens. She never liked Callum, was scared of him. What made her do it? With *him*?

Slowly, the terrible truth filters through his churning mind. It was because he had rejected her. Had been too scared that night to tell her he was gay in case his brother had found out. He'd left Ailsa vulnerable, and Callum was used to taking what he wanted in life. This had been no different.

'You forced her?' he says through lips numb with cold and shock. 'You *raped* her.' He lets go of Callum's collar and takes a step back. It explains why she's been so odd with him. 'Jesus, tell me that's not what happened.'

'That's your interpretation... maybe even hers.' The smile Callum gives doesn't reach his eyes. He breathes heavily through his mouth. 'Let's just say she didn't put up too much of a fight.'

Jonah feels the muscles of his face tighten. He's rigid with fury. 'You bastard. When we're back, I'm going to tell the police what you did. What you are. You know what? I'm going to tell them everything.'

He draws his fist back, but, before he can do anything, a wave catches the boat at an angle, catching him off guard. He feels his feet go, losing their grip on the slippery deck as he pitches backwards. His hip makes contact with the gunwale and, as the boat rocks dangerously, he throws out his arms in a vain attempt to grab something. Anything. But there's nothing to hold on to.

Just air.

Then freezing water.

His head goes under. Water fills his nostrils. His ears. When he surfaces, the boat is further away. It's bitterly cold. Dangerously cold. He must keep swimming. Keep afloat.

The icy water has saturated his clothes, weighing him down. It's like his very blood is freezing inside the shell of his body.

He mustn't panic. *Mustn't.*

'Callum,' he cries, his voice mingling with the wind. 'Callum!'

FORTY-TWO

CALLUM

Then

The water of the loch is black. Inky. The moon has disappeared behind a cloud and Callum can't see Jonah, can only hear him. The sound of his arms thrashing as he struggles to stay afloat in his jacket and jumper. His voice snatched away by the wind as he cries for help.

Despite the alcohol he's drunk, his body goes into automatic pilot, performing actions he's done hundreds of times before. Cutting back the throttle to almost nothing, he points the boat away from the sound, circling around and positioning it on the downwind side so there's less danger of the wind pushing the boat on top of Jonah. The only lights are the ones on the shore, tiny yellow rectangles and dots, too far now to make out individual houses. He needs to see.

'Jonah!' The wind snatches at the word. Carries it away.

Barely able to see through his swollen eyelid, he reaches down to the locker under the seat and searches with numb, fumbling fingers for the flashlight he knows is in there. The boat rocks sickeningly beneath him.

'Hold on.'

Coils of rope, an old fishing net, an empty whisky bottle... that's all he can find. Desperately, he pulls them out, flinging them across the deck. Jesus, where's the bloody light? He's about to give up in despair when his fingers feel something rigid. Solid. Thank God. Grabbing it out of the dark well, he turns the flashlight on and sweeps the light across the water until he sees his brother, the beam picking out his white face. He's further away than he'd thought.

'Keep swimming. For fuck's sake, keep swimming.'

Aware of the injuries a moving propeller can cause, and not wanting to get too close, he points the bow into the wind. Positioning the boat, he cuts the engine, letting it drift alongside his brother. He can see him clearly now. Can see his panicked eyes.

'Callum!' Jonah's voice is getting weak.

They both know how treacherous the deep water of the loch is at this time of year. Have had it drummed into them by both their mother and their father. In summer, it's best to be careful, but in winter the danger is magnified. It's not the waves accompanying a storm that are the silent killer on Loch Briona, nor the currents that run unseen below the surface. No, it's neither of these things – it's the cold water that can claim a life. Causing the body to go into shock.

In the beam of light, he sees the desperate lift and press of arms. The futile attempt to stay afloat in the icy water.

'Help me!' There's no disguising the fear in Jonah's voice. The naked fear.

For a moment, Callum loses him, then the torch picks him out again: long hair floating, head tipped back, mouth wide, gasping for air. Each breath too rapid. Hyperventilating.

Grabbing an oar, he thrusts it towards his brother, loch water dripping down the wood, but it won't reach. Then it's slipping, slipping from his cold hands, sliding away into the water.

'Damn!'

Jonah's face is deathly pale, lips tinged with blue. His body will be trying to keep his blood warm by moving it towards the centre. His blood pressure will already be shooting up. There's only a small window in which a person must leave the water before worse effects kick in. This is it.

'Callum. *Please!*'

His nose and eye are throbbing so badly he wants to throw up, but he can't. 'Don't worry. I'll get you, little bro.'

But however hard he tries, he can't get the vicious argument they've just had out of his head. He'd forced himself on Ailsa, had banked on her never telling anyone, but now Jonah knows. Like an idiot he'd told him. Jonah's covered for him so many times before, but this is different. Jonah loves the girl. Maybe more than he loves *him*. He can't trust him to keep this to himself.

'Callum!'

Jonah's getting weaker, his teeth chattering in his head. He's beyond the point where he can save himself, and Callum knows if he doesn't act now, his brother will die.

A hand breaks the surface again. Eyes wide. Pleading. He's closer now. Close enough for him to grasp if he just reached out a little further. Jonah's eyes are wide. Terrified. But instead of pity for him, a deathly calm envelops Callum. A terrible, calculating calm. Jonah's scared of him; he can see it in the dilation of his pupils in the torchlight. In the way he's calling to him. Begging for his life.

He can see his lips moving, but the only words he hears are the ones from earlier.

I'll tell everyone what you did. What you are.

You forced yourself on her.

You raped her.

His mother's voice joins Jonah's in his head. *You're getting more like your father every day.*

If you hear it enough times, it must be true.

He's a monster.

Evil.

Another minute and Jonah will inhale water directly into his lungs. That would be enough. No one would ever know different. He'd say it was an accident. No one would ever know the truth.

The white disk of his brother's face looks up at him from the loch. He's stopped thrashing. Is slipping lower. Lower.

This is his chance to ditch Callum forever. To be Jonah. The good one. The one they all love.

The boat rocks again, the sharp edge of the gunwale catching his shoulder. Jolting fresh pain into his nose. Bringing him to his senses. What the fuck is he doing? Jonah's his brother. His twin.

'Jesus!' He puts down the torch and grabs the second oar. Lowering his centre of gravity, he reaches out as far as he can. Desperate hands rise to grasp the blade. An arm circles the wood. Hand over hand he pulls his brother in until he's close enough to grab by the shoulders and with a loud grunt manages to manoeuvre him to the side of the boat.

'Come on,' he shouts. 'You've got to help. Hold on to the side.'

Reaching under Jonah's arms, he pulls with all his might, terror giving him super-human strength. His brother's head is over the edge now, his shoulders too. Holding the collar of his jacket with one hand, Callum reaches down and grabs the waistband of his jeans. Screwing up his eyes as he counts to three and heaves. He's losing his grip. The body's starting to slip back. In desperation, he wedges his knee between the blood-spattered bench and the rail and pulls harder, his face red with the exertion, until finally he manages to haul the rest of him over. The boat rocks, pain ripping through his skull as he falls back, his head making contact with the edge of the far bench.

Everything goes black.

When Callum opens his eyes again, he has no idea how long he's been lying there or what's happened. He sits up, his hand pressed to the back of his head. The boat's adrift, the engine cut. Why? Then it all comes back to him with terrifying clarity. Turning his head, he sees the deathly white face of the boy lying on the deck next to him. The blue lips. The rigid stillness of his chest.

God no!

Forcing himself up, his head thrumming with pain, Callum staggers over to him. He sits astride his brother's slim, muscular body, the heels of his hands finding the dip of his breastbone.

Nellie the elephant packed her trunk and said goodbye to the circus.

Before his eyes, Jonah's sternum dips and rises as the heels of his hands press to the rhythm. Over and over. Fighting the wind. The waves rocking the boat. His body exhausted.

Even when he knows it will do no good, Callum carries on. They're brothers. From the same womb. He can't be dead.

But even as he thinks this, he knows it's true. Those moments when he'd looked down on him in the water, hating him. Those wasted, twisted minutes, had been enough to kill him and he'd known it. Had wanted it.

Pushing himself as far back as he can from the body, Callum covers his face with his hands.

He's a murderer.

He knows it and God knows it.

He'd killed his father and now he's taken his own brother's life as well.

Cradling his head in his hands, he gives a deep moan. A primitive sound from the very depths of him. His mother's right. The islanders who talk about him in hushed voices are right. He's evil. The very devil himself.

He hates himself. Hates the child who'd entered the world

thirty minutes before his brother and who his mother had named Callum. It's meaning *peace*. *Purity*. What a fucking joke. He'd thought he'd loved himself, but now he realises that's not true. His hatred is stronger than his love. He hates everything he's ever done. Would be rid of Callum if he could.

He has to live each day knowing that everyone fears him and, however much he wants to deny it, sometimes, in the dead of night, he's scared of himself too. Scared of what he's capable of when he's had a skinful and the alcohol makes his father's bad blood course faster through his veins.

Like it did tonight.

They'd be better off without him. Isn't that what everyone says?

He stares at his brother's lifeless body. This is his chance to be rid of Callum forever. Be rid of the name that shames him. The name that he knows will follow him, dog him, for the rest of his life.

Jonah's life had been hard too, but he'd got brains. Despite his crap childhood, he'd managed to stay sane. Work hard. Find a girl who loved him. Get himself a place at university and with it a golden ticket to running the holiday lodges.

Jonah isn't a rapist.

Jonah isn't a murderer.

Jonah isn't a monster.

He leans forward and presses his forehead to his brother's, feeling the chill, wet skin. What if he wasn't Callum any more? What if he was Jonah?

FORTY-THREE

AILSA

The scales have fallen from Ailsa's eyes, and she sees Callum now for who he really is. How could she not have seen before? Not guessed?

That afternoon when she'd found him slumped on a bench outside The Stag and followed him to his brother's graveside – shouldn't that have been a clue? And when he'd broken down beside the headstone engraved with his own name, confessing in a moment of drunken weakness how he'd left his brother for too long in that blood-chilling water. Confessed he hadn't wanted him to live. Shouldn't she have seen it then?

But, of course, love is blind. It makes her no different to Moira. No better.

When she'd thought it was Jonah speaking, she'd felt compassion for him. Had justified his actions to herself. Callum had terrorised Jonah's family as Hugh had done before him. Jonah hadn't been thinking straight, had been in shock when he'd watched his brother struggling in the water. As soon as he'd come to his senses, he'd done his best to rescue Callum and, because she loved him, she had forgiven him those few treacherous minutes. The reason was simple. She was glad.

Even though no one spoke the words aloud, all the islanders who knew the family were thinking the same thing – they were better off with Callum gone. She'd seen it in their eyes when they'd gossiped about it at school. Her mum had heard it in the tone of their voices when, in the following days, they'd called in on Moira to give their condolences.

But this is different. This man who let his brother drown is Callum and not even Jonah knew the true workings of his brother's mind. They'd shared the same womb, had the same faces, but that was all. In no other way were they alike.

Ailsa's skin shrinks from the enormity of what she now knows and for a moment she forgets to breathe. Every nerve of her body feels stretched. She can't let him touch her again. Can't let him kiss her.

But he's staring at her, his eyes drinking in her face, and Ailsa realises there is something worse than his hands on her. More dangerous by far is him knowing she's found him out. On that clifftop Jonah had asked her never to tell Callum he was gay, and she promised she wouldn't. But, even if she'd wanted to, by the end of that night Callum would be dead.

Or so she'd believed.

Ailsa's hands are shaking, and she squeezes the fingers of one hand hard with the other. She can't give herself away. Not while they're alone at Loch Briona. Not if she and Kyle are to remain safe. She looks at the fire, the glinting glass of whisky, anywhere except at Callum. Inviting her up to the house was all part of his seduction. He's got a plan and she can only guess at what it is.

He'd taken Kyle, still in his funeral suit, out to the boathouse without her knowing and it kills her to imagine her beautiful, vulnerable boy in that vile place. Why had he done that? Why? She thinks of the motorboat where Jonah lost his life, the open loch beyond the boathouse doors, and her fear intensifies. A knot pulled tight.

What had Callum planned to do and what had happened to thwart that plan?

It's something she'll never know, but there's one thing she's sure of. She and Kyle have to get away from the house. Go back to the lodge and phone the police, Doug and Reyne... anyone. Get in her car and leave Loch Briona for a place of safety.

But Callum is reaching for her, his question about that afternoon on the clifftop swept aside by his drunken need to possess her again. The drink weakening him yet emboldening him. The result the same.

'Ailsa...' Callum leans towards her, the weight of him pressing her body against the cushions.

A voice in her head tells her she must play along. Pretend it's Jonah whose drunken fingers are fumbling for the buttons of her blouse, whose hungry lips are searching for hers again. But she can't let it happen. Not again. Anything... *anything* but that.

She's just wondering how effective it would be to draw her knee up. Whether the blow would hit its mark and cause him to roll away, his hands cupped to his groin, when she hears a voice.

'Mum, I want to go home. I don't like it here.'

'Fuck.' Callum raises himself up on his elbows and looks where she's looking. Kyle stands in the doorway, his Spider-Man pyjamas skimming his skinny calves, the tablet in his hand.

'You said you'd come up at ten o'clock. It's two minutes past ten, Mum. You lied.'

Ailsa sits up, straightens her blouse, wishing her son was still safe upstairs yet grateful that he's not. He's saved her, even though he'll have no idea that he has. She forces a smile, but still the horror threatens to overwhelm her. Because there's something else Kyle doesn't know. The terrible danger they are both in.

FORTY-FOUR

AILSA

Callum's neck is red, his eyes hard.

'Go back to bed.'

Kyle bunches the fingers of his free hand into a fist. 'No. I don't have to. Mum said she would get me at ten. It's been ten and now I want to go home.'

'I said—'

Ailsa gets up quickly. Places a hand on Callum's shoulder. 'Don't shout at him, Jonah. It will only make it worse. I'll deal with this.'

Callum looks up at her, and she sees how bloodshot the whites of his eyes are. How many times had he refilled his glass when she was upstairs with Kyle?

'I thought you said he'd stayed here before,' he hisses. 'That he liked it.'

'It must be because of Moira. Her not being here makes the house feel alien to him. It was your mother as much as the room that settled him when he was here.'

'Jesus Christ.' Callum leans forward, his elbows on his knees. His fist cupped in the palm of his other hand. 'How do you put up with it? You should be stronger with him. Stricter. You mollycoddle him and the kid needs to know he's not top dog in the house.'

Ailsa hears Hugh's voice fall from his son's lips. Remembers the marks on Jonah's skin. Callum's too. Her fear strengthens. They have to get out.

Her skin crawling, she forces her hand to move from his shoulder to his cheek. Lets her thumb caress the soft skin above his stubble.

'Come later. When Kyle's asleep. I'll get him settled back at the lodge and wait for you.'

He looks up at her from under his brow. 'How long?'

Ailsa thinks. Too short a time and she'll be trapped here, too long and he might be suspicious.

'An hour.' That should be enough time to ring Reyne and get over to her in the car before he leaves the house. 'Kyle will be asleep by then.'

Callum turns his head from one side to the other as though releasing tension. He stands and picks up his empty glass from the table. The smile he gives first her then Kyle is one she no longer believes in. He's back in his role now. Remembering what Jonah would have done.

'Glad you were able to come over for a bit, lad. Get yourself home now and into your own bed. As you say, it's late.' Turning his back to Kyle, he whispers in Ailsa's ear. 'I'll see you later. One hour.'

'I'll look forward to it.' Ailsa picks up her bag and goes over to her son. 'Come on then. Jonah's right, it *is* late.'

As Ailsa hurries down the concrete steps, Kyle behind her, she shoves her hand into her bag to find her phone. She feels the soft leather of her purse, the spiky ridge of her comb, Kyle's tablet but that's all. Sitting on the cold ground underneath one of the yellow lights where moths are fluttering, she turns the bag upside down, emptying its contents, but her mobile isn't there. She must have left it back in the lodge.

With an impatience that makes the job slower, she shoves everything back. She needs to find it. Needs to ring Reyne. When she reaches her lodge, she climbs the steps and fits the key in the lock, ushering Kyle in. Slamming the door shut behind them.

She stands with her back to the door and scans the room. Where would she have left her phone? Kyle's standing in the middle of the floor, rubbing at his eyes. Maybe he's seen it.

'Kyle, do you know what I did with my phone before we came out?'

'You unplugged it and put it in your bag. Then you told me to brush my hair. Then you—'

'All right. All right.'

He must be wrong. He has to be. Yet, Kyle never gets things like that wrong. His attention to detail is second to none and, when it suits him, he has eyes like a hawk.

There's a coppery taste of blood in her mouth, the inside of her cheek sore from where she's been biting it. She'd left her bag on the floor by her feet and it's possible that Callum took her phone from it while she was upstairs with Kyle. But why? Is it because he suspects she knows something or is it because he wants to keep her a virtual prisoner?

'Can I go to bed now?' Kyle has perched himself on the edge of the sofa, his coat still covering his Spider-Man pyjamas.

'No!' Her reply comes out too loud. Too sharp.

Going over to Kyle, she kneels in front of him. 'I know you're tired, but we can't stay here, Kyle. Not tonight. I don't have time to explain why, but you need to listen to me. We're going to leave everything here, take the car and go to Reyne and

Doug's. In the morning, I'll explain everything, but, just for now, I need you to do as I say without asking questions. Do you think you can do that?'

Kyle's rocking says more than his lack of an answer. This isn't going to work. The anxiety she's tried not to show, is affecting him. Confusing him. There must be another way.

In her bag, there's no phone, but Kyle's tablet is there with his favourite Minecraft game. She's never played it herself, but the reason she'd got it for him was because she'd been told one of its best features is it allows the user to be in control of the game, encouraging them to design solutions to a problem. In a world that doesn't always make sense to him, it's something Kyle enjoys doing.

'I want you to play a game with me. Would you like that?'

Kyle frowns. 'I don't know.'

Without making it obvious, Ailsa checks her watch. It was ten fifteen when they left. It's now nearly ten thirty. 'Come with me.'

She gets up and goes over to her bedroom door, pleased when she hears Kyle behind her. Beckoning him over to the window, she pulls back the curtain just enough for him to see out.

'You can see Moira's house from here... and the car park where our car is.' She points to where the car sits beside Moira's Range Rover and the old one she'd let Callum drive. 'I'd like you to find a way of getting to the car without being seen from the house. It will be fun. Could you do that do you think?'

'Of course I can. I'm not stupid, Mum.'

'No, of course you're not. I should have said *will* you do that? I don't think I'd be very good at it, and you're much better at problem-solving than me. Oh, and we have to get there in, let's see...' She looks at her watch again. 'Ten minutes tops.'

'Why?'

Ailsa drops the curtain. She hadn't expected the question though it's an obvious one.

What answer should she give? What answer *can* she give without worrying him?

But Kyle speaks first.

'Is it because of the man? Uncle Jonah?'

Ailsa hovers between the truth and a lie. Neither is ideal. 'Yes, it is.'

'Did he do something bad?'

'Yes, Kyle. I think he did, and I need to tell Reyne and Doug.'

She prays he won't ask what it was he did as she hasn't the words to explain... not tonight. Thankfully, he doesn't.

'I can get to the car in less than ten minutes, Mum.'

Ailsa smiles though her stomach's churning. 'That's my boy. But before we go, there's something I need to get.'

Under her bed is where she keeps her important things. Her passport and Kyle's. Their birth certificates. She can't risk leaving them. Lying flat on her belly, Ailsa reaches her arm under the bed. Her heart pounding. Knowing she has to hurry. At first her fingers touch nothing, but then she feels the cold hard metal of the tin. She pulls it towards her and pulls off the lid. The tin is the same one her mum used for the lavender bags she made for her friends at Christmas. The smell brings back memories of those days.

Fighting back tears, Ailsa takes out their documents and, as she does, sees the large envelope Moira gave her. When she'd given it to her, Ailsa hadn't questioned its contents. Had understood that it wasn't to be opened until after Moira's death and had wanted to believe that time would be somewhere in the distant future. She'd know when the time was right to read it, that's what Moira had told her, and she hopes she was right. Now, as she stuffs the envelope into her bag and zips it up, she wonders why she hadn't thought it strange that it was she who Moira had chosen to give the envelope to rather than Jonah.

She's tempted to tear the envelope open now, but there isn't time. The clock is ticking and in half an hour, Callum will let himself out of the white house and descend the steps towards their chalet.

They have to leave now. Before it's too late.

Ailsa closes the door quietly behind them. For a moment, her attention is caught by the loch below, its surface skimmed with silver moonlight, but there's no time to wonder at its beauty.

'This way, Mum.'

Kyle runs down the steps in front of her and ducks between two of the lodges. Ailsa follows, hoping she's made the right decision to let him choose the way. But she'd had no choice. It had been the only way to get Kyle out of the chalet when all he'd really wanted was his bed.

Bending low, Kyle runs from one row to the next, keeping to the dark areas between the security lights, turning frequently to make sure she's following. Up ahead, at the top of the slope, is Moira's house, the curtains at the windows shielding them from Callum's eyes. She can see the car, parked on the gravel above the wash block and the laundry. At some point, they'll need to cross the concrete steps to reach it, cut across the row of lights and duck into the shadows of the outhouse buildings.

Ailsa whispers for Kyle to stop and he does.

'When I give the word, when I tell you, I want you to run with me as quickly as you can across the steps to the grass on the other side.' She points to the dark bulk of the outhouses, their edges undefined in the darkness. 'We'll stop there by the shower block.'

Glancing up at the house, she makes sure that the curtains are still closed, no face at the window watching their progress. All is still, just a thin line of yellow between the living room curtains.

'Now, Mum? Now?'

A dark shadow moves behind the curtains and Ailsa freezes. Without thinking, she grips Kyle's shoulder. 'No!'

'Get off. Get off. Get off.' Kyle jerks away, and Ailsa swears under her breath. How could she have been so stupid? They're near to the car now but even nearer to the house. Will Callum be able to hear him?

'Shh, Kyle. Please. You've done such a brilliant job getting us this far. I'm sorry I startled you. It was silly of me.' She kneels beside him and points at the car. 'Look, we're almost there. You can do the central locking for me if you like.'

Kyle stops shouting and looks at the car. 'Okay.'

Ailsa unzips the outside pocket of her bag and pushes her fingers in to find the keys. Her heart misses a beat. They're not there. Trying not to panic, she feels inside the main body of the bag but even as she's doing it, she knows they won't be there either. If they had been, she'd have seen them when she emptied the bag onto the steps earlier when she was searching for her phone.

A sudden gust of wind rustles the Scots pines in the forest behind the outbuildings. Their fanned canopies look spectral, unreal, in the moonlight. No longer knowing what to do, she looks up at the white house. Callum has taken her phone and the car keys too, what other explanation is there?

Shoving back her sleeve, she looks at her watch. Only fifteen minutes until he comes out of the house. Only a few more minutes to get down to her lodge and find her not there.

Then he'll need to get back up to the car. It isn't long enough, but she has no choice. She and Kyle will have to go on foot. Keep to the edge of the road and take shelter if they see the headlights of the Land Rover.

'I've changed my mind, Kyle. It will be much more fun to walk. We can be explorers.'

'How will we see?'

Ailsa looks up at the flat disk of the moon, thankful that it's a clear night. No rain forecast. 'We'll have the moon, and our eyes will soon get used to the darkness. It's part of the game, Kyle. If we get to The Stag, Reyne has a special prize for us.'

Kyle frowns. 'What prize?'

Ailsa tries to keep the frustration from her voice. Aware the minutes are ticking by. 'That would spoil the surprise.'

The dark shape passes by the window again. The slice of light widens. He's looking out. Maybe deciding if he could leave a little earlier. Wondering if she'd mind.

Ailsa pulls Kyle back into the shadows, her breath releasing as the strip of yellow light disappears again. 'We have to go, Kyle. Now.'

Hoping he'll follow, she runs across the concrete steps and onto the grass the other side. Kyle joins her and they wait in the dark until Ailsa is sure that the coast is clear. There's a small, paved path between the outbuildings and the wire fence separating the complex from the trees. It's darker here, the moonlight not finding its way through. Keeping to the shadowed edge, they follow the path to the car park where the gravel drive to the road begins.

Ailsa looks at her watch. Just ten minutes more and Callum will be leaving the house. If she was on her own, she'd run but Kyle hates running. Hated PE lessons at school and refused to participate. Anyway, it would be foolish to think they could outrun Callum's car.

They've reached the road and Ailsa looks around her.

Maybe there'll be somewhere to hide if they see the headlights. They can wait until the car has passed before carrying on.

From their vantage point at the top of the hill, Ailsa can see down the long drive to the car park. Moira's old car is still parked next to the house, and she breathes a sigh of relief. She can also see the trail of white steps, each one lit. There's no movement. Nothing to show that Callum has left yet. Maybe he won't follow them at all. But she knows he will. When Callum's been drinking, he won't be crossed. She looks down at the forest to the right of the site – Seth knows that better than anyone.

'We need to go quickly, Kyle... to win the game.'

There are no cars on the road, but there never are at this time of the evening. Making sure Kyle is with her, Ailsa crosses the road. On this side, the springy turf quickly gives way to heathland and bog, but every now and again a scrubby bush or the stunted form of a rowan comes into view. Ailsa strains to see the lights of Trip, but there's nothing but the dark road ahead. It's too far. More than six miles.

More worrying than this, though, is how open the road is. Above their heads the moon that had been their friend as they'd weaved their way through the holiday park, is friend no longer. Its brightness treacherous. If only the clouds would blanket it.

Ahead, the road bends. It will make them less visible, but it will also mean she'll no longer be able to see Callum's car. An hour has passed since she left him and by now, he'll be taking the steps down to their lodge. How long will he wait on the deck before he realises she's not going to answer the door? How long before he lets himself in with the master key and finds them gone?

'Can you go a little faster?' she urges, panic spreading through the very being of her. 'Please, Kyle.'

She looks behind, knowing there's nothing to see. They mustn't stop – not unless they have to. Six miles isn't so far. Ailsa stares at the long dark road. Who is she trying to kid? Kyle has never walked that far in his life and soon he'll start to tire. Already, he's slowing. Dragging his feet.

'Let's play another game,' she says, over brightly. But what game can they play out here on the lonely stretch of road? 'I'll say something in a special way, and you tell me what emotion I'm feeling.'

It's a game they've played before, and Kyle quite enjoys it, but the night is getting colder. Kyle's struggling. She can see it in the way his head is down. In the way he wavers from the path into the road.

Soon they'll have to stop.

Her half-empty bag bangs her hip as she walks. She should have brought water, a snack even, but her only thought had been to get out of the chalet and as far away from Callum as possible.

'Kyle?'

He's pulled the hood of his coat up and all she can see is a mane of fur and a dark space where his face is. 'No, I don't want to.'

'Then we'll play something else. I know, I'll give you two numbers, hard ones, and you see how long it takes you to add them together.'

This time he raises his head. 'All right.'

'But we have to walk quicker. It will help you think better.'

She's spouting nonsense, but it's all she has and she doesn't care. Anything to make him go faster. It's nearly eleven thirty. What's Callum doing? Is he, even now, running back up the steps to his car?

'Five hundred and thirty-six plus two hundred and forty-one.'

The answer comes back, rocket fast. 'Seven hundred and seventy-seven.'

Ailsa doesn't bother to check if he's right; he always is. She'll have to make it harder next time. To their right and below them, is Loch Briona – just a shiver of silver giving away its presence. It's strangely comforting.

'Two thousand, three hundred and ninety-six plus seven thousand, nine hundred and twenty-one.'

When there's no answer from Kyle, she turns around. He's standing in the middle of the road. Just a dark shape, his white trainers the only brightness in the moonlight.

'I don't want to walk any more. I want to go home.'

Ailsa's ribcage tightens around her lungs. 'We have to. Please, it's not much further.'

But it is. It's miles yet and they both know it.

A helplessness like she's never felt before engulfs her. Far in the distance, she can now just make out the lights of Trip. Tiny dots that don't seem to get any bigger. The town so far it might as well be the moon.

Callum will be getting in the car, deciding which way they will have gone. Guessing correctly, as the other direction leads to nothing but mountains and glen until the road splits. Elgin or the sea. Neither one a choice for a woman and her son with no car to take them there.

Not knowing what else to do, she goes back to Kyle. Taking his arm, she half runs, half stumbles with him along the road. Kyle struggles to free himself from her grasp, but fear has given her strength. She manages to drag him a few more steps, but with Kyle resisting, it's hopeless.

Ailsa lets go of his arm and sinks to her haunches, covering her face with her hands. Callum will be here soon. He'll find them and, even if he doesn't know for sure, will guess the reason she left. That she knows his secret. What she doesn't know is what he'll do with this knowledge once he finds them.

'You're sad.' Kyle's voice comes to her through her tears. 'I'm sorry, Mum. I can walk some more.'

Ailsa lowers her hands and looks at him, his words making her want to cry all the more. Her son has just done something marvellous. Something she'd celebrate if they weren't in such danger.

She stands. Turns her head to look back the way they came, seeing the sweep of headlights round the distant bend in the road. Desperately, she searches for somewhere to hide, but the rowans on this stretch of the road are too stunted, the rocks strewn across the cropped grass too small, to be of any use.

Fear presses down on her. She was mad to think they could run from him.

The headlights are closer now, blinding her. She pulls Kyle towards her and this time he doesn't resist.

Callum will be angry.

Worse than that, he'll be desperate.

FORTY-SIX

AILSA

The car stops and Ailsa freezes, blinded by the headlights. There's nowhere to go. Nowhere to hide.

She hears the car door slam, the engine still running. Then there are footsteps on the road. Ailsa tents her hand to her eyes to shield them from the glare. What will Callum do now he's found them? He was always unpredictable, more so with a drink inside him.

It's not herself she's worried for but Kyle.

'Ailsa?' The voice is familiar, but it's not Callum.

'Douglas?' Ailsa thinks she'll cry with relief. 'Doug, is that you?'

'Aye, it is.' He steps out of the headlights. 'What are you two doing out here at this time of the evening?'

Ailsa looks past him, back down the road in the direction from which she's come. What can she say to him that won't sound mad? She doesn't know anything. It's just her instincts and the words of a loner who lives in a caravan in the forest. Who would believe her story? What proof does she have? It would be her word against his, nothing more concrete than that. As far as the island is concerned, Callum is dead and gone.

Buried in the graveyard along the road from The Stag... and good riddance.

No one would want to believe he was back from the dead.

And her need to flee from Loch Briona... how would she explain *that*? Callum hadn't done anything. Hadn't hurt her or Kyle.

Not yet anyway.

Doug frowns. 'Do yae want me to give you a lift back? It's lucky I saw yae. I had some deliveries to make in Elgin and was on my way home.'

'No. I don't want to go back.' The thought chills her and she has to think quickly. She glances at Kyle, then lowers her voice. 'The funeral, the change of routine, it's upset Kyle. He didn't want to be there... not without Moira. I wondered if we could stay at yours tonight.'

'Of course.' He looks troubled. Unsure what to make of her strange request. 'But where's your car, Ailsa? Why are you walking? It's nigh on six miles to Trip.'

'It wouldn't start.'

'You could have called, and I'd have come and got you. Or could you not have asked Jonah?'

She hadn't been expecting so many questions. 'I mislaid my phone somewhere and Jonah has been drinking all evening. It wouldn't have been safe for him to get behind the wheel. To be honest, I hadn't really thought it through.'

'I see.' Douglas turns to Kyle. 'Do you want to have a ride in my car, young man?'

Kyle says nothing. He's standing at the edge of the road, shielding his eyes from the headlights.

'Is the lad okay?'

'Yes. He's just tired. Kyle, come on. You like Doug's car. You can sit in the front if you like, and I'll go in the back.'

Douglas holds open the passenger door and Kyle gets in. He draws the seat belt across and stares out of the front window.

'I've got a book about cars. This one's a Mitsubishi. Did you know Mitsubishi means three water chestnuts in Japanese?'

Doug scratches his head. 'No, lad. Cannae say I did.'

Ailsa gets in the back. She twists her head to see out of the rear window, terrified she'll see the lights of Callum's car in the distance. Relieved when there's nothing but darkness. They'll spend the night in the pub's spare room and in the morning, she'll think about what she should do.

Ailsa goes through what she knows. Callum watched his brother succumb to the icy water, pulling him out when it was too late to save him. Sometime between then and running to his mother's house for help, he swapped his clothes with Jonah's. Then, for the next eleven years, using Jonah's documents, he'd lived as him.

And now he's back. Needing the money the holiday lodges brought in to pay off his debts. Still a drunk. Still a cold-hearted killer. Still a rapist.

With a glance in the rear-view mirror, Douglas pulls out onto the road and Ailsa leans her head back against the head-rest. She closes her eyes, fighting the panic and the fear of what will happen next. She may be safe for now but what about tomorrow, the next day and the next? Even to her ears, the accusations would sound wild.

She covers her face with her hands.

Her word against his.

Her word against his.

The car journey, which on foot would have taken over two hours, is quickly over. As they slow, the tyres crunching on the gravel of the pub car park, Ailsa opens her eyes to see the large sign with the stag's head. How will she explain why she's come here to Reyne?

As if understanding her dilemma. Douglas cranes his head round to her. 'Guest room is always made up. You and the lad make yourself at home. I'll square it with the missus.'

She smiles gratefully. 'Thanks, Doug.'

He hasn't queried why she has no proper bag. No things for a night away from home. Hasn't questioned her at all during the drive.

She and Kyle follow him into the public bar, and he switches on the lights.

'Through here.' He takes them into the small reception area, with a wooden coat stand and a reception desk, and points to a door on his right. 'Will you be okay here?'

'We'll be fine, thank you.'

He hands her a key. 'Then I'll see you in the morning.'

Ailsa lets herself in. There are two beds, and she points to the one by the window. 'You have that one.' She takes Kyle's coat from him and hangs it on the back of a chair, then turns back the covers. 'In you get. It's been a long day. Try and get some sleep.'

To her surprise, Kyle gets into the bed without arguing. He yawns loudly. 'Will the man come tonight?'

For a moment, Ailsa thinks he means Callum. 'No, he doesn't know we're here. He didn't see us leave.'

'Not him. The man with the dog.'

Of course, he's talking about Seth. His obsession with the dog pushing everything else that's happened aside.

'No. Not him either.'

She remembers Callum's reaction when, that afternoon, she'd told him she thought it had been Seth snooping around the lodges. He'd wanted to have it out with him there and then and would have if she hadn't stopped him. At the time, she'd thought it out of character, but now it all makes sense. What would have happened if he'd gone there? What would he have done to him?

He'd been sober then, thank goodness... but now?

She remembers the words daubed on the side of his caravan. *Guilty. We know you did...* and the smell of the burnt-out van that had lingered for days. Crimes that Callum had committed, but which had never been proven.

Now a terrible thought comes to her. When Callum had knocked on the door of their lodge and got no answer, when he'd eventually let himself in with the master key and found them gone, might he have suspected Seth could have had something to do with their absence? Maybe that's why he hadn't come after them – because he'd gone into the forest to find out if his suspicions were true.

Kyle is already asleep, and Ailsa quickly takes off her jumper and jeans and gets into the other bed. She's exhausted, but it takes a long time for sleep to come to her and, when it does, her dreams are of Jonah. He's floating on his back in the bitter water of the loch. The current taking him ever further from her. He's dead, she can see that, and as she watches, he slips below the surface. From the boat where she's sitting, his brother, Callum, looks on, his face passive.

Ailsa jolts awake. There's someone outside her door in the reception area. Pushing back the covers, she creeps to the door and puts her ear to it. They're speaking in hushed tones, but their voices still carry as men's often do.

'No, you can't go in there. It's gone three, and I won't have them disturbed.'

'I'm worried about them, Doug. Who in their right mind goes out in the night with only their coat? Why didn't she take the car?'

Ailsa presses her palm to the door. It's Callum she can hear. He's found them. Her heart beating in her ribcage, she looks down at the key in the lock. Thank God she thought to lock the door.

'She said it wouldn't start.' Doug says something else she can't catch.

'It's the boy I worry about the most. Taking him out so late. Expecting him to walk. And why? Did she say?'

'No, she didn't really tell me much. I thought it best to get them back here and let them sleep. It was Reyne's idea to ring you. We thought you should know, seeing as how you were once so close.'

'We still are. That girl means the world to me, but she's troubled.' There's a pause and Ailsa waits, hardly able to believe what she's hearing. 'I'm sure Ma must have mentioned something.'

A woman's voice now. Reyne's. 'I know she was concerned about the boy. Thought it wrong that she took him out of school.'

'That's what I'm saying, Reyne. She lives by him. Breathes by him. Ma told me, but since I've been back, I've seen it with my own eyes. The things she's been saying recently I dinnae know what to make of them. Things she's seen. Heard. She makes out it's the boy, but she just projects her delusions onto him. Makes the kid her voice. Ma suggested she see someone, but Ailsa's always been stubborn.'

Ailsa pushes her ear harder to the door. Such lies. How could he say these things? But she knows why. He's discrediting her. Sowing seeds of doubt before she's even got the chance to say her piece.

'Come back tomorrow, Jonah.' Doug's voice is placatory. Fatherly. He's always had a soft spot for Callum's brother. The gentle one. The one they'd always hoped would one day return to Bray. 'We can have a chat and see if we can't sort things out. I knew as soon as I saw the two of them at the side of the road that things weren't right. Don't worry, lad. We'll make sure she gets any help she needs.'

The voices fade and she hears the front door slam. Going to the window, she leans over Kyle's bed and parts the curtain.

Watches Callum reverse his mother's old Land Rover and drive away.

She presses her forehead to the glass and feels the tears run hot down her cheeks. They think she's crazy. No one's ever going to believe her.

Had Moira really said that or had Callum been lying? Thinking of her brings tears of loss to her eyes. She'd loved her like a mother. In her bag is the envelope Moira gave her the last time she'd seen her alive. She'd said she'd know when the time was right to open it. This could be it.

Going back to her bed, Ailsa switches on the bedside light, then crouches to her bag and pulls out the envelope. She looks at it a moment, scared of what it might contain, then tears it open. Inside are two sheets of paper. Ailsa slips them from the envelope and unfolds them, her heart aching as she sees Moira's neat writing.

She stands next to the bed and reads the first few paragraphs, but as their meaning start to penetrate, hitting their mark, she sinks heavily onto the mattress, the words swimming.

Moira has saved her.

Moira has given her a way out.

Callum thinks he's so clever. Knows no one will believe Ailsa if she tries to tell anyone her crazy story about the twins who changed places. He knows, too, that he can never be Callum again without difficult questions about Jonah's death being asked. Not to mention the circumstances in which Kyle had been conceived. He's forfeited the right to call himself Kyle's father... but she doesn't care.

He can be Jonah... just as he always wanted to be. And she'll say nothing.

Because it's what she wants now too.

FORTY-SEVEN
MOIRA'S LETTER

My dear Ailsa,

A few months ago, I received the distressing news that the headaches I've been having weren't caused by migraines as I'd thought, but by a tumour. Of course you know that already. Reading this letter, means that I am no longer with you and for that I'm sorry. You and that little boy of yours, who I now know is my grandson, have given me such joy over the years and helped to erase some of the blacker times in my past. But that's something I'll come back to.

I am writing you this letter after speaking with Jonah earlier today. A talk that confirmed his desire to see Loch Briona Lodges sold after I'm gone. Even though, as I told you, I will be letting my solicitor know that Kyle is Callum's son, in order for the estate to be divided between Jonah and Kyle (with his share in trust and you the trustee) that alone might not be enough. I'm sure you'll be asking yourself the question why and the answer is simple, Ailsa.

I love my son, but I don't trust him.

You love my son too, I know that, and I'm afraid it makes

you vulnerable. It will also make Kyle vulnerable too, and I don't want my grandson to have to move from here unless it's what you both really want. That's something for you to decide, not Jonah. The two of you are in this together and I've stipulated in the will that one will not be able to sell their share without the other. It's better that way.

You think you know him, but I don't think you do. He's always been a good boy, a sensitive, caring son, but inside him runs a seam of something that has been inherited from his father. Nothing obvious as with Callum, but there all the same. My husband and Callum called Jonah weak, but I don't think that's true. I've seen a side to him that is at odds with his usual, gentle self. Seen him make decisions that you wouldn't expect of him... and it's this I want to protect you both from. If you and Kyle are to remain here at Loch Briona, you need to keep my son under control and reading the contents of this letter is the only way you'll be able to do it.

The words you're going to read now will shock you, most likely sicken you, but it's not the words that are important but what you do with them.

The day I'm going to tell you about started like any other day. I had spent the morning in Elgin looking for some new cushion covers for one of the lodges and, when I returned, your mother was just leaving after working her shift. I went into the kitchen and looked out of the window to see if the boys were still working on the foundations of the shower block. They weren't there and a little nugget of concern lodged inside me, growing ever bigger when I saw they'd taken the boat out onto the loch. I didn't know where Hugh had gone, but what I did know was there'd be trouble if he came home and found they'd been slacking. I was just going out to warn them when I saw my husband walk past the window, heading for the steps that would take him down to the shore, his face like thunder.

I should have gone with him, but I was frightened. You see it's not just Jonah who's a coward – all my married life with Hugh I was treading on eggshells. Scared to stand up to him. Scared to defend the boys in case it made him worse. It's something I'm truly ashamed of and I hope, one day, you'll tell Jonah that. It's too late to tell Callum, as my boy is dead, but I do wonder whether he would have turned out as bad as he did if I had been a better mother.

But I'm digressing. I stood at the window watching. Saw Hugh march my sons back up to the building site. I saw everything: the way Callum stood up to his father, the way Hugh threatened to take the belt to him in return, the look of hatred on my son's face as he'd run at him, head down, pushing him backwards into the trench.

Neither of the boys knew I was there. Hugh didn't either. I've never told anyone what I saw, but it's important you know as it will help you stay strong for me and for Kyle.

For this is what I'm trying to say to you, Ailsa. Callum might have wanted my husband dead, but it wasn't him who killed my husband... it was Jonah.

FORTY-EIGHT

JONAH

Then

Jonah stares at his father in horror. He's dead. Callum has killed him.

He looks to the sky as if it might give him some idea what to do, then back down again. Through the shock and numbness, a thought starts to bloom in his head. Coming to the fore.

Yes, his father is dead... but he's glad. With him gone, the fear is gone too. The awful black cloud that hangs over him every morning when he wakes, already lifting. All his life, he's lived with the anxiety of not knowing what word will spark him off. What action. Without Hugh in the world, the family has been freed. His future, all their futures, will be brighter.

Covering his face with his hands, Jonah leans his elbows on the edge of the trench and sobs uncontrollably. Shock. Disbelief. Relief.

His father is dead. Hugh is *dead*!

Jonah's brain is still trying to digest the reality of what he's witnessed, and it's why he's not prepared for what happens next. Why the sudden vice-like grip on his ankle takes a while to register. To understand. He looks down at his leg. Sees the fingers that dig into the flesh.

The shock is physical. A sledgehammer blow that sends him to his knees.

'That kid will wish he'd never been born when I get him.' His father's voice comes as if from a grave. Its unexpectedness leaving Jonah winded.

He tries to stand again, but the fingers hold him tight. How could he have got it so wrong? His father had been so still, his face so deathly pale. And the blood! But he knows what it was. He'd seen what he'd wanted to see, that was all. As if wishing him dead had been enough for it to happen. He should have checked. He should have known.

In desperation, he looks up, searching for Callum. It will be worse for them now than before. So much worse.

'Help me up.' His dad pushes himself into a sitting position. Prods and pokes at the back of his head with his hand. His fingers come away red and sticky. 'I'll kill him for this.'

'He didn't mean it, Dad. He just lost his rag.'

Hugh rubs his bloodied hand on his jeans. 'Take that little shit's side, why don't you?' His lips twist. 'Always hiding behind your brother, too scared to speak up for yourself. Callum's a wretch, but at least he has a backbone. *You*...' He looks at Jonah with disgust, then spits into the trench. '*You* are a snivelling coward. Moira's little pet.'

Suddenly, it's as if the walls of the trench are pushing in on Jonah. A dark heat rises from somewhere deep inside his belly. Filling every muscle, every sinew, every cell of his body with poison. He presses his hands against his ears and shakes his head.

'Shut up!'

Jonah grabs the shovel Callum had been using to load the cement mixer from the side of the trench. He stares at the wooden handle, at the heavy metal blade caked in mud.

Hugh reaches out a hand. 'Put that thing down before you hurt someone and help me up, you pathetic little yellow-belly.'

'I said, shut up!'

Before he can understand what he's doing, he lifts the shovel over his shoulder, all sense gone from his head. All sanity. After what Callum did, their lives will be a living hell. Far worse than ever before. He can't let it happen. He *can't*. When he'd thought his father dead, he'd been happy. He's not afraid to admit that. He can't go back to how they were. None of them can.

'What are you doing? I said get me up.' The side of his father's face is covered in mud. His hair is matted with blood.

Jonah stares at the hand that reaches out to him. A hand that has struck him and his brother more times than he cares to remember. He's shaking so hard, his teeth are chattering in his head. His eyes move to the face with its broken veins, its small black eyes where kindness has never lived. Hating him. No, loathing him. He thinks he hears a sound and looks up, but there's no one there, just his overactive imagination. It's just him and his father.

Jonah's voice is cold. Ice. 'Do it yourself.'

'Why, you little—' Getting onto all fours, Hugh bends his knee to push himself up, his hand pressed against the side of the trench to steady himself. His back is to Jonah. The bloodied wound on the back of his head gaping.

Madness overtakes Jonah; he can think of nothing else to call it. Like an automaton, he draws back his arms, the shovel twisting with his body. Blanking his mind, he swings it in an arc with as much force as he can muster. Hears the crunch as it makes contact with the back of his father's head.

It's only when the older man collapses back onto the floor of the trench that Jonah comes to his senses. The enormity, the terribleness of what he's just done, hitting him.

Turning away, he retches into the soft mud.

Minutes pass. Jonah knows he has to look. Has to be sure. He turns and crawls towards the body. Wrenching him onto his back, he puts his ear to his father's chest, half expecting to feel the rise and fall of it, but there's nothing.

There's no mistaking it. No error. Not this time.

He stares at the lifeless body feeling nothing but a cold emptiness.

A movement makes him look up. Callum is coming back, a bottle of his dad's whisky in his hand. Quickly, Jonah grabs his T-shirt from the side of the trench and ducks down behind the earth wall, using it to wipe the blood from the shovel before shoving it behind him.

When Callum reaches the trench, he looks in. His face is impassive. Unreadable.

'He's dead, Callum. Dad's dead. He must have hit his head when he fell.'

Jonah knows he should tell the truth, say what really happened, but he doesn't. None of this is his fault. It was Callum who caused it all. He who shoved his dad into the trench. If he hadn't suggested they go fishing, none of this would have happened.

Callum crouches above him, a slow smile spreading across his face.

'Dead?'

'Yes.' Despite the sun, Jonah is deathly cold, the hairs raised on his arms. It's the shock. The horror of what has just happened. He can't think straight. Can't focus.

'What are we going to do, Cal?' He looks beyond him, a movement at the window of the house catching his attention. He covers his mouth with his hand. 'Oh, Jesus. What are we going to tell Ma?'

Callum gets to his feet. He walks over to the cement mixer where the wet, grey mixture is slowly turning and stands thinking. Ten seconds pass. Twenty.

'Callum. Fucking speak to me.'

Callum turns and looks at him, but even if he'd wanted to, he's no time to answer. There's a movement by the laundry block. Moira is making her way towards them.

Jonah stares, wide-eyed. 'Oh, Christ.'

Moira's face is white. She goes to the edge of the trench and looks down at her husband, at the blood on the earth beside his head that's drying to almost black. At his eyes staring at the sky.

'What have you done?' It's barely more than a whisper.

'I pushed him.' There's no sorrow in Callum's voice. No guilt. No remorse.

Their mother's eyes flick from Callum to Jonah, then back again. 'You killed my husband.'

It's a statement rather than a question.

Callum's eyes are steady. His mouth set. 'Yeah, I killed him. He had it coming. He deserved it.'

'We can say it was an accident.' Jonah steps away from his father's dead body, his mind racing. Yet, even as he's saying it, he knows the idea won't work. If the responders come, the police too, they'll see the gash on his father's head. His skull fractured. They'll know the blow that killed him couldn't have been caused by the fall alone. He thinks of the questions that will be asked. Ones that only he knows the answers to.

Panic takes hold of him, and he begins to shake again. His whole life he's tried to keep the peace, tried to shield his brother and keep him out of harm's way, but now, because of him, he'll be going to prison. His heart is beating nineteen to the dozen. He has no idea what to do.

But, in the end, he doesn't have to do anything.

Hugh's belt is on the ground, by the cement mixer, where he dropped it. Bending to it, his mother picks it up. She looks at it a moment, smoothing the cracked leather with the palm of her hand, then throws the belt into the trench. Her face is pained, her eyes swimming with tears. Both boys know that however much she hated her husband, she loved him too.

'No,' she says, turning back to her two sons. 'We won't do that.'

Taking a handkerchief from her sleeve, she blows her nose, then nods at Callum. 'That trench is too shallow. You've a few hours left of daylight to sort it out. And I'd add some water to the cement before it gets too dry. Rain is forecast and you'll need to get that filled while it's still fine.'

Turning her back on the two of them, Moira walks back to the house, her head bowed, her shoulders bent. Jonah watches her, his body still numb with shock, but Callum has already jumped down beside him.

He bends and picks up the shovel Jonah dropped, and Jonah doesn't stop him.

They have chosen their path and once they've finished doing what they must do, the lies will begin, and they'll go on with their lives as though it never happened. What other choice do they have?

And the worst of it, Jonah thinks, is he'll never be able to tell anyone about this day. Not even Ailsa. *Especially* not Ailsa. For no one must ever know what happened.

No one.

FORTY-NINE
MOIRA'S LETTER

For once in my life I took control, Ailsa. I had to, as there was no one else to do it for me. Jonah was a mess, still in shock from what he'd done. My husband was dead, and I knew I'd miss him until the day I died, because despite everything, I'd never stopped loving him, but I had to protect my boy. For if anyone knew the truth, he'd be taken away from me. Locked up and the key thrown away.

My head was spinning, thinking of all the possibilities, and the only thing I could be thankful for was that Callum didn't know the truth. As far as he knew, he had been the one to cause Hugh's death and that was how it needed to stay.

We couldn't risk pretending it had been an accident. The only way was to bury the body. Leave Hugh in the trench and fill it in with the concrete from the mixer. Everyone knew my husband was a philanderer and no one was taken in by his cover stories when he went to hook up with women on the mainland. We'd tell people he'd left. That I'd finally grown a backbone and thrown him out. Told him that his latest woman, whoever she might be, could have him. No one would be surprised that he'd left Bray as there was nothing left for him here. The lodges were mine and there was nothing he could do about it. Besides, everyone knew he was a bad lot, and it was unlikely anyone would miss him.

As I told the boys what they had to say and do, it was like I was someone else. Hugh's death had in some strange way released me. Despite my breaking heart, my head was clearer than it had been in years. I'd never see Hugh again. Never.

It didn't take long for the boys to fill the trench and when they'd gone up to the house to clean up, I went down to look. Saying a silent prayer for Hugh before pushing the shovel they'd left at the side of the trench with my foot. Watching it sink beneath the surface.

It was over... or so I thought.

What I hadn't accounted for was how my husband's death would affect Callum. Instead of releasing him too, it made him harder. Meaner. Hugh's shoes were big ones, but it didn't take my son long to fill them. I'd thought our secret might bring us closer, but it had the opposite effect. Jonah went more into his shell, but Callum walked around the place as though he owned it. He'd thought he'd single-handedly got rid of the tyrant who was his father, and it had gone to his head. He never laid a finger on me, that wasn't his style, but the emotional abuse was nearly as bad. I'd had it from my husband and now from my son.

It was why I never cried at Callum's funeral. Why I was glad it was him who had drowned and not Jonah. I wanted Jonah to stay with us, and I know you wanted that too, but after the accident, he was a different boy to the one he had once been. He could no longer live in the place where his brother had drowned and where his father lay interned under the footings of the shower block. Couldn't live with his conscience. He wouldn't have returned if he hadn't needed money and, do you know, I don't even care. It was that desperation that finally brought him home to me.

My boy.

My precious son.

But I can't trust him, Ailsa. I can't be sure that he'll do the right thing by you and my grandson, Kyle. The lodges must stay in the family, not sold to some fancy developer who'll rip the place apart. You must do everything in your power to see that it doesn't... for if that happens, Hugh's body will be found. Jonah's secret will be discovered.

So now you know the truth, Ailsa. Jonah, the man I know you still love, was capable of doing this terrible thing, but I want you to remember he did it in desperation. He did it because he was scared. He did it for me.

Keep this letter safe. Use it only if you have to. No one needs to know about it, but if Jonah ever tries to trick your son out of his rightful share of his inheritance, you may tell him what it contains. I know him, Ailsa – it will be enough.

My only regret is that I couldn't be a better mother to my boys, but I tried to make up for it with Kyle. I wish you well, Ailsa, and I mean that with all my heart.

Moira

EPILOGUE

Ailsa pushes the flowers into the plastic holder on the grave – daffodils and the vivid blue of grape hyacinths.

Swallowing back the tears, she rests her hand on the cool marble of the headstone.

'I'm sorry, Jonah. I had no choice.'

A breeze ruffles the yellow trumpets, making her wonder if they'll still be there by the end of the week or if she'll find them limp and brown, their stems beaten and broken by the wind and rain that's forecast.

As Ailsa crouches beside the grave, the tips of her fingers tracing the inscription on the stone's flat face, she tries not to let her frustration get the better of her. More than anything, she'd like to change that stone to one that bears Jonah's true name, but that will never happen. The world thinks Jonah's still alive and that's how it must stay. No one can ever know it's him who lies beneath the peaty soil. It's the price she has to pay.

Callum Wallace.

It's a name. Nothing more.

'I just hope you understand, Jonah,' she whispers. Sure that he would. For, despite what she now knows, Jonah was essentially good. It would have been desperation that made him do what he did to his father. And although she'll never be sure, he would have done it for his family. Something she understands.

It's likely Callum won't be back on the island for a long time. Fifteen years minimum, she'd been told. Not as long as if he'd committed the crime as an adult, or if there hadn't been extenuating circumstances, but still a substantial amount of time, nonetheless.

Of course he'll still have his share of Loch Briona, but he'll have to appoint someone to manage it on his behalf and by the time he's finished his sentence, Kyle will be an adult. That's all she wants... to give her son the stability he needs while he's young, in a place that he loves. Maybe then she'll agree to sell. Who knows? That's the future and nobody knows what that holds. She's found that out the hard way. They all have.

If Moira had known what she'd done, would she have approved? She likes to think she would. For hadn't Callum killed too? Allowing his brother, the son she'd loved the most, to die? It would be justice. Punishment for the terrible things he'd done to Seth. To Ailsa... for she's pretty certain Moira had guessed the circumstances in which Kyle had been conceived.

What it comes down to is this: if their mother had been alive to choose a son to stand in the dock and receive that sentence, which one would it be?

In her heart, Ailsa knows where Moira's finger would have pointed. Jonah had always been her favourite. More sensitive, less antagonistic of Hugh. Looking out for her as best he could. It's that knowledge that had allowed Ailsa to play her own part in Callum's downfall. And what will make it easier for her to live with what she did – even though Moira had no idea that the boy returning to the island was the one she thought was buried in this grave.

The morning after she'd fled from the lodges, she'd driven to Elgin and handed Moira's letter to the police. They'd questioned her about the circumstances in which she'd received it and asked her what else she could tell them... how well she'd known the brothers and whether there had been any building works at Loch Briona in the year Moira had mentioned. For the most part, she'd been honest. Keeping back only what she had to.

Ailsa fights back the tears. 'I told them about Kyle being Callum's son, Jonah. I told them about the rape.'

It had been hard, so very hard. They were words she'd hoped she'd never have to say. But, for her plan to work, she'd had no choice. A safeguard in case, one day, Callum decided to tell the truth – that *he* was the one still living. The policewoman had been kind, but with Callum dead, the only thing she'd been able to offer was sympathy, and the number for a Rape Crisis Centre.

Ailsa wipes the tears from her cheeks. 'Despite how he came to be in the world, I love Kyle with all my heart. What I did, I did for him. You know that, don't you? I've let Callum keep your name so that Kyle can live here in safety.'

She remembers the cold shock of disappointment when the police had told her Moira's letter couldn't be used as evidence. Unless she'd written it on a witness statement form or been alive to give evidence in court, it would just be classed as hearsay. But she needn't have worried. The things Moira had said, the details she'd given, had been serious enough for the police to start an investigation. And, despite Reyne telling her she shouldn't, she hadn't been able to keep away from the place.

Closing her eyes, Ailsa pictures the scene. Remembering how she'd parked on the road above the lodges and looked down on the site. There had been so many people, some in uniform, some in forensic suits, moving around the outbuildings. Disappearing into the shower block only to appear again to confer.

She hadn't been allowed to walk down the drive to the lodges, but the police officer at the tape had told her that the

Scenes of Crime Officers and Forensic Archaeologists, who had taken the ferry to Bray from the mainland, were planning to scan the ground with penetrating radar to ascertain if there was a body there. If there was, the whole lot would have to be dug up.

Ailsa gives a small smile. 'There were more people on the site than there had been all summer, Jonah. Ironic really.'

Taking her phone out of her bag, she checks for messages. There's nothing from Reyne, so Kyle must be all right. With a last look at the grave, she picks up her bag and walks back down the lane to The Stag.

She collects Kyle and drives the six miles to Loch Briona. Parking in the car park next to the white house, she stands and views the lodges. Five are occupied and there are more on their books. There's a light on in the window of the reception and Ailsa goes over and taps on it. Her assistant, Sarah, looks up from the computer and smiles. She smiles back. If bookings continue to rise, she might be able to increase the girl's hours.

'Let's go down to the water, Kyle. We can eat our lunch there.' Reyne had kindly fixed them something while she'd been at the cemetery. 'Good idea?'

Kyle nods. 'I want Marmite sandwiches.'

'Do you now?' She smiles and pats her bag. 'Lucky Reyne knows you almost as well as I do.'

'No, she doesn't.'

Shaking her head, Ailsa leads the way down the concrete steps. When she gets to the last one, she jumps down onto the beach and waits for Kyle, then, together, they walk along the shore. The rowing boat is upturned on the stones. The wood is warm from the sun and Ailsa leans against it. She unwraps the sandwiches and hands one to Kyle.

'I've been thinking. It's about time I taught you to swim. Would you like that? You can wear a wetsuit so you don't get cold.'

Kyle looks doubtful. 'I don't know.'

She doesn't like to think of him out on the water, but she won't be able to keep him off the loch for ever. It wouldn't be fair. Last week, she'd found him standing on the deck of their chalet watching two teenage boys drag the kayak to the water. One day, she'd like him to be confident enough to join them.

'It's not something you have to decide now.' She watches him eat his sandwich. In the distance, she hears a dog bark. Seth's dog. Her fingers rub at the inside of her arm, feeling the raised skin. 'There's something else I've been wanting to talk to you about, Kyle. I wondered what you thought about us getting a dog. It would be a companion to you.'

Over the months, his obsession hasn't waned. If anything, it's got stronger.

'A dog,' he says, his eyes fixed on the stones. 'A real dog.'

'Yes, a real dog.'

Kyle's head nods and a smile spreads slowly across his face. Ailsa's glad.

The dog barks again, louder now and Ailsa turns. Seth is walking along the beach towards them.

She places her sandwiches on the boat. 'Wait here, Kyle. I won't be a moment.'

Seth has got as far as the boathouse and, when he sees her hurrying along the beach, he stops. His dog sits by his feet, and he pets its head.

Ailsa stops in front of him. It's the first time they've met since Callum was arrested. When they'd found Hugh's body, the handle of the shovel buried next to him had elicited Jonah's fingerprints. The blade of it, his father's DNA. It had all fitted with what Moira had said in her letter. It had been enough. Of course Callum could have pleaded innocence and blamed his brother, but he hadn't. Who would have believed him anyway?

Both boys' fingerprints had been on the shovel, but Moira's letter had pointed the finger at only one son. His only hope would have been to tell the whole truth, but that would have dragged up a whole lot of other crimes. The stakes were too high.

Jonah or Callum.

He was damned either way.

Seth points to the boathouse where the motorboat is still kept. 'I seen it all. I know who he is.'

Ailsa crouches on the stones. Reaching out a hand, she strokes the dog's head. Feels how soft its fur is. 'I know you did, Seth.'

He rubs the side of his face, then attaches the rope lead to his dog's collar. 'Your boy. He's a good lad. Like the other one.'

'I know.'

Seth clicks his tongue, and the dog slowly gets to its feet. He nods to her. 'Take care.'

Ailsa watches them walk back along the sand. Waiting until they disappear into the trees. She goes back to Kyle and, as she finishes her sandwich, she thinks about the man in the caravan. She should be worried that he'll tell someone the secret they share, but she's not. Although he hasn't said as much, there was something in his expression that had told her he would keep it to himself.

Seth stands in the shadow of the trees, his dog beside him, and lifts his binoculars to his eyes. He watches a greylag goose graze the vegetation at the water's edge, then slides his binoculars away until they're trained on the boathouse. He thinks of the boy he saw pull his brother out of the loch. The one who changed clothes with him. They call him Jonah, but he knows it's not his name. He's heard he's been taken away to the mainland and will stand trial for the murder of his father. Knows he'll no longer be able to hurt him.

But that's not the reason he won't step forward to say

they've got it all wrong. That he isn't who they think he is. He'll say nothing because the girl doesn't want him to... and because he hasn't forgotten what he saw through the window of his caravan all those years ago.

A boy. A girl.

A random act of kindness to his beloved dog.

For him, it's enough.

A LETTER FROM WENDY

Firstly, I would like to say a huge thank you to everyone who has read *Childhood Sweetheart*. Without readers a writer is nothing, so I hope you realise how important you are to me! If you have got this far, then the chances are you've now finished reading my latest psychological thriller, so I hope you loved reading it as much as I loved writing it.

If you did enjoy *Childhood Sweetheart* and want to keep up-to-date with all my latest releases, just sign up at the following link. Your email address will never be shared, and you can unsubscribe at any time.

www.bookouture.com/Wendy-Clarke

Once again, setting has played an important role in my novel. For those of you who might have been wondering, Bray, where *Childhood Sweetheart* is set, is not a Scottish island you'll find on any map. It's a product of my imagination. The reason for this is simple: I wrote my novel the year after the Covid pandemic hit and my research trip to the West Coast of Scotland, and the Isle of Skye in particular, had to be postponed. By the time I was able to make my visit, I had almost completed the first draft of my story, which hadn't been the plan!

Needless to say, I had the most amazing holiday and instantly fell in love with the dark lochs, pine forests and swathes of heather-clad moorland. By now, though, I had a fixed idea of what I wanted from my remote Scottish island. The place I'd written about had two main towns, a limited boat service, a secondary school, a police station but no hospital. Despite loving Skye, the island was bigger than the one in my story and, while having some of the elements I needed, it didn't have them all. There were also parts of the mainland I wanted to incorporate – in particular, a road lined with rowan trees leading to a little cemetery and a pub just like The Stag.

The solution was easy. As in many of my previous novels, I decided to use details from the different and amazing places I'd visited, both on and off the island, to create my own new setting. In this way the Island of Bray was born. My only regret is that if you want to stay in the Loch Briona Holiday Lodges, visit the harbour town of Trip or the pub at Elgin, it will have to be in your imagination!

I hope you loved *Childhood Sweetheart* and if you did, I would be very grateful if you could write a review. I'd love to hear what you think, and it makes such a difference helping new readers to discover one of my books for the first time.

I enjoy hearing from my readers – you can get in touch on my Facebook page, through Twitter, Goodreads, Instagram or my website.

Thanks,

Wendy x

www.wendyclarke.uk

facebook.com/WendyClarkeAuthor

twitter.com/WendyClarke99

instagram.com/WendyClarke99

ACKNOWLEDGEMENTS

As always, I owe an enormous debt to a large number of people, without whom this book would not have made it to publication.

My first shout out is to my lovely new editor, Susannah Hamilton. This is the first novel we've worked on together and I am grateful not just for her patience and great insight, but for allowing *Childhood Sweetheart* to remain true to the original idea. Thank you for being a champion of my writing and for making the whole editing process so stress-free! Thanks also to my previous editor, Jennifer Hunt, who loved the idea of my new thriller enough to commission it. I hope you'll enjoy reading the final version (if you get the time with two little ones!).

Thanks also to the whole team at my wonderful publisher, Bookouture, who work tirelessly behind the scenes to get my novels in front of readers and to my brilliant cover designer, Lisa, who has done a fantastic job as always. I've loved all six covers!

Now I'd like to move on from the people who produce my books to those who support me (or at the very least tolerate me) when I'm writing them. Firstly, I have to thank my writing buddy, Tracy Fells, who keeps me going at our monthly meetups with sound advice and plenty of cake. Thanks also to Liz and my other writing chums who keep me sane and to 'The Friday Girls' who are a breath of fresh air when I've had enough of writing talk!

Childhood Sweetheart has a few police procedurals in it and once again it's the fabulous Graham Bartlett I turned to with my strange mix of questions. Thank you also to my sister-in-law, Mary, for the information on autism, homeschooling and the Scottish education system. Any mistakes are entirely my own.

My family are always there on the sidelines, asking me how things are going and reading my books when they are published... even if they might not want to! I'm grateful for your encouragement.

As always, my final thank you has to go to my husband, Ian, who's become adept at reading my moods while I'm in the thick of the writing process. He knows how to talk me through writers' block and is great at unravelling plot problems. He's also the first to celebrate my achievements with a glass of Prosecco!

I can't sign off, though, without mentioning *you*, my readers. For some of you, this will be the first of my novels you've read, for others it will be the sixth. Whichever it is, without you as a reader, I wouldn't be an author... so thank you!

Printed in Great Britain
by Amazon